Brett Edward Stout has done so
novel... Such rich personal deta
as anything but real.

Janelle Wilbanks, *ACCESSline Iowa*

An intriguing story that grabs you from the moment you start to
read... A fascinating coming-of-age story that should not be
missed.

Terence Jackson, *Thirty Days and Counting*

An often-disturbing examination of one young man's unabashed
self-involvement.

Eric Arvin, *The Rest is Illusion*

A page turner that compels the reader to know where the bridge
is going... I am hooked!

Shell Feijo, *Without a Net: The Female Experience Growing up
Working Class*

An enjoyable read... extremely well written... I would
recommend it.

Bookannelid Book Reviews

The smooth prose of a mature writer... Subtle and brutal in the
questions that it raises.

Ruth White PhD., *Former Iowa Director of Human Rights*

DAVID,

TO THE KILLINGEST, RUNNINGEST, SQUATINGEST, PUSHY PULLER I KNOW.

SUGAR-BABY
BRIDGE

Brett Edward Stout

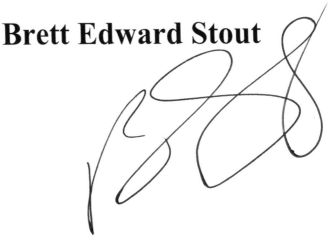

Sugar-baby Bridge
Edited by Janelle Wilbanks, Arthur Breur
Sugar-baby Bridge Copyright ©2006, 2009 by Brett Edward Stout
Excerpt from *The Lives Between* Copyright ©2008 by Brett Edward Stout
ALL RIGHTS RESERVED

Published in the United States by Breur Media Corporation
Printed in the United States of America
Cover design and photograph by Brett Edward Stout

Breur Media Corporation logo is trademark of Breur Media Corporation. All rights reserved.

Library of Congress Cataloging-in-Publication Data
Stout, Brett Edward
Sugar-baby Bridge : a novel / Brett Edward Stout

This book contains and excerpt from Brett Edward Stout's forthcoming novel *The Lives Between*. This excerpt may not reflect the final published content of the forthcoming novel.

p. cm.
ISBN-13: 978-0-9819474-1-9
ISBN-10: 0-9819474-1-7
1. Gay — Fiction. 2. Military — Fiction. 3. Coming of age — Fiction.
4. Road novel — Fiction. 5. Iowa — Fiction. 6. California — Fiction.
7. Title — Sugar-baby Bridge
TXU 1–305–957

www.sugarbabybridge.com
www.brettedwardstout.com

BREUR
MEDIA
CORPORATION

Breur Media Corporation
2643 Narnia Way, Suite 102
Land O' Lakes, FL 34638-7268
www.BreurMedia.com

This book is dedicated to
Dr. Ruth E. White

ABOUT THE FORWARD

Dr Ruth E. White retired from teaching after more than 30 years in 2000. Her life is filled with many accomplishments including the development of The Academy for Scholastic and Personal Success, headed the Commission on the Status of African Americans, and served as Iowa Director of Human Rights. She has since retired from her directorship and spends her time between her family, Cultural Competence, and sits on the Board of Directors of Diversity Focus.

FORWARD

A teacher never knows what from his/her tomes of wisdom students will absorb, take away and use.

Who would think that nearly ten years after the fact a student would remember a specific conversation, let alone produce the novel that the conversation spurred?   Brett Stout was a bright, bored student—no different from many other seventeen-year-olds. He had a curiosity that had led to astute contributions to class discussions, but he was less accomplished in writing. I recall using my red correction pen liberally on the papers that he submitted—lots of sentence fragments and awkward sentence structure. But Brett took to staying after class to talk. I remember one conversation during our architecture unit, during which he told me about having visited the Biltmore Estate. He had much to say, and his commentary led me to believe that his interest was real—that he had applied what had been presented in class to the actuality of his visit to an existing site. That much I remember. What I did not remember and what was related to me years later is that when he wrote his first novel, he said he intended to dedicate it to me. What I had done or said that connected with him in such an abiding way, I am still not sure. I do know that every good teacher hopes for connections of this

i

kind with her students. One hopes that something done or said in a high school English class will have some lasting, positive impact.

Brett's mother and I commiserated many times during his tenure in my class over our shared belief that Brett's capability was not reflected by his productivity. We both knew in our heart of hearts that Brett was capable of anything he set his mind to, and shared fervent hopes that he would one day come into his own.

After his high school graduation, I lost track of Brett's comings and goings until one day I stopped in at his mother's car wash business, and saw Brett and his brother's Marine photos on proud display. Brett looked so handsome—and serious—and disciplined! Service in the Marine Corps obviously made a significant difference in Brett's perceptions. From time to time I would receive updates as to Brett's whereabouts and progress. Years later, during a car wash stop, I received a manila envelope containing a manuscript, and requesting that I write the forward to Brett's first novel! He was enrolled at the University of Iowa, and was writing novels and screenplays—and he was on the Dean's List! I was proud by proxy! A promise fulfilled.

Teachers are much like parents in that they want only the best for their students. They, like parents, want their students to exceed what they themselves have been able to accomplish. We form bonds with certain students who show promise; we think we see potential—the budding artist, scientist, actor, musician, writer. I saw promise in Brett Stout.

In *Sugar-baby Bridge*, I see the smooth prose of a mature writer. There are many references to an Iowa upbringing, and even apparent recollections relevant to his high school education. *Sugar-baby Bridge* is a deftly drawn character study, in which I see Brett in many incarnations. In spite of the disclaimer that the work is entirely fiction, I remain convinced that the best writers

ii

must necessarily draw from their own experiences. How they may manipulate those experiences to fiction in the course of the writing process is subject for separate discussion. The experiences of the protagonist in *Sugar-baby Bridge* are reflected against Iowa memories and Midwest values and are in stark contrast to those of the foil. The protagonist's Marine service and station in Hawaii coincide with the life of the author. The protagonist's warm references to his mother and his recollections of her lessons and admonitions parallel what I know of Brett's respect for and relationship with his own mother. Even the several references to art and architecture are resonant of the author's educational experience. Themes relevant to the gay lifestyle, as contrasted with the regimentation and discipline of Marine training, choices of friends and partners, observations regarding the profligacy that stems from economic privilege, and even complications that emerge in families and among siblings, although these come from a more interior, and perhaps darker more complex place, are steadied against the solidity of a life in the Heartland.

At the same time, what we gain through our venture into this novel is insight into the pitfalls of relationships that we all experience in some way. The tentativeness of the approach, the re-ordering of our perceived beliefs in consideration of the other; the sojourn down unfamiliar paths—and the experience and wisdom gained for having done it. Our protagonist is not the Sugar-daddy, according to the colloquial definition of that term. Rather, he is the Sugar-baby—unsure, less than mature, and questioning himself at every turn as to whether he should venture onto and attempt to cross the bridge to a different kind of relationship with a different kind of person in a different kind of world. The metaphor of the bridge looms large in this regard. The idea of crossing over to a different series of experiences, constitutes one interpretation; another views the bridge as a connection between contrasting modes of existence. But that's what bridges do, and in truth, both interpretations have weight.

The novel is satisfying in that it does not answer all of the questions that arise. Good writing doesn't have to. It leaves us questioning, wanting more, and with much to discuss. *Sugarbaby Bridge* is both subtle and brutal in the questions that it raises and does not answer. And that is good.

As a one-time teacher of this young writer, I am proud. Proud of his development and determination, proud of the "way he turned out", and given that no one knows what inspires a student, proud that something about his time with me resonated and stuck.

Ruth E. White, Ph.D.

SUGAR-BABY BRIDGE

1

KEYS

His smile was predatory.

"Anything else in that?"

His expression exaggerated the wrinkles of his tanned face. He had thick, dark eyebrows over small, blue eyes and a receding hairline, partially disguised by being shaved. His clothes were intentionally worn and tight to show the lean physique beneath; the fit body contradicted the age that showed on his face. He had no belt and the top button of his jeans was left undone. I couldn't see them, but I was sure he had leather boots on his feet.

While I took in my observations, his eyes stayed fixed on mine. It had always seemed that men were easier to read than women. Women were far more evasive with their intentions. His eyes told me that flirting was his favorite part of the job. Listening to him speak, I imagined I could hear years of reckless passion that had left dents and scratches in his voice, but underneath, it seemed a resilient hope had survived. It was possible that it was his ability to control the alcohol content of people's drinks that had boosted his confidence.

Personally, I'd never really been into the whole "alcohol" thing. I'd always thought that getting drunk was something the popular kids did. Even though I secretly wanted to be one of them, in the way that every unpopular kid wants to be part of the "in" crowd, I spent my life avoiding their habits and I felt it hypocritical to participate in anything I associated with those who had rejected me on a daily basis. I knew it was a silly paradox to pretend that I didn't care what they thought, and then to let it affect my decisions through life. It did, however, make me feel like an individual who was somehow above mainstream thinking.

"That's all, sir," I replied with a smile.

The man left and came back with a frosty beer-mug filled to the top with milk. Some of it had overflowed and frozen to the side.

"So, being a good boy tonight?" He asked, exposing a mouth of perfectly straight, yellowing teeth.

"Always." I winked, and looked up and down the bar to see if anyone had mistaken my playfulness for actual interest.

He paused for a moment. I watched him watching me; his eyes scanned over my arms, neck, and chest, and lingered on my dog tags which were prominently displayed on the outside of my shirt.

"Let me know if you need a refill, or anything else." The edges of his grin sharpened and he winked again before moving to another customer, who had been waiting longer than I had. I picked up my drink. The warmth of my hand melted the frost on the mug's cold handle and the water dripped down the inside of my palm. In order to make the dangerously full mug more manageable, I took a few swallows of milk and then licked the thick residue off my lips. Bars usually kept whole milk for mixing creamy cocktails; the texture was silkier and the swallow more satisfying. Also, there was something that was decadent about drinking milk in its more natural state.

I took another drink and eyeballed the bar for a dark place from which I could people-watch. This would not prove difficult; in this bar, dark places were in abundance. The shadows of this bar seemed like a half-formed crowd all on their own, shifting nearer and nearer to the dim bulbs, flirtatiously occluding more intimate meetings, and providing constant companionship to those who drank alone. I chose a spot not far from the pool table and settled in. Using a few napkins, I wiped the half-frozen trails of milk from the bitterly cold mug until it was completely dry. Placing a napkin down on a ledge, I set the mug down, lifted it back up, and inspected it for a ring or other sign of wetness. When I saw that there were none, I knew I had successfully relieved the surface of any unwanted moisture or spillage that might leave my hands distractingly sticky.

The whole place seemed to move slowly to the rhythm of the deep bass throbbing out of the speakers, a sound that embraced the shadowy corners and disappeared into the black walls. Looking around, I surveyed the crowd that peopled the bar that night. Most of them were older men; they shaved their heads to disguise their true age. A few took a slightly different approach and wore baseball caps. I'd been in here before, but was pleased not to recognize anyone. Big city bars were always full of fresh faces and there was a certain relief in not having a prior connection to anyone there. Here, in the presence of strangers, I could be whomever I wanted without the consequence seeing them again or seeming out of character.

In the few years I'd been going out to clubs, I'd noticed that gay bars were divided in two by age and where there should have been a link, there was instead a chasm carved by disease. An entire generation was missing. Those who had lived through the seventies and survived the eighties were increasingly detached from the younger, lazier, and more flamboyant generation that was now exiting their closets in high school. I felt this divide separated bars into two generic categories: the new, brightly lit, pop-music filled video-bars with colored walls trimmed in brushed-metal, and the darker, seedier, older bars that clung to the nostalgia of an era predating the Stonewall Riots. I gravitated toward the second type, the type that typically

3

frightened away guys my age with their shadowy corners, trough style urinals, and black walls decorated with chains and Tom of Finland prints.

The Detour was one of these places and I was at home here. There was an honesty I appreciated about it. I guess to me, this place seemed to "get it." I reveled in their lack of pretension and blunt honesty about sex — but mostly, I felt comfortable in the rugged, frank, and masculine social environment and the company of the aggressive men it attracted.

I overcompensated in order to fit in. I was overtly blunt to the point of rudeness. I was especially harsh with anyone I didn't want to talk to. I was equally forward with anyone whose attention I had interest in catching. I felt like a jungle animal fending off threats and stalking my prey. It was animalistic, natural, and satisfying.

Strolling into the Detour that night, I was hoping to track down a bartender I'd once met. Nation was a memory, one I very much wanted to relive. I could still see the thick vein in the side of his scruffy neck, his barbaric forehead, his exaggerated jaw, and the stupid way he grinned at me. Bartenders were one of my many weaknesses. They always knew just how to play me; usually they just let me give away too much.

I have long believed that people slowly conformed to the aesthetic of their names. An Amanda tended to grow up to be soft, talkative, and caring; a Derek, on the other hand, was most often daring, cocky, and experimental. Personally, I'd never felt much like a Brad, but was lucky not to have been named after a vegetable or a car. Today's name pool seemed diluted with an uncountable number of bizarre names that permanently brand children with their parents' starvation for individuality.

Nation was a perfect example of someone who had grown into the coolness of his name. He was defiant and oozed a commanding sexuality that dared me to explore him. He did not strut — men like him did not need to — but heads turned to stare at him nevertheless and he cut a swath through a crowd.

4

He was not there. Either he wasn't working that night or he didn't work there anymore at all. My eyes wandered the bar and I took small sips of my milk to try to make it last as long as I could.

Out of the corner of my eye, I saw a man come up near me. I pretended to be engrossed in a game of pool between two men with shaved heads and leather chaps. A silence ensued while I stayed slightly turned away from him, frantically scanning for interesting details to distract myself with. I was amused with the cliché costumes of the men who were playing. This was the stereotypical image that everyone expected to find in a place like this. In fact, I would bet that many people thought all gay men looked like these two all the time, lounging around watching TV in a pair of leather pants, or cooking dinner in a harness and armbands. Straight men were all thought to be lazy beer-drinkers who watched football all day. From the time I'd spent in gay bars and the Marine barracks, I wasn't sure either side was entirely wrong about the other.

My unfortunate fidgeting caused me to swallow the last of my milk. I looked down at the empty bottom of the glass still thick with a white residue that pooled in a ring. Turning further away from whoever was next to me, I set the empty glass down and then leaned forward toward the pool players.

After several minutes, he still hadn't said anything. I could only assume that my strategy was working. It was a game for sure, but I detested men with no self-confidence. Both my father and my drill instructors had put it the same way; how could anyone take a man at his word if he didn't have any respect for himself?

As time passed, the number of balls on the table shrank but the score seemed to be even. Mostly, the balls bounced off the rails instead of sinking out of sight into the pockets. Not that pool was something I was any good at, but it seemed a single game between these two could go on for hours. Just as I started to favor the player with smoother skin and a pin-up girl tattooed on his forearm; the man who'd been next to me walked away.

I took the opportunity to give him a good once over while he wasn't looking. From behind, I could see that his hair was short, light brown, and well groomed. He walked with an exaggerated, almost awkward gait, but it was the fact that he was dressed in shorts and a clean, pressed polo shirt that made him stick out like a sore thumb.

Unlike this man, I had intentionally dressed to be noticed. I'd pulled on a tight white undershirt emblazoned with an iron-on eagle, globe, and anchor with USMC printed beneath it in bold capitol letters, all of which was squarely centered over my left pectoral muscle. My legs, lean from years of running in formation and calisthenics, were covered with faded blue denim. My combat boots were spit-shined and crisply reflected the colored lights that blinked and pulsed in the dark bar.

The pride I had in my appearance was also apparent in every other detail of my uniform. It was a uniform that I had been wearing since I'd stood in the middle of the night on that fateful pair of yellow footprints at MCRD San Diego four years ago. I could still hear the silent confusion of young men scuffling, and drill instructors shouting, as we were herded off white buses and then forced to stand, blankly staring for what seemed like hours. I could smell the stale air of the receiving barracks where I'd stripped off my civvies, packed them into a box, and was forced to stare off at the wall while they were carried away somewhere. I had been glad to be rid of them; I had equated them with everything wrong with me I was there to fix.

The balls on the table collided with a loud smack. My eyes wandered back to the pool game.

I hadn't seen the bartender approach. "This is for you." He set down another frosty mug of white that seemed to glow in the darkness. The milk inside rocked back and forth but did not spill over the edge.

"Really? Thanks."

It wasn't uncommon for anonymous men to buy me drinks. Through trial and error I'd figured out that it was best not to ask who'd paid and just drink. But I'd always end up playing the game in my head and look around to see who might have paid to keep my glass full.

Shooting me another devilish grin, he leaned across me inappropriately closely, to pick up my empty glass. As he reached, his eyes never broke with mine. Even in the low light, I could see his blue irises had small stains of brown near the pupils, and the whites revealed small irritated veins. I could smell his cologne, faded from a long night at work, and mixed with traces of body odor. After retrieving my glass, he turned away and casually walked back to the bar.

Picking up my glass, I took another drink of the cool liquid. I'm not sure why I found milk so satisfying, maybe it was because its opaqueness made more substantial than other translucent beverages or maybe it was some Freudian reference to my mother; either way each swallow was pleasant. My mouth was coated with the sweet taste of the milk that changed, as it warmed on my tongue, to a mellower flavor that lingered until I took another crisp, refreshing drink and started the cycle over again.

After waiting a few minutes, I started my game. There were a number of guys glancing in my direction—predictable since I had dressed specifically to turn heads. Any one of them could have been my anonymous opponent. Still, their brief looks or lingering stares were obstacles trying to block me from reaching my goal. My freshly cut high-and-tight was also quite popular among the patrons of the establishment, and they'd probably have still been looking at me even without my skin-hugging attire. The man in the polo shirt started to make his way over to where I was again. When I accidentally made eye contact, I immediately looked away and back at the other game the men were playing in front of me. I felt stupid for having done so, like I'd done something wrong, a foul that endangered my chances of winning.

The pieces fit that he was the one who bought me the drink. I let the image of his face sit in my mind to consider if I found him attractive. It had been a day since he'd last shaved. He had a strong jaw and small eyes that peered through the dark. His skin was tanned, his neck was strong, and the hair on his head had only receded slightly. His expression seemed sure with no traces of self-consciousness. He was definitely my type. I clenched my teeth together to keep from smiling.

"I'm Ron," he said with a deep, refreshingly masculine voice, and extended his hand.

I looked him up and down purposefully. Upon closer inspection I could see his clothes were not just clean but brand new, with small creases where they had been folded. He had meaty forearms that ended in durable but manicured hands with strong thick fingers.

"Brad." I resisted the urge to use my last name. First because of sports and then the military, I'd exclusively gone by it for the past several years. In fact, I'd rarely actually ever heard my first name since I'd been a high school freshman, and it felt weird to speak it aloud again.

Letting my smaller longer fingers enter the grasp of his; our grips tightened down on one another. His handshake was very firm and our hands fit perfectly together; we were both experienced hand-shakers. The skin of his hands was tough, but not callused, soft, but not sweaty. I'd gotten my firm handshake first from my parents making me practice it and then from the long, congratulatory lines at swim meets and later from promotion and award ceremonies.

"Marine Corps, huh?" He asked.

I smiled. I could tell he had been drinking, but he seemed to be holding it well.

"The real deal. But, I just got out actually." I purposely licked my lips and grinned out of the right corner of my mouth. Looking around the bar, I took a survey of who was watching us. Ron was definitely my type, but there was always the chance there was someone else even more appealing that I might prefer. Balancing back and forth between his feet, Ron seemed excited but calm. The anticipation of sex was always more thrilling than the act itself, which was already on the high end of my thrill scale. He took a drink from his cocktail. I think it was the only time I'd ever seen someone other than myself drinking something other than beer in a bar like Detour. "That's great." This time Ron was the one who checked the room. "Let's get out of here." His words were more command than suggestion. As it was an order, I simply obeyed. I'd told my friends before, if they ever wanted me to do something, they were better off just to tell me to do it than to ask me if I wanted to. "Good to go." I drank down the rest of my milk, wiped my mouth, and threw the napkin into a nearby trashcan as I followed him to the door.

We pushed aside the heavy rubber flaps that kept the weather outside while the door was propped open. Outside, we stood in the cold fog of the San Francisco night. The misty cloud suspended in the air hazed the lights and numbed the city like Novocain. All six lanes of Market Street were vacant except for a few cabs parked along the opposite side in front of another club. Music pulsed out into the air, and was swallowed up by the gloom. I could see skinny figures dancing on the balcony of the bar and tiny sparkling dots from the dance lights inside.

One of the cabs made an illegal U-turn around the wide median and pulled up in front of us. Ron opened the door and climbed inside, leaving it open for me. An almost nauseatingly sweet blend of air fresheners emanated from the plastic crown glued to the dashboard. When I looked out the smudged windows, my mind became fixated and I felt a need to get some glass cleaner so I could watch the buildings pass by without the distraction of looking through drunken handprints.

"What's your name?" Ron leaned forward and asked.

"Excuse me, sir?" The cab driver was startled that a passenger was saying anything other than directions.

"What's your name, buddy?"

"It's George, sir."

"You're a good man, George." Ron sat back against the seat. The warbling of his voice, and the unrestrained way he spoke indicated that he was drunker than I had realized. Ron gave him an address on Knob Hill.

San Francisco was divided in to a myriad of districts with appealing names. I was unfamiliar with the actual locations of most of them but I'd been here often enough to know my basic way around.

I'd first come to San Francisco nervous and excited that I would find this gay Mecca where everything was OK and nobody cared. My image of San Francisco was one of rainbow painted curbs, daily parades, bohemian coffee houses on every corner, and a gay population so numerous they were in positions of power that held open every possibly opportunity. What I had found was a gay ghetto where heterophobia was as prevalent as homophobia was anywhere else.

"You got kids, George?" Ron continued.

"Pardon, sir?"

"I said, do you have kids?" Ron's voice carried a tone distinctly signaling that while he was being personal with the driver, Ron would be steering the conversation.

"Yes, sir, three. Star, Karma, and Passion." I smiled as he listed these names, which proved the point I had made to myself earlier about the absurd titles that his children would have to endure for their entire life.

"Good man."

Ron continued to extract information from the driver about his family and history, never revealing anything about himself, strictly following a question and answer format and always in that same forceful tone. I'm sure George went along with it because it was different, and at least was better than driving strangers around in silence.

George's children were by two different women and he had hinted jokingly that there might be more beyond his knowledge. He had moved into the city from Oakland and gotten twice married and twice divorced. I didn't understand why Ron was interested, so I just listened. George had never gone to college but he had acquired his GED. It seemed stereotypical, all of it, like he'd picked up a status sheet for black, middle-aged men and signed up for whatever was at the top of each list. Ron had been looking out the window while he interrogated the driver. I put my hand on his knee and worked my way up his muscular hairy leg and half way up his shorts. Ron's reaction was that of a child who'd just been given a free chocolate bar. His skin tightened and he sat up a bit straighter. I could see the muscles in his jaw clench as he eyeballed the driver in the rearview as if he were afraid the driver might "figure us out." I knew George had us figured out ever since he picked us up together outside a gay bar in the Castro.

The cab slowed and I reached for my wallet. Ron pulled a small wrinkled wad of cash from where it had been stuffed into his front pocket and passed one bill up to the driver. "Take good care of Star, Karma, and Passion." I was a bit surprised that in his state he had remembered these names, which I had forgotten almost as soon as I'd heard them.

We stood under a long green awning that hung over an iron-gated front door. The neighborhood was high on a hill near downtown. The shrubs were well manicured, and there was no garbage in the gutters of the street.

We walked up to the gate and Ron fumbled for keys. After a short search that yielded nothing, he looked up at me. At first I thought maybe he expected that I had the keys, but then a sly grin crept over his face while he gawked at me. I raised an eyebrow and took a step towards him to encourage whatever mischievous thoughts he had brewing in his head.

We were interrupted when a well-dressed couple approached the door laughing and talking in voices that echoed down the empty city streets. The woman noticed us first, and she stopped babbling immediately. Her grip on the man's arm tightened visibly, and her lips pursed in a grimace of obvious distaste. Mid-laugh, the man noticed us. After a brief look of surprise and a slight move in which he placed himself between the woman and us, as though to shield her from our gayness, they both suddenly found the ground quite interesting. They

11

moved to the door, guarding it as the man put in his key, held the door open, and the woman scooted through. Ron attempted to follow them.

"I can't let you in!" the woman proclaimed and started pushing on the gate to close it.

"I live here."

"I'm sorry, I can't let you in."

The man looked at Ron and his expression changed as if he recognized him. He put his hand on the woman's shoulder to get her attention and interfere. The woman was looking out with cold eyes and firm lips and she did not yield and shut the gate virtually in Ron's face. They disappeared into the building and it was quiet again on the sidewalk.

Ron looked up at me, puzzled.

"I live here," he stated. "Ronny!" he shouted out into the night. "Ronny! I live here."

I stood silent and amused. Ron brandished a cellular phone from his pocket and began to look at it as if trying to remember what to dial. He then looked up at the door.

"Get in here!" he shouted again. There was a change in his voice when he was shouting. When he was shouting his name, the intonation went up at the end in a unique way. He was clearly mimicking someone from his past. I assumed it was his father's voice that was echoing out down the orderly streets of neighborhood. He paused for a moment, looked up, and walked over to the directory on the building. He began pushing buttons with a finger extended from the same hand in which he still held the cell phone. He was squinting at the numbers like they were in microprint.

"Hello?" A voice came crackling over the intercom.

"It's Ron. I…"

"Did you forget your keys again, sir? I'll be right out, sir."

Ron continued to stare at the directory as a man appeared behind the gates to the building.

"Ronny! Get in here! Ronny!" He still had the same upward intonation at the end of his name.

"Have you been waiting long, sir?" The man seemed very concerned, and ignored Ron's drunken belligerence.

"They didn't let me in!" Ron talked at the ground instead of looking at the man next to him.

"Who, sir?"

"The… the… the couple."

"The couple on nine, sir?"

"They shut the door in my face."

"I'll be sure to mention something to them in the morning, sir." The man ushered us into the building and rang for the elevator. Ron had put his hands back into his pockets and appeared to be searching for his keys again. He looked up suddenly at me, surprised and elated at my presence. I smiled back, wondering if he'd forgotten who I was.

The elevator doors opened revealing a small space with mirrored walls held up by an ornate, twisting golden framework. We entered and stood in the back of the little gilded room. The man climbed in, pressed the button, and the three of us headed up. I noticed that he had pushed the button for the penthouse.

When we reached the top, the man stood to the side and waved us to exit first. Ron stood in front of the door and put his hand in his pocket yet again looking for the key that wasn't there last time. I was very close to laughing at the sight of him digging so deep into his pocket as if his keys still might be in there hiding in some corner of his shorts he had not checked yet. The man, who I assumed was the building manager, and to whom I was aware I had not been introduced, produced a large ring with dozens of keys fastened to it.

The man unlocked the door; Ron entered, and headed down the hallway toward the only door. With the click of a switch, light too bright for any room but a bathroom poured out the open door and lit up the hallway. I turned around to the building manager.

"Thank you very much, sir."

"Don't mention it. Call me if you need anything, sir."

I nodded and shut the door.

I used the sound of Ron's urinating as a timer to check out my surroundings. The apartment disappeared around both corners and contained several white rooms with wide doorways opening into even more spacious rooms — all void of furniture.

When I heard my timer stop and the toilet flush I quickly repositioned myself back by the door. Ron emerged from the bathroom and stood in the light of the doorway. I walked down the hallway toward him at a deliberately slow pace.

I would have complimented him by saying something like "nice place," but the fact was obvious that his living conditions—while bare of art, tables, couches, or even a chair— were beyond nice. I came up close and loomed over him wearing what I knew to be a cocky grin. I was considerably taller than him, and he had to tilt his head far back to look at me. Looking up put him off balance, which he compensated for by grabbing me by the arm and neck pulling me down to kiss him. His kiss had the same forcefulness with which he spoke.

His lips were hard; he pushed them into mine with the force of his whole head. His tight hard lips barely opened and his body tightened. He kissed like man who still didn't know it was okay, and that God wasn't going to punish him for it. We stood for a moment in the hall, his hands almost painfully squeezing my arm and neck, and pressing those hard closed lips against my soft, relaxed mouth until he broke the embrace to breathe.

We moved into the bedroom in the middle of a long stumbling kiss. We broke to breathe and started to laugh as we wrestled out of our clothes. Neither of us could seem to strip fast enough. With my eyes now open, I saw that the bed was the sole piece of furniture in the room and was, of course, unmade. There was a tall pile of clothes on the floor against the wall and an open closet that revealed stacks of clothing all wrapped in drycleaner's plastic.

Ron's chest was strong and his body well built. He was short, with round muscular shoulders and a wide neck. His chest was hairy and his legs were thick, giving his entire form a well-proportioned, masculine look. He walked toward me naked, grabbed the back of my neck to kiss me, and then pushed me down onto the bed.

Almost immediately, he reached for a bottle of lube on the windowsill above the bed. Holding it in one hand he squeezed some out onto himself.

"Hey, stud, shouldn't we grab a condom?" I said.

Ron looked at me with a puzzled look that bordered on being offended.

"Aren't you clean?"

The question was pointed; even if I had an unfavorable answer it would not have been an option to give. "Of course."

Ron smiled and came at me to kiss me again. Here we were, facing each other from across the gay age-divide.

***

15

BRETT EDWARD STOUT

2

THE FAIRMONT

We lay in bed for a while afterwards, staring up from the white sheets at the white ceiling supported by white walls — all of which were tinted blue from the artificial light coming in through the tall windows.

"Let's get something to eat," Ron said.

"Now?"

"Aren't you hungry now?"

I laughed a little. "Well, actually I am I guess." I was shy on money, and I'd been getting by for the last few days on enormous cheap slices of cheese pizza found in abundance in small, somewhat seedy establishments in Noe Valley. At night I stuck to the liquid diet of milk that I had learned was an easy way to get some extra protein in a pinch.

"We'll go over to the Fairmont and get something."

He casually mentioned the place as though I was supposed to know what he was talking about. I managed to refrain from asking how far away it was, or if we'd have to learn the life story of another cab driver to get there.

Ron sat up and looked around the room. Disoriented, he searched the floor for his clothes. I couldn't remember where he'd tossed them either. Giving up, he went to the closet, ripped the plastic off a shirt and a pair of shorts, tossed the plastic onto the floor, and dressed without underwear or socks.

I watched him dress as I put my clothes on, amused at his lack of coordination. I knew exactly where my clothes were. We started down the hallway, me trailing behind him. He started opening the door and I spoke up.

"Where are your keys?" I asked him, embarrassed to sound a bit motherly.

Unfazed by my tone, Ron stopped, looked down, pointed his finger while he shook it in the air and shouted "Ronny!" He then walked into the kitchen, turned on the light, picked up the keys with a scraping sound, and flipped the light back off.

Since he hadn't reacted badly moments earlier I held out my hand. "Why don't I carry those, stud?"

Ron looked up at me with a grin, handed me the keys, and extended his hand through the open doorway indicating that he wanted me to go first.

Once on the street, I immediately took note of the fact that the neighborhood was as quiet at this time of night as my hometown in Iowa was. The only sound was the rushing of car tires on pavement made wet by condensation from the thick fog. As the cars drove down the streets, the sound would get louder and then fade off somewhere out of sight.

"Where are we headed?"

Ron did not answer. Instead he took off down the block. I followed, and hid my annoyance at him for avoiding my question. Even if he was drunk, he had no right to be rude to me. However, I also knew it would be pointless to point it out, or to argue with someone as intoxicated as he was.

We rounded the corner, and as we did a large building with cement columns, a corniced roofline, and decorative moldings above the windows and around the base came into view. Bright floodlights illuminated the façade, and its entrance was adorned with several flags of countries I didn't recognize. It was located on the top of a hill, and all the structures seemed to descend from this spot. In every direction, streets sloped down steeply toward the other slumbering neighborhoods of the city.

The lobby of the Fairmont contained luxurious oversized leather chairs with carved wooden legs, and settees upholstered in gold fabric, all positioned on large beautifully-shaped rugs. The clusters of furniture were finished with large palms in decorative oriental pots, and wooden tables with bouquets of peach, pink, and cream-colored roses that looked about four-feet wide. Golden marble columns ascended to a ceiling so high it seemed they were reaching up to touch, instead of support, the elaborately painted embellishments. The ceiling reminded me of the illuminated pages of an ancient text.

Ron walked in, determined and authoritative. He looked around, and made for the clerk at the desk.

"Good evening, sir, welcome to the Fairmont. How may we be of service?"

"We need some menus. We're hungry." Ron's speech was short and without patience.

Behind the counter the young man's mouth opened and closed twice, as if he had been about to say something rude but thought better of it. After another pause, he straightened more fully and spoke. "Um, at this time, sir, I'm not sure, but I think the kitchen is closed." I didn't like the clerk or his obsequious manner, but I still felt sorry for him. After all, he made his living being rudely talked to by people like Ron.

"Then get someone down here to make it open." Ron said, implacable.

The desk clerk was clearly intimidated but Ron seemed not to care. Ron stepped back from the counter without waiting for the clerk to respond. He idly looked down at his sandals while the desk clerk picked up the phone.

"Just one moment, sir," The clerk said.

Ron wandered away from the desk and I followed him. I continued to take in my opulent surroundings. Within three minutes a man dressed in a sleek, black, silk suit and a tiffany blue tie appeared and walked towards us. His shoes tapped against the marble floor and echoed through the lobby. The similarly-dressed woman beside him walked silently on the same stone. The man was handsomely groomed, about thirty, carrying a leather portfolio, and showing a smile that was polite but not inviting.

"Good evening, sir. May I help you?" the man asked.

"Yes. We need menus," He could have been addressing a McDonald's worker at a drive-thru and not a dignified manager at an expensive hotel.

"I apologize, sir but our kitchen closed at 10, and won't reopen until breakfast."

"Make it open. We're hungry. You will go get us menus and find someone to cook the food if the chef isn't here."

"I'm sorry about the inconvenience, sir…"

"My father is a close friend of Prince Alwaleed bin Talal." Ron paused. "Make it open."

The man looked to me with an expectant expression. What exactly did he expect me to do? I approached him and led him a few feet away from Ron. His female assistant walked over to the counter to the desk attendant, who was on the phone again.

"I'm very sorry, sir. We just came in for some food. I understand if you're unable to reopen the kitchen, but if there is anything you can do we'd really appreciate it. Thank you very much for assisting us, sir." My high school foreign language classes had prepared me for this moment. I was translating Ron, who spoke rude fluently, into a non-offensive form of English that was easier on the palate.

"Perhaps we can see if there is anything left in the fridge." The man smiled sincerely for the first time.

I looked over at Ron, who was wandering around, shaking his head. He shouted. "Ronny! I need some service here!" His voice echoed through the lobby, and he scolded his own loudness by shushing himself.

"I'm not sure that's gonna work for Ron. Is there anywhere you guys can order for us, while we wait?" I said.

The woman came back from the desk, gently touched the man on the arm, and then spoke into his ear. "Let us see what we can do to accommodate the both of you. Would you mind waiting in the Tonga Room while we get some menus for you?" The man gestured through an open door into the next room, leading deeper into the hotel and, more importantly, out of the lobby where we might offend anyone else who might come in. That anyone else would be coming into a hotel like this, at the hour that it was, didn't seem likely but I did as he asked.

"Yes, thank you, sir." Clearly Ron's story must have checked out. From listening carefully to the woman's whispers, I learned that the Prince was the new co-owner of the luxurious hotel.

We walked into the dining room, which was even more impressive than the lobby. Ron seemed completely numb to the lavishness of his surroundings. He simply stared at the floor, positioned in the chair as if he'd been thrown there. I could not act so indifferent, and I marveled at the space. The Tonga Room was filled with tables covered in thick linen and graciously spaced apart from one another. They were all arranged around a central rotunda, from which a chandelier hung and illuminated a spiral staircase that wound down into the floor in the center of the room. Marble Neoclassical columns capped with dark-golden Ionic tops broke up the vastness. They collectively supported the central rotunda. The soft light that fell individually on the center of each table added to the intimacy of the space.

Each table was set with stacked china and full sets of silverware. It was comforting to know the basic order in which I was to use the multitude of forks, knives, and spoons. My mother had taken care to teach me about formal dining. Crystal water and wine glasses, gleaming in the muted light, were overturned, and large pale-yellow cloth napkins that matched the marble of the columns were folded into large and intricate flowers and placed atop each plate. The entirety of the wall was painted in a faded fresco depicting tropical plants in front of a blue horizon.

I pulled up one of the heavy wooden chairs and gestured for Ron to sit. Off in the distance, a stout Hispanic woman holding a can of furniture polish was running a rag across the backs of the chairs. We waited in the quiet of the room, and I imagined that it would ordinarily be filled with soft jazz played by a quartet or piano.

"Have you stayed here before?" I was immediately embarrassed by the stupidity of my own question. I mentally scrambled for a way to turn what I'd said into something clever. Ron looked up at me, squinting, but he didn't seem to think a reply was necessary.

"I just wondered, since I'm sure they have furniture here." I waited to see if he would think what I had said was funny. He laughed.

The woman in the suit shortly brought us two menus. Since the menu appeared to be in French, I let Ron order for me. I didn't want to embarrass myself by ordering the roast chicken with mashed potatoes by mistake. "Two sirloins, mashed potatoes…"

"Oh, um…" I felt rude interrupting him and he looked at me as if I'd insulted his mother. "I'm sorry, I'm a vegetarian." I spoke softly and tried to look genuinely apologetic. Ron just looked at me for another moment as if asking, "What's wrong with you?"

Then he turned back to the menu and continued with the order. "Make one of those a pasta with steamed vegetables."

I was used to getting strange looks when I mentioned my being vegetarian. My experience had taught me that carnivores tend to have an attitude towards those who choose to go without consuming the flesh of animals. They generally think that we're all missing out on something, and make it their business to tell us, with great fervor, the error of our ways. Their advantage is that as a meat eater they can order straight off the menu at any establishment.

I'd stopped eating meat while I'd been in the Marines. I'd been dating a guy who was a vegetarian and a smoker. I was still under the impression he was just a bad boy whom I could influence or change. He'd made a bet with me that he would quit smoking if I stopped eating meat. Needless to say, he didn't quit smoking, but I rediscovered the flavor of food all over again. Before becoming vegetarian, my eating habits were filled with the same dishes prepared with only slight variation at each restaurant. Everywhere I went I'd order my "usual." When I stopped, I adapted and became creative. I didn't usually share this with people. Even in my own head, it sounded neurotic.

In addition to the order, Ron requested two pints of homemade ice cream, one with fresh strawberries and the other chocolate. While we waited, I watched the woman clean and wondered where she was from. How much did they pay her? Did she have a family here in US, or did she send money back somewhere? After Ron had interrogated the cab driver, I was mildly surprised that he did not do the same to the maid.

The woman in the suit came out the kitchen with our meals in a sturdy-bottomed plastic carry out containers, tucked in a paper sack that was so decoratively patterned that it approached the point of femininity. The ice cream came in smaller containers. It suddenly struck me that they had previously mentioned that the kitchen was closed. Did the cook live in the hotel? Surely the chef was not here this early the morning. Did the manager wake him up to prepare Ron's emergency fillet? Or did they slide out of their silk suit-jackets and cook it themselves?

The group of us made our way into the lobby again.

"Thank you for your patience this evening. Is there anything else we can do for you tonight, sir?"

"Yes." Ron paused and pointed his finger in the air again. "I want some golf balls."

The manager raised his eyebrows, puzzled not only by Ron's request for golf balls after three in the morning but also by the fact that he was still making requests.

"I'm sorry, sir, but at this time the Logo shop, Vendetta, is closed. But if you like, I can have the concierge arrange to bring you some in the morning."

"No good. Make it open."

The man's hand went into his pocket. His search turned up what I recognized as a Tiffany keychain. I stayed behind as he led Ron down to the Logo Shop for the golf balls.

"He's had quite a bit to drink tonight, hasn't he?" This was the first time I'd heard the woman speak above a whisper.

"Just a few." I laughed with her.

"Do you think there is anything else you'll be needing tonight?"

I smiled. "No, I don't think you'll have to worry about a return visit."

"Well, please let me know personally if there is anything more I can do." She slipped a business card into my hand.

"Thank you, ma'am, I will." We were both doing our best to watch our manners. Again I thought of my mother, who had always stressed that politeness in all situations was necessary. Any situation that might prove stressful to one or more of the parties involved was a necessary one. Ron returned after a few moments, staring at his golf balls with a smile of satisfaction.

"Let's get going before our food gets cold. Thank you again." I nodded to the man and the woman, who were now both smiling, probably glad to see our backs. I escorted Ron, who was stumbling a little now, back out into the glow of the fog that caught the ambient light reflecting off the building. I wondered what he'd be like sober, and then I wondered if I'd find out, and if I'd be staying the night or if, perhaps following more sex, we'd exchange awkward goodbyes. I'd have to figure out how to get back across town without any money.

***

3

WE ALL SCREAM FOR ICE CREAM

We reentered the apartment and I sniffled from the chill outside. My knuckles had turned white from holding onto the bags in the cold. Entering the kitchen, I flipped the light switch and set Ron's keys back down on the counter. I could hear Ron in the bathroom again, so I carried the bags into the next room — which thankfully had a dining table and chairs. I set the bags onto the table and removed the warm, moist containers from underneath a stack of monogrammed paper napkins. The napkins were so thick at first I'd thought that they were cloth. I smiled at the attention to detail. That axiom was one of the single most important characteristics of being a Marine. During Boot Camp, it had been hammered into our heads relentlessly and under the threat of agonizing punishment. Nothing was more important to a first impression than appearance. The Fairmont understood this and wanted everyone to know at all times, even if they had taken their meal to go, you were being taken care of by a first-class, five-star establishment.

Ron walked in rubbing his eyes just as I put the finishing touches on our dinner set-up. I had done my best to replicate a civilized table. Forks nestled on napkins on the left, knives on the right turned inward, and the lids removed and discarded. Ron sat down, picked up his utensils, and began to work on his fillet. I excused myself to the bathroom to wash my hands.

Coming in and out of the bright and dark rooms was starting to make my eyes ache. I found the soft, white, silky bar of soap and started to wash my hands. Looking in the mirror I saw that my face had become oily from a mixture of bars, walking, and sex. Turning the water up hotter I splashed myself. The oils quickly liquefied and I felt my fingers become slick and slimy. I squeezed my eyes shut and lathered my hands gently on the bar of soap and then lightly spread it over my face. I rinsed as thoroughly as possible, careful not to leave any near my eyes that would leave them disgustingly bloodshot. The last thing I needed was to emerge from a trip to the bathroom with a flushed face and bloodshot eyes. That was not an impression that would work to my advantage if I wanted to stay the night.

Turning off the water I patted down my face with a towel and dried my hands. The surfaces of my palms were red from the painfully hot water. By the time I returned to the dinner table Ron had eaten most of his plate. I sat down across from him and started eating from mine. The food was good, if a little cold from sitting, but the pasta was perfectly cooked and the sauce was creamy but not heavy. I did my best to catch up to Ron so that we might finish at the same time, but he was already eating the last bits of his food. While I was hurrying, I felt Ron looking at me. I looked up. I could not read the expression on his face. I swallowed, wiped my mouth, and then asked, "Do you want ice cream?"

"Sounds good." He sat back in his chair and looked around the room a little. I couldn't exactly tell what he was thinking about or observing. Maybe he was planning what exactly he was going to do to make this place look like someone lived in it, but somehow I doubted it.

It felt strange to keep eating now that Ron was done so I laid my fork down. I had only eaten roughly one quarter of my pasta, but wasting it felt less rude than making him wait for me to finish. The main course had ended so I took both our plates and discarded them in the kitchen. I started opening the empty cupboards to find where he might have stored bowls. Each one I opened was empty. I checked all the natural hiding places, but turned up empty-handed. True, there was no furniture in the apartment—but no dishes? Opening the less likely cabinets under the counter I revealed a cluttered stack of pots and pans and two mismatched bowls. Thinking the worst was behind me, I pulled the handle to the silverware drawer. What I found instead of flatware was that the drawer was stuffed with unopened mail. So much mail that it overflowed and had to be smashed down again before the drawer would close.

I resisted the impulse to laugh or scream at the absurdity of the situation. "Where are your spoons?" I called out to Ron.

I shook my head, baffled, and lost the fight with laugher. After there was no reply, I collected myself and continued rummaging through the drawers, all full of unopened envelopes. While I searched the cabinets again, Ron entered the kitchen and opened one of the drawers I had already checked. After lifting its contents as one solid mass he pulled out two spoons and handed them to me. He did this in a way that seemed perfectly natural to him, like he did it every day. Maybe Ron thought that everyone stuffed their kitchen drawers with unpaid bills and junk mail. I chuckled softly. I felt like I could get away with it at the moment while I served up the ice cream. He was looking at his sandals again, thinking, when I turned around and handed him a bowl containing a scoop of each flavor.

"Do you always go to the Fairmont at three a.m. when you want ice cream?" Ron was not amused by my comment. "How long have you lived here?"

"I don't always live here. I got the place a year ago, but I don't spend much time here." I wondered how long it had taken to accumulate the pile of laundry on his bedroom floor but I didn't ask.

"Where are you usually?"

"I spend a lot of time traveling for business." We both stood eating in the kitchen. Ron swallowed each time before he spoke. He held the bowl close to his face and his head hung down toward it. His posture was such that he looked to be guarding his food from any hungry lions that might wander by and try to take it.

"What do you do?"

"Loan stuff."

Ron's available wardrobe didn't look like he spent much time in an office. I imagined that most of his work might be accomplished via private golf outings or sailing trips. I romanticized his attitude and surroundings and that he might live a fantasy life that I had only theorized might be possible: one of leisurely power-brokering.

After eating the scoop of strawberry, he set it down on the counter with the chocolate scoop sitting in it slowly melting. Ice cream went down easy for me and I finished first. I put our bowls in the sink and ran water in them so that they'd be easier to wash later. It didn't occur to me that maybe Ron didn't wash his dishes and it might not matter.

"Let's go up for some air." Ron said, breaking the silence of the empty apartment.

"Lead the way, good sir," I replied playfully.

I hadn't seen any balconies on the building and I didn't know where "up" meant, but I followed him to the door. We exited the apartment and entered the service stairwell. It was undecorated, full of utility pipes, and lit with yellowed lightbulbs. Making our way up the metal stairs we came to a large door with a stainless-steel push bar next to a sign that read *Roof Access.*

The roof was covered in the typical black tar substance that felt soft under my shoes and made walking feel strange and mushy. There was a scattering of boxy air conditioning units. A yellow and purple haze created by the city lights surrounded us. The fog diffused the lights of the city like smoked glass. I could see surprisingly far at this height despite the fog. I'd never stood on top of a building in the middle of a city. It felt surreal, like being in a science fiction film, and aliens were about to blast me into oblivion. It wasn't hard to picture that the buildings went on forever into the distance and that the ground might be thousands of feet below. It was a powerful and progressive vision of the accomplishments of man.

Ron walked over a ledge and picked up a lighter and pulled out from some unseen pocket—or perhaps his ass—a half smoked cigar. "Come on." He started climbing a metal ladder that went up a copula-like structure in the center of the roof. It was another story up above where we'd come out of the stairwell. There was an open area on it with a domed top held up by round columns. The design appeared Italian. I couldn't see what was actually up inside the structure, but I followed him up the metal ladder.

As the top came into view I could see that the space was bigger than it had appeared. There was no railing around the edge and in the middle there was a hot tub with a large leather cover on it. The lavish possibility of how impressive parties could be held in this rooftop was the first thing that came into my head. The second was how scandalous it could be to have sex in the hot bubbling water in the middle of the day, and look out over the city while the masses were busy at work.

"This is the hot tub with the best view in the city." He said with pride. I wasn't sure if the statement was aimed at me or if he was just saying it because he liked the way it sounded.

"I can see that. Did you want to get in? I didn't bring a suit but I'm not sure that will be a problem." Making my way around the hot tub to the side he was on I bit my bottom lip and did my best to make my excitement easygoing. This would be a story worth repeating. How one night I came back to a guy's apartment and lounged in a hot tub on top of a building overlooking the entire city.

"No, I'm tired." Ron flicked his cigar off the roof of the building and headed back to the ladder. "I just wanted air." I never understood why smokers described going out to smoke as "getting some air." It was an oxymoron.

I lifted the lid and inserted my hand into the water. A whirring sound and some steam escaped. The warm scent of chlorine wafted up to my face. The water felt smooth and silky, unlike hot tubs I'd been in previously that left my skin feeling dry and abrasive. I shut the lid with a soft thump and, with disappointment, listened to the whirring disappear back underneath it. I checked to make sure Ron had gotten off the ladder safely before I went down it. In order to get back to the main part of the roof, I had to face the hot tub. Slowly I watched it go out of sight as I sighed.

In seconds it seemed like we were back in his bedroom and Ron had changed back to the same lustful animal he had been the last time. Grabbing at the back of my neck he started kissing me with his tensed lips. I smiled as he kissed me frantically. Reaching for his hand I took his wrist and used my strength to pry his grip from my neck. It was my turn to be in control. Amused, he fought back; a power struggle began. I smiled as he struggled to regain dominance. We were face to face like two wrestlers on television, holding him by one hand and one wrist, I muscled him down to the bed.

Lying on his back on the bed, he stripped off his shorts and then his shirt, which seemed backwards to me. He got back up on his knees as if he was ready to leap off the bed and attack me naked. I pulled off my shirt and threw it in his face. Letting my jeans fall to the floor, I jumped at him.

He was unexpectedly strong considering how drunk he was. There was a smile on his face, one of pleasant surprise: surprise that I was strong enough to manhandle him. I wasn't entirely sure I could have if he'd been sober. He was shorter, thus he had a center of gravity advantage over me. I straddled him on the bed and pinned his hands over his head. Ron's mouth snapped at me as if he meant to bite me. I growled back and kissed him. While I did, I grabbed the bottle of lube with my free hand.

After the excitement ended, I lay in bed staring up at the blank ceiling. Ron began to snore. He was sleeping far away from me on the bed. It didn't surprise me that Ron was not one who liked to cuddle. My mind wandered from topic to topic in the dark, quiet room. I wondered if Ron's parents were disappointed or proud of him or if they spoke to them at all. I knew that mine were proud of me, but thought little of the poorer decisions I had made. Like the ones I'd made tonight. As anxiety built about facing the disappointed looks of my parents I instead started to fantasize about telling friends about my strange night with a rude, rich, alcoholic. Another joy about vacation was that I could pick and choose the adventures I would share when I went home to face the life I'd escaped. They'd envy the dazzling view from the roof and the hot tub I could easily pretend to have lounged in. I could hear their laughter as I told them about the golf balls and the drawers stuffed with bills and I could leave out the more reprehensible details of going home with him after a few sentences and the unprotected sex.

Before long, I began to feel anxious about sleeping in. I knew that it was rude to sleep longer than my host... what if he didn't wake me up? What if he waited for me, getting more annoyed by the minute? But I wasn't prepared to deal with tomorrow yet, so turning onto my side, I counted my breaths and forced myself to sleep.

***

4

THE USEFULNESS OF PEOPLE

As I counted, drifting off into that hazy indefinable margin between sleep and wakefulness, I allowed myself to relive the last few days. Even though I'd only been in the city for a little more than a week, it felt like months. I'd decided to take a military hop from Hawaii and exploit the Marine Corps one last time. It was actually the first one I'd done. Taking a hop was something cheap everyone frequently talked about but rarely actually did.

The experience had been anything but pleasant. After waiting in the terminal for twenty-six hours, surviving on snacks from the vending machines, and exploring ways to sleep on the plastic chairs that had been fastened together in groups of four, I finally boarded. The flight itself was long, cold, and completely barren of the usual amenities: things like soda, little bags of nuts, or pillows. I sat facing backwards. The seating area on the cargo plane was on the upper deck, in the dark, and surrounded by bundled cases and canvas bags. The only windows were the ones on the exit doors and most of the light came from them and the tiny bulbs here and there on the cavernous hull of the plane. Nevertheless, it felt freeing to get away from prospect of my nebulous post-Marine life in Hawaii. My heart was hollow and light with indecision about what I'd done; leaving the Marines was a choice that could not be undone and it terrified me that I'd chosen wrong.

Rows of chairs were bolted down to large metal sheets with industrial carpet glued on. This gave the appearance that the area we were in had a solid floor, but underneath we all knew was a metal mesh just strong enough to hold our predicted weight. On the rest of the upper level the sturdy see-through metal floor was exposed. I could see down into the lower area where more bundles of cargo were stored. As for the bathroom, it contained little more than a toilet welded into place. It would suck the contents out into the upper atmosphere. The flight was cheap and I got what I paid for.

I hadn't brought much money with me, and I had traveled light. Packing to stay for a weekend was something I had grown used to from trips across the island to Waikiki, short vacations home, or to various destinations on the mainland. I had one bag with me; it was full of clothes with a little room in it in case I picked up anything. I intended to fill the extra space with porn, which was sold at a steep premium on the islands but while I was in the city, I could usually get a good deal. Thus the extra space in my suitcase. Gay porno tapes were alike in that their titles would invariably be a double entendre referencing some part of the male anatomy or sneaky sexdezvous: The Bigger the Better, Power Tool, and The Other Side of Aspen. I was not about to walk though an airport carrying a gaudy VHS that had such a self-evident title.

I was a little homesick in California. Hawaii had become a romanticized home that I found myself ignoring the difficulties of. Island life was certainly not all plumeria blossoms and palm-covered beaches. Milk and other perishables that had to be flown in regularly sold at four times the price that they did on the mainland. While it was relatively easy and cheap to get to and between the islands, getting back to the mainland was something that took time and planning. "Island fever" was not a joke, and many felt trapped and claustrophobic. I just thought they needed to get out more and see what else the island had to offer. I rotated between the different activities and different bar scenes, making sure to keep active and entertained.

Without bad weather to complain about, people focused their negative energy on other topics. Political corruption and the economic slump were popular choices. While the rumors of corruption had some merit, the slump wasn't actually a slump at all, but a normalcy that followed the dramatic boom of the Japanese economy. I had learned, from looking at photos, that Waikiki had grown-up almost overnight in the seventies and eighties with the backing of various Japanese companies. This accounted for Waikiki being a jungle of mostly ugly, plain, concrete, balconied towers.

Overwhelmingly, I like it on the island. Hawaii is home because of the people and the absent fear of strangers. When I notice a hitchhiker, it never crosses my mind that he could be dangerous. What does cross my mind is more like, "I wonder if he's going the same way I am." Instead of paranoia of unfamiliar people there was unity and a friendly camaraderie. Instead of locked up fortresses, I found open-air condos. I even knew people who never rolled up their car windows.

When I moved to Hawaii, I became a member of an international community of travelers. Every home is stocked with things for the accommodation of guests. Extra sets of bedding, places to sleep, extra toothbrushes and other toiletries. No one seemed to mind having people stay the night and any guest was expected to reciprocate.

Without this unwritten traveling law, I'd never have been able to afford to come San Francisco, or just about anywhere else I'd visited. I'd been in the past but never for this long. My accommodations this trip were the courtesy of Hal. I'd met Hal through a guy with whom I'd spent time in Hawaii. I'd given him a free place to rest his head. Hal and Vlad had been roommates at the time. Vlad was attractive enough to persuade me to find the necessary excuse to make a trip to the mainland to see him.

I understood very well that men as attractive as Vlad are rarely bored. He'd been busy most of the time since I'd arrived and he'd dumped me on his roommate. Neither of us minded. We hooked up after spending the day together and developing a mutual attraction. Hal worked in computers and was good enough at it that he had license to take time off of work. Being not so bad looking myself, I didn't have much difficulty getting Hal to help me out with anything I needed, financial or otherwise. This trip was one of those times I needed his help. I wanted to escape my life in Hawaii for a while and San Francisco was the preferable choice over Iowa.

My hop landed at Travis Air Force Base, several miles to the northeast of the city. Later that night I did my best to show him how grateful I was for the ride and place to stay. Hal paid what, even in Hawaii, was a ridiculous price for his apartment, but that's the way things are in the Bay Area. This time it felt like Hal was a bit more distracted by work. I spent most of my time on my own, walking over the steep hill from Noe Valley into The Castro.

As I ambled from store to store, I'd convince myself that I was not cruising, I was leisurely window shopping. I'd make my way back up over the hill for lunch, wash my face at Hal's apartment and then trek back into The Castro where I'd continue browsing the merchandise.

Each time I went, I had a list of destinations I would frequent in an order to maximize the amount of time it would take to get to all of them. When left with entire days to waste, I devote great effort to become increasingly inefficient at performing the same limited number of tasks. This was the bliss of an unplanned vacation to a place I had already been.

I would break my routine from time to time when I'd run into someone who remembered me. Living in a city where the people are constantly circulating in and out, I had usually

36

forgotten their name, how we'd met, if we'd had sex, or even their face, but it never mattered. It was among the unwritten rules of pretty people that such impolitenesses were dismissed. The pleasantness of my vacation was interrupted twice. First, when I was heading up the steep hill to Hal's apartment. Opening my cell phone to check my voice mail—I frequently checked my voicemail despite the fact that it seemed like no one ever called me—my call was interrupted with an error message condemning me to call the cruel time-sucking deathtrap the phone company called "customer service." After hours of talking to insufferably incompetent people and countless transfers, I had my service resumed. Apparently they had lost my payment, but were going to look for it. They told me this with the air of someone granting a huge favor, such as donating a kidney. The second interruption was moments later, when I went to the ATM and had my withdrawal denied due to insufficient funds—though the ATM still collected its two-dollar surcharge.

Once back at Hal's, I discovered that my final paycheck from the Marines that *should* have posted days earlier had not. I had forty dollars in my pocket, I was alone in one of the most expensive cities in the world, and I had only been in the city for three days and I had several more days until my flight. I was not, however, without means.

As the days passed by, I began looking more intensely for anyone I recognized and getting them to invite me out to lunch, dinner or agree to meet me at some club I usually didn't want to go to. Mooching was not something I was used to, but it was a level I was prepared to stoop to. It wasn't like I was hurting anyone. After another few days, I had my new routine down and life was once again good.

I hadn't often seen Hal at the apartment this trip, so one night I waited around for him to come home. My intention was to ambush him with an intimate encounter and perhaps get invited to dinner. It didn't seem completely right to me to use him as a hotel and I wanted him to know that I appreciated his letting me stay. When he did arrive, he came in with a smile and a friend. Since he had company my ambush was foiled.

We all greeted each other, and Dave introduced himself. Hal had forgotten to. I learned that not only were they good friends, but that Dave, conveniently, lived upstairs.

"So what were you doing all day in the city?" Dave asked.

I thought of an answer obscure yet specific enough not to reveal that I had been cruising for guys. My answer had to be evasive enough not to sound pathetically boring but not enough of a lie that would cause distrust were I figured out. Friends have a tricky way of influencing each other's opinions and I was not about to make a mistake that would leave me homeless. I needed Dave to like me. My answer was ready. "Just kinda loafing around, hitting up Hot Cookie and getting pizza up around the corner."

"Oh I love both of those places!" I realized when he answered that Dave wanted to be won over. Dave leaned forward on the counter, Hal unloaded grocery bags into the fridge and cupboards, and I pretended not to watch for things I could eat later.

"So what do you do? Do you work with Hal?"

"Hell no! I make real money, honey." Dave was one of those sassy guys who swayed their head from side to side to add emphasis. Dave was a mix of Asian. I couldn't quite place his ethnic origins. His voice was half stuck-up, half feminine, he was a little overweight, and he straddled that peculiar line between true attractiveness and humdrum. He was the type of gay man who had become successful in business by being smart, and successful socially by being even smarter.

Hal turned to Dave with his mouth gaping open, mimicking a gasp. The gesture was new to me; Hal was usually masculine around me. His relaxed manner was a further indication that Dave was not just a friend, he was a close friend. I later learned that they had known each other for years and that in the beginning Dave had a crush on Hal that he managed to overcome in order to forge the lasting friendship.

"Ouch, that was harsh."

"Well the second you want to stop selling your soul for minor dockets, let me hook you up." Dave snapped his finger in the air the way a sixteen-year-old girl would.

"Why don't you take him up on it? Sounds like a good thing."

"When my job stops promoting me, I'll consider it."

"Okay if you want to waste your time over there, I certainly won't stand in your way, honey."

"Hey, Hal? Can I borrow a shirt from you for tonight?"

"Um..." He paused, considering my request. "Sure."

"Awesome. Thanks." I went into the bedroom and intentionally left the door open. I tried to listen to what they were saying while I searched for something tight in Hal's dresser drawer. I found the white undershirt I had given him almost a year ago when we first met. Hal had listened to Vlad tell stories about Hawaii and about me that eventually coerced him into making a trip out to islands himself. I had been more than happy to play tour guide.

Positioning myself at an angle to the doorway, where Dave would be able to watch, I peeled my shirt over my head and gave my neck a good slow stretch from side to side. I could see out of the corner of my eyes that Dave, my target audience, was watching. I took as much time as I could, without being obvious, unfolding the shirt, checking it for dirt, and readying it to be worn. I put the shirt on while I exited the bedroom and watched Dave's eyes follow the shirt as it slowly covered my abdominal muscles. He looked up at me embarrassed that I had caught him. I smiled and winked causing his cheeks to flush red.

"What are you kids doing tonight?" I asked.

"Hon, who you' callin' kids?"

"What, like you're old or something?" The compliment was cliché, but in a culture obsessed with youth and beauty, no one seemed to get bored of it.

"Flattery will get you everything." His slight twist on the old axiom made me smile. "I'm going to be thirty-six years old this year."

"*Really?*" Hal exclaimed, covering his mouth with his hand, and widening his eyes.

"Oh, no, you *didn't* forget how old I am."

"Hal has a hard time counting in the double digits sometimes."

Both of them turned towards me in unison. I crossed my arms, cocked my head to the side, bit my lip, and arched my brows. I happen to know that I looked particularly adorable in this pose.

"Hal, I like him, we're keeping him."

"I found him first."

It seemed that I had made good with the best friend in less than minutes. I was both satisfied and relieved. As the conversation progressed I learned that Hal actually had plans that night. I suspected it was a date and he was worried I'd be jealous or weird about it. Not wanting to press the issue I took Dave up on his idea going up to his apartment to hang out.

We went upstairs and he unlocked the door. Dave's apartment spoke to his personality. It had nicer and cleaner couches and tables than Hal's cluttered living conditions. He also had several plants and it smelled of vanilla air freshener candles. The more I learned about him the more I was intrigued and comfortable in his presence. He was originally from the city and had moved to Florida to go to school only to return to work for a business not unlike Hal's software company.

"So, what are you going to do now?"

"I was just going to go over the hill and hang out."

"No, I mean now that you're not a Marine anymore."

I was suddenly speechless and aware of the silence in the room. I had defined every quality of my life for the last four years with the trappings of being a Marine. It's something that sailors, soldiers, and airmen don't understand. To them, the military is a job, but the Marine corps is something that defined me every moment of the day. It had never occurred to me yet that I was no longer really one of them. Who was I now? The quiet stillness of the apartment became claustrophobic. I had no joke, witty comeback, or way to escape the question I had no answer to.

"I'm not sure." It was the truth and it hurt to say. I still felt like a Marine, my clothes still fit the same and the cold on the back of my head reassured me that my hair was still well groomed and within regulation. What was going to happen to me, what was I going to do? What was I going to say to the countless strangers who would ask me this question or the classmates I would have to face at high school reunions? I felt my grip tighten as if I would need to fight to defend that inside I was still a Marine, that I would always be one, like the phrase said. I stood there, inelegantly frozen, in Dave's apartment. I was literally speechless.

After a moment, Dave broke the silence that had cornered me. "Well, you've got some time. Are you planning on going to school?" Dave's voice was soft. He communicated his understanding that with one question he had eroded the entire foundation upon which my personality had been built.

"I'd like to, I guess. I have the GI Bill and all. You went to school in Florida?" I was desperate to change the subject, and people find it easier to talk about themselves.

"Yeah, it was nice. I hate Florida actually. It's just a bunch of skinny Latin guys who talk like girls." I laughed at his making fun of feminine guys and considered how feminine they would have to be for him to consider *them* girly.

"Yeah, no doubt. What is that? I'm gay because I'm attracted to men."

We laughed together for a while and talked about movies, the city, and what turned us on. I felt guilty when I made up a reason to excuse myself. All I was going to do was head to a bar and spend most of the evening alone, watching strangers. He was offering fulfilling conversation. I did not want to invite him and hamper my chances of finding someone. I was not ready to build even the first floor of a lasting connection with anyone. I yearned for the mystery that the variables of the bar offered; I wanted the potential to meet someone else, someone new, someone like Ron.

The next morning dawned crisp and bright. I hadn't slept enough and tried to cover my face to hide from the light. This was always a tricky balancing act. The feeling of my breath reflecting back onto my face was something I found distracting and uncomfortable. After some squirming I usually managed to pinch part of a pillowcase on my nose. This way, it neither blocked my breathing nor allowed the light to disrupt my sleep.

Whenever I wake up next to someone, I always worry that they might ask me what I'd been dreaming about. I worry that I'll have to lie. My dreams were usually the same and admitting their contents was embarrassing. In my dreams I am well known, respected, and living a life where money is not an object, the casual life of a celebrity. Truthfully, I had always wanted to earn my own way and prove myself through my actions and be known for being good at something. I cherished nice things, but I didn't think I was overtly materialistic. At the same time, I wanted monetary recognition for my worth.

If I hadn't left Dave's when I did, it was unlikely I would have ended up in Ron's bed. I might have just gone back to Hal's and crashed in his bed only to cause a moment of uncomfortable excitement when he walked in with his date.

But here I was instead. Trying not to be awake in Ron's big, white, fluffy bed in his big, white, empty apartment. The sunlight was just coming over the buildings and the decision I had avoided was now too pressing to ignore. I would have to make up my mind or time would decide for me.

***

5

MY FIRST NEW CAR

I felt Ron starting to stir when it really hit me. I sat up suddenly the way I did when I'd tripped or fallen from a building in a dream. Looking around the room I tried to find a clock but didn't see one. Glancing over at Ron's side of the bed, I saw Ron was sprawled clumsily, limbs akimbo, as if someone had flung him there. There was no sign of a clock on his side of the bed either.

My dry mouth indicated how thirsty I was. I was always parched when I woke up. At home I kept a full glass of water next to the bed to drink in the morning. Surely the kitchen the stove had a clock on it. I could kill two birds with one stone by getting a glass of water. Getting up I walked naked down the hall to the kitchen. The bright green numbers glowed back at me. They told me that it was only seven fifteen in the morning. I didn't really know if I could trust any clocks in Ron's apartment. The time felt more like eleven, but I was tired like it was five.

I filled the glass completely, listening to the changing pitch of the water pouring into it. The glass had touched my lips before I remembered I was in San Francisco, and I hated the metallic taste of the tap water. I opened the fridge and was not surprised at its contents. There was an open squeeze bottle of mayonnaise, a jar of Grey Poupon, some slices of cheese, and a dozen bottles of Fiji water. Grabbing one I opened it and let the refreshing water flood down my throat. It was too cold to drink fast, and the first few swallows had already painfully frozen the roof of my mouth.

Standing in his apartment in the morning light, I felt a little bit like the squeeze bottle of Mayo next to the jar of elegant mustard. There were details that I could see in the light that I hadn't noticed before—carved, painted, wood trim around the windows and on the walls that gave the impression of wood paneling. I was out of place but it didn't seem completely odd that I was there.

Ron lifted his head to look at me when I came back into the room and then quickly put his face back into the pillow. Then he lifted it again and looked at me more closely. He squinted to see me, and a small grin grew on his face before he buried it in his pillow for the second time.

"Go to sleep." He mumbled into the soft padding.

"I have to tell you something."

"Can it wait until morning?" I wondered what time of day, in Ron's world, morning began. In Marine time, it was already lunch.

"Is there any way you can take me to the airport? I'm actually supposed to fly back to Hawaii today at nine-thirty. I'm already cutting it kinda close."

"Skip it and stay in San Francisco."

What did he mean skip it? I couldn't "skip it." I couldn't just... not get on my flight. Could I? I hadn't ever really given it thought. The idea of not sticking to my schedule or not showing up somewhere at the designated time was a bit terrifying. Why not skip it? It wasn't like I had to report back to base and I didn't have a boss waiting for me. But, what would happen to me if I didn't get on the plane? What happened to my ticket? Did I lose the money for the one-way ticket to Honolulu or did I get some sort of credit with the airline? The number of variables became exponentially dizzying the longer I thought about it.

"I can't just skip it."

"Call the airport and change your flight to next week."

"Can I do that?"

Ron didn't feel compelled to answer my question when he felt he had already answered with his instigating statement.

"I guess I *could* call." I said unsurely. What was I doing, was I nuts? What did I have to lose? If I could change my flight without penalty what would be the harm? Picking up my pants off the floor I pulled out my phone. What if Ron gets bored with me? I barely have any money. Screw it. I picked up the phone and dialed information. My heart raced at the spontaneity of the moment.

The operator came on. "San Francisco, California. United Airlines at San Francisco International Airport. Thank you." When I hung up the phone my heart was pounding even harder. I played it cool and climbed under the covers. My eyes were about to pop out of my head and I was definitely not tired anymore. I had just stood up my plane back home and I had no clue what I was doing. It felt great.

Ron shifted closer to me on the bed; he was awake now. Maneuvering himself he went in for a kiss. I pushed him onto his back, positioned my head over him, and looked him right in the eye only inches from his face. As I expected, I could feel how this made him uncomfortable. His eyes then started to look more closely at the details of my face. He had kissed men before. But I deduced that he had never actually looked at one up close. I moved slowly closer and he started to close his eyes. I stopped and waited for him to open them again. I could feel him almost ready to squirm to escape the intensity of facing me. He didn't. Smiling at him, he looked at me as if for the first time. I closed my eyes and lowered my lips. His posture changed, and his body tensed up as it had when we kissed the night before. I felt his lips tighten before I touched them. Wanting to show him what

45

kissing could be like, I let my lips go soft and lightly brushed them across his. Brushing back and forth slowly until he relaxed. Before long his mouth opened and formed to mine. It was, in all likelihood, his first real kiss.

The passion and softness swept over Ron and he became docile. His body surrendered and his limbs went limp like an octopus does when it gives up fighting. Pulling back from him, I looked at him. His eyes were still closed and small wrinkles formed on the edges where he had pinched them shut. His eyebrows were blond with darker hairs sprinkled through them.

His eyes opened and he smiled at me, a little shy and a little surprised.

"Hi." I smiled down at him coyly.

Ron sat up and pushed me back onto the bed. Pinning me down he reached up to the windowsill. He gave me a smile, cluing me in that, despite my having just been in charge, I should not expect that to be a common occurrence.

Later on he got into the shower. When he didn't invite me to join him I assumed he wasn't into showers for two. Some people can be funny about that. I'd always thought that was a little odd, especially after the intimacy of sex. I wasn't particularly bothered; I could use the time to explore the apartment.

Moving from the dining room into the next I found what would have been the living room had it not been completely empty. It was a large, and had the same tall ceilings found in all the other rooms, spacious enough that it could have been furnished in a way that would provide three separate seating areas. There were doorways at both ends and two more in the wall opposite the large windows facing east. At the far end was a fireplace, and with no furniture, the character of the old wood floor was exposed for exploration. Had it not been for the rich, dark wood flooring the room might have felt cold and sterile; instead, it felt full of memory and history.

The only object in the room was a stereo on the floor. It was sitting at an awkward angle next to a pair of speakers unevenly spaced from it. The helpless look of the carelessly placed electronics offset the crisp feel of the room. Reaching down, I slid the unit so that it was parallel with the wall then I moved each speaker so that it faced directly out into the room. Ensuring that they were evenly distanced from the stereo, I pushed them slightly back so that they would not to be flush with the face of the stereo. The disarray of the gangly wires was also distracting so I collected them and hid from view as much as possible.

Getting up off my knees I looked down at my project and was pleased with my work. Running my tongue across my teeth I realized how much I needed to brush them. My host didn't seem like the kind of guy who would share his toothbrush, so I resigned myself to the fact that I'd have to pilfer some toothpaste, brush with my finger, and check under the sink for mouthwash to kill the layer of fur that had grown in my mouth.

With the sound of the shower still running around the corner I continued checking out the apartment. The place was much larger than I had realized, occupying the entire floor of the building. All told it there were five bedrooms without beds, a couple bathrooms without toiletries, three living rooms without couches, a few empty rooms I didn't know what were for, and one room that the built in floor-to-ceiling bookcases gave away as the library. Had all the trim not been painted over white the rooms would not have felt as impersonal and empty as they were. The library was the furthest room from Ron's and I could no longer hear if the shower was running so it seemed like a good idea to head back.

New details emerged as I gave the place a second look. Even though it was a square layout, it felt more like one long, continuous home. Since the building was old, the kitchen was small with plain flat surfaces and it lacked the marble countertops most places had nowadays. Giving another look up I noticed that the ceilings were flat plaster that differed from the textured ceilings I was used to seeing. I wondered if, underneath the layers of thick latex paint, once upon a time the ceilings had been decorated in elaborate frescos. Maybe someday a future tenant would accidentally stumble upon the hidden treasure and spend the exorbitant amount of money required to restore them.

As I went, I listened carefully for the sounds of the shower. The large living room with the stereo was when I first heard the sounds of running water. When I got back I heard that it was the sink running, and not the shower. Peeking in the cracked door, I saw Ron shaving himself in short frantic strokes. I had a strong urge to interject my philosophy of proper shaving technique. I didn't.

"Mind if I get in the shower?" It was a question but I wasn't really asking for permission.

"I'll get you a fresh towel." Ron said in a gruff morning voice. I wondered if the towels were stacked in a closet wrapped in plastic.

"Thank you, sir." It sounded odd the moment I said it. I'm not sure if the formality of the apartment, my desire to be polite, or force of habit from the Marines that made me call him "sir." He paused for a second and I pretended not to notice that I said it. Making my way past him I climbed into the shower. Ron said nothing, finished shaving, and then returned with a towel.

Once the water hit me, my internal timer began. When I was in Boot Camp my hygiene time was limited. I still couldn't get myself out of the mode that a shower was anything but a task that should be quickly and accurately executed. Starting with a thorough scrubbing of my scalp I systematically soaped and rinsed my body from head to toe. It rarely took more than four minutes or so to completely clean myself.

While I dried off, I glanced into the bedroom and found Ron was almost completely dressed. His outfit was almost identical to the one he wore last night; right down to the creases where they had been folded. Watching him in the mirror, I saw him standing in khaki shorts and another polo shirt. It was a good thing I took quick showers or from the looks of it he might have left without me. Ron was putting on his watch when I finished scrubbing my teeth with a finger.

What were we going to do? Today was a day I had planned weeks ago, but with one phone call I had thrown away my entire itinerary. My schedule now was a clean slate ready for any idea or plan of action to be written on it. I had hurried under the assumption that his request for me not to skip my flight meant that he wanted to hang out with me more. I was not one-hundred percent sure this was the case; in ordering me not to leave, and fly out a week from now, I'd assumed he'd meant for me spend the week with him but I didn't really know. Now was a good time to bring it up.

"So. Now that I'm stuck here for another week, what are we going to do?"

"The weather is supposed to be good so I thought about going up to Lake Tahoe."

Did he mean right now? With no car of my own I had completely discounted the possibility of doing anything outside the Bay Area. It was Monday, so I asked the obvious question. "Don't you have work?"

"I'll tell them I'm going up to my sister's for a few days."

Was he going to see his sister by himself, or was he hinting that I would be going too? I wasn't sure. Following him down the hall into the kitchen, I waited for him to provide some more information. He gathered up his cell phone charger and his wallet. Despite having been through the room three times that morning, this was the first time I noticed that we'd left out the ice cream. It now sadly sat on the counter, melted in the containers, and surrounded by pools of condensation.

"So, we're going up to your sister's in Tahoe?" I was fishing to get him to acknowledge where we were going, and whether or not I was invited.

"My sister just built a new cabin up there. She wants me to see it." Ron walked into the big living room, looked out the window, and started winding his watch. I picked up the ice cream and placed it into the garbage can that was almost overflowing. There was no towel, no napkins to dry up the sweat rings with, so I left it, but walking away from it made me anxious. There was the possibility that I could return to the bathroom and use the same towel I'd used earlier, but I for all I knew I'd be using that towel again. Reusing a towel that I had wiped the counter with was more disturbing that leaving the wet rings there. The next best option was one of Ron's dirty shirts, but it seemed rude to do without his permission, and anal to draw his attention to my being anxious about it in the first place.

"I'd offer to make you breakfast but I know that your fridge is empty. Can I get you a water?"

"No, I want to get on the road."

"Sounds good to me. Is it alright if *I* grab one?" I asked, even though I had taken the first one without permission.

"That's fine." Ron looked down at his, now tidy, audio equipment on the floor. I was simultaneously embarrassed and proud he noticed.

"I see that there isn't very much here." Part of me expected him not to answer the question. There was a good chance that the response was personal and none of my business.

"I haven't had much of a chance to fix it up since I broke up with my ex." I didn't understand how someone who lived a life where he could spontaneously take a week off of work did not have a chance to buy furniture.

"Did you guys live together?"

Ron nodded while he spoke. "He was the one who did most of the decorating."

"Well, if you ever need an extra set of hands to help spruce the place up, man, give me a call." He didn't say anything back. "So you moved here after you broke up."

"Yeah, I let him have our old place and bought this one."

"You bought the entire floor of a building?" I muffled my astonishment with feigned disbelief.

"No. I bought the building." He laughed. I couldn't tell if he laughed at my suggestion that a floor of the building would have been enough, or that the idea of buying only a floor of a building was a bad investment. In any case, I understood that he did not take out a loan to do this.

"Are you ready to go?" My guess was this was as close as I'd get to him saying that I was included in his plans.

"Yeah, sure." We both headed for the door. The floor creaked slightly under our shoes.

"Oh, I almost forgot my water." I grabbed the bottle from the fridge and took one more look at the vast empty apartment before shutting the door behind me.

We took the elevator all the way down to the basement where the doors opened into a garage. Ron walked up to a glossy, grey Mercedes and opened the trunk. My surprise to Ron's oddity was starting to wear off so that when he opened the trunk to reveal more stacks of the same clothes wrapped in plastic it barely phased me. Pulling out a toiletry bag, also stashed in the trunk, he rummaged through it, inspecting it like a pack before going into the field. I guessed he was ensuring all the necessary overnight items were present and accounted for.

It was then that I noticed the car was sitting funny and walked around to the driver's side. The front driver's side of the car was quite literally crushed and the tire sat at an unnatural angle to the wheel well. "What happened to your car?"

"I hit it on the building when I was driving in. We'll go down to the dealer and pick up a new one until they fix it."

"You hit the building?"

He said nothing in response but I understood his answer completely, even if he didn't want to admit it. He had obviously been drunk when this had happened.

"Ouch. Such a pretty car." Given that I was on a roll of saying things that sounded stupid once they came out of my mouth there was no need to hold back. I didn't like the feeling saying the word pretty left in my mouth. Pretty was a word like fabulous. Only Sean Connery could say it and still sound masculine.

"We'll catch a cab." He shut the trunk and we walked out the garage, onto the street, and headed uphill around to the front of the building.

In darkness, San Francisco feels like an island miles from anywhere else. But in the day the sun illuminates the two majestic bridges that stretch themselves across wide bodies of water, connecting it to Marin in the North and Oakland to the East.

A man in a uniform, which was more of a costume, was stationed at the front entrance to the building across the street. "Good morning, sir. Can I get you a cab this morning?" The man shouted. His uniform was clean and reminded me of an old maroon bellhop from the fifties.

"That would be great, Frank." Ron shouted back.

Frank shouted down the street to a passing cab. The sound came out loudly and strong from daily practice. A cab's tires squealed a little as it U-turned too fast and pulled in front of us. We climbed into the same sweet smell held in by the dingy windows of the cab. Ron issued some directions to the Mercedes dealership on Van Ness. Performing another fast turn we embarked down the hill.

In the cab, Ron sporadically looked at me. He kept suddenly turning his head and squinting. He had looked at me this way last night also. He grinned and seemed pleasantly surprised each time he looked at me. What was he surprised about? Did he think he'd imagined our meeting? Was he expecting that without the filter of alcohol he would no longer find me attractive? Or, was he surprised that, despite his nearly intolerable rudeness last night, I was still around?

"What's your name?" Here we go again, I thought.

"Matt."

"Matt, we need some coffee and the paper. Stop somewhere close by." He paused and looked at me. "You drink coffee?" I think this was the first time he'd asked me a question.

"No, actually, I don't. I'd take hot chocolate."

The sneer I got in response meant I would not be getting my hot chocolate.

"One coffee and the Wall Street Journal."

Pulling up next to the curb, I was beside myself when the driver took the twenty Ron passed up through the slot in the barrier. The quality of Ron's command compelled the driver to actually get out of his own car and retrieve a cup of coffee and the paper for him. I could tell that taking cabs with Ron would never be a dull experience.

By the time we'd reached the dealership, he still hadn't touched his coffee. Maybe he only ordered it because that was just what serious businessmen were supposed to do. Maybe he just liked the act of having the coffee bought to exercise his purchasing power. We walked through the tall heavy glass doors into the bright lights of the dealership showroom. Air blew down on us from vents used to help control the climate inside. Instantly, a woman in a grey suit over a pink blouse appeared from nowhere and greeted us.

Ron pulled out his wallet and led her to a desk. I decided not to follow and just to wander around the showroom floor. With my military-trained senses I became aware of someone staring at me. Turning quickly I saw a salesman.

"Can I help you today?" He stood at the comfortable distance of ten feet from me with his hands together in front of him. I noticed he hadn't called me sir. Since I *was* inappropriately dressed, I decided not to take offense.

"No, thank you, I always let Ron do the negotiating." I said. It felt good to say this. There is a joy that I got from letting strange comments like this linger in people's minds. It gave me joy to think about the wild ideas that might have been swimming around in the old man's head.

"Let me know if you need anything."

When he walked away I was even gladder he hadn't come closer. My clothes smelled like a smoky bar, and I desperately needed to change them. Also, in the setting of The Castro my attire was appropriate, but once I got more than nine blocks from the corner of Castro and Market, I became a fashion disaster. I knew that both here, and in front of Ron's sister, my ensemble would not fly.

Ron strode over to me, and I realized that it wasn't actually the hills that made him walk with a funny determination. He normally walked that way. His steps were short and quick, his feet hit the ground forcefully and apart, and his gate was a little too wide for how short he was. His arm stretched forward and I naturally extended my hand to accept what he was giving me.

"You drive," he ordered. I looked down into my palm at the large black key with the Mercedes logo on it. Outside the door two men were holding the doors open to a new grey Mercedes SUV.

***

6

TRAVEL GAMES

"You drive."

Ron walked to the car parked outside. The handsome men who were holding each of the doors open flanked it. Me? Drive? I wasn't much of a driver. I had never had my own car before, let alone driven a brand new one. My mind raced with clips from television of foolhardy characters enthusiastically pulling out of dealerships only to be smashed by oncoming traffic. The image was overcome by my own enthusiasm, and hooking my toe behind my heel I spun around once and then walked out the doors, getting one last blast from the air vents as I went.

From the moment they shut the door to my left I felt awkward. It felt odd to have the door on the wrong side, and the wheel was obstructing my legroom. In other cars I'd been free to let my knees roam back and forth near the dashboard

"Are you alright?" Ron was more worried about his own safety than mine as he sensed my fear the way barely trained dogs guarding trailer parks do. I saw his nervousness echoed in his body posture but not so much so that it took away from his overall careless persona. He sat more upright with one hand on the armrest and an elbow on the window.

"Yeah, sorry." After fastening my seatbelt I pushed down on the brake and put the car in gear. I had seen this done before thousands of times and it was as easy as it had looked. Lifting off the brake and putting my foot lightly on the gas pedal, the vehicle started to move forward. Thankfully it did not lurch and give away my ignorance. Frankly, I was thrilled to be driving. Adrenaline was pumping through the blood in my veins and I wanted to push all the way down on the pedal, fly out onto the street, and fishtail around every turn out of the city. Instead I let the car coast up to the edge of the road. After looking both ways, I pulled out into traffic.

It wasn't until I was actually driving for the first time that I realized I'd never paid attention to where I was going or how I'd gotten there. While I'd paid close attention to the process of starting the car, I'd never really looked at the driver for the rest of the trip. As a passenger, I could always provide directions to the driver based on interesting reference points I'd observed, but the operation of the machine itself was not included in this.

The driver's seat was one based more on relevance. While it was important to know to go left at the elegant white marble building from the passenger seat, from the driver's seat it was crucial to know what lane to be in and where the turning signal was. To complicate my situation, San Francisco was a city without left turns. A friend of mine had described it as a place that every "no left turn" sign came to die. Now on the street I saw that they were affixed to almost every corner of every road traversing the metropolis. Maybe the city planners had some grand idea that making three right turns would boost the local economy by increasing traffic down secondary streets. All I knew was that it wasn't going to help me pretend to know what I was doing.

"I've never driven in the city before so, I'm a little nervous, sorry." It was the truth, technically, but not the whole truth. I prepared myself to lie if I needed to and say that I had driven a lot back home. True to form, thankfully, he merely grunted and relaxed into his seat.

"Do you know how the navigation system works? I'll need some help getting to the Oakland Bay Bridge. After that, I should be fine."

He looked at the glowing panel and touched the screen. A message came on stating that we could not operate the navigation system over five miles per hour. Understanding the practicality of it being disabled while the car was in motion I still found it inconvenient if I had a passenger who was capable of inputting the destination. I pulled the car over and Ron programmed in what I assumed was the address of his sister's cabin. A voice came over the speaker system.

"Ahead, one-hundred feet, turn right."

Guided by the computer's voice, I managed to navigate onto the freeway and we made our way onto the massive Oakland Bay Bridge that spanned more than eight miles of water that concealed the San Andreas Fault. I had memories of seeing the late eighties earthquake that had taken the lives of sixty-six people on the bridge when sections of it collapsed. Did those driving on the suspended concrete platforms feel the shaking, or had the world fallen apart all around them without warning. Would my luck be any better or worse crossing it? What exactly was I getting into anyway? I had postponed my flight and was driving hundreds of miles from anyone I knew with someone who I had met only eleven hours earlier.

The entire cab of the vehicle was alien from the driver's side. There were buttons, levers, and details I had never noticed before from my passive position on the passenger side. My eyes drifted down from the navigation to the familiar buttons of the radio. I was unsure that any choice of music I would make would have cross appeal with Ron. Worse than him just not liking my opinion of "good music" was the idea that he would override my choice with something *I* didn't like. What if he tuned into a country station, a familiar song came on, and I uncontrollably hummed or sung along? Country music was definitely uncool, and I'd done my best to shed any taste for it in my pursuit of coolness. The fewer uncool things I revealed about myself to people who didn't know me the more I could enjoy the privileges it provides. The benefits of coolness were many. For instance, if I tripped and someone saw me they would be laughing with me not about me. The advantage of joining the Marines is that I got to start over again from scratch. For all anyone knew, I was the coolest, richest, sexiest, smartest, toughest kid around where I came from. The door was open to rewrite myself.

"What's the story with your laundry?"

"My mother has someone come get it every so often."

I wanted to laugh at the grown man sitting next to me who owned his own building, bought a new car, and whose mother does his laundry. I didn't laugh.

"That's cool." It was actually not cool, but I didn't know what else to say. This brought up a good question: what other obligations did his mother take care of for him? Maybe she came in from time to time with a garbage bag and cleaned out bills from of his drawers, hired someone to come in and do his random assortment of dishes or polish the sprawling expanse of wood floors. I doubted that a man like Ron, a man who had to be worth millions, could ruin his credit with a few unpaid bills.

The long drive to Lake Tahoe became visually uneventful once we were out of the East Bay and crossing the state's central valley. I wanted to fill the silence in the car with conversation, so I said the first thing that came to me.

"My name is Brad, in case you don't remember," I said lightheartedly, just to throw it into conversation. Sadly it wasn't uncommon for me to spend an entire weekend with someone and not remember his name or vice versa. I'd become increasingly skilled at dodging phrases that would require using a name and deliberately skipped introducing them to people in hopes they'd introduce themselves and give me a second shot at remembering it.

"I remember your name Brad." His head rolled back ever so slightly and he adjusted himself higher on his seat. There was a detectable level of irritation in his voice. I'd insulted him with the blunt abrasiveness of my suggestion. Of course he remembered my name; he knew the names of our cab driver's children.

"So, how old are you, Ron?"

His brows contracted a little and he didn't answer right away, indicating that he wasn't used to answering this question. That point was fitting because I wasn't used to asking it. I had an affinity for older men and a tendency to operate in circles outside of my age bracket. I didn't want others to be self-conscious about feeling too old, anymore than I did about being too young.

"I'm thirty-two." He was telling the truth but alcohol and golfing in the sun had aged him a little. Still, he looked good; I wouldn't have gone home with him if he hadn't.

"Hot. So, do you *always* go to the Detour to pick up twenty-two-year-old Marines?" Ron's gaze slowly drifted to the right and focused on the landscape rolling by. The weeds on the roadside blew by rapidly while the fields jogged along in front of the perceivably still mountains.

Conversation, I guessed, was not Ron's forte. I was having a good time driving so I devoted my attention back to it. It's surprising how quickly I'd gotten used to doing it; holding the wheel, tripping the turn signals, changing lanes to make way for faster traffic. There was an artistic fluidity to the way different cars moved in and out of lanes or merged on and off exits; a mechanical ballet that extended out in front of me and into the far distance in the rear view mirror. I started exploring more "advanced" features of the car. Among them, I found cruise control the most useful. Once free of pushing on the gas I rotated my tired ankle, relieved to be out of its locked-up pose. The new problem was where to put it now. Alternating positions, I did my best to find the most sustainable and comfortable way to arrange my feet on the unfamiliar contours of the driver's side floor.

"Sorry if I'm boring, I'm having a hard time making conversation while driving. It's weird to be trapped in a car, you know?"

"I actually enjoy the quiet. The city's noisy." He said plainly.

"That's cool." Like the Oakland Bay Bridge in 1989, my hopes for conversation collapsed. I believed him; he seemed overwhelmed and almost uncomfortable in the city, not just interested in shutting me up. Maybe he was just hung over. He wanted silence so silence is what we had; that was, until he reached up for the radio.

***

7

GO FISH

Miles into our journey, it was Ron that broke through the monotony of soft jazz which I had been silently enduring. The vibration of his deep masculine sound was almost startling.

"Are you hungry?" I'd been hungry since last night, but I was a man with limited means who wasn't about to start suggesting meals for which I couldn't pay. Besides, it wasn't like I was starved to so badly I was ready to chew the meat off one of Ron's arms—and not just because I was a vegetarian.

"Sure, what did you have in mind?"

"We can stop by Tinsley Island on the way and grab something." At first a picture of a dark smelly harbor restaurant came to mind. A place where all the cooking instructions included the number of minutes it needed to be in the deep fryer.

"Sounds delicious." I gave him a sideways glance. "Where do I go?"

"There will be an exit coming up before too long. It's just after Stockton." I had no idea where Stockton was but I trusted in the idea that it would be obvious. My eyes panned across the flatness of the countryside and I remembered that we

61

were in the middle of the state, driving across a valley created by the most active fault line in the country. It was an interesting mix of serenity and danger but more importantly, in the middle of this flat irrigated plain, where in the hell would we find an island?

I conjured up maps of the state in my head and tried to remember if there was a vast lake I hadn't paid attention to, or perhaps the Bay came in this far and we would again meet up with it. But what about the Altamont, the high hills covered in windmills? It seemed impossible that the Bay could cut a swath through it and meet up way with us out here. No matter how hard I thought or how many details I scrounged up I was fairly certain there was no major body of water between the bay and Tahoe. This wasn't the first trip I'd made this way and I didn't remember seeing any bodies of water big enough to have an island. There was a feeling of impotence as I struggled against the limitations of my memory. A feeling that brought about a burning desire to find a map as quickly as possible and study it so intensely that I would know every detail of the region's geography.

Stockton came and went uneventfully. There were so many signs for the city that it seemed they were very eager to ensure we didn't miss it. The sheer quantity of them felt like a withering town's desperate pleas for company. Driving past it down the highway was like walking past a homeless woman begging for anything I could spare. After passing what I fervently hoped was the last of the signs to Stockton, Ron directed me to exit the freeway and down a two-lane road straight into the cornfields.

It always spurned me to see cornfields in other states. Growing up in Iowa, I picked up a pride for living in the "Corn State"—that the endless rows of tall stalks and razor sharp green leaves were something special and unique. I thought I'd left Iowa to get away from cornfields, but it turned out that these fields were everywhere, even on the southern tip of the Big Island of Hawaii. If corn was everywhere, I didn't understand what made Iowa so special. Not being special made being from there even less exciting that it already was. It was an uneasy feeling that reminded me of my own expendability, a feeling that I did my best to outrun in the Marines.

We came upon an area where the land quickly rose about forty feet. There was a long building on top and at a right angle to the road. The slope away from the structure was covered in rocks and dirt and ended in a parking lot with of a plethora of luxury cars arranged in tidy rows. Black BMWs were parked alongside green Jaguars and numerous silver Mercedes filling the lot. I parked next to the only ordinary vehicle, a beat-up Ford truck with faded blue paint.

My legs were stiff from driving and I practically fell over when I stood up. I reached down to hit my legs with my fist to rouse them so they would work. Standing there looking down at my legs a reality struck me. I was still dressed like a gay porn star.

"Um, Ron." I came around from the side of the car and saw Ron already to the road when he heard me and turned around. "Is there any way I can maybe change clothes?"

"We'll take care of it." I sighed and felt worried, relieved, curious, and then worried again. I had skipped town without taking anything with me and without telling Hal I was even leaving. The bag containing all of my clothes was sitting in the corner of Hal's bedroom. What would Hal think when I *didn't* come home for a few days? What if I didn't come home in a few days? Ron had never said anything about when we might go back. I pulled out my cell phone. No lights were glowing when it flipped open. I was sure it was dead but I held down the power button just in case I'd turned if off and forgotten about it. I jogged up the slope on my wooden legs and tucked my dog tags into my shirt to keep them from bouncing around.

At the top I could feel the last painful tingles fading in my legs. It was easier to make out from here that we were on a dike that held back the waters of a canal seventy feet or so across. The road ramped up toward and over it into the brown water where people could unload boats. The concrete was only visible for a few inches past where it met the lapping edges. Away from the long building, wooden docks reached out like fingers, causing ripples on the water. It's strange that no matter how dirty water gets it's still beautiful dancing in the sunlight.

The dock made hollow sounds under out feet as we walked out onto it. It harmonized with the pleasant sound of water splashing against logs driven deep into the mud to support the sturdy docks. Other than that, everything was quiet, almost disturbingly so. It's strange how the sound of nature interacting with itself seems simultaneously quiet and full of sounds. Ron moved as part of everything. The lines of his walk, his stride, even the way he squinted behind his sunglasses seemed to fit.

I took in the building, the dock, Ron, a few benches, and even the mountains crowning in the distance. What I didn't see was an island. For the most part the setting was unremarkable. The endless miles of cornfields in every direction infringed upon its normalcy.

At the end of the dock was a bench with a blond woman and an older man sitting patiently waiting for something. The two contrasted with each other in such a way that their differences caused an asymmetrical sort of beauty. The woman's skin was soft and revealed only the slightest traces of wrinkles. The small white and red horizontal pinstripes of her shirt exaggerated her enhanced chest. The man must have been her senior by fifteen years. He was plainly attired in clothes similar to Ron's. His hair was almost all grey, and his belly stretched his shirt a little. He had his arm around her in a way that made it clear that she was not his daughter.

She looked up and tilted the pair of thick Jackie O sunglasses down her nose, as if to see us better. She hardly glanced at me, but scanned Ron's outfit, casual posture, and expensive watch appraisingly. He must have passed her examination, for she pushed her sunglasses back up and spoke. "There's another one coming in about twenty minutes." Ron nodded and looked up into the sky as if he could tell the time by looking at the sun. I considered the notion that he might know her but dismissed it just as quickly. Surely not, or he would have remembered her name and engaged in conversation. That would have been the proper thing to do with an equal.

In my mind I began to play a game with her appearance. I tried to guess what her name might be. My eyes traced over her clean clothes, gaudy gold jewelry, and soft, well-groomed hair. She looked like a Barbara or a Bonnie. I watched her from about twenty feet away. After a few minutes of observation I noticed that she wasn't so still after all. She looked around a lot and fidgeted. Every few minutes she checked her slim golden watch, more like a bracelet than a timepiece, and frequently wiped imaginary dirt off her suede pants. She inspected her fingernails for dirt, and made sure, at least three times, that the seashell pink toenail polish had not chipped or cracked. It occurred to me she didn't like sitting here on the dock. She was definitely not an outside cat. She was not adapted to environments that could not be controlled by central air, and she was uncomfortable with the dirt and disorder of the natural world.

A black man and his son walked down the dock and sat on the bench opposite the blond woman and her husband. The son was in his early teens and was carrying two fishing poles. Their clothes were simple, colorful, casual, and slightly worn. The boy propped up the poles and his father set down next to him a small white Styrofoam cooler he'd been carrying. Playing the "name game" with them felt inappropriate; I didn't think it was fair. The names that came to mind were born of the same types of stereotypes but when it was someone outside of their race category it smacked of racism.

Fishing was something all boys are supposed to like. I always found it exceedingly boring. I didn't drink. I didn't like swatting mosquitoes for hours and coming home with itchy bumps all over my skin. And I especially didn't like stabbing worms with barbed metal hooks. Fishing was an easy excuse for fathers to give their sons their first buzz in the controlled environment of a boat where they couldn't escape or be caught by mom. I simply didn't see how sitting for hours in a small metal boat catching and releasing fish from polluted waterways could be any more fun intoxicated.

The demeanor of the pair was a mixture of different types of excitement. Easier to recognize was the boy's squirming. From now until they came back to the dock he'd have his father's attention all to himself. No distractions from adults, televisions, phone calls, or other children. This was his day. His father sat calmly with the corners of his mouth upturned with preemptive pride of the lessons he would instill in his son.

In the distance, I heard the familiar sound of exhaust bubbling behind a motor. I turned to look and was relieved that the woman had miscalculated the arrival time of the ferry. A pontoon boat with blue canopy and a man standing behind a ships wheel was making its way down the lake. My relief dissipated when I noticed the painstaking pace of the pontoon as it moseyed toward us. She had given us the correct time of arrival.

When it finally maneuvered up to the dock, two deck hands that couldn't have been more than fifteen secured it to metal prongs bolted in the wood with stained white vinyl ropes. Their slender bodies were athletic and tan. The man came out from behind the wheel and lowered a flap in front, creating a bridge across which we could safely board. The floor was made of green Astroturf reminiscent of miniature golf, which I preferred to the "real deal" since it was less itchy and less inclined to nurture stinging insects. We allowed the couple that had been waiting longer to board first.

We sat down on the aluminum benches that ran down both sides and behind the ship's wheel. The heat that the metal seats had absorbed from the sun permeated my jeans. A sudden shift in mood caught my attention. Looking around I saw Bonnie/Barbara's mouth open slightly. Ron, the woman's husband, and the boat driver all wore a look of peculiar astonishment. I followed their gaze to what they were looking at.

The man was situating his cooler under the seat and his son was looking for an out-of-the-way place to stow the poles. Coming back out from behind the wheel, the ferry driver walked over to the man. He placed his hand on his shoulder the man's shoulder and leaned in speaking into his ear too softly for me to hear. I saw the father's expression change from pride to embarrassed worry. Sitting down, staring up at the two, the boy's face silently said "now what did we do?"

"Wrong boat. Everyone here is headed to the Island right?" The driver shrugged and said with a smile and a laugh. They picked up their belongings and got back off the boat with the driver pulling the flap up behind them. It was sad to see the two of them take their seats on the bench again, especially the helpless look on the son's face; he didn't understand that he wasn't being punished.

Ron pulled a pair of sunglasses out of his shirt pocket and slipped them on. "No black person has ever been on Tinsley Island that wasn't carrying something." I was shocked and taken back by the openness of his racism punctuated by the smugness of his smile. I said nothing and released a small nervous laugh, careful not to show my offense. Having overheard what Ron had said, Bonnie/Barbara tilted her face up into the sky and laughed softly.

She checked her watch again just at the boat shook from the twin prop engines revving up. The woman perked up once we started moving. She sat up, looked around, and grabbed her hair as if she was wearing a loosely fitted hat, or maybe she was afraid the bulb of cropped blond hair might blow right off her head. After a little back and forth maneuvering, we were pointed down the canal to where the water widened and then forked. She wasn't alone in her excitement; I too was eager to move.

When we were far enough down lake that the dock had disappeared around the bend, a speedboat came powering towards us. Through the purr of the engine I could hear the tight vocal cords of teenagers shouting over the din. When they saw us, as was etiquette on the water, they slowed down. After passing us they came about, and pulled up alongside us. The pontoon began to rock gently as the remnants of their wake caught up.

"Hey, is this the Island ferry?" One of the boys yelled. The driver nodded. All together there were three boys and two girls aboard the sleek fiberglass craft. The boys were shirtless, wearing only brightly colored board shorts, while the girls revealed even more skin by wearing string bikinis. All of them were shockingly beautiful but younger than was proper to comment on.

"You guys get on. I'm gonna put the boat up." Without breaking stride with their conversation, the girls cooperatively reached over and grabbed onto the railing of the pontoon pulling the boats together. The two boys took over; their caramel-colored hairless bodies stretched and lengthened as they steadied the boats against each other. They cordially helped the girls as they crossed onto the ferry. The ferry sank down a little under the added weight. After both girls had safely switched boats one of the boys extended his hand to the other to help him over also but he slapped it away.

"Piss off, dickhead." Standing up on the seat he leaped forward, landing on the Astroturf with a loud thud. Bonnie/Barbara braced herself and gasped daintily.

"There's a lady on board, young man. Show respect," The driver said.

"Sorry, sir." The kid looked down and erased the expression from his face.

"No problem, son."

When the driver had turned back around, the two boys smirked at each other. Bonnie/Barbara curled her lips and shook her head in disgust.

"Nick, come on! I'm hungry!" One of the girls called while leaning over the rail and holding her hand up to block the sun. Her auburn hair was straight and pulled back into a shiny, lush ponytail. The thick, perfect hair seemed like it had been ripped from a shampoo ad.

The force of the leap had pushed the boats apart and Nick had almost fallen in. "Shit Brad. Get me back over there."

After repositioning the boat, Nick swung his arms and leaped straight at Brad who was caught off guard. The inertia of impact sent them stumbling to the other side of the boat and into the bench. They collided with it hard enough that Nick almost tumbled into the water again, only this time he would have taken Brad with him.

"Cut it out guys."

"Trish, Anna, you girls be good while I'm gone now." The driver of the boat who was the oldest and most handsome said back while winking with a clear blue eye tucked deep in its socket topped by a sandy blond eyebrow.

"Bye, Ken!" The girls said back in unison and waved as though they would never see him again. He preened and deliberately flexed his designer muscles before he took off.

"He's such a dork." One said to the other as they watched the boat return to full speed in the direction of the dock.

Each of them was different but they all moved and interacted with the same vibe. Similar enough that, out of the moment, it would be difficult to remember which face belonged to which name. They were at the age where they still referred to sex as "doing it." I was sure they talked about it with their friends a lot, but they probably had never progressed to actually following through. The dark-haired girl wore black with tiny polka dots and the platinum blond girl turquoise. The two boys on the boat were both athletic with strong abdominal muscles. The black-haired boy, Nick, had wider shoulders, a bigger build, and was paler than Brad.

By self-admission, I had always found my name to be a little snobbish but events in my life had provided me an escape from its stuffiness. I thought it was hysterical that these kids were actually named Trish, Ken, and Brad. Even in my game I wouldn't have been able to pick names that fitting. I could hardly contain my laughter; choosing instead to stare at the floor and bite my tongue.

We continued forward, taking the left fork where the lake widened. To the right of us the land was covered thick trees and shrubbery, including bushes full of plump blackberries. The opposing shore was further and further away, and was covered in tall grasses. I eyeballed the banks and looked ahead. I searched for features that would identify our island destination. Island is a word typically associated with palm trees and volcanoes; out here in the freshwater, I wasn't sure what exactly I was even looking for.

The boat started to slow as we approached a stream that split through the woodsy area off the right side of the boat. Slowly, the driver turned the pontoon and faced us into it. There was no motion in the water and I recognized then that it wasn't a stream at all. The inlet veered to the right and then back to the left around a corner out of site. Overhead was a small wooden sign that politely asked us to disembark with caution. It was suspended on a wire that ran between strong trees on opposite banks.

Pushing deeper around the bend, the air quality changed. All the elements of nature calmed down, the sun got brighter, and the sounds of water and birds became more soothing and harmonic. The water divided sharply in opposite directions. To the left and right were floating docks with massive and extravagant yachts tethered on to keep them from drifting away. There were so many of them that they disappeared around the gentle bend in both directions. Directly in front of us was a platform. Two more young deckhands waited with ropes. From the dock, a metal ramp led to a trail. Well-groomed grass led straight up and away from it to another wooden platform with two benches. At the top was an old gas lamp with three lights, and spanning the pathway was an arched sign that read *Tinsley Island*.

***

8

YOUR AVERAGE EVERY-DAY COOKOUT

When it was time to go ashore, I hesitated in order to let the woman and her husband go first. Our arrival heightened my self-consciousness about my attire. A jury of Ron's peers would soon surround me. Ron charged up the metal ramp pumping his arms the whole way. It was easy to imagine him climbing a hill on a golf lawn with a club in one hand and wearing one of those plaid hats that buttoned in front.

Stepping onto dry land always made me feel a little clumsy. My feet had quickly forgotten the feeling of solid ground; ground that instead of sinking under each step it slams back up at them. I took in my new surroundings. It was like a park in many ways. In front of us was a pool. There was a grassy lawn ahead and past it a large pavilion. Inside the pavilion was a stage, currently occupied by a live band. The music created a peppy ambiance. Far to the left stood a large square Victorian structure that was tall enough I was surprised I didn't see it from the ferry. Its red roofline was perforated by three small gables on each side and topped with a lantern room that made it obviously a lighthouse.

The trees were dispersed randomly but not so much they interfered with appearance that everything in this environment was under human control. Even the weather felt more regulated inside the shelter of the island. Looking up was a perfect blue painting in the air that was close enough to touch. Concrete walkways connected the most traveled routes between activities and structures, many covered with the same flat metal roofs. The arrangement had them positioned relatively close together without making them feel cramped. We walked to one that seemed an obvious place for a bathroom. The inward facing side was storefront that thankfully had racks stocked with shirts, shorts, hats, and various other island gear.

"Good afternoon Ron, sir. How can we help you today?" Ron turned and looked me up and down. I tried not to appear excited about getting new clothes but the anticipation of new stuff always has a little rush coupled with it. There was a special charge putting on fresh clothes knowing that no one had worn them before me at that moment. "I need a pair of shorts and a shirt. Is that going to be a problem?"

At first I didn't understand why that might be a problem, then I took a closer look at the racks. The tags in the collars of the shirts mostly contained the letters "L" with various repetitions of the letter "X" preceding them. I took a look at the clusters of rotund men laughing and sipping their drinks. Apparently the rich were better fed than I.

The overweight, balding man behind the counter started flipping through the shorts on the rack. "Let's see here. Well, could we fit you into a large?" I hesitated not sure I should speak until Ron and the man both looked at me waiting for a response.

"Um, yes, sir. I suppose I could wear a large." I would have plenty of room around my thirty-one inch waist to breathe but I could wear one.

"Ah, here we have a large that has a string on it. That might help." He pulled a pair of bluish-purple shorts from the bottom rack and laid them on the counter. I wanted to snatch them up and inspect them, so that I could approve or decline the selection. Ron stood motionless leaning against the counter with one elbow and watching the various clusters of people talk from behind his dark sunglasses. The man behind the counter wiped sweat from his forehead with his wrist and then started looking through the top rack for a shirt. After eyeing the majority of the available selection, he stopped on a white one with three buttons and a collar.

"And a large will have to do for the shirt also. Should I put this on your account?"

"That'll be fine." Ron crumpled the clothes into a ball and passed them to me like a football. I quickly found the hangers letting them dangle and checked them to see if his disregard had wrinkled them. "Are those hats new?"

"Just got them in."

"Give me one of those." Ron looked me up and down, lingering over my combat boots. "And a pair of those." The man picked a blue hat from the wooden hat tree and slid it across the counter. Ron affixed it on his head as we went around the corner handed me a pair of flip-flops he'd requested so that I wouldn't have to walk around in shorts and combat boots.

On the back of the building, as I had predicted, was the familiar set of gender-specific signs that meant I would have a private place to change. Ron held the door open for me and waited outside. Inside the restroom was a marriage of styles, part locker room and public restroom. The floor was a solid piece of concrete sloping to a metal drain in the center. There was a long bench and a row of metal lockers. They were painted white with combination locks hanging from a few of them. On the far end of the room were shower stalls, urinals, and toilets. The sound of water slapping the concrete in one of the shower stalls provided the final touch of atmosphere to the little room. It was somewhat dark as I'd expected but it was that it was incredibly clean.

I placed my new clothes on the bench and peeled my dirty shirt off my body again. The fabric was relaxed, warm, and stretched from hugging my chest, shoulders, and arms; I was glad to be free from it. Folding it neatly was difficult due to the way three days of wearing had warped it. Bringing in each sleeve, smoothing the fabric flat, folding it inward in thirds, then up in fourths, I placed it next to my new outfit.

After I unbuckled my belt, I checked the floor for water I might accidentally step in, slipped off my shoes, and let my pants fall to the floor. My new shorts were swimming trunks and therefore had a mesh lining so underwear would be both unnecessary and uncomfortable. I removed my boxers and just as I did, the shower stopped and curtain flung open. Standing there naked with the air blowing between my legs, I pretended not to care, but as a man, I was always a little self-conscious when other men can see my manhood in all its flaccid glory. A hairy, wet, heavy-set older man emerged from the stall drying his thin grey hair with a towel. I joked to myself, "I could have stayed in the Castro if I wanted to see this."

Standing in front of him, seeing his sagging aged skin I felt like a shiny new penny by comparison. He looked at me in the nostalgic way older men admire the tight athletic bodies of youthful men. There is nothing sexual about their staring; rather, it reminds them of their invincibility at that age, a time before they had been forced to confront mortality. Pulling up my new shorts, the clean fabric felt fresh against my skin; skin that had surely reabsorbed the yuck from the dirty clothes I had been wearing. I wanted to take a shower before putting on my new clothes but taking the time to do so seemed inconsiderate to my host, so I pulled my new shirt on too.

I hadn't noticed until washing my face that both my shorts and shirt bore the bold embroidered logo of the Saint Francis Yacht Club. Once I'd moved around in them a little the shorts had started to slip. They were virtually falling off even with the string pulled tight. Knowing that it was a fashion no-no, I tucked the baggy shirt into my shorts for practicality reasons.

Given how preppy the garments were, it worked visually well enough for me to live with.

I was giving myself one last look in the mirror when the door opened, letting the blinding bright light in and the old man out. As it closed I saw Ron come in go right for the urinal. The splattering sound of urinating reminded me that I needed to as well. He stood confidently in front of the urinal with both his hands on his hips as if he'd conquered it and was rubbing it in. I came up to the urinal directly next to him and pulled down the front of my shorts, ignoring the usual bathroom etiquette to leave at least one vacancy between myself and anyone else if possible. I smiled and bit my lip at the slightly erotic situation standing next to him at the urinals. As soon as I started to piss I squirmed a little. The feeling of piss splattering onto the bare tops of my feet in flip-flops was one I hated and found a little nauseating. Ignoring my discomfort I leaned my head back and slightly toward Ron. With my hand on my hip I let my elbow brush up against Ron's. "Not here." He said calmly which only made me smile harder. As I finished I stared at the ceiling, which was free of the cobwebs I usually found.

I placed my folded shirt and jeans on top of my boots in an empty unlocked locker figuring that there was no one here who might steal them.

Emerging from the bathroom, the daylight was bright enough it hurt my eyes. The sounds of children playing resonated in the air from an indeterminate direction. We walked around the building we'd come out of to where the shop was and then headed towards the pavilions. The smell of food deepened my hunger and we took our positions at the end of a line that lead away from the kitchen. The mood was upbeat and people walked in step with the tempo of the classic rock music that was being performed in the main pavilion. Scanning across the chatting faces I saw a crowd devoid of racial diversity. White faces stood in congratulatory groups of four or five with wives mutely in tow. They were the type of men I imagined had names like Jonathan, Rudolph, and Charles III. Even the staff that was

75

emptying the garbage cans and grooming the hedges had pale complexions. It was as if the entire island were a bucket of white paint no one wanted to disturb with an accidental dollop of color. The monochromatic congregation was past coincidence; this was a world where the people had been deliberately filtered so as not to muss the island's atmosphere.

"Ron, you rascal! How's your father?" One of the men ahead of us in line had recognized him and was engaging us in conversation. Ron's whole body became active as he took a step forward shaking the man's hand and smiling. It was as if Ron had been an inactive machine that someone had just plugged into the wall. The lights were flashing and the gears were turning. It was a bit startling.

"Hey, Gary. How the hell are you? He's doing well. Where's your wife Debra?" He said as he pretended to give a quick look around for Gary's wife and then stood smiling with his hands on his waist again. I laughed at the thought that he was just standing at the urinal in this same prideful pose.

"Oh, she's around here somewhere with the grandkids." The man patted Ron on his shoulder, grasping and shaking it with the last slap. From years of smiling on golf courses the man's face had become weathered and his tanned forehead had grown larger where his hair had receded.

"Don just had a birthday didn't he?"

"Yeah, just turned six. We had the family in from the east coast for it. Gosh, you haven't seen him for what? Has it really been two years since we've seen you?" Listening to him speak, I began to put together the story between the two of them. Ron seemed familiar with him and his family but the details he retained were things I didn't, but probably should, know about my own family. Comparing it to yesterday's experience in the cab, I was fascinated that Ron seemed to retain the minute details about everyone he encountered, right down to the birthdays of their grandchildren. I understood now why my suggesting that he didn't remember *my* name in the car didn't go over so well.

"Been about that long. You brought him sailing. In fact, you remember Cynthia, my sister? We're going up to see her new cabin on Fallen Leaf Lake."

"Oh, it's beautiful up there around now."

"Gary, this is my friend Brad." Ron stepped back and to the side to clear a path that would allow for our introduction. In doing so, Ron gave up the space that he had occupied and offered it to the two of us to use as our meeting ground. Our hands moved ritualistically toward each other. It was like a battlefield where each side was sending an envoy to meet the other's and decide if there was to be peace or bloodshed.

"Nice to meet you, Brad." All of a sudden I was smiling, shaking hands, and part of the conversation. When I was the unknown member, it's always my task to fill whatever personality void was missing.

"You also, sir. And, I agree with you. Tahoe is striking this time of year."

"Not much of a skier then?"

"No, not me. Winter is just something that gives you time to think about what you're going to do next summer. So, going out in the cold on purpose isn't really my thing." The void I was filing was that of the comedian; interjecting humor between statements and conversations that eased tensions, helped flow, and provided convenient distracting escapes if any uncomfortable moments arrived.

"Me too, never understood what made people strap those wooden things to their feet and try to kill themselves." The man's smile was joyous and non-threatening. There would be peace. His wrinkles were heaviest at the corners of his eyes and mouth, telling a story full of smiles. I wondered whether it was his accomplishments that had lead to so blissful a life, or if had he found happiness only recently in retirement?

"Brad just ended a tour in the Marine Corps." I swallowed a lump down my throat. Right off I knew it was a mistake for Ron to bring this up.

"Is that so? A devil-dog, huh?" Here it came. As a general rule I didn't mention my having served to older men. That was, I'd learned to keep it to myself if I didn't want to spend the next two hours reliving war stories from their youth.

"Bob and Charles here are Army." He gestured to the men next to him in line who turned around at the mention of their names and their service. Their faces brightened as the excitement of times past, better times and exhilarating times, illuminated their cheeks and eyes. Smiling hard, I firmly squeezed each of their hands as we were introduced. I was petrified as they introduced themselves by number of stars and first names. The moment was claustrophobic. Never had I considered calling a general by his first name. As I did, I did so nervously. I was sure that I would be struck down by lightning by the military gods at any moment.

The last wall of the trap was set when the man in line behind us joined the conversation. "One star, Air Force. Henry. Nice to meet you, Brad. I bet you've got stories to tell." As attention focused on me, Ron began to understand his mistake, but he was too amused to interfere. They were stern men, with small lips, silver hair, and hardened voices that had yelled speeches over formations of men that had then marched on to death and glory.

"I'm sure you gentleman have far better war stories than I do, sir."

"Oh, hell. We're all gentleman here. Call me Henry. Our best battle stories have nothing to do with bullets." I joined the men in laughing and wondered what level of detail I would be forced to endure of their sexcapades; tales of debauchery before rank made their lives too public to live scandalously.

"I remember when I went through Annapolis, that was the hardest thing I've ever done. My hat's off to any man that can put up with that." One of Gary's friends, I couldn't remember if it was Bob or Charles, gave me the same strong shoulder pat that Gary had given Ron. Earlier, standing in front of the old man naked in the locker room, it was easier to be distracted from the sadness of vicarious reminiscing. Here I stood in the company of great men whose eyes told me they would give anything to be me and have a chance to do it all again, if not for any other reason than to see what it would be like if they'd done it differently.

"Everyone faces difficulty at one time or another. What's hard for some is not for others." The implication almost escaped my attention. I had been promoted just by being there. They all assumed I was an officer, that I had been to Annapolis. I felt it important to maintain that illusion for mine and for Ron's sake. Besides, to point out their error just seemed rude. Also, it was better to be one of them rather than be the enlisted guy among officers. I was ascending through layers of the social atmosphere at a thunderous pace. We had escaped the heavy air of gay culture, traveled through the spheres of ordinary lives, and I was now skimming the outermost layers of the stratosphere. This was the highest tier of society, one so thin and faint that ordinary people only talked about it in the abstract and only the stars were intimate with. I had no idea when or if my rocket ship would land or if I had a parachute. I was fascinated by the moment and I felt like I deserved to be here.

All the tables in the pavilion were nostalgically dressed in a red-checkered tablecloth. We came to the front of the line where there was a table arranged with food. Hamburgers were beautifully assembled on white plates with bright green ruffled lettuce and generously thick slices of red tomato. Next to them on oval shaped buns were glowing pieces of glazed chicken breast, tiger striped with picture-perfect black grill marks, similarly and meticulously garnished. They were indefectible as if they had been mass-produced by some ad agency's food designer in preparation for a TV commercial. There was a silver chafing-dish steaming with soup and after it were the deserts. I was in a theme park where the rich had decorated and dressed up to pretend they were relaxing from a hard week of manual labor at the factory. It appeared their version of soup and salad was a flawless gourmet burger served with a bowl of lobster bisque with whole tails of lobster in it. Maybe the stresses of their life did warrant a little escapism but I felt a little insulted by their fabrication intended to replicate the culture of my income bracket.

"You want something without meat, don't you?" I thought it considerate that my host noticed the obvious lack of vegetarian options. Being used to this I was prepared to grab one of the painstakingly composed plates of salad.

"I can just work with what they have here, it's not a problem."

"The chef here is great. He used to be the head chef for the Four Seasons International." Ron set down his hamburger and led me around the table of food to the kitchen. The heat coming from the grills was warm on my face and bare arms. Despite the fact that I hadn't eaten meat in more than two years, I found the smell of it cooking quite tempting.

"We have a vegetarian here. What can you do for us?"

It was his first "we" I'd noticed him say. Maybe he only used it this time to reassure the chef that I was the weird one, not him. In any case, it felt good to finally have some connection between us acknowledged out loud.

The man Ron spoke to was a middle-aged man whose face was sweaty from standing over steaming stock pots and sizzling grills. His teeth were white as his tan face smiled at us, and atop his head was the cliché towering white hat. "Sure, no problem." He said warmly, his voice seasoned with a European accent I couldn't place.

The chef walked me through his kitchen with his hand on my shoulder. He described the ingredients that were particularly fresh that day and embellished his opinions and recommendations. I did my best to pay attention to his suggestions but I was distracted by the nuances of his accent and the way his curling brown hair crawled out from under his big white hat. All of his ideas sounded great and I pulled what seemed to be the best of them. After some negotiating my dinner was decided to be pasta in a sauce he would concoct from the lobster bisque with the lobster removed and a side of braised asparagus. Even if I hadn't been a vegetarian this seemed a better choice than a burger.

With my specially prepared meal in hand we sat down amidst the various clusters of friends, families, and couples. The men were relaxed and unconcerned as they chewed, swallowed, and chatted. All the women had bright glowing cheeks and white smiles. All looked about at least a decade younger than their husbands. In front of me I rotated my plate so that my asparagus was in the upper right-hand corner, moved my glass to the top left of my plate, and put my plastic fork on the left and plastic knife on the right. The red checkers provided a great measure by which I pushed the plate back two inches from the edge of the table. Then, I centered it from left to right so that it was evenly spaced across the fading red white and pink pattern; adjusting my knife and fork accordingly.

I looked down at my plate and filled my fork with some of the pasta. The taste was the difference between a symphony and a marching band. I knew it was better, but it was difficult to point out the specifics. The components fell perfectly into place under his direction; each herb and season added at just the right moment to maximize its potential for flavor.

Looking up from my food I made eye contact with the vocalist of the band. He was attractive with short black hair. I could see the holes from where he had removed his piercings in his lip and eyebrow. He wore long sleeves that I assumed covered colorful tattoos. The way he looked at me suggested that he somehow he recognized me as a fellow outsider. His eyes begged for empathy for compromising his sense of self. It wasn't hard to imagine him silently hating himself in some Indie coffee house somewhere as he trashed people for doing the very thing he was now.

Ron ate his food as if it were a personal mission. He was eating fast enough that I hadn't even seen him finish his burger. The movement of his fork from his plate to his mouth were precisely executed and followed by a regimented chewing and swallowing pattern. Compared to the lackadaisical setting, the speed at which he scooped up his potato salad felt out of place. I didn't want a repeat of the night before, so I put myself in high gear and pretended to be back in the chow hall. After he finished he placed his utensils and napkin on his plate, took a breath, and looked at me. Swallowing my last bite, I copied his motion and we got up leaving our plates where they sat.

On his feet, the hurry was gone again. Looking down at our feet I got in step with him and we strolled over to the pool. A fence surrounded the concrete pool deck. Sturdy white sun-beds and deckchairs were arranged around the glowing blue pool. The voice of my mother telling me I needed to wait thirty minutes after eating before getting in the pool nagged at me. Did the mothers here give this same message to their children?

Again, I took a survey of the crowd. The white sun-beds were occupied by the same slightly overweight men and their younger, more-fit wives. Many of them discreetly flaunted their new breasts. As the sun danced on the water, children splashed and tried to teach each other tricks. They dared one another to swim underwater the whole length of the pool and showed off how many summersaults they could do without taking a breath. It struck me that this was the manufacturing ground for the elite to come. While this was a place that congressmen came to play; it was also a breeding ground for the next generation who would inherit the earth that has been purchased by their parents. This was a place so distant from an ordinary life that I'd always assumed it was fictional. Somewhere they could put their children to bond with other children without the fear of infecting their world with ordinary people.

I wasn't sure why Ron had brought me here. Did he want to skate the fringe of scandal? Did he want to flirt with rebellion without actually going over the imaginary lines tradition had set? Or, most confusing of all, did he simply want me there? There were no answers in the way he stood there. His arms at this side, mouth upturned with the slightest contentment, and eyes hidden behind the dark tint of his glasses.

Having hurried through my meal I was now becoming stir crazy. I felt an overwhelming urgency to do something, and had nothing to put my energy into. There was no puzzle to put together, no book to read, no rifle to practice dismantling blindfolded. I was itching to accomplish anything. I'd resorted to playing with my fingers, hair, and shorts to compensate for the lack of something else to do. I could feel Ron's irritation at my fidgeting.

One of the deck beds scraped on the concrete and I saw him sitting down on it. He relaxed onto his back; his shirt was off, sunglasses and hat on sandals, tucked into the striped shadows under the bed. It didn't seem very considerate for us to be wasting time relaxing by the pool if Ron's sister was expecting us. I didn't particularly care about her feelings either. What I *really* cared about was having to deal with her being irritated and how that would affect my ability to be at ease once we got there.

Lying down on the bed next to Ron, my shirt folded neatly instead of thrown down like Ron's, my skin absorbed the heat from the sun-baked plastic. After staying still for a moment, I decided to try something, just to see if it worked. I stood up, stretched my arms overhead, walked to the edge of the water, and hopped in. Exhaling the air from my lungs I allowed myself to completely submerge. The cold numbed my body and my skin pulled tight over my muscles. I swam out into the center of the pool shutting my eyes and turning my face up to the sun. Sunlight forced its way through my eyelids, warming them, filling my vision with a gold and pink blur.

Exhaling again, I sank back down into the water. My feet touched the bottom and I opened my eyes. With strong, slow strokes I made my way back to place I'd entered. The cement warmed my fingers while I pressed my hands down onto the deck lifting myself out of the water and stood up. Without a towel in my immediate possession, I ran my hands over my head to push the water out of my hair and then down my chest and stomach to brush off the excess water. I looked up at Ron who was watching me with his mouth slightly open. I grinned, satisfied. I had accomplished my mission.

***

9

WHY WALK

Towels had been set out as a courtesy on small tables that were stationed at each of the two pool area entrances. I walked over and picked one up. The towel was new, soft, and smelled clean, so I pressed my face into it. It was so white that it reflected the sunlight and hurt my eyes. I could feel the pavement cooling as the dripping water pooled around my feet. Free of the droplets of cold, chlorinated water, the sun restored the warmth to my skin. Moments later a gentle breeze permeated through the trees and stole the warmth, so I did my best to cover myself with the insulating towel.

To keep the children from escaping, a wrought iron fence encompassed the concrete deck. It wasn't like they knew any better, but the fence had been designed as a cage for the sprightly creatures so that their caretakers could rest their worries. Around the pool the sun was beaming even more intensely, seemingly for the benefit of the sunbathers.

Ron was still reclining, pretending not to be watching me from behind his sunglasses. I pretended not to notice. Light reflected by my dog tags zipped back and forth across him as I slowly ran the towel down my body to soak up the water that was beginning to make me shiver. When I was mostly dry, I took my place on the bed next to him and folded my hands behind my head. In a matter of minutes I was dry with the exception of my wet shorts, and I could relax and enjoy the heat radiating down from the sky.

Time had slowed down, and I entered an almost hypnotic state. The laughter and splashing added to the surreal quality of the moment that was beginning to feel like a daydream, a fantasy. Life was pleasantly calm here to the point of being free of mundane worries that burdened the ordinary world. There were no ringing cellular phones, no squelching modems connecting, and no horns honking. I had overheard someone say that cellular phones were outright forbidden on the island; even silent they represented the outside world, and the outside world seemed manifestly unwelcome here on Tinsley Island.

In a place like this, the fantasy childhood we all hypothesize might exist could actually come true. My ears had become so cynical that if they were to hear someone describe growing up in such a place like this I would not believe them. I had heard that in Russia children should live free from the adult world and enjoy a fairytale upbringing free of responsibility and complications. The flushed youthful faces here were happily engrossed in sentimental games that didn't require the implementation of the latest gadget. The explosions of a Playstation were replaced with the gentle knocking of croquet mallets. It held a simplicity that I wish I could have enjoyed and been satisfied by at that age, or even now.

Parents, too, were available to play here free of the prying eyes of the common world. Cocktails and beer flowed freely with the assurance that the kids were near and safe. They could come here and leave the office behind. There was no worry that someone was trying to steal anything or swindle me out of jealousy. Listening in on various conversations, I also noticed that this was not a place to talk business. The usual talk of mergers and acquisitions was instead substituted with dialogue about vacations and family.

I wasn't sure how long we'd been there when Ron started to move. Had I not heard the scraping of his sandals being pulled out from under the bed, I might not have noticed him get up. Looking up, the perfect sunny sky I had closed my eyes on was being intruded on by the shadows of rain clouds. Normally the chance of rain would have dampened my spirits but in this moment it didn't bother me. I was so content that the sky could have broken open in a downpour and I wouldn't have cared.

"What's up?"

"Thirsty. I want to move around a little."

The pool-deck had become more crowded with small shivering bodies. Parents were coaxing children out of the water in case of thunderstorms. We waded our way through the short, wet, smiling mob and out onto the lawn. The Marine in me cringed as Ron led me out across the grass. It was another one of the instilled rules that Marines shouldn't walk across the grass if it could be avoided. Whenever I did, I felt guilty and looked around for a drill instructor who might jump out from behind a tree and punish me by sending me to the quarterdeck. Not being watched didn't make me feel any better as they also advocated that discipline was defined by doing the right thing even when no one was looking. Especially when no one was looking.

The flip-flops continued to smack up against my heels and I could feel the blades of grass tickling the sides of my feet. Underneath the canopy of the bar, I was glad to be back on a paved surface. Ron ordered a rum and coke and I asked for an orange juice. "Is pulp alright, sir?" The young man behind the bar asked.

"That's fine." I was getting used to disguising my befuddled surprise at unfamiliar questions. The young bartender moved with an assured grace as he composed our drinks. His lean, hairless forearms and hands moved with agility as he filled the glass to the top with ice, trickled rum over it from an unlabeled decanter, and topped it off with a fizzling stream of coke. Mixing drinks always impressed and fascinated me; it all seemed elegant and sophisticated. There was a certain sexy cool to being familiar with the elaborate bottles and provocatively named concoctions.

From the refrigerator, the bartender then pulled a glass pitcher of translucent orange fluid with several inches of dark orange sediment sloshing back and forth. He set it on the highly polished bar and stirred the contents with the wooden spoon. The pulp erupted in swirling currents through the sweet water. It swirled up until the pitcher became one continuous color. I watched as he held the pitcher steady with his hand and then used the same hand to steady my glass as he filled it, so I preemptively grabbed a napkin in case my cup would be sticky.

I waited until we had walked some distance before I took my first sip from my napkin-wrapped cup. Fresh-squeezed orange juice was generally a delicacy and to get it from a bar was a first. It was ice cold and the sweetness made my jaw ache. Swallowing, I softly chewed on the slippery pieces of pulp. It was difficult to imagine ever being satisfied with store-bought orange juice again. When Ron stopped to take a drink, instead of tilting the cup into his mouth, he put his hand on his hip and tilted his entire body back. His mouth formed to the lip of his cup and he took a modest sip. His eyes were open and peered off to the horizon as he held it in his mouth for a moment. It could have been that his tongue was moving the liquid back and forth, searching for balance in the flavor, scanning for inconsistencies or aftertaste. Whatever it was, I could see he was thinking hard about it.

My shorts had not completely dried and as we walked I was chaffing a little. I didn't want to complain, but the flip-flops were also starting to wear out the skin between my toes. Because of my discomfort, we were both walking with oddly wide gates; like two geese clumsily waddling alongside one another.

I constructed a layout of the island as we walked. To make the best use of the space, the island was divided into different areas for dining, swimming, a row of small floating houseboats, and between them all were games. The games were the same ones I'd seen on overly sentimental "Thank You" cards: horseshoes, croquet, and bocce ball (which at first, I mistook for shuffleboard). They were present wherever there was room in between other structures, such as the main building and the classic lighthouse that stood watch over it all. Attached by a gravel land bridge was another smaller island that was apparently used for utility purposes. There were rows of plants to replace any that might become unsightly, mounds of mulch to be spread on the various flowerbeds, a building that sounded like it housed a generator, and past the tractor at the far end were water treatment ponds.

In a rare moment of talkativeness, Ron told me about the residents of the small floating houses that floated on the backshore. Most of them I forgot as soon as he'd said them but one stood out. There in one of the quaint little boathouse lived an Olympic gold medalist. They had made him a home here so he could be on hand in case any of the guests wanted to steal him away for private lessons.

I took a drink from my cup and noticed that Ron was no longer carrying one. He must have finished and discarded it sometime earlier. I offered him a sip of mine, expecting him not to respond, and to my surprise he shook his head saying, "No, thank you." The words came out kindly and naturally, but from what I'd seen from him so far, they came out infrequently. I appreciated them the way I appreciated a hug when I haven't been touched for a week. The principle that the absence of something made its presence more potent almost made Ron's rudeness a profound way of ensuring people would take notice when he was polite or grateful.

I expected that should I explore the island, I would be disenchanted. Instead I became more and more fascinated the more I learned. Walking along the shore, I discovered that a long, circular-shaped island protected Tinsley itself. The only opening I saw was the one we entered through. This feature created a moat protecting the delicate world within. The wild brush and trees formed a high protective wall that hid and protected the retreat from any intruding eyes wanting to satisfy curiosity by stealing a look. Tinsley was a carefully planned and executed social fortress constructed to keep the unwanted out and camouflage its location.

We made another pit stop at the bar so Ron could quench his seemingly endless thirst, and then we ambled in the direction of the island's most prominent feature. The lighthouse was nestled into the narrowest part, giving it the feel of an oversized chair tucked into the smallest corner of a living room. As we walked along a hedge, I noticed small, green, tube-shaped droppings; presents left by geese. I avoided them and continued to listen to the conversation. The hedge stood three feet tall and more than two hundred feet long. It helped to visually separate the houseboats from the other activities in the same way five feet of grass between a street and front lawn distracted passersby from how close it really was to the road.

Just before contentment over its appropriate placement and pleasing shape set in, my eyes focused on a six-inch patch of the vertical side that protruded. The blatant imperfection was out of character for what I had seen so far on the island and defaced the beauty of the feature. I looked around for someone I could alert to the oversight, but there was no one conveniently at hand. Besides I was sure Ron would have thought it tasteless for me to point out the mistake.

Moving past it, I refocused on the sound of Ron's voice, which was deep and masculine. With him talking so much I got the chance to listen to its nuances and the subtleties. There were rough patches in his vocal cords that matched the growing five o'clock shadow on his face that from time to time he'd reach up and scratch with the palm of his hand. Down the sides of his neck were thick bulging jugular veins that pulsed as he talked. I couldn't help but feel a bit of romance from the moment. I wanted very much to come up close to him, put my lips on his neck, feel the scruff from his face and the pulse of his heartbeat through those thick veins and smell the dark, shielding smell of his skin. But we were behind enemy lines, and that would give away our position.

I got so lost in looking at him that I felt guilty about losing track of what he was saying. I came back to reality when he pointed across me; he had begun to tell me the story of the lighthouse: that it was completed in 1905 and originally guided ships away from danger in San Francisco Bay. In 1959 the Club had purchased the Southampton Shoal Lighthouse, lifted it with massive cranes onto a barge, and had brought it up here. The act of relocating it was a mix between ostentation and the unwillingness to let go of a romanticized era where great industrial barons ruled and the poor knew their place. All this was done under the guise of preservation and restoration as opposed the more likely motivation of the ultrawealthy's flamboyant profligacy. Ultimately it didn't feel like that big of a deception, since the structure would have otherwise sat unappreciated in the bay until chance destroyed it.

We entered the lighthouse, not through the main entrance, but through the kitchen's small narrow doorway that had never been intended for use by the privileged. Ron discarded his empty cup into a small waste can and I threw away the rest of my orange juice. Like his apartment, the kitchen evoked design elements of a bygone time. It was cramped with all the plain wooden surfaces coated with a century's layers of white paint. Out of the kitchen the hallway widened and the rooms were more gracious. It reminded me more of a Victorian house than what I thought a lighthouse should be. Silk ropes prevented visitors from sitting on the furniture and rugs protected the majority of the hardwood floors. The tall plaster walls showed the occasional but forgivable cracks, indicating that underneath were historical plaster and lathe instead of contemporary drywall.

In the main hallway was a narrow wooden staircase that we climbed up to the second floor. My hands felt the grooves that had developed over generations of keepers carrying oil to keep the light burning. The second-story hallway was quite constricted and the doors to the all the rooms were proportionally thin. I wasn't entirely sure what purpose they once filled; presently they functioned as boarding for visiting guests.

Next we climbed the metal stairs up into the lantern room. The lantern room was hot and dry inside from being baked by the sun all day through its glass walls. We didn't dwell in this uncomfortable area long, instead we stepped out onto the balcony and took in the view. It was then I saw why I had not noticed the lighthouse earlier. Even from three stories up, the natural battlements of the island blocked the view to almost everywhere.

Looking down and over the roof, the layout from above was more simple and orderly than it seemed on our walking tour. The lighthouse sat on the southern horn of the island. It grew and spread northward. There were actually two more openings in the barrier island that surrounded it. I assumed their existence was a result of security giving way to convenience. As he leaned on the rail, I peered down the stairwell behind us, to make sure no one was watching, and then took a healthy handful of Ron's butt in my hand and squeezed it, startling him.

He looked around behind him terrified someone had seen and gave me an almost angry glare that dissipated as he shook his head and smiled a little.

"You need to behave." Ron said calmly and quietly, as if afraid the lighthouse might hear him.

"Afraid they'll toss us in the brig?" I winked at him and leaned my chin onto his shoulder by the tanned, thick skin of his neck.

"*You*, they'll just toss out. But, *me*? I wouldn't be able to come back."

Permanent exile didn't seem like a fair trade for public groping so I gave in, let go, and resisted the natural impulse to kiss him in this ideal setting. Taking another look back again to make sure we were alone, I decided I'd settle for just looking right into his eyes. We were standing quite close to each other and he didn't resist my gaze. His eyes were blue and quite vulnerable, for all the confidence he exuded outwardly. The corners of his eyes and mouth eased into a smile and a grin uncontrollably came over my face. Even though I wasn't entirely sure what he saw in me, we fit together pretty comfortably. I was used to politeness and following orders, he was used to taking charge and giving them, a combination that had made sex the night before incredible. It was then that a droplet of rain touched my cheek. We both looked up and reluctantly went back inside.

On the way back down we ran into another group who were headed up.

"It's starting to get a little wet out there." I offered this advice to the woman, but it was more so that I could hold onto the moment of Ron and I being up there alone a bit longer without clouding it with the comings and goings of other people.

"Oh, really?" The woman said with a sour note. She turned to the small party with her and shrugged. "Well, there goes that idea." I smiled to myself; the moment together would be allowed to linger there, unspoiled for at least a few more minutes.

We went around them and headed back down the stairs while the group of them debated the options of not going up, going up and staying in the lantern room, or boldly braving the rain.

"Are we going to stay here much longer?" This had become a longer lunch break than I had anticipated. If we were leaving, when, after what else, and what would we do next?

"Not much longer." Ron said, answering only the question I had asked and nothing more.

Downstairs, we started our own unspoken debate about going out in the rain. Ron looked out at the rain, then at me. I looked at him, then out at the walkway, which disappeared into the haze of the rain and then back at him again. We both looked out together and then walked away from the door.

I found some plastic cups and poured us each a glass of tap water. Other than the orange juice, I hadn't drank much water and if I didn't start drinking some I'd have a headache before long. Two refills later – I couldn't get enough of it once I'd started – the woman giving the tour and her friends rejoined with us.

Her hair was soft, short, well groomed, and white. Her gold seashell earrings as well as her eyes sparkled. I could tell she was used to taking the helm in domestic situations and when it was called for; she was a tour guide who could probably fascinate me with her knowledge of facts and lore. Ron had assumed this position because he felt it was necessary at the time, but under normal circumstances he would have allowed someone else, someone like this woman, to take over.

I assumed that moisturizer, with the assistance of a facelift, was responsible for the youthfulness of her face. Accordingly, she was stylishly and conservatively dressed in a subtle nautical theme. Her shirt had horizontal stripes and was tucked into her Navy trousers. The red stripes loosely pulled across her chest, which could have been described as perky even on a woman twenty-five years younger. Her necklace matched her earrings, and her buckle was in the shape of a ship's wheel.

Her feminine gestures and perfect posture kept even my eyes focused on her. She was the only one worth noticing in the group she had led up and down the stairs and had now herded to the open door like mega-wealthy sheep. After some hesitation and laughter, she grabbed a magazine off a table, held it over her head, and the group of them attempted to run out into the rain.

It was borderline hysterical to see the group of them, with an average age of sixty, shuffling along with hands on their heads trying to run through the rain without getting wet. I wondered if one of them would end up falling and initiating my instinctive training to run out into the watery war zone and pull them to safety off the battlefield.

I felt a little like a pansy being showed up by the group of seniors who had fearlessly faced the rain. Either picking up on my wounded pride, or due to his own pride being wounded, Ron headed for the door.

We had barely made it twenty feet in the downpour when it came almost to a halt. Slowing down, I felt a little foolish. Changing to a brisk walk we headed for the bathroom. I took a few paper towels and wiped the water out of my hair. One of the advantages to the military haircut was that it was easy to dry and, for the most, part no muss no fuss. The sound of conversation and the occasional booming laugh came in over the top of the wall.

Everyone's voices were amplified as they echoed under the cover of the pavilions, until it all became a rushing sound that was even more intense when we came out into the crowd.

Now that the rain was over, people were taking their drinks and resuming the games and activities they had been involved with before it had started. The children were smiling again; they had not understood why they'd had to get out of the pool in the first place; if they were already wet why did it matter?

The smell after it rains is a calm and pleasant one that I forget every time until I smell it again. Ron came back with his third drink, this one more yellow. I guessed perhaps a gin and tonic, but his other hand, which would have been nice to be holding something for me, was empty.

We continued to stroll through the people and a surge of bright energy livened up things in the pavilion when the sun started to break. The grass and trees sparkled in the mid-day sun and we escaped again out the back end of the pavilion.

We walked down to the dock and took survey of the boats that were there. They seemed to increase in size as we went further. The wooden planks squeaked and were slippery under my flip-flops. My feet were slightly wet, which annoyed me. I used to walk everywhere when I was growing up and I hated every time I had to walk with wet shoes in the rain. My flip-flops squeaked and became slimy at an exponential rate. The further I walked in them, the more yuck, sand, and sweat built up in dark gritty pools between my skin and the foam.

"That's what a beautiful boat looks like." Ron stated, pointing, and I joined him in admiring the massive multilevel boat with wooden floors, lush furniture, and marble countertops. At the bottom, near the ramp that rose to the first deck, was its name. Ron explained to me that the boat had cost an excess of fourteen million dollars and was so large that it was hardly worth having on the manmade lake it could barley navigate.

The name struck me as fitting and funny: "Why Walk." Why, indeed?

***

10

EQUAL FOOTING

"Now that's a damn fine boat!" A stranger exclaimed. He strolled toward us down the dock, and tilted his head at the Why Walk. He carried a cooler under one arm, and a small bit of belly showed through his shirt. He had the soft tan of a wealthy man that had nothing to do with rough living or skin cancers, but everything to do with tanning booths and long lazy days on private islands, like this one. I couldn't see his eyes; they were obscured by sporty sunglasses but I knew underneath they sparkled with Old Money naiveté.

I understood from being around the culture of the rich before, it was rude to be envious of other people's things; instead they preferred to compliment the object as if it had purchased itself and then accidentally fell into the owners hands.

"Randy, how the hell are you?" Ron asked, striding forward to take his hand.

I had noticed it was also custom not to respond when people complimented each other's things.

"I could complain, but who'd want to listen?" It surprised me that on the small island we could still run into people we hadn't seen yet.

When I had hung out both with Marines and with homosexuals, I found myself constantly surrounded by people that defined their formative years as that of the recluse, the outcast. People avoided talking about the time before they earned their title, the time when they were unpopular and uncool—or at least *I* tried my best to forget about it. I had gotten used to never running into the jocks, cheerleaders, or the valedictorians; there is a safety in the knowledge everyone had had it just as bad as me, albeit in their own way. The popular kids disappeared from the map; I assumed they were hidden behind boardroom doors, or occupying obscure political offices. Their absence gave my world a feeling of normalcy. Seeing someone like Randy show up reminded me that the popular kids were still out there somewhere; they had that same cool smile on their face. That smile that meant everything still worked out for them just the way it had been planned by their parents.

Randy was followed by two beautiful women who were just as tan as he was. The first was in a pink bikini; her breasts were about to pop out. She had straight hair and she had bleached the color out of it. Behind her, the other girl was equally busty. Her teal blue bathing suit showed through the thin fabric of her white T-shirt. Her auburn hair curled around her delicate face. I admired girls who dared to change the color of their hair to something different. I'd come to think of blond as a blank slate compared to the character of brown, black or, if the girl was ready to really make a statement, red. I decided right then I'd like the second girl better, but it was hard to look at either of their faces with their distractingly large breasts pointing at me.

"Hey Ronny!" The blond girl called out taking off her glasses. "What are you doing here, you sexy shit? Give me a hug damn it!" She leaned forward and weakly hugged Ron around the neck, careful not to smash the huge orbs that clung to her chest against him. Ron allowed her to hug him, but he didn't hug back or even look at her much. I considered that maybe I wasn't the only one afraid that her breasts might explode. "What's up, stud?"

"Just headed up to the lake." Ron's response was apathetic and cool. Beautiful girls still made me nervous and I usually ended up saying the wrong things around them. I played the indifferent tone of his voice over and over in my head and hoped I could recreate it. I'd had a long standing theory that beautiful girls were like dolphins, if I pretended I didn't want anything to do with them, their curiosity would drive them into my company.

Paying attention to what Ron had said, I started taking careful notes of the code words that were being thrown around, so that I might sound natural using them later. Apparently, Lake Tahoe, or maybe it was the nearby Fallen Leaf Lake was "the lake" that was being referred to. Whichever lake it was, everyone clearly understood what he meant but me.

"This is Veronica, Jim's wife. We kidnapped her because she hadn't been up here yet and we needed a break from the city." Randy smiled as he talked; his white teeth contrasted the black of his sunglasses. What exactly were these women escaping from? I wanted to laugh as I scanned across her smooth and tanned skin, her delicate manicured hands, and her hair that was expertly layered and cared for.

"Hi." When she finally spoke Veronica's voice was higher than I'd imagined it would be.

"This is Brad's first time up too." Ron stepped aside to allow the girls through to shake my hand. One at a time they extended their soft hands to meet mine, but only slipped a few fingers into my grip. I resisted the urge to correct them and teach them the grip of a proper handshake or to squeeze my hand shut around their limp fragile fingers.

"Nice to meet you..." I swallowed the word ladies at the end of my sentence. As I spoke, I attempted Ron's uninterested tone and I did my best to smile in a way that wasn't too flat and wasn't too big.

"I'm Tonya, and my friend Veronica, and the *horrible* brute of a man over there is my husband."

"Hey now, I know where you sleep," Randy joked as he set the cooler down on the dock and began to unfasten the cover on one of the boats.

"I'd shut up if you plan on getting any tonight."

Randy held his hands up like someone pleading not to be shot at.

"What are you doing right now? Nothing? Well, if you're not busy, you should come out with us! We're gonna teach Veronica how to ski. You should totally come!" Again with the skiing, I thought.

"It's an open bar Ronny, get your ass on the boat." Randy said.

"This is great; we can have another expert on hand to give Veronica some pointers." Apparently it was decided for us that we were going boating.

The uncovered boat was Randy's. It was clean, long, and polished. It rocked back and forth gently as we climbed in. The seats were wet with dew, and from a hatch underneath of them, Tonya produced a handful of crumpled shammy towels that she gave to Veronica and me. Ron had wasted no time getting a beer into his hand, I hadn't even seen or heard the cooler open or a can pop.

The shammies were too dry at first at first to soak up the water, but became more cooperative before too long. After about three or four minutes we had dried off the sitting area and Tonya opened the cooler.

"Veronica, hon, what can I get you?" Tonya asked with exaggerated hospitality.

"I'll have a Guinness."

In my mind, I could see the heads of the Marines back on base turn with interest, lust, and pride for a girl who preferred dark beer.

100

"What about you, hon? Brad right?" She said looking at me with her hand hovering over the bottles and cans of beer peeking through the ice. I didn't really want to answer her question since I knew that my asking for a non-alcoholic option would require an explanation.

"You have any soda?" I said after a pause, hoping that the disinterested tone in my voice sounded natural.

"Just a Coke, hon?" She said back with a predictable confused intonation, as if she was sure she'd heard me wrong or to signal to me that it was okay to drink their beer.

I didn't respond at first, too distracted by her choice of words. Growing up in the Midwest I naturally called it pop but, as a means of conformity, I did my best to break this habit. Tonya, it seemed was from Texas, where all soda was called Coke. I never really understood this. To me, Texas had always seemed a hyper-patriotic state, making Pepsi's red, white, and blue the natural choice over Coke, (whose color scheme always reminded me of communism.)

I paused and shook my finger. "I'm the designated driver." This response had worked for me in the past when, with no car, it had been a complete lie.

My first roommate in the Marines had discussed with me what the other Marines thought about my choice not to drink. He said that, while he found the choice admirable, those who did drink usually did not trust those who didn't. There would be times and places to disguise the fact that I didn't drink *ever* with the half-truth that I was not drinking right then. I felt reassured that, this time, while not the reason I wasn't drinking, it was at least a true statement.

"Good man. We're keeping you around." Randy said as he fired up the boat and laughed. At the sound of the exhaust gurgling up through the dark water and we all took our seats.

"You done with that?" Veronica reached out for the shammy I was still holding. Looking down I handed over the towel. I was embarrassed to notice that I had neatly folded it into a perfect square. Taking it from me, she analyzed it, stacked it on top of the other towels and shut it away beneath the seat.

The boat slowly backed up from the dock and I took a sip of my lemon-lime soda. After weaving our way past the dock and back out the island's clandestine entrance we were back in the normal world. Out on the lake, the air felt different again, as if it were possible for the wind to be organized or unorganized. We picked up speed and motored around the turns of the manmade lake. The faster we went, the more uncomfortable the wind became. I had always hated wind. I found it a loud, obnoxious, and distracting phenomenon that instilled a constant paranoia about taking a bug in the eye or mouth.

Behind us, the water surged out away from the boat and then rushed back in to meet the whitish jet of water emerging from the engine. We cut through the lake, leaving a wavy trail of bubbles and a wake that widened and made its way towards the shore like a mini tidal wave.

"So, Tonya says you're quite the stud on a pair of skis." Veronica's voice was carried down wind and sounded miles away.

"Tonya exaggerates almost as much as her husband." Randy teased.

"Is it hard?" Veronica asked.

Tonya flipped her bleached hair. "What?"

"I've never done it before. Is it hard?" Veronica asked.

"You'll do fine." Tonya reassured her, nodding like a bobble-head Barbie.

I found it natural for humans to compete against any forces of nature that might try to intrude on daily life. Listening to Veronica and Tonya have this ordinary conversation, shouting at the top of their lungs to overcome the wind, reminded me of this. There was no urgency to have this conversation at that particular moment, but they were going to have it anyway.

"This place is great. I'm glad I came up. Are you staying here?" Veronica kept moving her hand through her hair, patting it, attempting to tame the windblown tresses. She was fighting a losing battle.

Ron answered. "No. We're just here for lunch." Again it felt good to be part of the "we."

"Brad. Where are you from?" A delicate question that required an answer carefully designed to dissuade further inquiries.

"I've been living in Hawaii for the last few years."

"What?" It was harder to shout upwind, and I thought it was silly to be shouting, but I went along with it.

"Hawaii." I shouted.

"I'm sorry, what?"

Ron came over to lend a hand since he was closer. "Hawaii."

"Oh, I love Hawaii. We were just there last year. It was beautiful." The engine died down, the wind backed off, and the rush of the water became clear as the boat slowed. The end of her sentence came as all of this occurred and she put her hand on her mouth to feign embarrassment for the unladylike behavior of shouting.

"Who's up first?"

"Bring it on, Brad." I wasn't sure why I was targeted as first. I was a little nervous about the whole thing. I spent a lot of time in the water, but I had always been afraid of failing at sports. It was a fear that had let me live on Oahu for years and never learn to surf. Tonya ushered me to stand up, opened the seat beneath me, pulled out two water skis, a rope with a handle at one end, and a d-ring on the other that she clipped to a hook on the back of the boat. I snapped into a bright yellow life-vest and tightened its multitude of straps. The thick padding hugged and stuck to my skin. She passed the handle to me and stepped onto the back of the boat which was a platform that led off into the water.

"Jump on in." I didn't like freshwater. I didn't mind pool water and I loved the ocean, but even the name "freshwater" was oxymoronic.

When I entered the water I did so gently trying not to submerge my head or get any water on my mouth or sink down far enough to touch the muck I knew was lurking beneath. My feet stung where there used to be skin between my toes. The smell of exhaust percolated through the water.

"Swim over to the side." I moved out of the way so that they could drive the boat off without drowning me. After pulling away slightly, they came up next to where I was floating. At the end of the rope I felt like a bobber on a giant fishing line.

Ron leaned over the side with an enthusiastic smile on his face. Normally, his expression conveyed that he could care less about what was going on but, at that moment, he was filled with joy and excitement. "What you want to do is point the skis up. Hold them out in front of you. When you feel the rope pull, keep pulling up with your toes, bend your knees and let the rope pull you up." I knew these simple instructions would prove harder to implement than they sounded.

The boat revved up and moved out. I gripped the rope tightly as the momentum of the boat pulled it across the water. The pressure increased on my hands and I maneuvered my feet so that the skis poked through the water in front of me. I was careful to ensure that the rope was squarely between my legs, and not threatening to tangle with my body and break my bones.

"You ready?" Someone called over the roar of the engine, I was unable to discern who spoke, probably Randy; who asked had no affect on my answer. I removed one hand, waved, then quickly replaced it on the handle. The pressure increased and I was pulled forward. My feet vibrated as the water moved past me. My body started to lift from the water. I couldn't believe it was actually working. The tips of the skis started to come back down to the water as the majority of my body came up, out, and into view from the murky lake. Perhaps skiing wasn't so bad after all.

My pleasure was instantly replaced with a variety of unpleasant sensations. The skis sank back into the water and the rope pulled me face forward through the water as I instinctively

104

clung to the handle. My legs jerked back as the skis fell off and I finally let go spitting out a mouthful of the brownish, brackish water.

Everyone laughed, and my anger intensified. I loathed failure and, under normal circumstances, I did not allow it. My attempts at various tasks seemed spontaneous, but they were generally preceded by careful consideration leading to dismissal of anything I thought I might not be able to do spectacularly.

I could only be glad that my father was in Iowa and not on the boat, watching me. Memories of my childhood were punctuated by my father's indifference to anything that mattered to me, his disappointment in a boy who was not exactly like the others, and his barely disguised revulsion at who I grew to be. I proved my mettle when I joined the Marines; however, in some ways, I was still seven telling him I wanted to be a magician when I grow up.

The lighthearted noises from the boat distorted in my ears to self-destructive thoughts. I'd messed up. I had rushed into something and I had failed. The boat came back up next to me. "Are you alright?" Ron was asking leaning over the side with Veronica's arm around his shoulder.

"I'm fine." I muttered. I was so consumed by my frustration that, despite my attempts to suppress it, it bubbled up through my words.

"It's alright. It's your first time. You'll get it." Tonya reassured me, beaming her beauty pageant smile. I wanted to smack the perfect white teeth out of her pretty little mouth.

Veronica chimed in. "Yeah, don't sweat it, if it was easy, it wouldn't be any fun."

How the hell would she know? We'd already established she'd never done it before. To make matters worse, I realized my ultimate potential for defeat would not come if I couldn't get up on the skis, but if I couldn't and she could.

"Grab the rope. We'll pull you back to your skis." Randy called from the wheel.

I smiled the biggest fake smile I could. "Let's do this!"

My second attempt was even less successful than my first. I barely emerged from the water before my face impacted it, stinging my eyes as momentum pushed the putrid water under my closed eyelids.

The attempts began to fade into each other after that. Each time the boat pulled me back to the skis; each time Randy drove the boat in an increasingly irritated manner. It was like I was participating in take after take of a wipe-out montage. I didn't know why I was being made to try over and over again. Maybe Ron wanted to get back at me for siding with the old general who hated snow skiing or maybe he just wanted to show me how to do something he did well.

"Alright, we're gonna go one more time. Remember, knees bent, toes up, let the rope pull you up." Ron really did want to see me do this and to prove to himself that he could help me.

Pushing the negativity out, I tried to relax back into a virgin mindset. My progressive attempts had only produced less worthy results. Instead, I cleared my head of the ideas I'd been collecting and assuming would help.

This was a trick I had learned from physical fitness challenges: if I forced my way into a genuine smile, my performance usually improved. I searched around for something I could draw humor from. Facing forward, I focused on the pointy tips of the skis on either side of the rope and imagined them to be the pointy plastic ears of a rabbit waiting to jump out of the water naked.

"Ready!" I shouted to the boat and the rope pulled me forward.

While I could not have been going more than a few miles per hour for a few seconds before my face once again plunged into the disgusting lake water, I was pleased. I had straightened my legs so, technically, I had just water-skied.

I was happy to be back on the boat. It was nice to be out of the water, to be free of the life-vest, and to know that I wouldn't have to be dragged behind a boat at the end of a rope again. I asked for another soda and a bottle of water. I then poured some of the water over my head to rinse the grime from my face before voluntarily putting any soda in my mouth.

A smaller, bright-blue life-vest was being fitted to Veronica with Tonya's assistance. They were telling each other a joke that I didn't hear and were laughing. I was still too energized to sit down and was pacing slightly on the boat. Catching myself fidgeting, I sat down even though I didn't want to and tried to squeeze some of the water out of the bottoms of the legs of my shorts.

Tonya helped lower Veronica down into the water and they double high-fived. Coming about, we came along side her the same way they had done for me, only this time, Tonya took the role of coach. Again the instructions were repeated. "Alright, hon, skis on each side of the rope. Toes up. Bend at the knees and let the rope pull you up."

"Got it." A loud masculine belch followed Veronica's reply.

"Oh my God! She's ready, let's go."

I looked back at her as the rope pulled again from a large arch into a straight line pointing directly at Veronica.

"I'm ready, let's go!" Her vibrant overconfidence would add to the satisfaction watching her flail around when she fell into the water. Taking a sip of my soda, I almost spilled it on myself when the boat lurched forward. The skis started to spray water out away from them as she moved through the water. Then smoothly, she stood up.

I changed my mind and decided from that moment that Veronica would not be the one I liked best. Tonya cheered for Veronica who had astonishingly managed to master in seconds what I'd spent the better part of thirty minutes failing at. I looked up at the clapping Tonya with her chest bouncing up and down. I didn't like her either.

"Don't be so hard on yourself." Ron's warm breath carried the smell of beer and entered my ear, making me shiver. I almost didn't recognize Ron in this environment, but then again,

I didn't really know Ron. I had spent so much time acting casual, like we'd been friends for years, that I'd forgotten we had yet to know each other for an entire day. All this was not to mention that fact that I was about to be introduced to his sister and pull off the same charade.

After a few seconds I relaxed a bit. I was enjoying the ride on the nice boat with "people of quality." Coasting along, I worked out a temporary truce with the wind. The terms: if it didn't sling any juicy insects into my eyes, nose, or mouth, I would allow myself to be friends with it. Casually taking a drink from my glass, I drank in what had been one of the most enjoyable days of my life. I wasn't about to let a pretty pampered girl upstage me. I was going to have to duke it out with her in conversation and somehow overshadow her successful debut performance.

The boat slowed down and we coasted up close enough to retrieve my soon-to-be-defeated rival's body from the water. Competition didn't end once I'd won or lost something; once I achieved it, the harder battle to maintain my position began. I was ready to take Veronica on.

"Ouch." The temper of a group immediately changed when one of the herd cried out.

"Oh, God! Randy, help!"

"Ouch." As a Marine, I reacted to every emergency with the same urgency: from dropped cell phones to dropped limbs, without hesitation, I immediately picked it up and tried to help. In a split second I was helping Veronica up into the boat and sitting her down.

"What the hell happened?" Randy looked back with one hand still on the wheel.

A fishhook had snagged her. It was only a superficial cut, just under the skin, the amount of blood was minute. It ran quickly though, thinned by the wetness of her legs. I held her legs and noticed how clammy and cool they were. Women always had a softer, colder feel than men did. It was a quality that incited them to curl up beneath men while they slept; men were like furnaces and it was convenient to sleep beside them, especially during the winter.

"How did that happen?" Ron leaned over, confused.

"Does it matter? Fix it! Help her!" Tonya was clearly not well adapted to handle stress.

"Would you?" Veronica asked. She was no longer the victor and I the defeated. We were again on equal footing, looking at each other face to face.

"Where is the first-aid kit?" I asked Randy. He looked back at me with a look that signaled he had no idea what to do in this situation. Tonya handed over the bright red package and I opened it, and then set it down beside me.

"I'm going to take it out. It's going to hurt. Then I'm going to put some disinfectant on it, which will also hurt. Okay?" I tried to sound reassuring as I looked into her eyes. Her eyes were no longer brave and wild like her hair; she was like a balloon that had blown into a rosebush, frightened and quivering.

She didn't complain while I removed the small shiny metal hook from her leg, preferring instead to bite into her lip.

"Oh, God! Don't hurt her!" Tonya whined. She sounded like she was in more pain than Veronica was.

"Shut up, Tonya." Randy was watching from the driver's seat with great interest.

Pulling out the bottle of peroxide I then handed a band-aid to Ron.

"Get this ready for me." Emergency situations gave me license to boss people around without them questioning me. The clear liquid fizzed at the red openings where the blood still slowly flowed. I held out my hand for the band-aid and saw Ron staring at the package, perplexed.

Minor cuts and scrapes were a natural occurrence that, in the life of ordinary people, I'd learned to deal with. Observing him now, holding the band-aid, was like watching an aborigine who had just been given a knife and fork. Did Ron avoid learning basic survival skills because he didn't need to, or had he seen them but simply not paid attention? It was not unlike driving and never having paid attention to the small nuances of completing the task, it seemed Ron had been a passenger to life.

I gently took it back from him, placed a cotton ball directly on the tiny wound, and fixed it onto her skin with the band-aid.

"What a champ!" Randy clapped. Clearly, everyone was making a much bigger deal out of the situation that was warranted.

"I played lacrosse in college. I could kick your butt Randy." I found it amusing that she was hardened enough to take it while I pulled a metal hook out of her leg but she still used the word butt when issuing her threat. "Do you think I should get a tetanus shot?"

"Yeah, that's a good idea." I told Veronica with the best "you're gonna be alright" tone I could manage.

"Thank you *so* much. Brad, you're so sweet." Tonya cooed.

"Thanks Brad." Veronica said. "Somebody get me another beer."

"Guinness?" I asked.

"Your friend is turning me on. First he saves my life and now he's waiting on me." I laughed as I pulled the bottle from the ice. "And he's got a nice ass. I'm gonna have to trade in my husband."

"Well, alright then." I handed her the beer and sat down next to her giving an exaggerated stretch and putting my arm around her and slowly moving my hand as if to grab her boob.

"Oh yeah! I could get used to this."

Compliments, once I'd become used to getting them, were sometimes hard to swallow. They left me wondering "what does this person want or expect from me?" But, coming from a girl, they were a gay man's ultimate source of flattery.

The sky darkened as another bank of clouds cast its shadow on the boat. Collectively, we decided to take the boat back in. The trip back was further than I remembered. The lake was a long series of forks, wide spaces, and narrow channels. We

110

stayed between the buoys that marked the deep channel and slowed to minimal power coming back through the openings to the inner moat of the island.

We drifted through various conversations that required a lot of talking and little disclosing on my part. It was beyond the simple pronoun game that gay men frequently engage in to tell stories about their love life without having to directly lie about the gender of their partners. I had to take this idea a step further and talk about what I had done without revealing where I was from, that I went to public school, or that I knew Ron for less than twenty-four hours.

"Are you ready to get back on the road?" I asked Ron.

"Yeah, let's go." I said, but suddenly remembered the flaw in the hedge I had seen. One last time, I looked for a grounds-keeper I might tip off before someone else noticed, but again, there was no one nearby.

The ferry was already docked and about to leave when we passed back under the welcoming arch. Unlike before, it was nearly full with mostly older couples clustered together in groups of two or four. They were quiet and their faces were as content as if they'd just been to a paradise but were too drunk on it to talk. Ron and I took one of the last available spots for standing and the ferry driver turned the next group of four away.

Heading back to the car, there was lightness in my companion's step. It seemed Ron couldn't have been more pleased by my natural arrogance, which proved to be the perfect camouflage. My particular brand of arrogance was accepted unquestionably. The grace of my mannerisms was elegant, not feminine; my direct eye contact was standard, not suspect; and my speech, intellectual instead of homosexual. I felt completely accepted, despite being a stowaway. As long as I continued to watch my step, I could avoid any questions that might expose me. The true test of this was still to come and Ron's sister was family; she would not be easily fooled.

***

BRETT EDWARD STOUT

11

THE ART OF CONVERSATION

We arrived at the car and it was dirtier from the trip than I remembered. Bugs had splattered on the hood, windshield, and side mirrors. A layer of yellow dirt slightly dulled the would-be silver sides. I reached into my pocket for the keys and realized my first mistake. I could have unlocked the car by simply pressing the button from several feet away. When I was opening the door and about to get in I noticed my second. I had opened the passenger side door. I moved out of the way, pretending I had intended to open it for Ron. The gesture was out of place and we both knew it. A man did not open a car door for another man; it simply was not done. Both of us looked around out of the corner of our eyes to see if anyone was watching.

I tossed my clothes, which I had retrieved from the locker in the bathroom, into the back. Ron climbed into the SUV. I knew it would only make matters worse to shut the door behind him. I let him do this himself and walked around to the other side that was still locked when I pulled up on the handle.

I was a bit melancholy getting into the car knowing that I might not be getting back out of it for hours. I knew beforehand that my butt would become sore and my knees would start to hurt. I could already see myself readjusting my legs again and again without relief; this combined with being in the driver's seat, I was not looking forward to.

When the key twisted in the ignition, nothing happened. Putting my game face on, I pushed harder on the brake and tried again. Nothing happened. I could feel Ron looking at me, waiting to patronize and expose me as a fraud. Eyeing the gauges and the steering wheel, I began to systematically try to recreate my successful ignition at the dealership. I tried turning the key back and, for a moment, I even wondered if I needed to put my foot on the gas instead. Just as my foot changed pedals I looked down to see the glowing outline around the letter D. Putting the car into park I turned the key again and the car returned to life.

My mind was filled with the possible looks Ron was giving me; from contempt to frustration to disgust, but I never looked at him. As if the moment hadn't been trying enough, I was further irritated when jazz screamed out of the radio, loud music that had been used to overcome the ambient noise of the road. I turned it down. I did not want to turn it off; that might be rude.

The straight road stretched out in front of us past the horizon between the cornfields. I sped up the car to five miles an hour above the speed limit. It was actually a pleasant sensation to feel the gears change through the pressure of the pedal.

Remembering my way out of places I had gotten into on foot had always been easy for me. Driving seemed to be no different. I found the highway and rolled to a stop next to a sign that said "Stockton," pointing to the right; we went left. We were once again pointed toward the same destination with the same uncertain outcome.

A few miles down the road I began to squirm a little. My butt was becoming uncomfortably warm and starting to sweat. I turned on the air and, in doing so, earned one of Ron's questioning looks.

"I'm getting a little warm."

He looked down in the center and pushed a button that had the shape of a chair with heat waves coming up through the seat. He then turned back down the air conditioner and turned up the radio.

I shifted my weight onto my left side to try to let my shorts breathe underneath. It was difficult to do and I had to pull the seatbelt out a little to accomplish the task. Looking over at my passenger, I saw that Ron was not wearing his. I was almost certain that he hadn't been wearing it the entire trip. It didn't seem as much an act of defiance or desire to live on the edge, as much as he probably just didn't care.

There is a point I often reach when I'm around someone when, if I haven't spoken up, it no longer feels natural to do so. As Americans, it felt like we avoided conversation at any serious level. When I see a group of people gathered in a circle on the street, I know it was the result of some form of violence and that they were not trying to listen in on a compelling argument. I remembered my teachers in school always going on and on about how America had forgotten how to have an argument; that we were too busy talking about the mechanics of daily life and nuances of pop-culture to explore any meaning behind any of it.

I enjoyed the rambling banter of my teachers more than I enjoyed chatting with other students. At least they made me think about important issues, and did not make me feel behind the trends. Encouragement from sources other than the faculty was rare. When my classmates heard that I intended to join the Marine Corps, I was met with outright resistance and verbal hostility.

"*You* want to join the *Marines*?" Was the typical snide tone I had been met with. The implication being that I was not good enough, or *whatever else* enough, to succeed at becoming this abstract idea they had only heard on the news and generally revered.

School ended, my service began, and suddenly I was on the other side of the country and miles away from the people I'd spent twelve years with and who had helped teach me to hate myself. I never missed them once. When I would see them when I was on leave back home, I swelled up with pride when I had forgotten their names, and satisfaction when they remembered mine.

The dodging of communication seemed to also be echoed in our dating culture. When I had taken dates out, I usually went to some destination where I wouldn't have to actually talk to them. At dinner, I could coast through the discomfort by distracting my date with the menu and ordering process and, once the meal arrived, occupy my mouth with objects that made it impossible to talk.

My preferred destination for non-talking dates was a movie theatre. It was possible to sit in the dark where I was not allowed to speak or even look my date if I didn't want to. I also enjoyed that it allowed me to observe them once they were engrossed in the film. I get to see them completely unaware that I was watching them, completely candid, gaping mouth and all. It was Ron who finally broke the truce of silence that had carried us since we left the Island.

"I should swing by and visit my friends in Sacramento." The 'we' was gone again for now, and I felt once more reduced to being Ron's chauffer.

"Sure, but don't you want to get up to the Lake?" It felt safe trying out my new code word that I still wasn't entirely sure meant Lake Tahoe or Fallen Leaf Lake.

"It'll still be there." Ron pulled out his cellular phone and started looking for a number in his contact list.

"No problem. I just didn't know if you were planning on being there by dinner or anything." Our trip was becoming quite perforated with stops. It was easier to handle skipping my flight when I had a clear plan of action; the plan was becoming hazier and hazier by the hour, compounded by how long the day already felt.

116

"Hey guys. Where are you?" I started to wonder who these friends were when he greeted them with "guys." Did he actually mean they were guys, or was he using guys in the general sense? Did this mean they were gay? Ron didn't strike me as the kind of guy who kept gay friends. My curiosity was piqued.

"Who are these friends of yours?"

"A couple of good guys I know from way back." I was starting to feel that he was being intentionally evasive.

"Do you have many friends in Sacramento? Did you used to live there?" This was part of my new mission. He was proving quite difficult to get details out of, a game that women understood and few played well. Ron was an expert because his apathy was genuine. He remained silent.

"I've never been to Sacramento. I've driven past it. Do you need to call your work or anything?" I went back into useful mode, as it seemed I got better responses this way.

"That's a good idea." *Of course* it was a good idea; I'd brought the subject up hours ago, when I first thought it was a good idea. I wasn't one for being late to things and if I wasn't going to make it to an event, I always called. Missing work was an absurd notion in any circumstance that didn't involve severe bleeding. (Especially if that job had words like "AWOL" and "Desertion" to describe unexplained absences.)

He raised the phone up to his hear again. "Hey John, this is Ron. Yeah, I'm going up to visit Cynthia for a while..." I found myself very interested in how long *a while* might be, but I knew that at least it meant the duration was open ended. "It's never gonna happen, you son of a bitch." Apparently he was on more familiar terms than I'd ever been with my superiors, assuming that Ron had superiors. "Alright, I'll see you then." When, I wondered, when was this "then?" I was failing at my mission. Instead of answers, I was accumulating more questions at a rapid rate.

"I wish it was that easy for me to take time off."

"Well, I don't have to be in an office to do my job."

"Must be nice. I bet it's nicer than the back of a Hummer too." I felt us slipping back into the limbo of travel silence again. "Where do I need to go to get to your friends?"

"They're at the Marina. I'll tell you where to turn off once we get into town." Our destination was yet another marina. I thought, "again with the boats, again with the water." What kind of boat would they have? Part of me expected to walk up to a giant ocean liner converted over for personal use; the kind of boat that boasted a chandelier in its ballroom.

Moments later came the first sign for the California State Capital, Sacramento. Ron steered me off the highway and down streets that became more and more residential as we went.

"You can park anywhere on the street." There were no meters and I looked for a "No Parking" sign. It was hard to believe we had found a place in the state where I didn't have to pay to stop driving.

Judging by its position, the sun was an hour or two away from setting. Opening the door, I noticed how dirty and unswept the parking lot was. There were rotten French fries not far from where I stood. They were smashed into the pavement and still inside their carton. Cigarette butts were littered through the grass that was barely alive, and the condition of the pavement itself was shabby.

A high chain link fence ran the length of the hill on the far side of a set of train tracks. The embankment sloped steeply down and out of sight to where the docks were. The huge blue metal roofs that covered the dock made the marina look more like a divided warehouse than a place to store boats.

We walked up to a metal turnstile with a call box on it. Ron pushed in a code and a slightly effeminate but deep man's voice crackled through it.

"If you're not hot you better be huge."

Apparently the "guys" were gay.

***

12

THE AMERICAN

The gate began to buzz, softer than I expected. Usually, buzzers sounded an abrasive challenge, rather than a welcome. The turnstile squeaked as I passed through it. The dry dusty metal made me shiver, the same feeling I got when I ran my fingernails across blackboard.

In order to descend the steep hill that had been created when they carved into the landscape to widen the Marina, we had to make our way down a metal walkway. The earth was held back by concrete retaining walls that stood as another monument to man's dominion over the natural environment. Our feet made clanging sounds as we made our way down the long, sloping, metal walkway.

My eyes panned around looking for any movement other than the soft undulating rows of sailboats, motor yachts, and the occasional bird. In addition to the squeaking turnstile, the smell was another aspect of the marina I didn't much care for. Breathing it into my nose made me feel like I was being invaded by the dirty liquid and I found myself trying to breathe less. I had learned the full extent of the stupidity of this in the Boot Camp gas chamber. Holding my breath to escape something surrounding me in the air was counter-productive. Eventually, I would have to take deep breaths to replenish the supply of oxygen to my brain.

I blew out what I'd been holding in and forced myself into even breathing, despite the awfulness in the air. I tripped, and looked up to see if Ron had noticed but he was ahead of me by several feet walking the way he always did. A turtle swam a few inches beneath the surface and I remembered the number of living things that would spend their entire lives submerged; it seemed depressing. It would be like living in a city where the sun was perpetually hidden behind the clouds and every day was monotonously overcast.

Ron made a turn ahead, down one of the rows. The boats were all shadowed under the lofted roofs overhead with the kind of huge light bulbs that took ten minutes to warm up hanging from them. A shadowy figure stepped into view, spoiling my endeavor to find them before they noticed us. The man was a little overweight but not fat. He wore khaki shorts and a polo shirt, as if he had pulled clothes from one of the plastic bags in Ron's closet.

"He doesn't look anything like the ad!" The man called. Now that I was closer, I could see he was clean-shaven, his black hair was bald on top, and he had thick Italian eyebrows and dark brown eyes. His smile was bright and his teeth were nearly perfect. Extending a hand and opening an arm to the side for a hug-shake (as I called it), they embraced, smashing their hands between them and slapping each other on the back with thuds that resonated in their torsos. Most striking of all was the deepness of his voice. It struck me deep in the gut. I found him strangely appealing.

"How the hell are you?" Ron asked.

"Oh, you know, same old tired life. I wish sometimes that I made a little money to make it easier." They both began to laugh. "Oh!" He turned his attention to me. "You must be the one we called for."

"Hi. I'm Brad." I shook his hand, which was impressively large and made me self-conscious about the size of my own hands. I'd always admired large strong hands; they always seemed more useful than the long thin fingers of my own.

He continued to shake my hand and look right at me.

"I'll need the money up front, if that's all right." I asked, hooking my thumb in the front of my shorts.

He laughed again from his belly. "Holy shit, Richard, we've got a live one!" He called toward the open door that led below deck.

"We'll, don't scare this one away then." Came another voice, a tenor. A man was framed in the doorway, but the light coming from the cabin occluded his features. "Come on board."

The boat was not as big as my imagination had conjured, however, it was very impressive. It looked to be about forty feet long with a lower deck, a seating area in back, a larger one on top just behind the bridge, and a long nose with an area to lay out on the bow. Its white surfaces and long sweeping grey decals were clean to the point of being shiny. The pristine surface was delightful and elegant, the cleanliness of it made me want to touch it but afraid if I did, I might diminish its spotless purity. There were no leaves, cobwebs, or dust in any of the crevices of the padded seats. It could have been brand new but I suspected it was just well kept.

Ron headed up to the upper level and plopped himself down onto one of the grey built-in seats along the side. He opened a refrigerator, revealing a variety of beverages.

"What can I get for you?" The higher pitched man asked.

"I'll just take a diet, please."

"Anything with that?" He responded like every other drinker, as if I'd forgotten to mention three shots of vodka or meant to imply it.

"No, I've got to be the responsible driver. Ron will have a rum and coke." I felt the need to assert myself with Ron's friend whose name I still didn't know. Ordering his drink would help the illusion that we knew each other for less than a day.

121

"You've got them ordering drinks for you now, I see." He laughed again and winked. He was charming, but I didn't like his comment. It made me feel like just one in a long string of men he might have introduced to them.

"What am I having?" Ron asked.

"A rum and coke!" I shouted up, and the battle to define myself as worth remembering was on.

"Sounds good to me." Ron nodded and I added a point for the home team to the scoreboard in my head.

The man turned with the fizzing class of dark soda over ice and extended it to me. The escaping carbon dioxide tickled my nose a little as I drank from the glass. A few moments later, he handed me Ron's drink and I made my way up the short stair to the upper deck. I handed it to Ron and sat down next to him, not touching, and put my arm over the rail, so that my hand was behind him.

"What are you doing down there? What are you having?" the man shouted down the ladder well.

Richard's voice was muffled through the deck. "Another Corona." I was beginning to wonder if everyone who was successful started drinking in the middle of the day and I had never noticed.

"We just got back from Greece. Richard's sister has a place there. It was *amazing*."

"We're on the way up to Ron's sister's on the Lake." My assertiveness felt off this time.

"Oh, is this your first time since she finished the place?"

"First time." Ron answered and took a deep swallow if his drink.

"And, the both of you are going?" He laughed again, and I got the impression he laughed a lot. "Is she still mad at you?"

Mad at Ron? The situation that I was being led into was becoming more complicated.

"I guess I'll find out." He shrugged and took another drink.

"When are you going to get one of these for yourself?" The man smirked.

"When would I ever use it?" I found his argument slightly ironic. By nature, all yachts such as these were impractical. What did it matter how much he used something that was, by nature, designed only for show?

"Not to mention that he'd probably crash it into the dock when he parked it." I added. Making fun at Ron's expense was a gamble but he didn't have any discernible reaction to it.

"You haven't gotten that fixed yet?" The man arched his brows.

"Haven't found the time."

"You haven't made the time. Call the service shop and have them come pick it up at your garage." I was glad to hear him say out loud what I'd been thinking.

The sound of footsteps came up from below; a head of sandy blonde, well-combed hair emerged. Richard was also tan and, while he was not wearing a shirt, he was wearing the staple khaki shorts.

"There's my favorite Dick."

"I thought we were getting out on the river?"

"You want your beer?"

"That's why I asked for it." I liked the honesty between them. Once coupled together, two people frequently stop with politesses. Conversations they had usually sounded more like two people who were annoyed with each other rather than in love. "Hi, I'm Richard."

"Brad." Richard's hands were much softer than his partner's were. His body was muscular, well defined, and completely free of hair all the way down to his forearms and hands.

"Robert, let's get this show on the road, already. We'll miss it!" A weight was lifted from me to finally learn the name to the person I'd been conversing with since we arrived. I assumed they meant the sunset as the light was rapidly becoming more golden.

Robert got up and set his drink in a holder next to the helm. The boat almost silently started and he began to check the gauges as if he were a pilot preparing for takeoff.

"Oh! Brad, help me out a second." All Marines, myself included, can be resistant at times if *asked* to do something; however, if it's an order, we tend to obey. Seconds later I had followed Richard down and off the boat.

"Undo us down there by the bow. Just toss the rope on board!"

I unwound the wet ropes that had grayed with soil, and tossed them up onto the vessel. The boat started to move forward slightly. I quickly undid the other rope and ran back to the stern. They were already a few feet out so I jumped. I leaned up against the railing, breathing heavily for something that was a rather minor exertion. I could easily have fallen right into the dark churning water and been sliced up by the boat's engine.

Their spot was almost in the very back of the marina. We made our way down the row and turned left toward where it opened up to the river. The wake made a pleasant splashing sound like long waves crashing upon an Oahu beach as we moved along the manmade finger of land that separated us from the river. Small waves have a more pleasant sound than their larger, angrier cousins.

The water of the Sacramento River was brackish, compared to the calm lagoon we were leaving. Once in it, the bow raised up as Robert brought the boat up to speed. It was a wide river and its water was heavily soiled. Up top, the air broke around; the windshield in front deflected most of the irritating oncoming wind.

We approached a large drawbridge that looked like the skeleton of an oddly shaped skyscraper. Across the river stretched a grid of steel girders riveted together into two towers and a similarly constructed span with a separation in the middle where it could be pulled up. Birds flew in and out from under it where they had made their nests. I picked up my drink, putting my hand over the top, discreetly hiding my fear that a lucky piece of droppings might land in it. It wasn't that I was afraid of birds. I just didn't like them flying overhead for reasons that had always seemed obvious to me.

A passenger again, I watched the buildings on the bank pass and, on the eastern bank, the buildings of downtown reflected the hot, blinding, yellow light of the sun. I let my eyes close and savored the heat of the sun's rays on the back of my head and reflecting onto my face from the glass curtains of the city.

The next bridge we went under was also a drawbridge, but of a different kind. It rotated from the center, which seemed more dangerous to me with its giant mass of concrete and steel freely swinging out over the water—an act that could cause its destruction with only a slight imbalance of weight. Once open, all of its ends dropped straight off into the water. With the other kind, at least the end of the pavement was hoisted up out of the way and leaning back on its own weight.

The ride was smooth. I leaned against my seat with my drink in my hand, and felt almost regal. This was the glamorous life of the super-rich. It was something I could easily get used to.

Ron had moved up into the seat across from Robert and was looking out over the bow at what was coming up. His blue Tinsley Island hat fit snugly onto his head. His arm dangled over the side. Richard was much the same as I was, but facing into the sun, as we headed north; he frequently turned his head from one side and then to the other to avoid looking straight into it. His legs were out in front of him with one foot on top of the other, and he reclined slightly with his hands spread out as if he had his arms around two invisible dates.

Standing up, the angle of the boat was awkward, and it would be all too easy to lose my balance. I came up past Ron and lightly touched him on the shoulder, giving it a gentle squeeze. The act seemed natural as I let myself stop resisting the fantasy life I was borrowing.

"You have to take off your shoes." Robert told me and I did so. Apparently there was a strict code of conduct on board.

I climbed out and found a large mat. The railing around the bow was only a few inches or so and the drop to the water made it feel like I was standing near the edge of a cliff during an earthquake. I positioned myself for stable footing and slowly pulled my shirt up over my head.

Reversing it so that it was right side out again, I managed to fold in the arms, then the sides, and finally up the middle even in the strong wind. I wanted to turn around to insure that everyone was watching me, but doing so would ruin the idea that I wasn't doing it for their benefit.

Lying on my back on the front of the boat was incredibly relaxing even though my bare feet were exposed to the chilly air. I wished I had brought my drink with me, but I didn't care enough to actually go get it.

The engine's purr lowered to a growl, and we reduced speed. The wind weakened and the heat of the daylight more easily permeated my skin, warming it. I leaned up onto my elbows to look.

I could see that we were approaching a fork that was the mouth of the American River. Where the two rivers merged, I saw a beach covered in people wearing bright bathing suits. The late day sun gave their bodies a golden glow. Those on the shore gawked at the beautiful piece of nautical machinery that made its turn in front them. Their faces, even from a distance, were star struck. They squinted and held their hands over their eyes to keep the sun from obscuring their view of who might be aboard the elegant vessel. Some of them pointed and I could hear them debating amongst themselves who it was they thought they could see on the boat, not knowing that none of us were anyone that would interest them.

Where the waters met was a fascinating display. The soiled Sacramento River consumed the cooler blackened water of the American in swirls. Even the surfaces of the water were different. The American was less hurried, almost moving like a continuous sheet into the choppy waves of the Sacramento's current.

We passed the beach and headed up river. I was bored of being up front, now that we were facing away from the sun. As I stood up and climbed back, I noticed the intense way Robert watched me. He smiled and looked over at Ron when he saw that I'd noticed. There was a safety in seeing him do this. I could tell his attraction to me, but also that I was protected by the respect he had for his friend.

We navigated out way around a few gentle bends of the river and, the further we went, the less evidence there was of civilization. I could see trails that zigzagged through the trees and brush on the high southern bank of the river.

Robert got up when we had slowed to a stop.

"You want me to get the anchor?" Richard asked. When Robert nodded, he made his way up onto the bow and cast the anchor over the front.

Everything was very quiet again, which was nice, considering the symphony of noises from combustion engines we'd been listening to during the course of the day. The four of us all got up and prepared for the transition from the journey to the destination. Drinks were replenished, towels were taken out, and we all took seats on the comfortable upper deck.

"So, where did you guys hook up with each other?" Robert asked, the golden question that both Ron and I had dreaded and hoped to avoid.

***

13

FRIENDS SHARE EVERYTHING

"So, where did you guys hook up with each other?"

I smiled to cover the awkward moment, and took a sip of my soda. "Oh, Ron picked me up last night in a leather bar in the Castro." My smile dissolved to a smirk. I could feel Ron's mortification radiating from him. His building embarrassment was calmed when the guys started to laugh wildly. Their laughs harmonized with each other, which happens frequently when two people are together for a long period of time.

"Seriously though, where are you from?" Richard asked, sobering up. I knew the absurdity of the truth was outrageous enough to be beyond belief, allowing me not to lie and them to make up a less interesting story of where we'd met. It was another point in my favor in my game where I was the only knowing participant.

"I've been living in Hawaii for a few years. I just got out of the Marines and I'm taking a little time to consider my options," I didn't want to come off to them as someone who had just had their identity shattered and had no vision of what my future might look like. Also, mentioning Hawaii was still useful at disguising my income bracket, even if they suspected.

"We love Hawaii. We go to Maui every year!" Richard sat up with excitement displaying his enthusiasm for the Islands.

"We love Marines too." Robert added. "Good place to have a command." Like the men on Tinsley, they assumed I had been an officer.

"I didn't know you guys went to Maui every year." Ron was taken aback, as though even he knew he ought to have known this about his friends.

Richard cocked his head in a gesture of overdramatic confusion. "We've been going for years. You didn't know that?"

"We've got property on Maui." Robert agreed.

"How long were you in the Marines?" This time, the mistake of mentioning the service was mine. I felt the conversation coming. Once I figured out what every gay man wanted me to tell them about, I started loathing even mentioning being a Marine. I'd worked very hard to be a Marine, and it bothered me that it was reduced by most to a tawdry fantasy.

"Four years." I replied.

"Wow, what was it like? Being gay in the Marines?" I knew what he meant, but I tried to dodge it by answering from an emotional perspective. "All those young guys willing to take orders from you."

"It's hard to be forced lie to your brothers one minute and be expected to give your life for them the next. The Marines are great. I just don't see what the big deal about being gay is. I guess maybe they're afraid of all the money they'd have to pay in marriage benefits. You make, like, twice as much money if you're married."

"I bet you had a lot of hot times in the barracks?" Here it was. I knew my answer would suffice for Richard, but Robert wanted the juicy details.

I laughed as I always did, like I'd never been asked that question before. "I had some good times."

"Oh, yeah. Now this I've got to hear."

"Nah, let's just say I had a Marine knock on my hatch in the middle of the night more than once saying: 'Man, I'm really drunk.'"

"Wow, I bet that was hot." The persistence shown at getting more details out of me was more irritating every time I was forced to provide any.

I dug down into myself and did the only thing I really could do to escape the trap of telling raunchy sex stories about Marines, for whom I'd endured hell, and for whom I held mutual love and respect. I brought up philosophy. "I don't understand what the big deal is. People are too obsessed with this gay/straight thing when really there is no such thing. There's a spectrum of sexuality. Just because you've had sex with guys doesn't make you gay. But, if you're attracted to someone else, regardless of their sex, and you don't allow yourself the option of acting on it because of what other people think... You're an idiot."

The seriousness of my point was the perfect mood breaker. No one said anything for a moment as they considered what I'd said.

"I feel the same way," Richard came in. "People should act however they feel is right."

Again, no one said anything for a moment. Apparently I'd done more than broke the mood; I'd killed it. I didn't want to be a serial killer of fun, so I had to make up for my rant.

"That doesn't mean I don't have any hot stories. Let me tell you how I lost my virginity..."

I told them the sexy story of how I'd lost my virginity, in the summer before high school, to a popular football player. Nobody at school even knew he knew my name. I told them how one night he'd spent the night and had slept completely naked. As just kids, how I'd asked him if he'd ever been with girls before and if he'd ever be with a guy to which he replied; "I'd try anything once." Our secret affair lasted all the way through our senior year. As time passed by, and we started constructing lives that were more complicated and contained obligations like

131

work, we had less time to get together behind closed doors, and the romance faded.

"That's the hottest thing I've ever heard." Robert said. I knew he wasn't serious but the graphic story didn't leave many other options for comment.

What I didn't tell him was the very unsexy silent torture it had been to be so intimate and liked by someone, who ran in the circles that I idolized, and to pretend that I didn't even know him when anyone else was around.

"Who's serving drinks on this boat? Ronny! I need some service here! Ronny!" Ron had managed to get drunk for the second time in less than a day only this time he'd done it without anyone even noticing. It appeared that Ron might be an alcoholic, but it didn't seem to slow him down in life any. Ron stood up and was having trouble walking. He changed directions a few time before sitting back down on the opposite side of the boat.

"Ronny needs a drink, Richard," Robert aimed the request at him since he was next to the refrigerator, apparently refilling my glass, which I'd emptied and he must have picked up. Richard looked up at me as if to ask my permission to give another drink to my "boyfriend." I raised my eyebrows and shrugged. It wasn't as if I could stop him and, if I tried, I ran the risk of being exposed and voted off the boat. I liked it here and I didn't want to leave just yet.

"Ronny! Get in here!" Ron seemed to be laughing at his own parody of his father, but the laughter still carried sadness and pain.

I pondered the absurd question of why this river was named the American River. Was it somehow more patriotic than other rivers? Patriotism and Americanism were indefinable terms and, for the most part, useless.

Richard came back up with the drinks, handing one to Ron and then to me.

"Thank you very much, sir." I'd slipped again.

"Oh, sexy, you don't have to call me that."

"What the hell is this? This is weak!" Ron's tone was both loud and rude. He handed his drink to Robert who took a sip and got a sour look.

"Richard, get Ronny a proper drink." Richard made a face at me that said "oh well, I tried." and then took Ron's glass and tossed its contents overboard where it splashed into the river below with a splat.

Once he had his drink in his hand, Ron pretty much entertained himself. He sat quietly and mostly stared at the floor. I wasn't sure what Robert was doing to keep busy, as he'd temporarily gone below deck, but Richard was laying out on a towel on the back of the boat with his shorts hiked up to expose his upper legs.

I walked onto the bow of the boat. Richard had moved around it as fearlessly as if he were walking on flat land when he'd retrieved and slung the anchor into the river. The boat was downstream, at the end of the rope that was not pulled tight by the current. It was difficult even to pretend to walk around naturally on the bow. I was not so fearless about falling as he was.

"You gonna get wet?" Robert asked. He was above deck again. I looked behind me and he was moving like he was going to climb up onto the bow with me. I didn't see Ron anywhere.

"Is it deep enough." Jumping would be an easy escape.

"Oh yeah, we come out here all the time. Sometimes you can watch the guys in the trees." The trails he gestured to in the woods, I now realized, must be a hook-up spot, used by people's fathers, bosses, and ministers, for anonymous sex. Places like this were almost unknown to those of my generation; I hadn't seen them with my own eyes as much as I'd heard about them. The woods were empty now. I was alone with Robert. "You're procrastinating." He said.

"I don't procrastinate. Procrastination implies that you actually get anything done." I gave him my best sexy smile, pulled tight the drawstring of my shorts, and dove off the bow of the boat headfirst into the American River. I counted this not as a point, but as pass interference.

Diving into the water, I quickly remembered again how disgusted I was by swimming in freshwater, but the appearance of my enjoyment was a necessary performance for my audience. Robert smiled down at me, backlit by the glow of the late day sky. What he didn't notice was that I was only really staring back because I was trying to pull up my shorts from where the dive had moved them to at my ankles.

Beautiful boys were expected to endure the uncomfortable, and parade about as if was the most natural thing in the world. Our world's entire sense of beauty seems to be based on beautiful people torturing themselves for show.

My disgust was overwhelming me and I used my best form I could, while keeping my head out of the water, to swim to the stern. When I arrived at the ladder, I had the taste of the river in my mouth. At that moment, it felt as if the water was growing and crawling on my skin. I decided to rename freshwater in my head to the more fitting live-water.

I came around the stern where the deck was only a few inches above the surface and Richard was laying prone. He lifted his head to look at me wondering where I'd come from. Maybe he didn't hear the splash when I jumped in. Ron was reclined on a seat with his drink in hand on his chest.

"It's the creature from the black lagoon!" Richard said flirtatiously, and then laughed.

"Or just the black river." I placed my hand on the deck and pressed my way up trying not to lean my dripping frame over him or his nice beige towel. "Can I get a towel?"

"Yeah, sure." He sprung up and hustled below deck. A breeze snuck up from behind me, and I was suddenly cold everywhere. When he came back with the towel I had crossed my arms over my chest to ease the shivering.

"Do you think I could take a shower?" I asked.

"Oh, yeah, sure."

He led me below deck. The cabin had a low ceiling but other than that was spacious. Just at the bottom of the ladder well was an almost full-sized kitchen that eased into a dining and living area. At the front was another doorway to a stateroom. The bed extended all the way into the tip of the bow and there was a row of narrow windows. The windows in the main cabin were larger and let in light despite the heavy tinting that made them black from the outside. Mostly the light was of a reddish-gold color that came from recessed lighting under the cabinets and dotted along the ceiling.

The countertops were granite with a matching backsplash. The stove was electric and only had two burners. The sink was deep and next to it was a dishwasher. The inside of the boat was just as pristine as the outside. The hardwood floors were polished and every pillow was in its place.

"Right in here." Richard opened a door behind me and to my right that hid the bathroom. I was holding the towel in front me, still shivering a little. I hadn't wanted to dry off and get any river water on the towel I would be using once I'd finished showering.

The bathroom would have been small in a house, but was huge considering it was on a boat. The shower was all glass and the same granite from the counter tops made up the floor sink and the walls of the shower.

"Let me know if you need any help with anything." It was easy to tell that Richard was joking when he said this, and not just because he gave me a slow wink.

"Oh, I will." I promised. It was easy to play along when he was too.

I started the water to let it get warm and shut the door. The sink was strewn with various bottles of lotion, aftershave, cologne, tubes of toothpaste, and toothbrushes that were sitting on the stone instead of in the holder next to them.

First, I arranged the bottles in descending order of height along the back left of the sink. I placed the tube of toothpaste in front and parallel to the row. The toothbrushes I placed in their holder and I used a piece of toilet paper to give everything a nice wipe down. It was the least I could do to repay them for their hospitality.

I let my shorts hit the floor with a flop and reached my hand in to check the water. It was perfect so I climbed in. It was harder to perform the ritual of showering in cramped showers like this one and I considered how I would maneuver myself during the process. I never asked if it was ok to use their soap, but I figured what was the difference if I used a few cents of soap on their two hundred thousand dollar boat.

About four minutes later, I finished rinsing and was ready to turn off the water when I realized my shorts were sitting in the middle of the bathroom floor, still soaked with the grime I had just liberated myself from.

Trying not to spray water all over the bathroom, I reached out and snatched up the shorts letting, them fill with water. The sound of the water changed as it impacted the fabric and a thick stream of water made a loud splatter at my feet.

Just then the door slowly slid open and Robert stood in it smiling. He didn't say anything, just watched me through the foggy wet glass door of the shower. I wasn't sure if I should pretend not to notice or pretend not to care, so I did both. I stayed facing the wall and rung out my shorts, turned off the water, and wrung them out again. My hand squeezed the twisted fabric and I tried to get as much excess water out as I could. I turned around and opened the door to get my towel.

"Hi, what's up?" I thought it least provoking to act natural, like I stood naked around everyone all the time.

"Just admiring the view." He grinned slyly. I laughed as if he was flattering me and stepped out, running the towel down my skin. Since I was already facing him, I didn't bother to turn back around while I dried off. It's funny how much more self-conscious about myself I was when someone wanted to watch. In the gang showers of Boot Camp, I had never been self-conscious because I had never actually thought about looking around; time was too limited, and those men were my brothers, and we were all living in hell together.

I hung up the towel, ran my fingers through my hair and stood looking at myself naked in the mirror for a moment. If he was going to look, I decided I was going to try not to be intimidated by it.

Picking up my damp shorts, I slid them on. They were harshly cold, once the wet breathable mesh came into contact with areas particularly sensitive to sudden drops in temperature. Again, I was covered in goose bumps. "Do you mind if I get by?" His smile showed that the ball of control was now more in my court than his.

He moved out of the doorway and gestured to let me by. Grabbing the towel and draping it around my neck, I went out, took a bottle of water out of the indoor refrigerator, set the towel under me, and I reclined on one of the built in chairs.

"You're something, you know that?" Inside I thought perhaps he only thought so because I was with Ron; that, only by association was I intriguing and worth coveting.

I smiled. "And maybe someday I'll find out what."

"You know, you could stay here with us. I'd make it worth your while."

"You think you could afford me? I don't do one night or one week gigs." I was playing the part he expected me to play, and hoping I was getting it right.

"You could have almost anything you want." The look in his face softened and I knew he meant it. I wondered if he felt guilty or if he was betraying his friend Ron and if he'd let Ron get drunk on purpose to corner me down here. I also wondered if Richard was in on it, or if he'd be jealous. Strangely, the power and confidence he was exuding was wildly attractive and I could see what might have attracted Richard to begin with.

"Thank you, very much. The offer is very flattering. But I earn my way in life. I'm with Ron because he's hot and what he does to me, not what he does *for* me." The words flowed out much easier now that I had given in to my own illusion that we were boyfriends and had been for some time now. I wasn't sure I believed all of what I said, but I wanted to. Getting up from my chair I hooked a thumb in the front of my shorts, pulling them down slightly, and swallowed the rest of my water. I crushed the bottle in one hand, walked up to where he was standing against the counter, and set it gently in front of him.

"You're pretty hot though." I walked over to the fridge, grabbed two more bottles, and headed back up the ladder well.

***

14

THE TWENTY-FOUR HOUR YEAR

I'd completely adjusted to the smell of the river and I drank my water sitting on the upper deck looking up at the sky, imagining the sun slowly melting into the horizon. I had to imagine it because it was out of view behind the trees. The light filtered through them, and the leaves seemed to cast a muted green glow. The shadows of the day could no longer be described as long: they now blanketed the landscape in their gentle grey.

My companion was in the same position, now on the upper deck, that he'd been in on the lower—almost as if someone had lifted him up and set him back down there as if he were an inanimate object. The way the glass rested in his hand on this chest kept me ever ready to leap forward, in a moment best captured by slow motion, to catch it before it fell without spilling a drop.

The conversation seemed to have come to a close for the moment. I was disappointed. I still had so many questions for them. I had spent too much time worrying about the way I presented myself to notice I hadn't asked much about them. But still, I didn't want to interrogate them. One-sided conversations are tedious for all parties involved. I didn't want to bore them. I might've pressed them had I not met them through Ron.

Being liked by new people was important to me. There was a joy in it. An altruistic self-image was once again possible. Everything is new and they haven't had enough time to become tired of me or hear me tell the same story more than once. I could ignore my faux pas and tell myself that I was different now, that I had learned from the past, that I would not do the same next time. It's the rapture in these lies that make *short* vacations the best.

I was getting tired. So much had happened, and I was still uneasy about the events yet to come. I felt the anticlimax of returning to the road coming on before we'd even docked the boat, let alone gotten into the car.

After some very short goodbyes, we headed back up the ramp, across the bridge, and through the squeaking turnstile into the parking lot. I had been continuously reminding myself not to walk up to the passenger side door, but instinctively walked towards it anyway. I caught myself at the last minute, changed course, and hit the unlock button on the transponder twice.

Robert's invitation echoed in my head. "The both of you should stop by again on your way back from Fallen Leaf." He referenced the undetermined return to the city I was trying hard not to think about. I had also noticed that his statement was targeted at *us* and not just at Ron.

It was already dark enough that the navigation system was uncomfortably bright. Ron put in an address and, after a few seconds of processing, the calm voice of the car began to speak again.

Getting gas was high on the priority list, so we ignored the protests of the car and made our way down the most logical streets and located a service station without much difficulty. Ron stayed in the car while I stood at the pump. The sweet smell of gasoline wafted up my nostrils. I knew many people were put off by it, but I actually enjoyed it. I'd heard people say that it meant

I had some type of nutrient deficiency, but I don't remember ever finding it repulsive, even as a child.

The gas stopped flowing with a loud clunk and I opened the door leaning in. "I need something to help me stay awake. You want to come in and pick up any snacks or anything?" Really what I wanted was him to come in and get something himself so I could slip the things I wanted amongst his purchase and not feel as guilty about spending his money.

He opened the car door and got out. He seemed a little tired and I knew that he wouldn't stay conscious for the remaining leg of the journey. I would be driving alone in the dark to somewhere I'd never been. At least I had the voice on the navigation system to keep me company.

Inside the convenience store it was bright. The standard Kenny G was playing, and I felt like I was in a giant elevator, full of isles of candy, and going nowhere.

Ron perused packages of nuts for about ten seconds or so and snatched up a bag of pistachios. My decision was more difficult. I found myself in front of a grand display of beverage choices in lit coolers with full-size glass doors. My choice was going to be observed and filed away into Ron's infinite memory under the heading "Brad's Decisions." It was important for me to locate the beverage that best described me as a person, but also that was appropriate to my statement that it was a requirement for me to drive. It was important to indicate with the selection that this was not a matter of recreation, but a choice with functional purpose.

I found diet sodas quite pleasing despite the rhetoric going around that they were supposedly bad for my bones. I didn't think there was much point in trying to further argue that carbonated sugar water was bad for me. But diet seemed a little too girly. Water would be the smart choice. I knew that I would need some later, but it also didn't have the caffeine kick. Additionally, I already had most of a bottle I'd grabbed from the boat. I'd given the second bottle to Ron in hopes that he might drink it and thus suffer a milder hangover the next morning. He had yet to open it. While tea in any form would carry a pleasant flavor, enough stimulant, and some nutritional value, it was totally out of the question. By choosing tea, I would run the risk of revealing my affiliation with the Democratic Party and provide my company with ammunition for a future character attack. There were the fruit-flavored sodas that were too adolescent, the colas were too boring, the caffeine fortified ones were too nerdy, and the organic concoctions were too granola and would arouse the same suspicion as tea. Despite being a vegetarian, I am not, nor have I ever been, a hippy. I firmly believe that flag-burning stoners have caused normal people to be repulsed by actively maintaining a healthy lifestyle.

I opened the cooler and retrieved what seemed like just the right mix, a Diet Mountain Dew. Mountain Dew carried a reputation as containing particularly high levels of caffeine. It was diet, therefore more sophisticated, but I also knew that this particular choice had only a slight variance in flavor from the original and I could always justify it with the proposition of a taste test.

Ron was waiting for me, reading the paper at the counter. I placed my bottle next to his item with the label in full display towards him. He handed over his credit card without even a glance at the bottle I'd chosen.

Once back in the car we hit resume on the console. The highway that the navigation system directed us to was not the one I had taken before, and approached the lake from the south side. As we pulled out of the station Ron reached up and turned on the radio.

"Hey, I don't mean to sound rude, but I'm gonna be driving in the dark for a while, do you mind if I change the station."

Ron looked at me with a little surprise and he was considering what strategy to use. He understood that my request was reasonable but he wasn't sure he wanted to give in to it. His hand retreated from the dial.

I assumed the coast was clear and I made my move.

Flipping through the stations I found a pop music station and
pulled back, mission accomplished.

Ron made the same scoff he had made at my hot
chocolate and reached up for the radio ambushing what he knew
would be my first move.

"Hey, now, I thought it was *my* turn?"

Flipping only a few times he came to what sounded like
a more upbeat permutation of jazz. This was not what I had
meant by something else. The moment his hand left the dial I
scanned through the stations and stopped on a mellow soft rock
song. I hadn't even pulled my hand away before Ron had
retargeted and fired, destroying my second choice. I heard the
same laid back instruments flowing from it. I started to move my
hand when the composition came into focus and the mannish
melancholy voice of Nina Simone came from the speakers. She
was singing "Little Girl Blue" a song Janis Joplin and I both
loved. Silently we agreed to a cease-fire and the battlefield of the
radio was calm. However, just like moments of peace, the
potential for future conflict was eminent. Moving along the
highway we entered the trees and gained altitude as the
mountains rose up around use. Before long our station would
disappear and we would have to engage in battle once more.

I was beginning to understand what Ron was saying
without words. Even under the influence of alcohol, he wasn't
really all that difficult to read. And, it wasn't that I said any more
than he did, he just talked less. He formed whole sentences with
his posture, gestures, and facial expressions. He also answered
many questions quite effectively by staying silent. Still, I wanted
to create more verbal interaction between us. "Should you call
your sister and let her know we'll be getting there pretty late?"

"Why?" He grunted.

At last, he asked a question. "I didn't know if she was
holding dinner up or anything."

"No, she doesn't know I'm coming up yet." I knew he
wasn't kidding and wished he was. I knew they were family, but
even so, how could he simply show up without an invitation? It

was an unfathomable oversight, like when kids from school had said they quit their jobs by simply not showing up or calling; how could they not even call? How could Ron simply show up?

"She doesn't know we're coming." I managed to keep my voice calm.

"She doesn't know about me either so you're gonna have to..."

"Ron. I was a Marine. I'm not a flamer or anything. I know how to be a man a 'real' man, don't worry about that." It was a turn of tables for him to be stating the obvious to me. It was also almost an insult that he would question my masculinity. Why would he think I would after my conduct back on the island? Or was his comment more about the way I had carried myself on the boat? But we'd been among men who understood; despite the opulence of the surroundings, I'd been in my natural environment.

I had never been very attracted to guys who had feminine mannerisms. It was a contradiction to me. I was gay because I was attracted to other men and the things that personified what it was to be a man. Being gay had never meant assuming a feminine role to me. What was he afraid I was going to do anyway? That I would strut in and start redecorating the place? Flick my wrist? Start talking like my tongue was attached to the back of my incisors?

The idea of him questioning my masculinity quickly faded when what he had just said sunk in. His sister didn't know. How was he expecting to explain me exactly, then? Here's my young attractive Marine friend and traveling companion. The ten-year age gap seemed to be more obvious than any accidental wrist flicking that might occur.

His sister didn't know. Would she be hostile towards my presence? Another question flooded into my deepening sense of dread. Where were we going to sleep?

I still found it confounding that Ron was planning to drop in on his sister unannounced, in the middle of the night, drunk, and dragging his new play toy. The strangeness of the scenario was dizzying, but not so much so that I let it interfere with my driving.

My ears popped and suddenly the radio sounded clearly, not as though I was listening to it from the bottom of a pool. I'd heard the song before, and I knew it was by Cole Porter, but I didn't recognize the singer. Many of the songs were ones I'd grown up with. My parents didn't agree much, but on the subject of Cole Porter, they were in perfect accord.

Ron's relationship with his father in particular intrigued me. I wondered why he fell into spells of mimicking his father yelling at him. I wasn't sure what exactly he was reliving, but he seemed both amused and saddened by it. It sounded as if he was being scolded and bossed around by this absent father whose expectations were impossible to live up to. It was a feeling I understood from personal experience.

I glanced over at him, saw his attention had faded again, and he looked almost asleep with his eyes open. His head was shaking back and forth loosely as we moved along the contours of the highway.

The air had become crisper and colder. I could feel the cold gliding down the window trying to make its way into the safe, temperature controlled cab of the car. The darkness this high in the mountains seemed denser and the trees were as still as silent sentinels. I watched as the random branches of the deciduous trees melted into spikier pine obelisks as we continued to climb.

I had long finished my soda and its empty bottle now rested on the floor behind me. It bothered me that I had littered in Ron's new car. It went against all my training. But I had missed the cup holder, and it would have been dangerous to attempt to reach all the way behind me while I was driving a dangerous mountain road. My water was low; only a small swallow quivered at the bottom of the ribbed plastic container. I took the last drink, which was small and unsatisfying, leaving me thirsting for more.

Giving Ron the other bottle was now a decision I found myself regretting. He hadn't appreciated it. He could have bought his own if he'd wanted one or I could have suggested one at the gas station. He hadn't drank any of it. Just at the moment I was wondering if he'd notice if I went ahead and drank it, he lifted the bottle out of cup holder, broke the plastic seal with a crack, took a miniscule drink from it, and returned it to its place.

I was anguished at my hesitation. If I'd moved sooner I could have taken back the bottle. Somehow, I didn't get the sense that Ron was willing to share. I accepted my defeat and refocused my attention on the road. Maybe we'd cross a fresh stream on the way. I could stop the car, crawl up to the edge, and drink from it on all fours like any other thirsty creature of the forest.

I knew we were close to our destination when we started to go back downhill. Having become so accustomed to leaning back, the downward angle felt exaggerated. The navigation screen was still bright and uncomfortable to look at. Doing so temporarily blinded me when I tried to look back at the road. There were few lights, and most of those did not come from streetlights, but from oncoming traffic, which presented its own problem. I was relieved to see that we would soon be turning off the highway. Then I remembered that we were driving somewhere uninvited and questionably welcome.

After making the suggested turns, we were guided onto a narrow one-lane road that wove back and forth as though the planners had not wanted to tear down a single tree or blast away any part of the mountain. The winding motion awakened Ron. He sat up and crossed his arms. We appeared to be the only moving objects, although it was hard to tell through the impenetrable darkness. Off in the distance, here and there, I could see lights from what appeared to be floating windows in the black. To the right I could see the luminescent surface of a lake that stretched out to the north and out of sight.

I swallowed hard when the car chimed that our final destination was ahead, marked on the screen by a red dot only a short distance away. It was fitting that it was red, the color of stop, of danger, and of blood. The cabin it seemed to indicate, to my relief, still had light coming from a few of its windows. At least we would not be waking them up.

We drove the car just past it and turned right into a parking lot. I brought the car to a stop. My hands were shaking when I opened the door. In the night, sounds were intense and I could hear the crunch of every small rock under my feet as we started down the path.

The cabin was a large, two stories, and covered in wooden siding. It had a number of gracious windows. Smoke dissipated into the night over the roof from a chimney on the far side. It seemed improbable, in a state plagued with wildfires, anyone would let a fire burn overnight.

The moonlight was actually quite bright due to the clarity of the mountain air. I could even make out the huge shadows cast by tall trees. The grass glowed with a gentle blue. We crossed on a burbling stream that joined the parking lot to the yard by way of a small wooden bridge. Even in the dim light I could see that it had been professionally aged by a skilled carpenter, but it lacked the character and imperfections brought by actual age.

We walked up to the door. The thuds of Ron's knocking resonated through the calm of the night. I could hear the slap of approaching footsteps. The door opened and the silhouette of a woman came into view. We stood in front of the door in our shorts with no luggage. Ron said nothing.

"*Ron?*"

***

15

JUST IN THE NEIGHBORHOOD

"*Ron?*" She sounded surprised, not angry.

"Who is it?" A man's voice — her husband, I assumed — came from down the hall.

"It's Ron."

"Who?"

"Ronny, Harold." She moved out of the way to allow us to enter. Harold's bewildered face came from around the corner. When he looked Ron, he closed his mouth and disappeared again.

"What are you doing here?" Again, I was expecting this question to be posed with a tinge of resentment, but it sounded joyous and confused. She had asked an excellent question. The obvious response would be to jokingly say that we were just in the neighborhood and wanted to stop by. They embraced in the hall.

"It's nice to see you, Cynthia."

"It's nice to see you too, Ron," This was something they had repeated before as part of required family etiquette; it sounded a bit uncomfortable and formal. Cynthia then turned toward me and stopped. She looked mortified and at a loss for words. Who was I? Why was I there? Why was I with Ron? I reached out my hand to her. She didn't take it right away.

"Hello, ma'am." She smiled a broad fake smile and looked me straight in the eyes.

"This is my friend. Brad."

"I'm the designated driver that made sure Ron got here safely." Ron looked back at me and gave me a look, silently asking why I'd said that. Cynthia turned to look at him, still smiling, and I gave him a wink. He smiled out of one corner of his mouth and headed deeper into the cabin.

"It's nice to meet you, Brad. Please come in." She pulled her hand back and waved me in.

I went inside and into the draft of heat that was escaping through the open door. The hallway was as wide as those in buildings with handicap access. The walls were an orange terracotta color, separated and trimmed by smooth wooden logs that were curving slightly, revealing the shapes of the trees they used to be part of. It was quite large and spacious. In the hall was a stairway, made of smaller pieces of the same wood, leading up to the second story. The floor was concrete, but stained into a dark, blackish-green, watery pattern with random impressions of leaves in it.

At the end of the hall it opened up to a high ceiling. I was relieved to see that Cynthia, unlike Ron, had furniture. There was a seating area with three suede couches facing a central coffee table and a large limestone fireplace with randomly patterned rocks climbing its way up to the wall.

There was also a kitchen that was large enough to comfortably fit an island. Magnificent polished stainless steel and copper cookware hung above black granite countertops. Two wine glasses, one empty and one mostly empty, were the only dishes on the counter, and a wine bottle sat open and nearly drained.

Ron picked up the bottle and read the label. He apparently knew what he was looking for. I'd seen wine bottles before, of course, but the list of names seemed as endless as the roster of professional football players. It would take someone who was truly obsessed to be familiar with them all. I could care less about football, but I wished I knew more about wine. It fascinated me despite the fact that I'd never touched the stuff. But being a connoisseur was sophisticated and elegant, characteristics I strived towards.

There was a dining area with a solid-looking wooden table with six chairs stationed around it. Near the table were three floor-to-ceiling bay windows—all of the windows facing the lake were large. Most of the wall was made of glass panes that in the daylight, I suspected, provided a spectacular view of the waterfront that was presently hidden by darkness.

Harold was in the living room on one of the couches. He was smoking a cigar and staring into the fire. Ron carried the bottle of wine over to one of the cabinets, opened it, retrieved a wine glass, and filled it with what was left of the wine. I wasn't sure, if he hadn't been here before, how he knew where to find the wineglasses, but I guess if it had to do with drinking, Ron was pretty resourceful.

Cynthia had followed me down the hall after shutting the door. She picked up her glass from the counter, took a sip of it, and folded an arm across her chest.

"You're staying with us, I take it?" There was the resentment I'd been expecting.

"That's the plan."

"We didn't realize you were coming."

"I like the new place."

Harold stood up, put out his cigar, and walked over to the stairs where he stopped. Cynthia set down her glass and followed her husband up. "There is a guest bedroom upstairs at the end of the hall. We're going to get to sleep. Make yourselves at home."

"Thank you very much, ma'am."

"It was nice to meet you, Brad," They went up. We both know it was to talk about us, and what we were doing there.

Cynthia and Harold looked and acted exactly as I'd expected a Cynthia and a Harold to look and act. Her hair was dark brown and just below shoulder length, pulled behind her ears to reveal large diamond earrings that were quite possibly from Tiffany's. Harold was a little overweight with a balding head, hair speckled with bits of grey, a button up shirt, and clean-shaven. Like Ron, he didn't speak much, but when he did, I was sure it was with authority.

Before they got all the way up the stairs they stopped. "Just be quiet, the kids are asleep." She said in a hushed voice. Apparently there were children present.

Ron took a large drink of wine, raised his glass in the air pointing his finger slightly, and nodded. His posture prepared me to shush him as I thought he might start to imitate his father again and begin shouting. He didn't. Instead, he took another sip of wine.

Cynthia and her husband made their way upstairs. Their bedroom must have been above the living room. I could hear the floor moving above us. I looked around at my new and interesting surroundings, and decided to explore a little. I sat down next to the fire near where Harold had been sitting. There were bookshelves built into the wall where the stairway disappeared. Normally, bookshelves in wealthy homes were full of classics and encyclopedias all bound in matching leather bindings. However, their collection appeared to actually be books that they had read.

There were a few dead animals that had been stuffed and mounted into lifelike poses. Next to the fireplace was a skunk and on the coffee table in front of me was a chipmunk, apparently in mid leap. Why it was necessary to keep the remains of animals like this confused me. Maybe this was what republican stuffed animals looked like. It did seem a little more macho and a bit of a throwback to a more traditional time when people hunted to feed the family. Maybe they kept the critter as evidence they'd killed it themselves and wanted permanent proof of it having been slain by their hands. The murder of a chipmunk seemed less than heroic to me, but it was only a theory.

The overall feeling was both authentic and homey. The artifacts, artfully arranged here and there, appeared Mediterranean and African and presumably were real. Even the meandering wood, which at first seemed out of place, I already couldn't imagine any other way.

This was what they considered a cabin, but it wasn't what Thoreau had in mind. Even by house standards, it could be considered posh. My mother's cabin had been a one room building that teetered along the edge of a muddy manmade lake. In the winter, we'd have to turn off the water and drain the pipes to keep them from freezing and bursting. I stroked the softness of the suede beneath me, and was sure the inhabitants of this place did not have such a mundane problem.

While looking at the curvy spindles that supported the banister leading upstairs, my thoughts wandered back to what Cynthia had said. She had told us that we could use the guest bedroom at the end of the hall. If she didn't know Ron was gay, why was she boarding us in the same room?

I glanced over at Ron. He was staring out the window, transfixed. I allowed my eyes to adjust to the darkness and could see the faint outline and a shining streak that gave the water's surface almost a glow.

The absolute stillness and quiet of Lake Tahoe was something I had forgotten about. Even time was suspended in the air over the alpine lake. My other trips to Tahoe were all to the northern end. Until I'd seen it on the navigation map, I hadn't even know that this auxiliary lake existed.

Despite the mild feeling that we were unwelcome, Ron appeared at ease. I wasn't sure how he could be, but then again, I didn't even really know what was going on. They didn't seem mad but, at the same time, they didn't seem all that friendly. She had embraced him, but maybe she was only being nice for my benefit.

I was starting to get a little too warm on the left side of my leg that was near the fire. The golden glow from the dim lighting, the dancing of the fire, and the pristine surface of the water was actually quite romantic. It wasn't hard to see myself sitting in a setting just like this, holding a glass of wine, and watching the moon cross the sky.

The spell he was under must have broken suddenly since he quickly turned, set his glass down on the countertop and walked over to the stairs. I got up to join him since I assumed that meant we were going to bed. He ran out of energy about halfway up and slowed down a little and I almost ran into him. Being that close to him I could once again smell the tangy sweet smell of alcohol coming through his pores.

On the second floor there was another hallway that went down and to a T-intersection. The walls upstairs were all of smooth wood paneling. Black and white family pictures were hung sporadically. The contrast of the images was high to the point of being artistic, and the images were beautiful.

One image was of a little black-haired girl about five; I assumed it to be Cynthia, smiling candidly right at the photographer. She was in a loose dress that had pleats with lace trim and puffy shoulders. The expression was of utter joy that only children have. One of her chubby arms was reaching up to stroke the long dark nose of a horse whose head dwarfed her. Five chubby little fingers were hovering inches away from the short silky hair of the giant head. She was fearlessly happy in the presence of the ominous animal.

Did she maintain this fearlessness all her life? In the hallway I could hear her hushed voice as she talked to her husband through the door. No question what was the topic of discussion: us. I wanted to creep up to the door and put my ear to it, just to get a heads-up on what I should expect from the coming morning.

Our room was a door at the opposite end of the hallway. Once inside the dark room I understood why it was not inflammatory that we both stay there. On opposite sides of the room were two small, matching, separate beds. Maybe this is where children would spend the night on sleepovers yet to come. When I laughed a little at the sight. Ron looked up at me as if he'd forgotten I was even there.

"It's gonna be a little cramped to have sex in a bed that small." The risk of being caught was thrilling, a little enticing, and the context of the setting felt almost naughty. We had been reduced to twelve-year-old kids getting their rocks off as quietly as possible, fearful that mom might hear them.

"We're not having sex here."

"Is that so?" I walked up to Ron and came within kissing distance hovering over him using my height as an intimidation factor.

"Yes, it is." Ron walked over to the door and shut it. It was a little surprising that the night before we had sex three times and now sex, or kissing for that matter, seemed to be off the menu.

Ron disrobed and crawled into his bed lying face up. Sex might not have been on *his* menu, but that didn't mean that I wasn't hungry for it. I walked over to my bed, pulled back the covers, and turned towards him. Stretching my neck from side to side first, I slipped off my shoes and slowly lifted my shirt.

I smiled at Ron. He was both excited and nervous. He opened his mouth slightly as if to speak. At first he didn't, and then he did.

"Stop. Go to sleep." My body shook with disappointment as he turned away from me and I sighed again, only this time with defeat. The bed was cold under the blankets and I started to shiver.

Maybe he didn't want to continue out of fear that the yet unknown number of children who, from the drawings taped to the outside of the door, were apparently in the room next door. Or maybe that Cynthia and Harold would hear. Were they as curious about us as I was of them? At that very moment they themselves could have been outside the door, ears pressed to the wood, trying to piece together through sound what might be happening inside. Then, a new problem entered my head.

"I'm going to need some clothes."

Ron rolled back over to me, puzzled.

"I don't have any other clothes. I'm going to wake up tomorrow and have to put on the same clothes. That's going to look a little weird after a few days." I threw out the idea that we'd be there for a few days just to see if he'd counter it.

"We'll go into town for some."

That wasn't a no, so I'd take it.

The bed was beginning to warm up and felt new and unused. It was quite likely that I was the only person who had slept in it so far. After a while in the military, I had gotten used to sleeping in different beds. Eventually a point came where I lost the concept that any bed could actually be claimed as my own. I'd become a perpetual guest. This bed was no different, and I felt no more or less at home in it than any other I had slept in for the last four years. My nomadic state had a comfortable feeling of normalcy to it. Going back to the same bed in the same room every night was confusing, and boring. Tomorrow, maybe I'd get more insight into just how long I'd be a welcome occupant of this particular bed.

***

16

COFFEE?

I knew it was early the second I opened my eyes. I looked up at the wooden ceiling, and my heart leapt out of my chest in terror. The ceiling was unfamiliar and the room was one that I had never been in before. Where was I?

The pounding in my chest intensified and I sat up quickly. Clenching my fists tightly, I gazed around the room, looking for something familiar, something that might give me a clue. I sprung onto all fours and readied myself for anyone who might come at me. I would kill them. I would use my hands to tear their throat and kick them to the ground. My face filled with heat from adrenaline.

Who put me here? My chest was heaving with excitement and panic. Why didn't they attack? The door to the room was open and the bed on the other side was unmade. Who had been sleeping there? My hands were shaking.

My dog tags were lying on the nightstand beside the bed. Did I put them there? Memories started to return. Yes, I had put them there. I could see my hand wrapping the chain around them and placing them on the wooden surface. My clothes were on the floor, folded. I had taken them off, folded them in the darkness, and placed them there. The person who was sleeping in the other bed had been someone that I knew, but who? I sat back down. I relaxed my fists where my fingernails had made deep impressions into my palms.

My whole mouth was dry and I badly needed water. There wasn't any near me. Standing up I unfolded my shorts and put them on. The floor was cold. I had gotten these shorts recently.

Just then a man walked into the room, fully dressed. He was handsome. *He* had been sleeping in the room with me.

"Good morning." Hearing his voice, I remembered his name was Ron.

"It's definitely morning." But morning where?

When he walked in, he brought with him the scent of eggs and bacon: breakfast. We were at his sister's cabin. We had arrived here last night. I was supposed to be here. I could relax.

"There are towels in the bathroom."

"Yeah, it's probably a good idea to shower." My unclean teeth were compounded by my dry mouth and I felt that if I could move my lips into a smile, it would have been green and yellow. "Do you have an extra toothbrush?"

Ron looked at me, looked to the side, and then headed back down the hall. He didn't know, but he was going to check for one. I followed him.

The door directly across from out room was open. The door was decorated with a crudely drawn picture of smiling stick figures dancing in front of a cabin. A child's room. Inside there were two bunk beds on one side, a window over a nightstand, and a single bed flush against the opposite wall. All of the beds were made, and the room was void of the clutter of toys that must have been hidden in the large toy-chest at the foot of the single bed. It was a certainly boy's room.

I didn't completely understand why they'd not chosen the room we were in to be the children's room. Ours had

158

windows on three sides and seemed to be more spacious. Maybe the windows just posed too much problem to position the bunk beds, or maybe they felt the hospitality of the more graciously sized room should be reserved for guests.

Ron produced a green toothbrush wrapped in clear plastic not unlike the free ones passed out at a dentist's office.

"Thank you, so much. You just saved my life." I smiled, and moved to grab his ass with gratitude. He backed away. I remembered Ron's secret.

I grimaced apologetically, moved into the bathroom, and shut the door. The air was still heavy with steam. Finally I would be able to brush my teeth. How long had it been? It didn't really matter. I squeezed a healthy portion of toothpaste onto the brush, as if the more toothpaste I used the more it would be able to remove the furry coat on my teeth.

Other people's toothpaste always tastes funny to the point of being wrong. It's either too minty, too gritty, or a flavor that just seems odd, like orange or vanilla. This brand was definitely too gritty, apparently due to its incorporation of baking soda. I learned this fact from an excited circle on the packaging that seemed to shout it at me from where it was lying on the sink.

For the most part, the bathroom was remarkably clean. Much like the rest of the house, it seemed to be this way not just because it was new, but because it was well maintained. The floor was made of brown swirling marble tiles. The array of lights over the mirror lit the room by itself, but strategically placed recessed lighting ensured that none of the corners were overlooked. From the presence of only three other toothbrushes with the heads of cartoon characters, I understood that this was the children's bathroom. The toothbrushes all tilted, the faces looked up and down, as if the group of them were soldiers standing guard over the bathroom. Turning each one of the little heads away from the sink to the left, I arranged them so that the handles made even, parallel lines. For a moment, I considered whether it was more appropriate that they face toward the sink rather than away, but their little noses seemed more balanced facing the door; also this way they could greet the children when they came in to brush. I unrolled a few pieces of toilet paper and wet it, letting the water rapidly absorb into the thin fabric, and then wiped the spots off the surface of the sink and shined up the faucet head.

My image was blurred in the mirror, and I could only see a diffused version of my face. It was more of a, orange and tan dispersion topped with a dark patch like a lid that was screwed on to keep my identity from spilling out should I turn my head too quickly. Since I didn't have a razor, there was no need to clear the condensation, and I turned my attention to its source.

The shower water was still warm so I climbed in. I surveyed the locations of soap and shampoo and began my shower. I also took notice of a yellow rubber ducky smiling up at me from the ledge. It was easy to maneuver in the large shower. I soaped up and quickly rinsed down. But something felt off, I had missed part of my morning routine. The water cascaded down my body, feeling like a caress, and I knew what I'd forgotten. I usually got off in the morning.

Masturbation is a pastime that grows from loneliness and boredom more than sexual prowess. Prowess can influence frequency, but it was more that: when I had nothing else to do, it was the cheapest form of entertainment. My need however, at this moment, was different. This was routine and without it, the rest of the day might be off. While the entire day need not be regimented, there were a certain number of steps that were imperative or else missing them would distract me.

The water felt great and the pruning of my hands felt awkward as I wasn't usually in the shower long enough to experience it. The sensation was gratifying and empowering but doing it while standing was always difficult. A concern crept its way into my head. Should I wait to do this with Ron? It felt that he had some sort of right to my orgasm, at least as much right to it as I did at that moment. But the feeling was so good…

I had endured a stressful morning. This would help. I was so close already. Maybe Ron would walk in and help me out or even get in the shower himself. I'd definitely make it worth his while. He should be there for it though; I should wait. I did my best to prolong things. I took my time slowing down with the motions of my hand and backing off before I'd taken it too far.

Taking so long in the shower might be obvious and Ron might realize what I was doing and become angry with me. Saving it would actually be healthier; before competition or before any physical fitness tests I always held back from getting off to save my energy. The testosterone also helped in the building of muscle and distribution of fat, as I had learned in high school. Saving it would be good for me.

But I'd be able to make more and Ron had made it pretty clear that he wasn't comfortable doing anything in this house. Who knew how long it would be before we had a chance to go at it again. I could always go more than once, but I knew that the longer I waited the more impressive it would be. With almost angry reluctance I slammed off the water of the shower. I knew already that this was going to be an off day.

I opened the door to the shower and stepped out. I didn't know which towel was mine. I was standing naked in the middle of the bathroom with a hard-on, and the door, on the other side of which might be children, was not locked. The logical choice was the folded towel tucked onto the bar on top of the other ones that seemed to be more naturally at home there. I used it with no guilt. Its softness made me think how nice it would be to snuggle under a blanket naked on the suede couches downstairs. The soft, shaggy rug that lay on the floor equally comforted my feet. I didn't understand how anyone could keep such a large mat from molding in a moist bathroom, but it didn't seem that either cleaning or just buying a new one was really anything the owners would worry about.

It felt a little dirty putting on the shorts I had been wearing before. There was no deodorant laying out specifically for my use. The spray deodorant seemed the most unobtrusive, so hoping that no one had his or her ear to the door; I thought I could get away with using it and no one would be the wiser.

I came out of the bathroom shirtless and holding my towel. The air was cold, not heated by steam, and I shivered. This was consistent with the pattern of getting wet and being cold I had noticed before on Robert's boat.

My pants from yesterday, or actually the day before yesterday, were half unfolded on the bed where Ron must have tossed them. With jeans on and the same shirt, at least I'd look a little different so as not to give the appearance that I had no other clothes with me. I stood and looked back and forth between the two unmade beds, trying to remember how they'd been made before we'd gotten into them. I remembered from undoing them, that the top comforter had been both tucked behind and under the front of the pillows. The sheets stopped half way up where the pillow lay. In only a few minutes I managed to reconstruct them as they'd been.

The smell of food was delightful, but the smell from my now day-old socks was not. I begrudged my stale outfit. Having no other choice, I fastened my belt and headed downstairs to breakfast. The stairs were sturdy under my feet, and I bounced down them a little, I wondered if anyone saw or thought it was childish. Everyone else was already too engaged in other things to even notice that I was there. Ron and Harold were out on the deck overlooking the lake. They were both reading the paper. Harold was holding it widely up in front of him. He was leaning back a little, indicating he was either near or far sighted, but I could never remember the difference. Ron had his section folded again into a narrow half-page that he seemed to quickly flip through, reading it through his dark sunglasses. Harold turned the last page after glancing at it for a moment, presumably because there was nothing interesting, and then folded it shut. As he did, both men started to move harmoniously. Harold continued folding it down the way Ron favored it and passed it to him; at the same time Ron unfolded his section until it was fully open, and passed it over to Harold.

Cynthia was in the kitchen, and I could see she was overwhelmed. I knew that breakfast had been underway for some time as I'd smelled it cooking before I'd taken my shower. When I saw her standing over the stove, I understood why.

She was meticulously measuring milk to go into the bowl that contained eggs. Apparently, she did not know how to cook or usually had someone else do it for her. Either way, she seemed determined to get it right, dripping drop after drop into the dry measuring cup that was nearly at spill level with milk. Stubborn but persistent people surrounded me. It would take some finesse to gracefully offer my assistance and not offend.

"Good morning." She turned around revealing a pair of thick, black-framed, rectangular glasses and a prideful smile that said "See, I told you I could make breakfast."

"Good morning, Brad. We weren't sure if you were going to wake up in time to join us."

"Oh, I'm used to getting up early. Is there anything I can help you with?"

"Oh, no. I'm fine."

"Well, let me know." She was now trying to decide out how best to pour oregano from the small bottle into a tablespoon. I shifted my eyes out to the deck where the sun was bright and the lake alive with tiny waves. I held in the laughter towards the image of Cynthia squinting at the herbs.

The door opened with stiff smoothness; it too was new. Outside there was a different smell that reminded me of wet spring. It was the kind of scent that reminded me of the first day I could run outside without a coat and not get yelled at by Mom. Walking around, I pulled out a chair, leaving it slightly askew from the table so that I could stare out at the lake. Sitting in it, I was careful to sit upright like my drill instructors had taught us.

"Coffee?" While Harold has asked the question, Ron was the one looking at me with a questioning look and expecting an answer. I hated coffee.

"Yes, please," I replied politely. Ron went back to his paper after I issued my affirmative response. The scoff he had given me the day before had clearly indicated that a "no" in this environment to the offer of coffee was strange and unacceptable.

Asking for hot chocolate instead was also not an available option. Perhaps declining coffee was even stranger than the fact that, when they offered me breakfast, I was going to have to reveal my status as a vegetarian.

"Cynthia! Another coffee!" He was yelling, but his voice was still cordial. "The paper, do you read it, Brad?"

"Yes, thank you," I enjoyed questions with answers that were both true and deceiving, and it was clear I was going to get practice at this. I did read, and sometimes, I did read the paper, but he assumed I meant daily and that was not my fault. He handed to me the section he had finished. It was the headlines.

The only headline that seemed interesting was one talking about United Airlines attempting to buy US Airways. Maybe they would be too busy to care if I missed my flight a second time.

"Did you sleep well?"

"Yes, sir. Thank you. The shower was also nice. I take it that's not your rubber ducky in there?"

He didn't say anything and I felt Ron eyeballing me from behind his glasses asking me where I was going with this.

"I just saw it and it reminded me of volunteering for the duck race down the Ala Wai in Honolulu."

He set his paper down and Cynthia opened the door with a cup I knew would unfortunately be filled with coffee. I would simply have to drink and pretend to enjoy.

"Duck race, huh?"

"Yes, sir. It's a charity benefit for cerebral palsy. They hold it annually. I've volunteered twice now for it. I get a real kick out of the shirt they gave me that has big block letters that say 'duck volunteer'." He seemed interested that I participated in charity work. I suppose I seemed nobler.

"Interesting."

"Cream and sugar, right here." Cynthia gestured to the small matching white ceramic jars in the center of the table. My impulse reaction was to empty them both into my cup so that I could disguise the flavor as much as possible. The reality was

164

that, while I knew that the containers were right there, I was not allowed to use them. Cynthia walked over to her husband and gave him a kiss on the forehead.

"I'll take orders in just a few minutes."

I lifted the cup to my lips. The black, nearly opaque, substance shook back and forth, looking back up, grimacing with yellowed teeth and laughing at me. I took a drink. The hot bitter liquid ran across my tongue, drying it out. It rushed into every corner of my mouth, between my teeth, along my gums, and against my cheeks. Swallowing, I leaned back with the cup still in my hand and the most honest looking grin I could find.

"Wow, that's hot." Was the only thing I could say.

I never really understood coffee drinking. Everyone always told me that coffee, like beer, was an acquired taste. If something tastes so bad that I have to adjust myself to a level of tolerance until I can bear it enough to claim I enjoy it, what exactly was the point? I took another drink of hot awfulness. On the bright side, at least it wasn't bad coffee etiquette not to finish the whole cup.

Sitting at the table in the morning calm had me bored in a matter of minutes. I wanted to bounce my leg but I held it in. Arranged in the center of the table were a paper napkin holder, salt and pepper shakers, and a small bowl of water with opened yellow roses floating in it. They were placed as if they were meant to be in the center of the table but the visual balance between the objects was off. The napkin holder and the bowl were touching and slightly left of the center of the table and the salt and pepper shakers were far towards Ron, haphazardly sitting on a seam in the wood, which made them cant slightly. It would have been quick to center them, space them comfortably far apart, and nestle the shakers near the space between and away from the spaces between the wood. I did nothing. I tightened my grip on my knee and held my hands firmly in place. I had already learned the importance of sitting still, or at least the importance of the appearance I was capable of sitting still. Restlessness was an obvious tell of both youth and immaturity, and either of these qualities would have adversely impacted the tension already present in the cold morning air.

After a few more minutes Cynthia emerged from where I was sure she had been silently freaking out in the kitchen. "What can I get everyone? Ron?" Ron asked for bacon, eggs, and toast, Harold had the same with the exception of hash browns instead of toast. I lucked out on revealing my vegetarianism by simply asking for eggs and hash browns.

"You guys barely missed the kids this morning." Cynthia said. This did not disappoint me. I'd never been much of a fan of children. It was easy to assume that my traveling companion felt the same.

"How did you and Ron meet?" Again, there was the question. My previous comedic, yet truthful, answer would be more than inappropriate at this juncture. This was an inflammatory subject and the simple truth was out of the question.

"Through friends in the city. So, you guys just built this place?" It was a cheap move and she knew it. No matter how much she wanted to explore this idea to expose us, she wanted to talk about her shiny new cabin even more. She knew I knew this, but she also knew she couldn't help herself from telling the story.

"Well, we'd always loved it up here..." I easily navigated the conversation, asking questions at just the right moment to lengthen the story. The more she talked, the less I would have to. Her story of how they'd chosen the lot, the color, the Brazilian wood that had impressed me last night, and the furniture, lasted long after everyone had finished eating.

"Breakfast was wonderful. Thank you." Wonderful was definitely an exaggerated description for overly buttered hash browns and slightly burnt eggs. I stood up and started to collect dishes. Cynthia reacted predictably by telling me that I didn't have to.

"It's the least I can do! You made breakfast."

"That's very kind of you." She stood and started collecting plates with me. We carried them in, leaving the other two to continue soaking up the morning.

"You really do have a nice place here."

"So, what will you and Ron do with yourselves today?" It struck me that, in the present moment, her new question was even better than her last. This one had an easier answer.

"I have no idea."

***

17

COMPETITION AND SPORT

"I have no idea. We'll probably just hit a few spots on the lake and enjoy the weather."

"It's a gorgeous day." She agreed. Talking primarily in niceties made it hard for me to figure out what she was actually thinking.

I hadn't gotten very far with rinsing off the dishes when Ron came in from outside. He walked up to the island and leaned against it. "We're gonna take off for a while."

"Will you be around for dinner?"

"Not sure. "

I washed the soap from my hands and dried my hands on a kitchen towel. "I feel bad leaving you with all this work."

"It's perfectly alright. Thank you for your help."

Ron was already at the end of the hallway by the door when I walked around the corner. He opened the door and walked out. I followed him down the stone path and across the little wooden bridge. The ground of the parking lot made less crunching sound under our shoes as we approached the car.

169

"So, what are we doing today?"

"I have no real agenda."

We opened the car doors, which I had unlocked. I was proud: I had finally walked to the driver's side on the first try. We climbed into the high cold seats of the SUV. I wanted to ask Ron more questions about our day but felt inhibited. Once inside, there is a mandatory break between the conversation outside and the new conversation in the cabin. I'd always thought there were outside-the-car questions, and inside-the-car questions. Maybe it's ingrained in us from watching movies. It is a logical place to end a scene since they couldn't very well have the camera follow them in with one long take. Outside, "where to" is more of an abstract that could encompass the whole day? Inside, "where to" has deliberate meaning that needs to be answered so the driver can proceed to the destination.

"Where to?"

"We'll go up to the main road and take a left." Apparently "where to" was somewhere north and on the west side of the lake.

The windshield was beginning to look a little dusty. I tried to balance taking my eyes off the road so I could look at the various symbols marked on the levers and dials around the steering wheel. Doing this was difficult to manage, as the road was quite curvy and the markings small. Finally I found the washer fluid.

Getting back to the main highway took longer than I'd remembered. When we met up with it, I turned us north. I took survey of the cleanliness of the car. A small haze of dust had accumulated on the dashboard. This was impossible dust. No matter how many times I wiped it away, hours later it would be there again. In the barracks I had learned to save these surfaces until last before an inspection. Moisture had collected on the inside of the wasted water bottle left in the cup holder overnight. I knew my empty bottles were on the floor behind my seat, and on the floor in front of Ron was the wrapper from his pistachios.

I debated leaning over to pick it up, weighing doing so against the risk of colliding with oncoming traffic. I let it be, for the moment, to sit on the floor and stare up at me until we could stop and I could move it to somewhere out of sight.

We were on the road for a few minutes heading up the pristine western shore when Ron broke the code of silence.

"You scored major points this morning with Harold." He had a smile that said "You done good" as he watched the trees pass.

"What do you mean?"

"He has cerebral palsy. You didn't know that?"

"Really, wow. How could I have known?" I wanted to say, "You never talk! Of course I didn't know!" But the answer I gave seemed to be the wiser, less inflammatory choice. It wasn't that I was mad at him, as much as I thought it was funny.

"Is there anywhere in particular we're going to?"

"I wanted to stop by the club for a while to relax." By relax, he meant drink. It was now afternoon and in Ron-time that meant it was appropriate. In Brad-time it was barely after twelve. I didn't protest. I knew better than to speak up about it. My survival instincts told me it was imperative to preserve the balance between conforming to Ron's wishes and asserting my independence. I rolled my eyes and turned my thoughts back to the road.

Tahoe was greener than I remembered, but not the lush green of somewhere tropical. The leaves on the trees and grasses all appeared slightly dirty and bleached by the sun. My memories of the local landscape were of blinding snowdrifts pierced by towering evergreens that seemed black by comparison.

I hadn't decided whether or not to tell my stories of being here before to my present company. This wasn't the first time I had been a guest of a man up here. A close-knit circle of military officers regularly had me as a guest, and on one occasion I'd even brought my nervous roommate with me.

171

It's fascinating how many different things the same place can be to different people. I doubted that I was the first guy that Ron had brought up as company. I was the one that was here with him now, though; I was going to make the most of it.

"We're going to pull off up here on the right." From where we were, the lake was not visible. There were trees and houses on both sides of the road.

"How far up?"

"Just around another turn."

He directed me into a parking lot next to a fenced-in vacant lot. The earth had been excavated and was held back by what appeared to be a large, broken foundation. We had parked on the high side of the hill and started walking along the road. In the center were what appeared to be three massive engine-like objects. They were heavily rusted and one of them was lying on its side, as if time and abuse had defeated it. It looked like they had crawled there to keep one another company. Who knew how long they'd been there or would be? At least they weren't alone.

Next to the fence at the bottom of the road was a driveway. It led toward the lake and ended at a parking lot next to a cluster of buildings nestled comfortably under the shadow of towering trees. The parking spaces were filled with the same species of cars as I'd seen at Tinsley Island, but these were a different breed. Instead of sedans and SUVs, these were their flashier cousins: Corvettes, Ferraris, and even a lime-green Lamborghini. Some of them had the windows rolled down and all were, almost without exception, incredibly clean. Music came from over the top of the building where the fluttering leaves of the trees overhead seem to catch it and keep the sound from escaping.

We walked into the building and were hit by a blast of noise. Most of the din was composed of voices attempting to shout above the music. At the end of the hallway we were outside again, on a pier twenty feet above the surface of the lake.

I was apparently the only one not on Ron-time. The bar was full of people that covered the pier-like structure. Not just ordinary people, but young and beautiful people. It reminded me of what spring break looked like on MTV. While I had never been to college, and didn't know exactly when spring break was, I was fairly certain it was not in the summer. Maybe they didn't know it was summer? What they did know, apparently, was how to have fun. I'd wondered before when I'd met Randy back on Tinsley where all the cool people went to after high school. I didn't anymore. I was drowning in a rippling sea of their well-groomed heads.

"Do you want me to get us something?" If I got the drinks, it meant he would have to give me the money and I'd be able to get something for myself also. He pulled sixty dollars out of his pocket and handed it to me. "I'll be right back. Will you be here?" He nodded, but didn't request anything specific. I took that to mean he trusted that I'd make the right decision.

The bar was easy to find, as it was a point at which heads were facing like insects transfixed by a streetlamp. The streetlamp here was an endlessly flowing stream of beer that poured out in a thick syrupy stream into the bottom of plastic cup after plastic cup.

I waited my turn in line, amid the youthful faces, and listened in on the conversations. Most of them had to do with the goings on at some party, or someone who'd had work done to them that turned out good or horror stories of times it hadn't. No particular voice stood out.

I finally arrived at the bar. It was wet with spilled drinks and attended by two overworked bartenders no older than those in line. I ordered a captain and Coke and a plain Coke. The bartender was fit, tall, and had angled features with dark hair and eyes. He smiled with a wide white smile that seemed to radiate happiness. Breaking his spell, I gave a quick look around to see if anyone noticed me looking at him; I was in the clear.

"Put them in the same kind of glass." Usually when I order something that isn't spiked, they put it in a stupid glass that says, "Look at me! I'm the dork who isn't drinking!" They also usually look at me stupidly, like this guy was, as if not doing this was simply impossible. I usually had to explain to them that, yes, it is actually possible to put a non-alcoholic drink in the normal glass. Resisting my request really made no sense. If it was the opposite, I could understand. If I was trying to disguise an alcoholic drink as one that was not, the resistance would be defendable. Ultimately however, arguing reason with someone whose job is to pass out beers was only dumb on my part.

Ron hadn't moved very far when I found and handed him his drink.

"Now that's a drink." He said after a sip.

"See, I have my uses!" The grin on his face let me know that he was in a good mood.

We started to walk around and waded deeper and deeper into the smiling heads of perfect white teeth and smooth tan skin. Breathing became higher on my priority list as I swam across them on our way to the shore. When I got there I also got the unexpected perk of being able to move.

I wasn't sure I'd ever taken in so much happiness as I was now. True, the happiness wore beer-scented perfume and was underage, but I had to admit it was a little exhilarating. This must have been what all those high school parties I'd never been invited to felt like. All the popular people, carefree, drinking, hugging, and laughing at each other's jokes. My resentment stemmed from their not feeling the shame and loneliness I'd endured through adolescence. I didn't want to hate them anymore. I felt like I was finally one of them now.

Ron was next to me staring back at the walkway along the building. Following his eyes, I saw what he was looking at. There was a tall dark-haired boy who looked twenty-one only because of the beer he held in his hand. He had dimples, a strong jaw and piercing eyes. I'd always been complimented for my eyes, and I recognized from this that Ron was attracted to him. The shirt he had on was missing its sleeves, which were torn all the way down his sides. I could see when he moved that his build was solid and athletic without being bulky. He looked like a Jake or a Zack—a short abrupt name that could easily be shouted down a crowded school hallway and had few enough letters that a cheerleader could easily spell it. At first I pretended not to notice the way Ron's gaze followed him through the crowd. Jake/Zack's stature made him stand out and his smile made me like looking at him.

"This place is interesting." He didn't respond to my comment. "I've been up here before but never when it was warm." He looked up at me, took a drink, and then back at the other boy. I caught myself chewing the ice from my soda and spat it out, watching as it spiraled on its way down to the water below.

"I'm gonna hit the john." I wasn't sure if he put it that way by accident or on purpose.

"I'll be here."

He'd been gone for only a minute or two when I looked for Jake/Zack's sleeveless arms again. There were so many handsome faces with cheery blond girls gleefully adoring them. He wasn't where he was before. Had he gone to the bathroom and Ron followed him there? I knew the idea was rude to think, but it wasn't implausible. What wasn't in question was that I didn't like the idea of Ron running into him without me there.

A new feeling, worse than jealousy, started to fill my gut; it was fear. What would I do if he didn't come back? What if he left me here? The thought was completely irrational wasn't it? He wouldn't have driven all the way up here with me only to leave me at some bar.

I found myself wanting to be wrapped in the tailored safety of my uniform. It was my armor. Everyone wanted to look at me and be around me when I was in uniform. At least that was the case when I was in a town that didn't have a military base. In uniform, I represented a hero. To them, I had fought every war that had ever been won. I was deadly, strong, sexy, and admired. Now, I no longer had the option to wear that uniform. No one was looking at me or depending on me anymore. I was floating on the outside of the people who had wounded me all through my childhood and I had been stripped of my armor.

Ron had been gone no longer than a minute or two, my drink was empty, and I didn't want to move for several reasons. He might come back and expect me to be here. I didn't go look for him because I might see him flirting with another guy. True, we had only just met, but coming up here had been his idea, after all. It was quite possible that I was disposable. I didn't get another drink because, while he had given me the money, he might still expect the change back.

If drinking made stress easier to cope with, now felt like a good time to start. Why didn't I drink? My reason started to seem childish. Refusing to drink because I felt like I had a rough childhood; everyone had a rough childhood. This was not a category I was alone in. It seemed such a minor part of my identity, but I loved the reaction I got from people when I told them. If I started drinking I might not be special anymore. I'd be just like everyone else. Was that so bad? Being part of the crowd had never been what I wanted. Ironic that I wanted to stand out so much, but I had joined an institution in which I'd line up in a formation of hundreds of people who looked, dressed, and talked exactly alike.

I chewed my last ice cube and looked down into the cup. It was completely empty save a few droplets of water that I couldn't manage to get out. Looking up I saw Ron next to me with a fresh drink in his hand and staring out across the lake. I wondered where civilians learned the "thousand yard stare."

"How much longer do you want to stay?"

"I just got a drink." Biting my lip I resisted the urge to comment that it wouldn't last very long. "Are you alright?"

"I'm just kind of starting to feel gross wearing the same clothes for the third day." This would be hard to argue against. Ron nodded and understood; after all, this was his second day in his.

We started to walk around and I was relieved. We would be heading towards the door. Walking past the bar, I decided to ogle the bartender again. His button-up shirt was surprisingly free of any accidental splashing. There were thick veins that ran

along his neck and his clean-shaven jaw. I looked over at the
female bartender and I knew I was busted. She looked at me
disgusted, with the top of her nose wrinkled. She knew the way I
was looking at him from personal experience. I wanted to move
past her more quickly, but the bar traffic was moving against us
and had bottlenecked.

I tried to laugh at the situation and gave her a little
shrug. She let out a grunt and put down the bottle she'd been
pouring from. I saw her softly put her hand on his arm and the
potential for the situation to escalate increased. Her hand was
wrapped around his bicep in a way only a girl can get away with.
The muscles of his arm were larger than I'd realized and almost
filled his sleeve. Leaning down she looked at me out of the
corner of her eye and whispered into his ear. As her comments
sunk in he began searching the faces in front of the bar. I looked
ahead of us and the group holding us up was still laughing and
negotiating how best to get past each other in the bottleneck,
while still talking and keeping the easygoing attitude of the bar. I
considered starting to push people, just to get them out of my
way. I checked the bar again, and saw that it was too late. The
girl was looking at me scowling, and the bartender looked
annoyed and confused, unsure if he should be flattered or
offended that I had been checking him out. "I'll see you around,"
one of the guys in front of us shouted and we started moving
forward again.

At the end of the walkway was a path that led through
the grass and back to an area shaded by the trees. Through a
large hedge I heard a splash. We came around the end of it to see
that the hedge had hidden a pool. When we started walking
towards the opening, my feet became heavier. I really didn't
want to get into the water again. This was not the remedy I had
in mind when I said I was feeling gross. Thankfully we
continued through, around, and out the other side of the topiary
walls of the pool area.

Everything was disappointing me and I was beginning to
feel like a drag on Ron's style. His drink was empty and he

tossed it into a wastebasket as we passed. Winding our way into the building, through a few hallways, back to the one we had first entered, he turned right again and guided us back to the pier. The location had lost its fun for me, but I also didn't want to complain anymore than I was by walking around in a virtual mope. After looking left, looking right, and then looking at me he caved in. We headed back out the way we originally came in.

The parking lot was livelier now. There was a group of scantily-clad girls being heckled by two guys in a hyper-masculine blue sports car with two-foot-wide white racing stripes that ran up the hood.

We made our way past them, and out from under the cool shade of the trees. The sun was strong and I realized how warm it really was now that I wasn't feeling the breeze near the water's edge.

Rounding the turn near the road I glance back at the rusted grouping of old engines and smiled. I wondered what memories they had, what jobs they had done, and if they told each other stories.

"Where to?"

"On up north to Agate Bay."

"Where's that?"

"Just keep going north." Ron calmly ordered.

After we climbed into the car our new conversation began. "That place is pretty cool." Ron issued his usual response of silence. It was a short conversation.

The blue-and-white sports car sped out of the parking lot and passed by us, followed by a jeep full of girls. I turned out of the parking lot and pointed the car back north on the road. Their cars disappeared around a corner.

A yawn escaped my mouth and I remembered the state in which I had woken up. I felt a mixture of disbelief and frustration with my reaction. I'd forgotten about it as quickly as it had happened. The whole thing embarrassed me. At twenty-two years old, I shouldn't be scared to wake up in unfamiliar places. This morning's reaction was not an isolated incident. In fact, it wasn't even the first time I'd woken up that way since I'd gotten to California. In fact, I'd woken up strangely for the last several years.

My first night home, after graduating from Boot Camp, I was sleeping. I had moved from the bed to the floor unable to cope with the softness of a real mattress. In the middle of the night my drill instructor came in and ordered me to sit up. I did. I sat with legs crossed, my fingers straight, chin up, and back inline. I must have sat there for an hour and a half before I realized that I was in my old bedroom and my drill instructor hadn't actually been there. In the dark, for a significant chunk of the night, I'd sat there and never doubted the existence of my imaginary drill instructor or the order he'd given.

However, this morning's moment had passed and Ron hadn't seen it. There wasn't much point in stressing over it now. New curiosities were the perfect distractions. Today I would get a better understanding of where I stood with Ron. The amount of clothing we'd purchase would help determine how much time we'd be spending here. At this point, I still had no idea.

***

18

WHO WE ARE AND WHAT WE DO

Tahoe is remarkably simple to navigate. The perimeter of the lake is surrounded by, in essence, a single road from which grow a few offshoots lined by houses and cabins. All of the buildings and roadsides were constructed in a way that facilitated the accumulation and removal of the large quantities of snow that fell each year.

Getting out of my stale clothing was a priority second only to my need to eat. The most interesting thing I tried to ignore about hunger were the irrational thoughts I considered in my quest for food. I was familiar with the advice that I definitely did not want to go shopping on an empty stomach. They should probably add that people shouldn't drive that way either.

"Are you hungry at all?" Since it was Ron's money we'd be spending I felt the need to justify his buying my food simply as an auxiliary expense. He thought about it for a moment. His head tilted to the side in quandary.

"We could grab a bite." I was still counting every time he used the word "we." "There's a McDonald's just up here." I knew I was listening to him carefully but I was sure I heard him wrong. When he started pointing to the white building with a red roofline—yes, there were the golden arches—he removed my doubt and my heart sunk into my empty stomach.

Even high in the mountains, the country was saturated with the grease of fast food. The arteries of our dining culture were clogged with McDonald's and Burger Kings. I was as baffled by the fact that Ron actually had ever eaten at a McDonald's as I was by the fact that he thought that I did or that I'd want to. What exactly did he think I was going to eat there?

"I'm not really sure they have anything for me to eat." The turn came faster than my protest and I felt a sense of doom in having already entered the parking lot. Would we go through the drive-through? The image of the Mercedes parked in front of the window manned by a kid with a greasy face passing out food was as nauseating as my past experiences with fast food had been.

"They have salads." Ron pointed out.

Contrary to what Ron must have believed, a salad is not what most vegetarians I'd met considered a meal. Salads were a phenomenon that gained popularity from girls who were either trying to get skinny or trying to stay that way. It kept them from feeling guilty about avoiding eating. I wasn't a vegetarian because I was trying to avoid food. I loved food, and flavored leaves were not my ideal eating experience. Food is an experiment of taste. It should be interesting, and the permutations I had discovered off the printed menu were what I cherished most about my eating habits. This was not a place where I would be able to negotiate ingredients outside of choosing ranch or Caesar dressing.

"Are we driving through?"

"No, we'll go inside." I felt a little mortified someone might recognize me there despite the fact that I didn't know anyone for hundreds of miles in either direction.

"Alright, then." Maybe I'd get lucky and they'd have a veggie-burger as I'd heard the ones in New York City did.

Stepping around the dried up packets of ketchup that had been run over in the parking lot, we made our way to the door. As I opened it, I was struck with the warm odor that years of cooking french-fries had coated the walls with. It was a smell that permeated through everything and I knew the fabrics I was wearing were quickly absorbing it.

I got into line behind a man whose scalp was sweating into his long white hair, so thin it was like cobwebs. This definitely didn't fit into my vision of a glamorous trip to Tahoe. I couldn't help but stare at the random pattern of large and small freckles on the old man's head. How could he possibly be sweating when it was just a hint above being cold outside? He didn't seem like someone who would have been running. He also didn't seem like someone who did much heavy lifting. Maybe just walking down the street was enough to wind him?

When he placed his order, I also wondered how he'd survived as long as he had. He'd paid the extra to increase the size of his fries and his drink. He'd also ordered a second sandwich. I wondered where this skinny old man was going to put all that food. The joke about a hollow leg rang uncomfortably true.

When the man stepped to the side it was our turn to approach the counter. It looked like it might be sticky. I didn't touch it.

The girl behind the counter was black and young. She was a little pudgy, and had tight braids that ran along her head up underneath her purple cap. Her expression was both bored and defeated. "Welcome to McDonald's can I take your order." Her words walked out of her mouth dragging their feet. The drudgery of her tone revealed how degraded she felt by her job.

Scanning over the items, it seemed that this would be a very confusing menu to list alphabetically since almost all of the products started in Mc and none of them ended in veggie patty. This was a temple where fat America came to worship meat, grease, and mayonnaise and I was a heretic amongst the devout.

Ron spoke up and ordered a Big Mac while I continued to read my limited menu options. I'm sure if he could have ordered a cocktail with it, he would have. I wasn't sure if I was being punished for wanting to leave the club, but it sure felt like I was being reprimanded for something. Looking at Ron, I got a different message. He seemed a little excited to be here, like this was some kind of special treat for him. It could be that my discomfort was overshadowed by his giddy attitude at the chance to grab a burger and not be judged.

"Whenever you're ready, sir." The girl behind the counter was not in any sort of hurry to be anywhere, but she was in a hurry to stop feeling humiliated by having us stand in front of her. She was anxious to turn around and face the kitchen, face the drive through, face the deep fryer, face anything but another human being on the other side of the counter.

Literally Ron could have written her a check that would have allowed her to quit this job she hated and leave this town that was surely full of rotten, run-over memories like the ketchup packets I'd seen outside. It wasn't that her job was demeaning in nature. Her job was demeaning because I could see that she loathed it. I was scared of ending up just like her now that I was out. I had to figure out where I was going to go and what I was going to do.

"I'll have a salad and a large fry."

"What kind of dressing with that?"

"Ranch, please, ma'am."

"Anything to drink?"

"Just water."

She rang up the total and I turned around to see that Ron had taken his soda and had sat down the dining room.

"That's going to be for here." I gave her one of the twenties that was still in my pocket. It was a little sad to watch it go to something I really didn't want.

In a matter of minutes, our fast food had filled up the tray and I carried it over to Ron. The tray was wet either from being clean or from not being clean. It was hard to tell. "I'll be right back. I'm going to go wash my hands."

Entering the bathroom and looking around, it didn't feel like an environment suitable for cleaning even my hands. The sickly odor of the air freshener made the air thick. Its sweetness made me feel like I was breathing candy, which, in a bathroom, was disgusting. The water warmed up to being just hot enough that it hurt a little. I wanted to climb into it and wash the smells off of me but I couldn't. I washed my hands with a healthy squirt of soap from the wall-mounted dispenser and dried them with the blow dryer next to it. While I was as environmentally conscious as anyone who had spent the last several years in Hawaii, I lamented the increasing lack of paper towels in public restrooms. When I got to the door I faced the dilemma for which, despite the thousands of times I'd been in public restrooms, I'd never found a solution. I grabbed the dirty door handle with my freshly clean hand and went back to our table.

Ron had already finished most of his fries by the time I'd arrived. This was now behavior I expected from him. I sat down and popped the lid off my cup of leaves, poured on the dressing, and shoved a fork in it. The pleasure my dining partner seemed to get from each gigantic bite of burger made me a little jealous. I speared some more leaves and put them in my mouth, washing them down with water. My mouth was at least partially satisfied by the salty, warm fries, which almost gave the sensation I was actually eating.

When he finished, Ron sat back and his eyes stared out at the lake. I hadn't noticed how pale and blue they were until now. I would often know people for months and months before ever noticing the color of their eyes in detail. Even if I'd spent considerable time looking right into them, it wasn't something that I committed to memory. Everyone else it seemed noticed almost immediately the green of mine. I was proud of my eye color; it went well with my uniform. Other people however, wouldn't spend as much time as I did looking at the jaw, neck, and hands. I had seen and admired all of these features on Ron already, but now I noticed his eyes.

They were a grayish blue, which made his stare quite cold and unfeeling. They were impenetrable and clandestine, almost to the point of appearing cruel. Even here in the plastic booth, they were beautiful.

"Are you all done?" Following his nod, I stood up, collected the trash onto the tray, and grabbed it again by the sides that still felt slimy. Walking over to the trashcan, I pushed the tray into the flap that had "Thank You" printed on it where I was used to seeing "Mahalo". I tilted it to the side so that the garbage and my half-eaten salad fell into the bottom. I placed the tray on top, careful to line it up correctly with the others and center them evenly to the edges of the trash bin.

It was good to smell the clean alpine air again. There was a hint of burning cedar that was surely coming from a fireplace nearby.

"We'll keep going this way and head further into town." I unlocked our doors and we climbed back into the car.

"What's in town?"

"A place we can get some clothes."

Driving through town was not unlike driving through Iowa. The buildings were no taller than two stories and most were huddled together in little strip malls. The only difference, really, was past the buildings: the vast lake and the mountaintops that encircled it. There were grocery stores, little shops for knickknacks, and an abundance of businesses peddling winter apparel and ski gear. The edges of the road had trails of sand that had accumulated from what was spread for traction during the long winters.

There weren't a lot of people walking around, so the traffic was mild. A woman walked out of a store bearing a giant sale banner, and across the front were several pairs of skis. The man holding open the door waved at her as she smiled and stumbled her way back to her car with an awkward load.

186

This was the end of the lake to which I had been before. The first time I was here I was scared and in awe of the lake. Lake Tahoe was one of those places that, growing up in Iowa, seemed far away and almost imaginary. The memory that stood out most to me was sitting in a hot tub naked in the yard of the cabin the group had rented. The cabin had been very high in the mountains and had enough trees around it that privacy allowed nudity. I relaxed alone at the edge of the steaming bubbling water and let my arms hang over the edge and hands play in the snow.

Even now it's hard to think that any time I had spent here was real. My recollections all seemed far-fetched like they were manufactured and printed into the pages of a novel. "This really is my life," I thought. Even if I had any friends back in Iowa to tell it to, they wouldn't believe me.

"Pull in just up here on the right."

We drove down a steep driveway and into a parking lot. Looking around, I didn't see anything I recognized as a clothing store. Ron opened the door and started walking back up the hill. I was still a little nervous about the whole shopping experience. This was a little more than a meal, soda, or pair of shorts. We were talking about a wardrobe. Rounding the front, we walked up to the door and I almost started to laugh. It was another yacht club.

Inside, the air was warm and the floor made hollow noises under out feet. There were stairs lined with pictures of men, their names on small placards at the bottoms of the frames. Straight ahead, the room opened up to the left and right. The wall was made of windows that stretched the length of it and revealed rows of undulating masts. They looked like bobbing straws in a giant soda. I cemented a smile on my face since it seemed better than laughing out loud.

"How can I help you gentlemen today?" An old man walked up. He was balding and wore a jacket with numerous pins of what I assumed were other yacht clubs on it; I scanned them for one that matched what was embroidered on my shirt.

187

His jacket opened in the front to reveal a button-up shirt that stretched over his round belly.

"We need to pick up a few things."

"Let me know if you need any assistance." The skin of his face was loose and quivered when he spoke. His ears were both occupied by small tan hearing aids. He smiled at us and Ron started to meander toward the clothes.

"Thank you very much, sir." I raised my eyebrows in victory when I finally found the St. Francis pin just below the buttonhole on his lapel.

None of the clothes on the various racks were that remarkable. All of the colors were flattened, all of the pants and shorts were khaki, and all of the shirts were either button-up or just like the one I was wearing. I could see now that it wasn't that everyone Ron knew dressed the same intentionally, they didn't know any other kind of clothes existed.

I flipped through the shirts looking for something that would fit and that I wouldn't be embarrassed to wear. Most of the shirts had a patch, button, or embroidered yacht club insignia on them. It made more sense now the question of why Ron didn't own a yacht. I didn't know he didn't own one really. Maybe he already had a sailboat and Robert meant he should diversify is nautical holdings to include a motor yacht or two.

Ron already had an armful of shirts and shorts by the time I had found my first. It was a clean sea-green button-up with long sleeves. Due to the length of my arms I'd have to roll up the cuffs, but I'd gotten accustomed to doing that anyway from wearing camouflage utilities every day. That he had picked out clothes so quickly was not unexpected, but what was and shouldn't have been was that he took the stack and walked it over to the counter without trying anything on. I'd been trained by my mother and the military to always check for the proper fit of garments. Appearance is of critical importance to daily life.

Ron made his way back to me and continued to eyeball the racks. When he picked up a shirt and brought it over to me, I looked over to see if the clerk noticed. He didn't. The gesture seemed out of place. He had refrained from any public display that might suggest the truth of our relationship to others. While it was subtle, it still seemed that holding up a garment to another man, fit the description of that kind of behavior.

"You like this one?"

"It would look good on you." He spoke in a hushed tone. From the feel of the fabric he was probably right. The shirt was white with a blue trimmed collar and two buttons. I took it from him and hung it over my arm with the few other items I'd picked up.

"Why don't you try on this one?" While I posed it as a question, it wasn't one. I really wanted to see how he'd react if I did the same to him and if I could get him to break his habit of "grab and run" shopping. This time, Ron did look over to see if the man behind the counter was watching. We were now both concerned with the opinion of an old man who probably couldn't see us from this distance anyway. He snatched the shirt from me. "I'm gonna try some of this stuff on."

I entered the dressing room. Pulling the shirt off, I could still smell our lunch on my clothes. I took a moment to look at myself in the mirror. Until I'd joined the Marines, I'd never thought of myself as good-looking. My dismal lack of popularity in high school reinforced the statements of my classmates that I was unattractive. Years later, I was approached by a photographer who asked to take my picture, and I discovered otherwise. When the photos were shot and I was again alone with my thoughts, the joy of the moment turned sour. I hated the kids of my past even more for making me hate myself.

Undoing my belt, I let my pants fall to the floor and stood for a moment in front of the mirror completely naked. First, I tried on a pair of full-length khaki pants. When I pulled them up, I was surprised by how well they fit in the back. I'm tall, so it's hard to find pants that show that I do actually have an ass. I paired it with the shirt Ron had chosen and I knew already that it was going to be my favorite outfit and the one I would wear out of here.

The sound of a hanger being replaced on the metal rail of one of the racks outside indicated that Ron might have returned.

"You out there, Ron?"

"Yeah, I'm out here. Are you done yet?"

"Just another second I'll be right out." I really didn't want to be rushed and it didn't sound like we were really doing anything after this. We wouldn't be late for anything. Shopping for clothes was usually something I did by myself, and I liked to take my time feeling the fabric before I spent the money. I stuck to myself quite a bit, and I've learned to take my time at certain things. Since this was not my money, some of my justification was missing, but I still wanted to look good. I tried on and critiqued every shirt and every pair of pants or shorts.

While I was adjusting the price tags so that they didn't distract me from formulating my opinion of the outfit, it occurred to me that I hadn't even looked at them. I'd simply grabbed the clothes without considering their cost or comparing them. I felt a little rude in doing so, but at the same time, the final total would also be a test of Ron's limits concerning me.

When I pulled the last shirt on and tucked it in, I performed the usual turn to the side and posed a little. Facing directly into the mirror I realized what was happening. Inside the confines of this tiny dressing room I was being transformed into what Ron wanted. This was the store he had chosen in the city he had come to. He'd even picked out some of the clothes. Did I really care? Looking at myself, I liked what I saw. The look was fitting. I wasn't sure why I hadn't started dressing like this sooner. At least I was becoming something, I was with someone, and I had a purpose. As long as I was with Ron, doing this, doing anything, it didn't feel so bad not to be a Marine anymore.

In my new persona, how would I answer the question "What do you do?" the next time someone asked me? I was used to the glow of respect in people's eyes when I answered that question over the last four years. In the Marines we would say, "I am a Marine." When people were in the Navy, Air Force, or the Army it's something that they do. Sailor, airman, and soldier are job titles. The institutions were things that people were in and that they worked for. The Marine Corps is different. We say "I *am* a Marine" and when we do, we become taller and no one ever questions why.

Emerging from the dressing room in my new favorite ensemble, I held out my arms to invite Ron's opinion of the shirt he'd picked out.

"Let's get it rung up."

"I'm gonna need some socks and underwear."

"You have flip-flops. You don't need socks for flip-flops."

This was not something I would settle for. "I'm not going to wear flip-flops up here in the cold. I'm going to need a pair of shoes and a belt too." I knew this was pushing it and he tilted his head a little, trying to decide if I was joking.

"What do you need shoes for? You have shoes."

I laughed a little. "What I have are jungle boots, and that doesn't quite work with khaki pants." I pointed down to the wide black leather boots sticking out from the openings of the off-white fabric. It was interesting that he had been perceptive enough yesterday to preemptively buy me flip-flops, but not understand the oddity of military footwear with business casual attire. Combat boots and shorts, I supposed, were more obvious. He was a bit disgruntled walking over to where the socks and shoes were. I followed his lead and picked a pair of brown leather shoes in my size and two packs of socks.

"Why do you need so many socks?" I wasn't sure what the big deal was. It was only an extra five dollars.

"What? I hate having dirty or wet socks on. You're the one who keeps taking me around water." He shook his head and grabbed a small handful of medium-sized boxer shorts I guessed were for me, and led the way to the register.

"Are you fine gentleman ready?"

"We have these too." He gestured to the clothes I was wearing.

"Yes, I see, sir." I didn't realize until then that it probably did seem a little odd in a place like this that I was wearing clothes out of the store. The standard practice when shopping was to take things home first and wash them once before wearing, but I had never actually known anyone who did that.

"Oh, we should get two of these." Ron looked at what I was pointing to and nodded. I grabbed two of the gym bags and set them on top of the pile of clothes.

"Anything else gentlemen?"

"No, that's it." Ron signed the receipt and I never saw the total.

We came out of the store into the late-day sun and I could have spun around and sang it felt so wonderful. I was covered in fresh clean clothes; my feet were wrapped in new socks and nestled into new shoes. "It feels so good to finally be out of those dirty clothes! Thank you!" I beamed at Ron.

"How on earth did you ever make it through the Marines if you hate being dirty so much?" He raised his brows.

"Well, it's like this. In the Marines, when you're dirty, you're dirty. I mean, really dirty. Beyond dirty. The mud in my boots made disgusting sucking sounds and my cammies were caked in mud and yuck. But when I was clean, I practically sparkled. My uniform was crisp and starched, my haircut a centimeter away from my head, and my shave was perfect. It was a matter of pride, and I'm addicted." Ron nodded, considering what I had said.

Unlocking the car, I opened the back hatch of the SUV. I took the gym bags and set them out. Ron got into the seat and waited while I did my best to quickly fold the clothes and put them into the bags.

"Where are we off to next?"

"I thought we'd head back."

I knew we weren't entirely avoiding interaction with his sister, but I thought by leaving so quickly this morning we were at least trying to keep interaction to a minimum.

192

Once I'd finished with the bags, I zipped them shut and grabbed the sacks we'd walked out with. After I tossed them away I came back and shut the hatch. I smiled at my work. I didn't know how long we were welcome at Cynthia's cabin, or how long we'd be staying. Her smile was hiding whatever it was that had transpired between her and her brother, but it was difficult to tell for how much longer. I had enough clothes for the next five days gently packed into my new bag. When we returned to the cabin we would have separate bags of clothes to lie at the feet of our separate beds.

***

BRETT EDWARD STOUT

19

ATTENTION TO DETAIL

The way back down the western shore was made even longer by the quickly setting sun. The shadows cast by the mountains extended the twilight, making time hover between day and night. Winding from left to right, the road made its way back and forth from the lake's edge.

I'd managed to find my way through the labyrinthine streets and buildings of San Francisco without a map, I could even plan the route from Ron's place back to Hal's without knowing the names of the streets. Finding a place in the dark I'd only seen once in the daylight presented a challenge. Without the sun as a basic reference of direction, the undulating highway was starting to get the better of me.

I was relatively sure that by the time the sky had completely gone black, we were headed east along the southern shore. But the turns were unfamiliar, the buildings were new, and unique landmarks like a tall totem pole were things I was sure I would have noticed before. How long should I continue before I alerted my passenger that we might be lost? Flipping through mental images of stop signs, deer crossings, restaurants, and turn off signs we'd passed, I was fairly sure I didn't pass an exit south to Sacramento. On the down side, if I spoke up now it might make me look worse than if I waited.

Looking down at the navigation system, the compass indicated I was still headed east. But it offered little comfort. The left half of the screen was blue and the right was green. A long black line ran down the middle and an arrow indicated the car and that I *were* on a road. It was about as much help as a pointing finger that said, "I think it's this way."

We crossed through another intersection that seemed vaguely familiar, but after a while, all of the intersections started to look exactly the same. The single-story roadside taverns with empty parking lots and small windows with neon beer signs all resembled one another. The worry I was lost was growing deep in my gut after rounding each slow bend in the road revealing nothing I could definitively identify. Surely I'd have seen the sign south. Surely there would have been one. Wouldn't they have marked an important turn like that? Maybe I *was* too inexperienced of a driver to pay attention to both the swerving pavement and the posted signage. Maybe I'd failed again and I could feel the burning on the back of my neck as if my father were actually there behind me, ready to yell or shake his head and say nothing.

When the angles of the left turns started to outweigh the turns right, it became obvious that I was in fact headed back north. At least I knew that the casino lights of Reno would become visible before too long so I could be sure. On the other hand, if I drove into Reno I'd be inviting harsher criticism from Ron. I could easily imagine him breaking his silence to chastise me for driving too far, not asking for help, and being generally incompetent.

"Hey, Ron?" I said quietly.

He looked groggy as his eyes opened. He blinked up at me. I smiled and just then as I came around a bend, I saw the sign for Sacramento. Ron still looked from under his eyelids with tired expectation.

"You want to pull over somewhere?" I winked and grinned while I bit the side of my bottom lip. He just shook his head and looked back out the window. As I went back and forth between watching him and the yellow lines of the pavement zipping by me, I realized that the radio must have been playing soft jazz the entire trip.

Making our way down the familiar road to Cynthia's cabin, I could see the lights inside the general store fully blazing.

"Do you mind if we stop for a few things?" My voice warbled around a frog that had formed in my throat.

"No. There a few things I need, too." Ron sat up slightly, brushed his hands down his shorts, and wiped his eyes by pinching them between his thumb and index finger.

The movement of the car softened when we pulled into the newly paved parking lot. I was glad to be rid of the noise of the drive. Outside, the quiet was shocking, making it easy to hear the cracking sounds of the engine cooling and hissing. But the forest sucked the sound of the engine and our feet up into the darkness, leaving us in a vacuum of near silence.

There was no music playing on an overhead speaker system as we went inside. It was almost jarring to have left the darkness outside, where trees reached up and disappeared into the stars, and enter the shiny room divided by aisles of colorful packages. The lights of the store exaggerated the reds, oranges, yellows, and blues of the glossy plastic bags of chips, candy bars, and baby wipes. The remaining walls were composed of steel-trimmed coolers stocked with endlessly replenishing beverage bottles. While I'd never cared for the usual choice of music convenience stores played, I found myself missing it. The lack of soundtrack gave a feeling of intrusion to our shopping trip. Without it, I wasn't sure how to act or how fast to walk through the aisles.

There wasn't really anything I couldn't have done without, so I made my way to the toiletries and began looking for anything I might need. I scanned over packaged nail clippers, emery boards, and tweezers. Below them, I saw deodorant, razors, and shaving cream. It was either the chill of the store or the excitement of new grooming tools that sent a tingle down the back of my head and neck. My mother often said "life has enough obstacles in it already, why be grungy and complicate things further?" Per her advice, I'd learned that people listened to me when I spoke, as long as I kept my hair cut, my teeth brushed, breath and body fresh, and face cleanly shaven. The world respected those who groomed themselves. From there, it was up to me to have something worthwhile to say.

My choices of shaving cream were limited to only the generic brand that I knew would come out white and fluffy, leaving my skin dry and irritated. Still, it was preferable to the Boot Camp method of going without, so I took it. Shaving my dirty face at four in the morning, in the dark, with only water and no mirror had been a substantial test of will and pain.

When I got to the counter, Ron was already there with a tube of chapstick and a two-liter bottle of Coke. The woman behind the counter smiled with her pink mouth and appreciative eyes and the demeanor of a Clair. Her neck was wrapped in a fuzzy white turtleneck, the rest of which was hidden under a denim over-shirt. Her hair was thin, delicate, and most of the brown had long since left it. Her teeth had white porcelain veneers and she smiled broadly with them.

"How are you nice boys tonight?" Clair asked, with a voice as soft as her turtleneck.

"Very well, ma'am. How are you?" Clair's smile became more genuine when I asked her this and her head canted, as she looked right at me with her pale blue eyes. I smiled back, amused at the reception to what was meant as a deliberate kindness.

"I'm very well, thank you for asking. Such a handsome young man." Her voice was like that of a warmhearted Midwestern women, not like the arrogant preoccupied Californians I'd become accustomed to. She might have passed

198

for the average, middle-American mother if she hadn't reached out with a hand adorned with a massive diamond ring. I was never very good at distinguishing carat weight but it was roughly the size of a small marble. I knew there was more to a diamond's value than its size. Mother's voice came into my head again "a big ugly diamond will always be a big ugly diamond; a beautiful diamond will always be beautiful no matter how big it is." She had imparted this advice when I was considering marrying a girl before heading to Boot Camp to stand on those yellow footprints, and before I really knew who I was.

The ring on this woman's hand was both big and beautiful. It perfectly refracted the hues of blue, green, yellow, orange, purple, and red and was hypnotic. It was not the ring of a woman who worked a cash register in order to put food on the table; I assumed that working was merely a hobby. She was no longer Clair, the name did not match the beauty of the ring, and I renamed her Diana. I began to wonder how far the saturation of wealth soaked through the community surrounding Fallen Leaf Lake. The implication of the word "fallen" was something that was conquered or left to the wayside; this place was neither.

We walked out of the store with our goods in the bottom of a thick paper sack. As I thought about the woman, another idea came to me. Having not been lost after all renewed my faith in my accompanying Ron. What still wasn't clear was what reason he had brought me here for. I had a new test to try out on Ron to see just how serious he was about my being there and what role I was supposed to play. Now all I needed was the right time and opportunity to present itself.

***

BRETT EDWARD STOUT

20

CHILDREN

We pulled up to the cabin where the lights in the living room were burning bright as they had the night before. Smoke was coming up out of the chimney and there was a general feeling that people were moving inside, but no clear evidence of it. I popped the back hatch and went back to the bags. The air was more brisk than it had been last night. I grabbed both of them, put them on my shoulders, and came around to where Ron was just getting out of the car. If I hadn't volunteered, would Ron have expected me to carry them? It was silly to wonder this now and I followed him up to the house.

He opened the door, without knocking, and entered like he'd been here a hundred times before. I made my way up the stairs and Ron headed into the kitchen. The Coke was still in my possession and I was hoping he wouldn't notice. Not really that it would matter as there was an abundance of wine in the little cubby holes at the end of the kitchen island. Cynthia was in the kitchen washing vegetables in the sink and Harold was sitting on the couch facing the windows, apparently listening to classical music coming from speakers I didn't see.

"How was your day, guys?"

Ron didn't answer so I did. "It was beautiful out. I've never spent much time up here when it wasn't all frozen." I figured that not spending any was not that different from not spending much.

"I know. Gorgeous weather we're having." Standing in the stairwell, the straps of the luggage digging into my shoulders I was wishing that either she would excuse me from the conversation or that her brother would start talking in my stead.

"The weather up here is always gorgeous." This was not an adjective I liked to use as I felt it made my speech sound mushy.

"Harold and I went into town and then for a hike. It was just serene."

"Really? Are there any trails within walking distance?"

"A few, I think. Harry, isn't there a trail..." As Cynthia's voice trailed off, my mind fixed on how Harry seemed too casual a name for the man I'd had breakfast with. Harold was definitely more fitting.

"Oh yeah, if you just go down the road a bit there is a nice one."

"Have we ever done that one?"

"I know I have, didn't you come with us when..." This was my queue to escape up to the room.

I put the bags down as I had planned. One at the foot of each bed and checked them to make sure that each had the corresponding clothes to the occupant. Detaching the long straps from the ends, I folded them and tucked them into the zipper pouches in the front. The smaller straps I folded across one another on top and then centered the bags to the posts of the bed.

When I got to the door on my way back down, I decided that I liked the shirt I was wearing too much to just wear it half a day. I took it off, refolded it, and selected a new one. Tomorrow I would wear the shirt for the full day that it deserved. While I had been changing, the sounds of Cynthia's feet had made their way up the stairs and into her bedroom.

Wearing new clothes always gave me an extra degree of confidence. Strolling out of the room in my new duds, I started to descend the stairs but found myself again sidetracked by the photos that hung there. The image of what I assumed was my host was still my favorite but I moved on to others. Almost all of them were pictures of children and many of those were of young Cynthia. Horses played a common theme too. They must have horses put up somewhere.

The morning I had woken up with Nation he had taken me to stables I'd never known existed in the middle of Golden Gate Park. The handsomeness of him and the great virile animal was intoxicating. It forever shaped my image of horses, watching him, this rough muscular man, react to the pacifying presence while he fed it an apple.

I couldn't imagine Ron in the same role but, then again, I really didn't know. I could hear Cynthia coming out of her room and my initial instinct was to continue down the stairs and pretend not to have been snooping. Instead I decided to stay.

"Isn't childhood wonderful?" she was close enough I could smell her perfume.

"Well, I didn't have horses, but I can remember quite a few wonderful times that didn't involve livestock." My nervousness about her proximity forced out a joke. I was hoping would make me sound witty.

"We used to have such a time at Dad's farm." I wasn't sure, but it seemed *her* nervousness kept her from laughing. So, the sprawling estate of pristine buildings connected by perfect white fences was their version of a farm. Mine was clearly different and included muddy lots with dirty animals clamoring to eat from troughs under the shadow of a collapsing barn.

"Where is that?"

"It's out East, in Connecticut."

"Is this you?" I pointed to the glowing girl with the horse.

"Oh, yes. I was only five then. Ron hadn't even been born yet." She was standing right next to me but didn't look at me. Her left arm was out at an angle with the back of her hand on her hip; a pose only woman looked natural in. The frame of her eyeglasses up to her lip as if she were thinking about biting it.

"Where's Ron? Is he in any of the pictures?"

"Let's see... There. There's Ronny." The picture she pointed to was one I hadn't noticed. The angle of the stair put it just above eye level and she pointed at it using her eyeglasses. In the frame were two boys; the one that resembled a tiny Ron was fittingly dressed in a sailor outfit. He too had the jubilant smile I associated with children. Next to him was a taller boy who appeared in his young teens. He wore a button up shirt tucked into his pants, had dark hair, and his smile was somewhat diminished.

"Who is that with him?"

"Harry." Did she mean Harold?

"Harry?"

"Yes, back when he still had hair." She laughed lightly, as if her husband's receding hairline was somehow comic. "We all had quite the time getting in and out of trouble." She started to walk down the stairs but I was transfixed by the image. There was an age gap between them of what could have been ten years; the happy Ronny next to the adolescent Harry. Looking at their comfort standing so closely together, practically touching, they must have been friends.

Was the population so limited among the "people of quality" that they actually all knew each other and grew up together? It was hard to imagine a world so small. Did that make it easier to remember people's names if there were only so many to know? Wouldn't an existence like that become dull and incestuous? What trouble did they get in together? They all seemed quite ordinary, at least while sober, and at what point did Cynthia and Harold's relationship develop into the one they shared today? I scanned across the pictures for one of the three of them, but when I didn't find one, I went downstairs.

"Where are the kids?" Ron asked before he noticed me coming down. "Grab the Coke and bring it down."

I returned to the room to fetch it and started back down the stairs. Stopping on the stairs again, I took another moment to look at the photographs. Reaching up, I straightened the frame of a photograph of Harold and Ron in mid-run near the entrance to a barn. The image I had of Harold with his pipe in his mouth and Ron with a drink in his hand slowly transformed into these two obnoxiously loud, spastically moving, infinitely innocent children chasing each other just for the joy of it. Looking at their plump unwrinkled faces I could see them panting for breath, daring one another to commit acts of mischief, and persistently asking the adults around them "why." In the games they played I wondered who won, if either of them remembered or if Harold, being the older stronger one, ever held back. I'd seen children like this before, but I had no evidentiary photographs like this, in fact, I was certain I'd never had the chance to so be unrestrained, so full of hope, or so happy.

The Coke was beginning to hurt my fingers, so I left my imaginary version of Ron's family childhood and brought the case down, setting it on the island. The music was a little familiar, it sounded like something I'd studied in humanities class in high school. I'd listened so hard and long to the tapes my teacher had given hoping to impress and get her attention. She was a woman who possessed an ethereal intelligence I had always admired.

"Is that Beethoven?"

I suddenly had Harry's full attention. "Are you a Beethoven fan?"

His tone required some form of affirmative answer "I like what I've heard. I also like his story." He stood up and walked over to the bookshelf.

"Take a look at these." I made my way over to where he was kneeling. His head was a little shiny even in the gold, glowing, interior lighting. "Do you listen to much classical?"

"What are you cooking?" I overheard Ron ask in the kitchen.

"I would like to be familiar with more. My favorite is Scheherazade by Rimsky Korsakov." This was my best answer, since it was obscure enough to be interesting without being so obscure it might be considered pretentious. It also usually led people to believe I know and was familiar with a lot more classical music than I was. That people assumed this I didn't feel was my fault.

"That's an excellent piece. Have you ever heard this?" He pointed to Beethoven's third symphony. I had assumed such a thing existed since I knew of the fifth and the ninth.

"I haven't decided yet." Cynthia answered.

"It's getting kinda late. Don't you think you should decide?"

"I don't think I've heard it before. I'd like to very much."

He stood up. "Cynthia darling, I'm going to change this one out."

"Do you need some help in the kitchen?" If I was in the kitchen I might be able to distract Ron.

"I could find something for you to do."

Cynthia was lost in the kitchen. She'd washed potatoes, carrots, and she'd even washed a few onions. "What are we making?"

"Well, I wanted some vegetables and I was thinking of chicken."

I knew she was inept in this room and she would probably never admit it. "Well, I know some great recipes. Do you mind if I check out what all you have?"

"Be my guest." I already *was* her guest. What I was trying to be was something a little less temporary.

206

"This piece is truly remarkable. You should listen." I hadn't seen where he'd put the CD and I still couldn't tell where the speakers were.

Opening the refrigerator the sight there was a bit comical. The ingredients, condiments, and various items themselves were unremarkable. What was funny was that they were all almost entirely unused and unopened. There was more of the same in the cupboard. Cynthia finished half a glass of red wine while she pretended not to scrutinize my thumbing through her pantry.

"You have pasta. We could make some chicken and pasta with a side of vegetables?"

"I could do that." I wanted to say back to her, "No, *you* can't, but I'm not opposed to giving you credit in exchange for peace."

"Jesus, just decide already and let's eat."

At that moment Harold asked Cynthia for another glass of wine and I retrieved some ice in a glass for Ron to mix his own cocktail.

Usually when I cooked I would entertain myself with a little television. The lack of such a device was something else I hadn't noticed the night before.

"You have three children?"

"All boys. They're with friends of ours." Again, I wasn't sure if the kids had been exiled for their protection.

After I filled the stock pan with water, I set out a cutting board, put the chicken next to it, and started filling a bowl with some flour. When she didn't take the hint that I wanted her to slice it, I pulled out the proper knife and sliced open the tight plastic that covered it. After I'd gotten through about half of the first one I figured that she'd seen enough for me to delicately pass off the task to her.

"Shoot, I really should start getting the skillet ready."

"Oh, I'll finish this." The cooking lesson had begun.

We continued interacting like this as we made our way through the ingredients. We talked about food and thing's we'd eaten, restaurants we'd liked, and who in our family we felt was the most inspiring in the kitchen. I'd half expected her to say something like "My father had the best cook at his farm in Connecticut." But, her response was the same cliché as mine. I wasn't entirely sure why we always considered our grandmother's to be such good cooks. Maybe we were so young at the time we didn't know any better, or maybe they really were the superhuman master chefs we remembered them to be.

My mother had never been much of a cook and was frequently busy at work so I started to explore the kitchen during grade school. However, it wasn't until I joined the Marines that I was exposed to the art of cuisine. The complexity and artistry of it was beautiful. I remember vividly the first time I watched a real chef prepare a meal in a small restaurant in California. His hands moved with precision and just enough inconsistency to give each dish a unique quality.

Our conversation was a long string of small talk, completely devoid of anything approaching real substance. That she was trying to pretend to be at home in the kitchen I found odd. Was this her version of slumming? Was she just trying to pretend she was just another housewife, happily at work preparing the family meal? I wasn't sure she was fooling anyone but herself.

"Where do you live the rest of the year?"

"We spend most of our time either in Carmel or at our place in the Hamptons." This living situation seemed cliché to me, but she had no reason to lie so it was believable.

"You never learned to cook? I learned to cook because my mother didn't." I hadn't meant it to sound insulting, but after, I realized it was. It was bad form to point out that I had noticed she couldn't cook when she'd cooperated so well. She put her hand on her hip this time with palm facing in.

"I thought everyone knew how to cook in Iowa." She said a lot with her statement. Usually when I mentioned my family people felt compelled to comment on their own, she was avoiding talking about her mother on purpose. She was letting me know that she was offended enough to ignore my question. And, she was also trying to insult me by letting me know that she felt Iowa was simple and poor place full of people who couldn't afford to hire people to cook for them.

"No." I laughed pretending that I thought she was being funny.

I lifted the stockpot off the stove. She had been standing close to the sink and backed up quickly when I had come toward her with the boiling water. I poured it out into the sink. Steam barreled up to the high ceiling where it danced in the light.

"Oh, careful. Hot water." I felt this was threatening enough to be effective, but not slow, in order to let her know I was not about to be bullied by her; even if I was her guest.

I replaced the noodles into the pan from the colander and set them aside. When I removed the lid from the chicken that had been slowly cooking in a mixture of wine, onion, butter, and seasoning, the kitchen filled with the sweet aroma.

"This you have to try."

"It smells wonderful." I used a wooden spoon to retrieve a piece of chicken from the simmering pan. "That's fantastic." I appreciated her compliment and genuine surprise at tasting what slow-cooking on low heat could produce and that it could be done in her own kitchen by a "kid." "You have to try some. You've outdone yourself, Brad."

"I'll take your word for it. I'm a vegetarian actually." I wasn't sure if she was confused because she didn't know if I was kidding or if she was confused that a vegetarian had just prepared such delicious meat. Either way I had invited criticism.

"You're a vegetarian?" Which meant; "Are you a democrat?"

"Yes, ma'am." This was my way of saying "Not exactly."

"Why are you a vegetarian?" or "Are you a tree-hugger?"

"Well, I actually stopped eating meat as a bet with an old ex of mine." This is usually where I would stop to allow the pronoun game to ensue.

"An ex?" Cynthia did not want to play.

"Yeah, my ex-girlfriend was a smoker. I told her I'd quit eating meat if she quit smoking. Well, at least one of us can keep their word." And there it was. She'd called me out and I'd lied. She now understood that I was serious about protecting the secrets necessary to protect. She knew I would not embarrass her brother by exposing him or, more importantly, embarrass her. "I enjoy it actually. So, you like the chicken?"

"It's terrific. We should have you back to cook for my birthday."

"You have a birthday coming up?" About two months before my birthday each year I would stop mentioning it. It was partly a test to see who truly would remember and partly so I could use it to make people feel guilty about forgetting it.

"I'll be forty-five."

"I'll refrain from the obvious statements about how you clearly don't look forty-five." This was a silly paradox but also a flattering one that she wouldn't object to. Truthfully, I hadn't realized that she was so much older than Ron. She really did look a lot younger.

"I can't believe you're a vegetarian. That's so funny." I wished she would let the topic go.

Why *was* I a vegetarian? It brought me more grief than it did happiness. I was starting to feel off balance. All the traits I'd depended on to describe me were being questioned. If wasn't a Marine anymore, could I just as easily let go of the other things I'd been clinging to?

"In India—Indian food is my favorite—everything is actually reversed. We make fun of vegetarians *here*, but they make fun of meat-eaters *there*. They call them non-veggies."

"That's interesting." I felt somewhat vindicated.

"Now we have the fun part." I explained to her my opinion that food was an expression of art. That, living in Hawaii had given me an added appreciation for the esthetic experience of food. I helped her ladle the farfalle onto the plates and drizzle the homemade alfredo over them. I told her about sushi I'd seen and other edible sculptures I'd witnessed or eaten.

We were starting to bond a little, which was a sharp contrast to the general attitude moments earlier. I handed her a small jar of paprika and had her hold it high above the plates. Apparently we'd stumbled into a temporary cease-fire.

"Now, this is a great finishing touch." Through gestures and sound effects I told her how to tap the bottom of the jar to allow sprinkles of the red spice to fall onto the white plate as the period at the end of our entree's sentence. She couldn't have been more pleased if she'd prepared the entire meal herself.

Harold came in from outside where he'd been sitting with Ron.

"Things just about ready? Would you look at that," He whistled. "Darling, that looks wonderful." I had capitulated earlier that I would let her take the credit for this meal since it was technically the product of her kitchen.

"I'll set the table." I arranged the plates around the table; forks again on the left, knives and spoons on the right, (even though we wouldn't need them.)

"Aren't you going to have any chicken?"

"He doesn't eat meat, Harry."

"You're a vegetarian?"

***

21

TAKING SIDES

"You're a vegetarian?"

"Yes, sir."

"How is it that you were a vegetarian in the Marines?"

I never completely understood exactly what conflict people thought would have prevented me from being a vegetarian and a Marine, but everyone seemed to think it impossible. Did they think that there was some regulation that requires the consumption of animal flesh? The two things had nothing to do with each other. In fact one of the biggest toughest Marines I'd known was a vegan bodybuilder. I lacked the discipline to give up cheese and ice cream.

Their disbelief set my imagination loose. I envisioned a pit of sleeping, shirtless, Marines into which a side of raw beef was flung. The smell of blood would cause them to stir and encircle it like hungry lions. Pouncing on it like wild animals, they'd tear into the flesh, clawing over one another, their eyes fixed and enraged, their faces and limbs smeared with dirt and

213

blood, until the bones were picked clean. After they'd finished they'd drag the remains outside, dig holes, and bury the kill. This had never occurred in my unit and ultimately I didn't mind people's concept of Marines as viscous carnivores. It was exciting to be recognized as dangerous.

As the dinner conversation continued, Cynthia brought up what I had said about non-veggies and India. Hearing her repeat my trivia I recognized how nerdy it sounded. Harold responded with something about maize, which I later learned was what the rest of the planet called corn, and said something about a guy named Borlaug. I did my best to feign knowing what he was talking about. Since the nerd factor of his trivia trumped mine I was no longer worried about it.

"What did you do in the Marines?"

"Every Marine is a rifleman, sir." This response felt better than admitting that I had been a "pogue," one of the world's deadliest paper-pushing gardeners.

"You really should try this." Cynthia placed a fork that had stabbed the poor little defenseless piece of chicken wrapped in paprika, flour, and oregano. Non-veggies insistence on getting me to eat meat with them exposed a paranoia that bordered on phobic towards vegetarians.

But eating meat *had* become something I was afraid of. Was this a step I couldn't turn away from? If I ate it now, I didn't know if I had the intestinal fortitude not to do it again. I might start sneaking around when people weren't looking and gorging myself on animal products. It was scary to lose the image of being vegetarian, of being different. Everyone was watching to see what fate I would deal the impaled chicken. I could have almost cried through my smile as I picked it up and ate it to satisfy my audience. In my mouth the innocent morsel turned to poison. I silently swallowed my regret. After it was over I wondered why I'd done it in the first place. I was so preoccupied with hiding my emotions that I never even tasted it.

After dinner things had calmed down. We were all a little docile and slow moving with our bellies full. I still needed a break from the family environment so I suggested a walk outside. It might not have been the smartest move since I hadn't thought to bring a coat with me to California in July. I actually no longer owned a coat, having thrown them away my second year in Hawaii.

"Your sister is nice."

"She's a bitch." I wasn't sure how to respond. Was I supposed to recant and agree? "Oh yeah, she's totally a bitch." This wasn't something I was sure I believed yet. I still knew nothing about what happened between them.

"So you've known Harold for a long time then?" He answered by not answering. He didn't want to talk about it.

Distractions were coming at me from all directions. The night was beautiful enough that it made me not want to spoil it with human voices. It was cold enough that I was becoming more and more uncomfortable. My hands were shoved deep into my pockets trying to get close to my legs for warmth. I was full but I still wanted to eat. Deserts were usually perfect recreational foods. It wasn't that I wanted to eat more; I just enjoyed tasting, chewing, and swallowing. The sensation of it satisfied certain pleasure centers in my brain.

The conversation wasn't going anywhere and, while I didn't really want to hang out in the discomfited air of the cabin, it was at least warmer air. Turning us around I was tempted to reach out to hold Ron for warmth. He didn't seem to be phased by the frigid lake air. It could have been the alcohol in him that had either warmed him up or just gotten him to the point where he didn't' care. I felt bad making us head back. He was at peace, strolling along at the leisurely pace we'd used to tour Tinsley, and I didn't have to be distracted by the smacking of flip-flops, so I could enjoy the slow speed.

We got back to the door and I opened it for him. I hadn't noticed before how heavy and thick it was. The door was very solid and the lock reminded me of security doors I'd seen in the military. There was a security panel the same color as the wall that I hadn't noticed before. Now that I was looking, all of the

215

windows, at least from what I could see near the door, seemed made of a thick glass that was probably security glass. Even up here in the woods there was worry about security. I remembered the woman who had shut the door in Ron's face. Did she ever find out who she'd locked out? If she did, would she worry or regret doing it?

"I never got your opinion on the symphony." Harold commented.

I felt bad in not giving the attention to something he'd gone out of his way to introduce me to and was clearly excited about. I made a few comments I wasn't sure were smart enough or even applied to the music, but that did at least let him know I didn't intentionally blow him off.

With disappointment I poured Coke into a glass filled with ice and then topped if off with a few shots of rum that was still sitting out on the counter top. Ron accepted it without a thank you and I replaced the bottle of rum into the cupboard promising myself that if he ordered another I would offer water as an alternative beverage.

With no more cooking, no more eating, and no television I felt a little naked and lost. My customer had taken his drink out onto the deck back outside and left the door open which I closed behind him and sat down across from Harold who was listening to what could have only been more Beethoven over the phantom sound system.

"I know this is an odd question. Where are the speakers?" Harold's eyebrows arched with that "I know something you don't know" expression and stood up motioning with his head after another puff from his cigar.

He revealed to me that the speakers were hidden behind panels in the walls and inside fake stones in the mantle. I hadn't seen them because they were camouflaged: tactically hidden troops of modern technology that had infiltrated the rustic setting. I had known that certain extremes had been taken to disguise the modernity of the dwelling but this was by far the most interesting yet.

216

"What would we do without our toys?"

"I wouldn't say this was a toy and music is not a game." I could tell he'd said this before but I didn't know if he was quoting someone.

"It's an interesting world we live in. At least it is for now."

"I take it you have a pessimistic view of things to come."

"I'm not sure pessimism is the word for it." This was a conversation that could quickly go bad but a good argument always gave me a little thrill. "I feel like American leadership is lost. We used to be the forerunner of human rights but now, it's like all the great leaders; JFK, Martian Luther King, I'd go as far as to say Malcolm X, are all gone."

"That doesn't mean there are no strong leaders left or that we're not making progress in human rights."

"What I'm trying to say is that I don't see any of these great people who really propelled things and made a difference today. Everything seems watered down. I mean where are the people we make holidays for anymore? I don't see them." I was second-guessing myself and not sure I was using all of my words correctly.

"I see. But is legislation really proof of progress in human rights?" Harold was clearly better at this than I was. I decided to make a bolder statement.

"I know this might paint me in a bad light, but it seems to me that the Christian Right is undermining all the good that has been done."

I was nervous about arguing with my host. I folded one leg up onto the couch. I was trying to look comfortable but sitting like this was actually almost painful to my hip and my hands were firmly glued to my leg so he wouldn't see my hands shaking.

"A slow progression of human rights process is favorable to chaotic, radical, and violent change. Keep in mind that JFK, Martin Luther King Jr., and Malcolm X were all assassinated."

"I see your point." It frustrated me to feel like I had lost an argument, especially on something I believed in, but I did see his point. I just didn't want to believe it.

"America has a notion that everything has to be accomplished in this lifetime." It almost sounded like he was putting down America; that seemed out of character.

"Just because someone goes to church, it doesn't mean they buy into a position of oppression." He seemed to be telling me that perhaps he and Cynthia were cosmetic Christians, that they only attended church to maintain appearances.

We both had bigger things we wanted the other to learn about one another from this battle. I wanted Harold to know that I was not the type of liberal who only went to independent documentary films or used the word "cornucopia" to describe everything. Harold wanted me to know that he was not the kind of conservative who attended Christian coalition rallies or used the phrase "new fangled." We both had our opinions, but were not intellectually stubborn enough to deny the validity of the opposition's perspective.

The end of a discussion is always strange. Everyone wants to have the last word and it usually trails on for several more minutes with one person either continually capitulating or with all parties crossing their arms, looking away, and putting up their nose. It felt good that that didn't happen.

Since we had returned I hadn't seen much of Cynthia, and until Ron walked in I was worried they were outside beating one another senseless. When he looked at me and Harold sitting across from one another he let out a huff.

"Your friend has an interesting point of view."

"That's because he can decide things for himself." I quickly stood up and took Ron's glass from him.

"I'll get you some water." Cynthia couldn't have picked a worse time to reappear from wherever she'd been hiding. Maybe she smelled blood and was hungry for it. She had an empty wine glass in her hand and was casually making her way into the kitchen where the mostly empty bottle was. "Can I get anyone else some water?"

Harold nodded and I looked at his wife who looked right back since I was between her, Ron, and the bottle. She stared for a moment, lost in whatever it was she was thinking about and then blinked.

"No, thank you. That's kind of you."

"I'm pretty tired." This was tricky, under different circumstances I would have just invited Ron up with me following that remark. Since we were just "friends" going to bed had to be done either separately or we mutually would have to agree that we were tired for our own separate reasons, and not going to bed "together."

After another huff from Ron, he set down the water I'd handed him without drinking it and turned towards Harold. My knees started to shake and at just that moment the symphony that had been the soundtrack of armistice went silent. A loud pop escaped the fireplace and no one moved. Everyone stood breathing. I found myself hoping that another track would begin and end the silence that had exposed us all and stripped any excuses that prevented us from addressing the sibling conflict I knew nothing about.

Ron started to walk forward, Harold stood his ground, Cynthia kept her eye on me and I swallowed hard. When he turned for the stairs and up them, the air resumed with music of our own making. Harold adjusted himself on the couch and the glass Cynthia had been holding was set on the counter with a clink. Feet pounding up the stairs provided a drumbeat; their mellow tempo put an end to the palpable unease that had thickened the atmosphere of the room.

When I myself made it up to the room, he was already asleep. Who would have ever pictured the two of us together? Matchmaking wasn't all that easy for gay men. There were different levels of compatibility that needed to be considered. We were a demographic defined by sexuality, but being gay was not the primary characteristic I wanted to be known for. I knew it was possible to live in an area like the Castro where I could go all day and never see a straight person. This, to me, was a depressing scenario. It paralleled people I'd heard about who spent their entire lives in Makaha, on the leeward side of Oahu, and never saw Honolulu. I didn't understand how people couldn't be interested in exploring what life had to offer inches in front of their nose.

He lay on his side; his breathing was slow and audible. I considered crawling up next to him in the small bed. Interrupting his sleep wouldn't go over that well and he'd been pretty clear about his discomfort with being physical inside these walls. The idea hadn't been in my head for more than a minute before I disliked that I'd even thought of it. I remembered how it had felt in the past when I'd been woken up similarly. I didn't know how to react to it. Part of me liked the attention and part of me felt raped, but once they'd started, I never told them to stop.

My worries about being here were not settled. I'd expected them to be gone; I'd hoped I would have been made welcome. In all actuality, they were getting worse. How long would it take for Cynthia to snap? What would I do if it came down to an ultimatum that either I go or he does? She was family and I was entertainment. Wasn't I? Was it only a matter of time or would the opportunity pass by uneventfully.

I still had my question I wanted to ask Ron. While the time and place had not yet presented itself today, I would keep a look out for the right moment tomorrow.

***

22

MORE COFFEE?

It was as beautiful as lunchtime weather could be at the outdoor café. The breeze was just gentle enough to keep the air fresh, but not forceful enough to blow the napkins off the table. I tilted my head back and let the sunlight filtering through the white sun umbrella kiss my face.

The street on the other side was peaceful other than the occasional car, which casually motored by. A couple at one of the other tables was pretending not to recognize me but their hushed voices gave them away. I didn't mind. I'd chosen to sit outside because I had wanted people to see me, to recognize me from pictures or interviews they'd seen.

The waitress, wearing a crisp uniform, made her way over to my table. She stopped right next to me and leaned in; she was holding a white ceramic teapot. I looked up at her, smiling, until I saw her face.

Cynthia reached for my cup "More coffee?"

My eyes opened and I was alone in the room. Ron had awakened before me and I could hear what I assumed was him in the shower.

This morning the evidence that he had been there went beyond his unmade bed. Hurricane Ron had destroyed the neatly folded environment I had carefully constructed in his bag. Hovering over ground zero, I surveyed the devastation. At first, I couldn't decide what to do. Shirts and khakis hung out of the bag like a disemboweled animal. I knew that half of him expected I would clean it up, but I wasn't sure if I should just leave it be or repair the damage. As I stood thinking I decided that this was not about him, this was about me, about restoring the order that I had created. I made an executive decision. It was time to call in the Marine for the clean-up effort. I extracted the contents, refolded them, and arranged them as I placed them back in the bag. When I finished, I zipped it closed and neatly crossed the straps.

Coming out into the hallway, I noticed the absence of the smell of food. The door to Harold and Cynthia's room was open. I paused near the stairs and listened. After I was sure I'd heard both of their voices I softly walked into their room.

Inside, their room was the size of ours and the children's room combined. The bed was large and adorned with rows of beige and white pillows of descending size. There was a matching Hawaiian quilt that reminded me of home, dripping from the sides of the California king. The sight of the massive overdone bed reminded me of a giant wedding cake. On the door to the master bathroom were two hooks on which were hung terry cloth robes.

The broad carved and polished dresser on the opposite end of the room and closest to me had an equally broad mirror that reached up nearly to the ceiling. The surface of the piece was covered in silver and brushed-metal-framed pictures, and was free of any trace of dust. At the foot was a headless white fur rug and I thought "more dead animals." I wondered what people did with the head if they didn't leave it attached to the rug. Did the less fortunate in the towns the animals were skinned in receive the industrial leftovers? Into my head popped the image of a floor covering comprised entirely of the menacing faces of murdered animals. While morbid, I still found it funny.

When the shower stopped I quickly retreated from the room without thinking to look down the stairs first before returning to ours. What if they'd been coming up the stairs at the time and had seen me come from the direction of their room? I stood in the doorway looking down the hallway where the dresser was in full view. When no one came from the area of the stairs, and I didn't hear any retreating footprints or whispering, I relaxed and laid back on my bed.

I wasn't sure why I'd gotten up in the first place. I should have just laid in bed and patiently waited for Ron to finish. When I'd been waiting for the eternity of ten minutes and the water was still running in the sink I stood up and headed for the stairs again. Whenever I woke up I was thirsty, my body having used the available water while it repaired itself during sleep. About three steps down, I remembered that I still hadn't shaved. What kind of Marine would they take me for if I came down looking so unkempt? When I returned to our room I took as much time as I could making the beds again and then carefully laid down. I resolved that I would have to wait despite my thirst for water, to be moving around, or talking to someone.

The door opened after a while and snapped me out of the daze I'd been in. I had practiced going into this trancelike state when standing at attention in formations. Ron's face was moist and there was a little redness on his neck still. A small glop of shaving cream clung to his earlobe.

"Good morning." I sent a wink in his direction. He smiled, looked down at the bag at the foot of his bed, and smiled again. I resisted my urge to leap from the bed and dash into the bathroom before it was occupied again.

Ron walked over to the nightstand, picked up his watch and put it on, twisting his wrist back and forth so it did not catch on his arm hair.

"What are we up to today?"

"I'm thinking about going up to the hot springs." This sounded more like the high-class fun I was expecting from the trip.

"Awesome. Let me get ready."

I got right up and quickly brushed my teeth looking once more at the blurry face hidden behind the steamed up mirror. Since I knew the water would be warm again I climbed right in and turned it on. Just before I stuck my head under the stream I remembered that I should check for a towel. Turning the shower so it sprayed against the tiles on the wall, I pulled back the curtain and checked. There was no towel tucked into the rack, as there had been the night before. I supposed I should use the one I'd used yesterday that was folded over my footboard in the other room.

I tiptoed over to the door trying to get as little water on the floor as possible. It was unlikely that walking like this would make any difference but the effort made me feel better. Opening the door I peeked out looking left and right at the open doorways at either end of the hallway. The coast was clear.

Emerging into the hallway, cold and still dripping, I continued tiptoeing down the hall in full view of the hallway windows. I made my way down past the children's room, hoping no one would pop out of it and scream in terror at the sight of the tall, naked, wet Marine sneaking past. Permanently traumatized, they might fall to the floor covering their eyes as if they'd been tear-gassed and it would be all my fault for having forgotten my towel.

I snatched up my towel and wrapped it around me. The children were apparently still not back from wherever they'd been shipped off to and my conscience was clear. I made my way back to the bathroom, attempting to use the lowest extreme of the towel to wipe up the water as I went.

In what felt like record time I completed all the required tasks in the shower and emerged proud of my accomplishment. When I toweled dry, I ensured to not to use the end I had used to clear wet footprints form the floor. Shaving was not something I

224

enjoyed; I found it painful and my skin was angry afterwards. But it was a necessary pain, according to my mom's philosophy on appearance. Showering softened the skin enough to make shaving tolerable, but the longer I waited, the dryer and more irritating shaving would become.

The items I'd gotten the night before were tucked into the side pouch of my new bag. Using the towel again I slowly ran it down the mirror revealing my face. It was the first time I'd seen it in three days. I looked more tired than I felt, and my hair, which I usually cut every week, was just long enough that I could see it on the sides of my head, but not so much that it lost its prickly texture. A shadow of facial hair gave the appearance the sides of my head simply continued onto my jaw and neck. While this was a look I enjoyed on others, I hated it on me. Looking at this reflection, I felt considerably dirtier than I had staring at the blurry version.

The shaving cream even felt cheap as I rubbed it over my skin and started to scrape across it with the cheap orange safety razor. Straight razors had always both interested and scared me. They interested me since they seemed more traditional and sophisticated, they scared me for the obvious reason that coming at my neck with a razor I didn't know how to use would. My only actual experience with them was when, on a rare occasion, I went to places that would cut my hair and follow up by shaving the back of my head. Not only did the haircut last longer, reaching back and feeling the sticky thick skin of my scalp was invigorating.

I cleaned the sink when I finished by splashing water to rinse away the little black hairs. Leaning closely in I exaggerated my lips from side to side and stretched my neck to give myself an inspection. When I was certain no embarrassing patches had been missed I went back into the room and put my new favorite shirt on.

It was too late now that I had showered, but I was itching to get some exercise. I had gone running up and down the steep hills of the city while I'd been there, but here, I didn't even have running shoes. Pushups, sit-ups, and other basic calisthenics were an alternative, but one that would have to wait for another time. I was upset at myself for not having thought of it sooner.

Coming downstairs I felt fresh and brand new. The sun was out, the lake was glittering, and the air seemed energized. Everyone was sitting outside on the deck reading the paper and drinking coffee.

"Good morning."

"Beautiful morning." Cynthia corrected me, smiling. She was holding her hand up like a salute to block the sun from her eyes. She stood up when I pulled out a chair to sit. "Now that everyone is up, should we fix breakfast?" I suspected she'd waited for me to wake up for reasons other than courtesy. It also seemed we would not be leaving as soon as I thought.

"Just something light." Harold was the only one to respond and patted his stomach while he did. Ron continued reading his folded paper. I looked at her, shrugged, and followed her inside. She poured me a cup of coffee and set it down in front of where I stood by the island. I picked it up and pretended to be delighted to drink it. Harold, who had followed us in, picked up the coffee pot and took it outside and filled his cup. Without looking up from his paper, Ron held out his cup for Harold to refill. As Harold sat down, Ron poured some cream and sugar into Harold's cup. Harold filled his pipe with tobacco from a small pouch and, by the time he was finished, Ron had passed him an unfolded section of paper and a lit match. Watching them was like watching a ballet about male bonding; they were two apes in a jungle picking bugs out of each other's fur.

"What should we make?"

"Breakfast sandwiches would be light."

It seems that we had a truce where neither of us would try to be rude, instead preferring to move from one insignificant topic to the next. I walked her through the ingredients of toast, butter, eggs, mayonnaise, cheese and the bacon (which I would leave off

226

mine.) Giving her the whisk and the eggs, I let her break and start to mix them while I warmed up the toaster and skillet.

"Did you sleep well?"

"Very well, ma'am."

"You don't have to keep calling me ma'am."

"Sorry, it's just force of habit I guess." I took another swallow of the bitter coffee. My plan of attack was to drink it quickly and get it over with. Each drink I took got harder; this was a taste I was not acquiring very well.

I couldn't help myself from correcting her on how to beat the eggs to maximize the amount of air into them. Putting her instead in charge of making toast and spreading mayo seemed more suited to her.

Telling her stories about making these for my parents and times I'd burned things helped pass the time and she laughed at all the appropriate moments. We arranged all the plates and carried them out to where the men had been talking. The conversation broke to make way for breakfast. Compliments were passed out to the team of chefs and eating commenced. Harold passed his paper over to me and I set it down weighting the edge of it with my plate. I stared at it pretending to read between bites and casual comments on cooking and the weather.

"I should have brought my running shoes with me. It's a beautiful area to go for a run."

"It's too bad you didn't. The air up here is so much cleaner than the city."

It was occurring to me that everyone was acting bizarrely normal and ignoring all controversial topics or mention of last night's tension. The situation reminded me of a picture I'd been shown once of a friend's baby girl. I could clearly see that the child's forehead was so covered in hair that her eyebrows seemed to be the start of her hairline. No matter how much anyone wanted to talk about it, the cuteness of babies was non-negotiable. The relationship between Ron, Cynthia, Harold, and me was an ugly baby. We all worked to perpetuate the brittle happiness created by evasion.

Finally swallowing the last of my coffee I stood up.

"Is it alright if I get a glass of milk?"

"Brad, you don't need to ask. Just get some." This felt out of place coming from Ron. I was desperate to get the taste out of my mouth. I took a swallow of it before I'd even put the jug back into the refrigerator and another before I went back to the table.

Sitting back down with everyone, they all seemed to have been laughing. The smiles were still on their faces and they were catching their breath. I wasn't sure what about but it was too late to ask and get any pleasure out of it for myself.

Pulling a paper napkin out of the holder on the table I set it under my glass and looked over my shoulder at the lake. Lakes always seemed peaceful but this one was especially so. The trees seemed to gather here just for the purpose of enjoying the view and the quiet. Even in the daylight, silence was the prevailing sound. In the distance somewhere I head the laughing of children playing.

"Where are your kids?" Ron asked.

"Julia has them. We're changing schools and we wanted them to know her children since they'll be attending together."

"Well that's gonna screw 'em up good."

Cynthia stood up "Ron, I'll have you know, was an excellent student. I was so proud when he came home with his first report card."

Ron looked down as if he was ashamed of having done well. I was little confused by this reaction. In school, I hadn't been that great of a student, but I'd happily receive any A.

Cynthia went inside and I smiled at Ron but he didn't look up to see my expression. Why Ron was so concerned about Cynthia's children changing schools I wasn't sure. It was understandably hard, but it seemed like having the kids get to know some of their new classmates was a good thing. Surely she wouldn't put them in a school that was worse off for them.

Lifting my glass the paper napkin stuck to the bottom and Harold reached for the center of the table.

"Let me show you a trick." He shook out some salt on the napkin. "Now your napkin won't stick."

I didn't believe him at first, thinking that the water would just dissolve the salt. I set the milk down on the napkin to test the theory. After a few moments I lifted the glass again. "Thanks." How I'd gone twenty-two years and never learned this I wasn't sure. The simplicity and practicality of it made me a little giddy inside, and I wanted to find someone else to impart this wisdom on.

"What a beautiful day." I stared at my glass and turned it clockwise and back feeling it rub on the tiny crystals beneath it. Cynthia appeared out of nowhere next to me and I looked up at her. This time, I had to hold my hand up to block the sun.

"More coffee?"

***

23

THE OFFER

After I recovered from my déjà vu, I declined, stood up, and began helping Cynthia collect the dishes and other things from the table. Stacking the plates on top of one another I followed her back into the kitchen.

"Thank you again so much for helping out."

"It's not a problem, ma'am. Sorry, I can't seem to stop that."

"You're mother must have raised you right."

"I wouldn't be who I am without her."

Picking the napkins from the plates, I threw them into the trashcan under the sink. Cynthia started running the water and placed a few fingers into the stream to gauge the temperature. When it was sufficiently hot I began handing her plates one at a time. She systematically ran them under the faucet and then placed them in the bottom of the deep sink.

Out the window I could see where the car was parked and I was ready to be in it. There were people with large bags coming out of a cabin that was close enough not to have been completely covered by the trees. One of the bags was five foot long or so. I wondered if there were skis in it. I didn't really know how people transported skis but a bag this large would have accommodated them.

I went back out onto the deck where Ron and Harold sat in complete silence, Ron with his sunglasses on and hands behind his head. His eyes seemed to be shut and his body was positioned to maximize exposure to the warm sunlight. Harold had his hands folded on his lap and looked out across the expanse of the water with a slight grin on his face. Neither of them paid attention while I gathered the cups, saucers, and glasses from the table.

"I really regret not having brought running shoes. The weather is perfect." I liked how I'd made it seem like my coming here was deliberate, or even planned.

"You could get a pair in town I'm sure." Cynthia suggested.

"I suppose that's an idea." Except I'd had enough trouble getting Ron to buy me the shoes I was already wearing. Justifying running shoes would be more difficult. I suppose I could give it a shot later.

I watched the bubbles swirl around in the filling glasses one by one before being dumped out into the sink and spiraling down the drain. Behind me I heard a chair move and looked up. Ron came inside and went upstairs. I excused myself and followed him. When I got into the room I sat down on the bed. He was pushing buttons on his phone.

"Are we gonna get on the road here?" My voice might have been a little too excited but the idea of laying around in luxurious hot springs was my idea of a good time.

"In a while." This was not what I wanted to hear. "A little while" wasn't even "in a little bit," or "in a few minutes." The word he used was while, and the idea of waiting an indeterminate amount of time didn't sit well with me. I resisted asking him if we were talking about an hour, two hours. Being

232

pushy about going somewhere to relax and waste time seemed counterproductive. But, how long was a while to Ron?

"Well, let me know when you're ready." I did my best to keep my tempo upbeat and optimistic. What I really wanted to do was grab him by the wrist and shove his watch in his face asking "When? Tell me when!"

Back downstairs Cynthia was bent over pulling out bottles of wine. Apparently, it was her day to join the rest of us in wearing khakis; maybe she felt left out. She had arranged the bottles on the counter in a perfect row with all of the labels facing forward. It looked like I had put them there. She stood back up with two more bottles and added them. I counted seven in all.

"Planning on having a really good time?"

She turned around and there was an enthusiasm in her demeanor I hadn't encountered yet. "I want to bring up some special bottles for tomorrow."

I took it to mean she was having some kind of party. It was an appropriate time for a housewarming, but I'd always been taught that the guests should bring the wine to an event like that. What did she mean bring them up? I didn't like the idea that she meant from the store. Being alone with her in a moving car with no escape did not seem like fun.

"Want to help me choose some?" Why did she want me to take part in this? She must want to get me alone. I didn't want to know what she'd have to say in private or what she'd ask out of earshot of others. My stomach became a little upset as I inhaled to answer her.

"Sure. That sounds like fun."

I walked behind her down the hallway, regretting step after step as I went. She stopped at the doorless closet that housed a number of coats. Reaching into one of the pockets I heard the jingling of keys.

She opened the door and I looked with sadness at the small sporty car that was one space down from where we had parked. The car was sleek and masculine giving it an appearance that it was still in motion. Its grey color was infused with a blue tint.

When she turned from the path I was confused. There were stones embedded into the grass in a footstep pattern that made their way along the cabin. Until now I hadn't seen them. We walked halfway down the cabin where there was something else I hadn't seen: a stairway that led to a door. The stairs were stone and were clean except where mud had splattered up on the side of them from the rain. The entire foundation was equally muddied to match.

The idea of a cabin having a basement was odd. I wanted to go back inside and find a dictionary and look up the definition of the word "cabin" so that I could debate the idea that they could label this structure as such. Although, it could have been described as a cellar. Could cabins have cellars? Was there enough of a difference between the meanings of the words "cellar" and "basement" to ensure that this cabin could remain a cabin and not be a "rustic mansion?"

The door opened into a lower level with only an eight-foot ceiling compared to the tall rooms of the main and second levels. We were in a hallway that had two doors on either side. One of the doors was different from the others and it was this one she stopped in front of. It was made of redwood and had a small square window in the top center. She unlocked and opened it. On the inside it was what I had expected. The walls were lined with straight and zigzagging racks full of hundreds of dark bottles. I'd never seen a stockpile of anything as substantial as this in any home I'd ever been in.

Inside the wine cellar, the air was dryer than it had been in the hallway and smelled sweetly of the fresh wood. I shut the door behind me since I wasn't sure if it was bad to let the outside air mix in. Three small lights along the ceiling lit the cozy, almost romantic, space. The racks were custom fitted into the space and extended from floor to ceiling, from corner to corner. There was a barrel near the end with a hole cut in the side for an internal shelf for small wine glasses of various shapes.

234

Mounted to the top was a massive metal arm reaching up. It had handles that seemed to be for the purpose of gripping bottles and a large metal lever and a spiraling metal screw at its core. She began looking through the racks as if she knew what she wanted but she couldn't remember where she'd put it.

"Do you like wine?" This was not the scary risqué discussion I was anticipating.

"I don't drink actually."

"Did you already tell me that?"

"I'm not sure. I find wine fascinating, though." I wanted her to know that I was interested in what she was saying without giving the impression of a wide-eyed grade-schooler.

"That's because good wine *is* fascinating." The implication in her words was that ordinary people drank ordinary wine. What she had was something else, something special, something more valid than an amateur had.

There were things I wanted to say. I thought it was great she'd managed to so prolifically pursue something she enjoyed, but I knew it was bad to talk life lessons with someone older. No matter how sound or heartfelt the statement would be it would seem immature.

"How long did it take you to stock this place? You just moved in didn't you?"

She let out a small laugh. "I moved the wine before I moved my clothes. I wasn't about to come up here without it. Most of what is here was just extra bottles we had at home." I better understood her priorities; alcohol came before food and clothing. People who drink wine rarely consider themselves alcoholics. They see alcoholism as something that is fermented in less sophisticated bottles. The classy beverage seemed too important to be considered as just another alcoholic beverage. Instead those who overindulged were called connoisseur or oenophiles.

Between silently reading the labels on bottles she pulled out, she elaborated on the first night she'd spent in the cabin. They'd only brought up small bags with a few pairs of clothes and a set of sheets for the bed that was the only piece of furniture they had at the time. The rest of the car was apparently filled with cases of wine. She added interesting details that made the story fun, like how none of the grass had grown in around the foundation, so carrying the cases of wine across the mud has ruined a pair of her shoes. Finally she punctuated the tale with the two of them in folding chairs, at sunset, on the small dock, drinking Dom Perignon from plastic champagne flutes.

She motioned to one of the racks where I saw a stack of what I knew were expensive bottles. She'd already set out one bottle on the barrel but the label wasn't turned towards me so I couldn't read it. Her hand was on her hip again with the palm facing out and her glasses were at her mouth. Standing like this she was elegant, thoughtful, and in control. This was her ship and she was the captain. It wouldn't have surprised me if *she'd* been the one who'd asked Harold to marry her.

"I think we'll choose the seventy-six Krug for the champagne and the fifty-four Beaulieu Pinot Noir for dinner, but I also want to bring up something else to celebrate with. You could take one or two back to the city with you if you wanted, there is plenty here. "

She handed two more bottles that took significantly less deliberation and handed them to me. I didn't even know if back to the city is where we'd be headed, but it would be nice to mail something back home. I felt guiltier for leaving my mother in the dark about where I was than I did up-and-vanishing on Hal. Before we left the room I looked at the stately labels that read "Inglenook Cabernet Sauvignon, 1948" something in me knew this detail was worth remembering.

Walking out behind her, she shut and relocked both doors. My eyes still had not adjusted to the day when we got back to the kitchen. I was little afraid I'd stupidly stumble into something or trip over Cynthia. Feeling my way with my feet and trying to look into dark corners to help me adjust, I succeeded in arriving at my destination without incident. We put

236

the bottles in the empty holes of the cabinet wine rack and it was time for something new.

My host produced a small tray of paper towels, furniture polish, and window cleaner. The two of us made our way from surface to surface wiping them down. I was starting to have a good time and, since she was with me, I didn't have the stress that she and Ron might be getting into it in another room.

I'd just finished with the countertops and was about to start the windows when I heard a knock at the door. A short, smiling, Mexican woman came in. "Hello." Her accent was quite cute. I wanted to pick her up like a little doll and pinch her cheeks. Her shoulder-length hair was pinned back and had streaks of silver. The clothes she wore were clean but plain and utilitarian. She came forward into the dwelling with cautious half-steps and hands at her sides.

"Hello, can I help you?" I didn't know what else to say.

"Mrs. Cynthia?" The formality with which she addressed the mistress of the residence revealed that she was here in a subservient capacity rather than a guest.

"Hello." Cynthia had been removing her long rubber gloves. The blue material squeaked and snapped as she did. "We'll be out of your way in a moment."

"Okay" the small woman said with an exaggerated nod.

Was this the cleaning lady? She opened a closet in the hallway, put on an apron, and by doing so answered my question. What the hell? Why were we cleaning if she had someone else to do it? Maybe it helped reinforce her delusion that she was just an ordinary housewife? If she was a housewife at all, she was a hypothetical housewife.

"We should probably get out of Maria's way." The idea crossed my mind that her name might not actually be Maria and that might just be what Cynthia wanted to call her. I wasn't sure how exactly someone could target hiring a Mexican cleaning lady. It seemed like it was a stylish thing to do and I found the practice derogatory but there was nothing *I* could do about it. Where exactly did they even go to find someone like Maria? It wasn't like there was a store where people could rent cleaning ladies from other countries, at least not in the world I lived in.

A mix of feelings had me off balance about the situation. It was probably wrong of me to assume that she was Mexican. I should have known better from the guys I'd worked alongside in the Marines. We'd discussed before the unfair way that everything from of Texas to Antarctica is lumped together as Latin Culture; we further defined this culture as one of sex. I didn't know if that made it any better or any worse, but I too was guilty of stereotyping people this way. My opinion of stereotypes varied, depending on the case. Systematic categorization is a mechanism that facilitates like humans to find other like humans. It seemed more a form of cultural coping than of cultural discrimination.

"We're going to take out the boat today, would you like to come?" Cynthia asked Ron.

"What boat?" More and more evidence was piling up that Ron and Cynthia were just a brother and sister that always spoke rudely to the other. I agreed with Ron's question though, I hadn't seen or heard anything about their having a boat. The small dock at the water's edge was large enough to accommodate one, but there was not one there.

"Svetlana and Dad got us a boat as a housewarming present." Admittedly this was a better gift than a bottle of wine. Apparently that must be what to give someone who already has plenty of wine in their cellar. I wasn't sure who Svetlana was but it didn't seem like the right time to ask.

"We're taking off here actually." I felt like a puppy whose master had just asked him "Wanna go outside!? Outside!?" but I held all my tail wagging and barking inside.

"You should join us for a late lunch."

"I'm sure we'll be busy." I don't think it was my fault that my jaw dropped open a little when he said this, but I quickly closed it.

"Well you came all the way up here; you could at least have lunch with us, Ron."

He gave a huff and went inside leaving me standing there under the scrutiny of a confused Harold and an annoyed Cynthia. Again I was at a loss of what I should do, so I shrugged and went after him. I wasn't overly enthusiastic about her company either, but lunch didn't seem to be that big of a deal.

Ron was waiting by the front door and was ready to leave. It wasn't until we'd actually reached the car that I realized I didn't have the keys. Now it was Ron who was looking at me annoyed. He told me to hurry and I ran back inside, up the stairs, grabbed the keys out of yesterday's pants, and back downstairs.

"Brad, just a minute." Cynthia stopped me. "Thank you so much for helping out earlier." What at first I thought was a handshake wasn't. She pressed three twenty-dollar bills into my hand. I was mortified.

"Thank you. You didn't have to."

"Oh please, you've been such a help." She beamed at me, as if she had not just insulted me.

With a simple gesture she'd made it clear she looked at me as no more than hired help. I wanted to punch her in the face and spit on her. Instead, I took the money and headed back to the car. As far as I was concerned, the truce between us was over.

***

24

IN SEARCH OF HOT WATER

I was either too mad or too embarrassed to tell Ron that Cynthia had given me money. The anger made me drive more aggressively, and my hands squeezed down on the wheel as if I was ready to rip it out of the dashboard. I didn't want to let her get to me and not enjoy the hot springs, so I focused my attention on relaxation techniques. I started by loosening my shoulders with a couple circles in my seat. I twisted my neck to the left, to the right, and then hyper extended my fingers to loosen my death-grip on the steering wheel. After a good deep breath, I threw a big fake smile on and started to sing cadence in my head. "Left, left, left, right, left; in the early morning rain; that is where I like to train…" I'm sure I could have talked to a psychologist and found out exactly what emotional mechanism I tripped by singing these cadences, but I didn't want to take the mystery out of it.

"I didn't know there were any hot springs up here."

"Not many people do."

The exclusivity of the places Ron frequented made them even more mouth watering. Tinsley Island hadn't been so over the top that the walkways were paved in gold; it was that only the royalty of America were allowed to walk them. I knew this was superficial but I didn't care. It still felt exciting and cool. I was so wound up about our destination that even the prospect of an hour-long journey to the sounds of jazz trumpets and saxophones didn't bother me. I looked at it this way: I'd lived through worse, in the barracks every day I woke up and came home to the same songs by Sublime and AC/DC.

We turned right and headed up the eastern side of the lake. I'd never been there before and had a mild curiosity if it would be somehow different. The area around us quickly became filled with commercial and residential buildings. We entered a small business area even before we'd seen the lake. We headed straight toward it until there was a sharp turn. The car swerved when we caught the full gust of the wind. This was another surprising nuance of driving.

"Where are we?"

"South Tahoe" I'd never actually heard of the place but the evidence suggested that it did exist. Everything seemed to be exaggeratedly patriotic with more than the normal number of flags and red, white, and blue bunting but, given the generally republican feel of the area, this made sense. After passing through what I could have called a downtown there was a large sign on the side of the road, welcoming us to Nevada. Right after it I could see the Eldorado Casino rising into the sky in all its glory. Gambling was one of those pastimes that I just didn't get. I would have almost thought Ron would be the type to frequent the roulette tables, but he was too apathetic towards money to get excited about winning big.

We passed through the city with little fanfare and continued on the road up north. I kept the fact that I was hungry to myself until I was sure we were far away from anywhere with a drive through.

"Are you hungry?" I wish I'd thought of a more clever way to bring it up, but this was all I had at the moment.

"There's a spot up here." A "spot" sounded more like somewhere that would cook food that didn't come prepackaged. Just about anything would be an improvement on yesterday's lunch. Being that it was already past lunchtime I guessed that we didn't stay for lunch at the cabin because he wanted to get away from Cynthia.

When we stopped, it was in a parking lot outside a brown building with a steep roof and a stone fireplace that ran up the center of the wall. The windows had shutters with dark green trim and there was a gated-off seating area outside, busy with the clamor of customers eating.

Inside it was clean with wooden tables and thick-legged wooden chairs. The beautiful stones of the fireplace were sadly covered over with a smooth layer of concrete. It was actually a little crowded with not much room between tables. The windows went all the way down the room with a row of smaller windows that were open on top letting the breeze inside.

"Hello, darlins, how I can help you today?" The woman's hair was a little disheveled and her face was worn from long days of smiling for tips. She stood in front of us with her hands folded across her chest, holding menus. She had on an apron that was mostly free of stains and her hands were decorated with gaudy gold rings with colored stones.

"Two for lunch."

Her walk was active and she led us through the dining room. She sat us down next to a window and set menus in front us.

"Just let me know when you folks are ready."

"Thank you very much, ma'am." I did my best to be polite to let her know I appreciated her perky gusto. The lunch portion of the menu was filled with a variety of actually quite appealing sandwich options. Scanning over the descriptions, I checked the variety of cheeses they had and discovered they were plentiful. She returned to our table not long after both of us had set down or menus and she set glasses of water with lemon on napkins in front of us. She asked us if we were the ones who came in off the boat and I looked out the window. Down where the parking lot met the water was a dock with a few boats parked at it. Boats, yet again; no wonder Ron knew about the place. It wasn't even necessary to drive a car to get here, there was water-front parking. He ordered a steak sandwich and I eagerly brokered a special grilled cheese with Colby, Swiss, and Muenster on multi-grain bread. Ron cocked his head a little to the side, which I anticipated and mocked by doing the same. She walked off, and with my hands on my hips I leaned back in my chair smiling.

With Ron's attention out the window I looked around a little more. There were old photographs in wooden frames on the walls. The scenes they revealed were, I assumed, of historical Tahoe. Pictures of a lake with higher waters and no casinos; a time before ski lodges brought traffic and disrupted the tranquility of the mountains.

I'd finished half of my sandwich before I'd thought to slow down and taste it. So far, I'd been good, I felt, at watching how quickly I ate. Usually time was a precious resource in the chow hall and I didn't waste it actually tasting what I put in my mouth. Eating slowly and taking breaths and drinks between bites, I let Ron catch up to me. I don't know why I was trying to be so considerate when Ron had started and finished eating before me at every meal we'd had together. It just felt right, and waiting for him was something that didn't bother me. The Marines had cultivated in me that I should lead by example, which I translated into *live* by example. I tried to impress this idea upon other young and impressionable Marines I'd run into without trying to sound patronizing. Partly I did this because it made me feel like I was helping them; the other part of me was doing it because it was the only way I felt like I outranked someone.

Ron spoke up when I was nearly done and suggested I have a milk shake. At first I thought he was mocking my being young but then he elaborated that they were especially good here and was going to get one himself. It was one of the best suggestions he'd made the whole trip. Sitting in front of the window that looked out over the blue waters of Lake Tahoe, I wondered if anyone would have ever guessed the two of us would be here together. We were in many ways oddly matched, but we were also not so bad of a fit.

When we did finish, the check was paid with the same familiar credit card in the same manner where I never saw the total. Once he'd put ink on the receipt I said my last "thank you very much" to the waitress and we were back in the car.

Not far to the north, the road divided and the northbound lane passed through a tunnel in a tall needle of jagged rock. It was spectacular and menacing. There was an interesting metaphor passing through the dark hole in the monolithic stone. Would the risk of the danger and the mystery of the blackness prove to be worth it when we would get to the other side?

"I'm having a good time." Ron's usual lack of response brought my awareness to the rushing sound of the tires on the pavement. "I think I accidentally pissed your sister off last night." Again, this was a statement more than a question, so it didn't really require a response on his part. I was starting to wonder if Cynthia was the reason I had been brought here. Maybe he knew that bringing me would piss her off. I wasn't sure if I liked the idea of being used like this but I recognized the effective statement my presence was.

Ron puffed out half a laugh. "I asked about why she hadn't learned to cook. Are you sure she hasn't put two and two together about..." I paused here to throw a glance at him, "...who exactly I am." This was based partly on my assumption of the answer that I was anything to him. It was his sister after all and I wasn't in much of a position to argue about her feelings. He clearly knew her better than I did, or at least he thought he did. Still, he said nothing.

We'd been driving so long I was getting the impression we were taking the long way around. The road had moved far enough away from the lake that the blue color was no longer displayed on the navigation system.

We were developing a pretty comfortable routine of drive, stop, drive, and stop. It felt like we were in a transient state, but weren't really headed anywhere in particular. Even the road was nonchalant, meandering back and forth through the trees more than it had on the western side. It too felt like it was in less of a hurry to get to its destination.

Driving the highways of Oahu, I always got the sensation that I was on a road that was on the outside of something. Here there were the mountains on one side and water on the other but I was instead on the inside.

"How far is it?"

He explained that there was a peninsula that extended southward from the northern shore of the lake. He had friends who lived near there and we would park at their place and walk. This confused me a little. I'd gotten the impression that we were headed to an established location. This made it sound like it was a hidden phenomenon, which was dispelling the idea that someone would be bringing me my glass of milk while I reclined in the warm natural waters with a towel over my eyes. The idea also occurred to me that unless we were planning to be exhibitionists, a possibility I was not opposed to, we'd need to get something we could get wet in.

"I just realized we don't have any swimwear." There was a look of discouragement on Ron's face that I couldn't quite pin down. He was upset in having not properly planned, having to spend more money on me, or having to spend money in general. For someone with so much money, he certainly didn't like to think about it or use it much. This was a personality trait of someone who lived in a family and society where flaunting money was not necessary. Ostentatious displays of wealth were in bad taste.

We would have to overshoot our destination and head into Tahoe City for a little shopping. It was my opportunity to be bold and enact my plan I'd been formulating.

246

"You know, I could use a pair of running shoes too. I'll have to get some exercise if you want me to keep this body you like so much." I smiled out of one side of my mouth and bit my lower lip with the other. He looked at me considering if he felt that my request was unreasonable.

"We'll see." This was more difficult to handle than his usual responses. It was quite clever actually. He had neither said yes or no. He'd given me a maybe and that, was much more difficult to argue with. I wasn't satisfied.

"You know, as long as you're buying me stuff, there's this great men's ring that Tiffany's sells." When I had originally thought of this plan it seemed better than it did when I said it. I'd played out that I wanted to ask for something expensive, and jewelry (which I really didn't wear much of besides my dog tags) seemed the logical choice. The fault I suddenly became aware of was that I was asking him for a ring; an item that carried symbolism that I was not going for.

"Why would you want something from Tiffany's?" The fact that he didn't say no took a back seat to my mental scrambling to escape from my accidental implication.

"I've always liked the quality of the stuff they have." This was getting worse by the moment. Anything I might say about the Tiffany & Co would undoubtedly cause the silver image of my masculinity to tarnish in Ron's mind; not to mention that I'd just referred to the inventory of the most respected jewelry company in the world as "stuff." I was glad that he didn't respond but the toxic aftermath of my well-planned test lingered in the air like smoke over a battlefield. The stench of it nauseated me. I didn't know if I'd pushed Ron too far. The funny thing about people's limits is that once I'd crossed them the line became blurred, harder to approach, more sensitive, and closer than it had originally been. It wasn't like he hadn't provoked me into asking this question though. He'd invited *me* into this situation. Isn't this what he wanted, me to be dependent on him?

That I hadn't even considered the money disparity between us had no bearing on his spending time with me in his mind, made me feel like a rotten person. The plight of our relationship was beginning to come into focus. If he liked me for who I was, it was difficult for him to express emotionally. If I liked him for who he was it would prove even more difficult with the fog of money in the way. It was now my intention to sit as still as possible and draw as little attention to myself for as long as I could stand it.

My driving trance ended when the frequency of buildings we passed increased. I assumed this meant we were approaching town. My joints ached from motionlessness, but I dreaded getting out of the car to shop with Ron after what had happened. I hadn't realized how dry my lips had gotten so I ran my tongue across the sticky dry surface. My resolve of motionlessness also included silence so I would continue to drive until he said something. It wasn't all that long before he did. When the car actually came to a halt in the space, I was tempted to let him just go in by himself and pick something out. When he hesitated outside his door waiting for me and stretching out his legs, I understood that it was expected that I join him.

The first pair of plain blue shorts I found in my size I pulled off the rack. Ron seemed relaxed and was perusing not just the shorts but also everything else they had. While he was flipping through a rack of sports jerseys I remembered that Ron hadn't had anything to drink yet today; in fact this was the longest I'd seen him sober. A smile came across my face but I corrected it when I recalled that I had put myself in the doghouse for my tactless request. Then again, why shouldn't I cheer up? This was self-imposed punishment and time with Ron might be short. Just like that, I'd had my time-out.

I left the store with a new pair of shorts and Ron left with two, another polo shirt (minus yacht club logo), and one of those squishy stress balls. This was cute, I thought: finally an admission that Ron was stressed out too. That he had revealed a moment of vulnerability to me I championed. I wanted to give

248

him a big hug. When we got into the car I put it in reverse and he handed the stress ball to me. He smiled and I wanted to give him an even bigger hug. Pulling out of the parking lot I steered with one hand and did my best to crush the poor little squishy sack as well as I could with the other.

My excitement was somewhat renewed as we were finally traveling towards luxury and relaxation. There were still a lot of unanswered questions about where we were going. I didn't know who these friends were and I didn't know exactly what the springs would be like.

I'd been to a hot spring once before, but it had been when I was too young to have the slightest interest in relaxing. What I remembered I remembered vividly. I remember bashfully changing into my swimsuit in a large concrete locker-room full of steam. The lockers were double my height and painted white; rust reddened the edges of the metal grating. Everything in the room dwarfed me in a way that made me aware of being so small. In the center of the next room there were stairs that descended into the source of the hazy humidity. There was something about being indoors and stepping into water so hot it almost scalded. One foot at a time I dipped my toes in, afraid that it would be cold like other pools I'd been in. I'd never been much of a fan of the cold. Heat was better. Ahead of me was a curtain that dipped into the water and it was slightly darkened and mildewed. The sunlight outside filtered underneath it making the water glow blue; casting dreamy ghosts on the walls. The smell in the air was metallic and once I was in up to my head, I learned the smell matched the taste of the water. The sensation of the water was like being loved from every side. I felt like a prince; all the inferiority and insecurities soaked out of my body. The pain of the water so hot that it reddened my skin was nothing in comparison.

It was interesting to learn how different parking lots actually felt. The size of the spaces, widths of the aisles, speed bumps, the landscaping, and any curves or hills all differentiated them. Pulling through the condos where his friends lived, we came to one of the nicer parking lots I'd been in. It curved to the contours of the land and there was plenty of room. The area was nice and well taken care of, like every other place we'd been to so far. What did Ron's friends know about him? Were we visiting more gay friends of his? I thought not, since I was still a little in shock he was even friends with Robert and Richard.

Inside the car we changed into our trunks, which was a lot more difficult on the driver's side with the steering wheel in the way. Ron had great legs and I couldn't help but sneak a peek at him while he swapped out bottoms.

With me at his side, we walked up to one of the buildings. There was a heavy smell of burning pine that wafted through the neighborhood. At the path up to the door he stopped. He seemed lost. He looked up and down the row, verifying from past visits that he was in the right spot and then marched up to the door. With a strong hand he knocked. I wondered if he always showed up unannounced at his friend's doors. The expression on his face let me know he was a little excited to see how they'd react. Everyone we'd seen so far, excluding his sister, was generally cheerful and glad to see him. No sound came from inside so he knocked again. When there continued to be no response he pinched his mouth in mild disappointment.

"Not home?"

He looked down the road and cut across the grass to head down hill in the direction of the lake. This was the second time we'd cut across the grass and I still felt uneasy about it, I looked out of the corner of my eye for any bystanders that might recognize my haircut and shame me. I continued to follow him down a sandy path that went along some tennis courts. In front of me I could see the blue lake that filled up the entire view. Once at the end of the path we went down a short set of stairs and it was my turn to make a face of disappointment.

There were several concrete structures full of steaming water. The insides were covered in a growth of orange and green algae and they were all topped with rusting metal grates. A walkway extended out to them and the ground was rock that

250

once had been underwater. There was a large triangle seawall of piled stones that enclosed the area. It appeared the stress ball was the only relaxation I was getting any time soon.

"That sucks."

"This doesn't look like that much fun." I couldn't help it, the day had been too much so far, and I started to laugh out loud.

"They've been having a drought up here for a while and the water level has gone down." He further explained that the cold water from the lake was five feet higher the last time he'd been here and splashed over into the pools of hot water regulating the temperature. Wooden seats were lowered in just below the water level to make natural hot tubs. Legend had it that when the lake receded a drunken man had strolled down here and decided to take a dip, boiling himself alive. After that they had covered them with these industrial grates for safety. Ron had assumed that they'd solved the problem in some way and we'd be able to enjoy them. Today, we were not that lucky it seemed.

"So, I guess we won't need our bathing suits?" Laughter came out of my mouth again.

"Alright, ass."

He headed back up the stairs and down shore along the tennis courts. I ran up behind him. "It could be worse: we could have forgotten the shorts and run down here naked to find out they've been sealed off for the last decade."

As he went he calmed down and slowed his pace. I tried to match my steps to his as I did when walking with almost anyone. Marines were to always walk in step, it had a meditative quality; it also made it easy to pick us out walking down city streets.

We turned out onto a broad dock and started to walk down it out into the lake. I had always loved going down to Waikiki at night, going out on the surf break, and looking back on the sparkling lights of the hotels that grew out of the beach.

"Did you always not get along with your sister?" The question felt relevant to both of us.

"She used to knock the crap out of me as a kid."

"Really?" As an only child, sibling rivalry always had been incomprehensible.

"She'd beat me pretty good. She was older. There wasn't anything I could do about it." Maybe having a common enemy in her strengthened the bond between us.

"That really sucks. Guess I have another reason not to like her." I nudged him trying to knock him off balance. The immaturity of the act fit the conversation perfectly. "What happened between you and your ex?" This also seemed relevant.

"We just had several differences of opinion." I scanned his words for tones of bitterness. He seemed hurt but not angry. The sun was starting to set and we were alone at the end of the pier looking back out on the mountains that boxed us in on all sides. I walked up to Ron and put my hand on the back of his head touching his hair. He backed up and looked around a little but I stepped right on forward to continue to close the gap between us.

"If anyone you know sees us out here, hundreds of miles from where you live, in the middle of Lake Tahoe, they deserve to catch us." I leaned forward, hovered right in front of his face. "Have you ever kissed before outside in the daylight?" When he shook his head I leaned in and kissed him. His lips were not hard like they'd been, and his hand gently touched the back of my stubbly haircut.

It was brief but didn't feel cut short. We were standing in the sunset; the best time to see the color of someone's eyes. I'd taken too long before to notice Ron's but I paid close attention to the way the looked at me now. In this moment they were emboldened by the sunset and focused directly on mine. And, they were happy.

Since leaving the cabin we'd been in search of, up to the edge of, I'd gotten myself into and was assuredly now out of hot water. There are some moments that deserve to happen during a sunset at the end of a pier. This was one of them.

***

25

THE WARM-UP

Opening the door to the car I debated whether the risk of being caught naked from the waist down was greater than the discomfort of contorting myself to get my shorts on in the driver's seat. The choice was easy and in seconds my shorts were on the pavement and a draft came up between my legs. Ron, who was already buttoning up, chuckled.

"It would have been easier to climb in the back." When he told me this, I felt a little dim not having realized that I had other options that didn't involve public nudity.

The temperature was already starting to drop and I was glad to finally be dressed and back in the car. I felt my outfit had gone a little wasted since we'd spent most of the day in the car again. Ron suggested a restaurant in Tahoe City; I said it would be fine. It felt good that he brought up food this time instead of me nagging him about being hungry. He flipped open his phone and spoke to what must have been the restaurant, telling them that we were about thirty-five minutes away and asking if they could squeeze us in. This meant that we where we were headed likely required reservations and we were going to have a proper meal prepared for us.

We'd completely gone past anything that bore resemblance to the city when we turned onto the highway that went to a town named Truckee. I was hoping that we were not going to go that far before we could eat. It's funny that when ambiguously hungry and eating is an idea that I knew I would get around to eventually, I'm not overly worried about eating. When I had a fixed time that I planned to eat, it was different. I would watch the minutes go by on the clock and when the alarm goes off I expect to have the first bite already being chewed. We'd been en route for thirty-seven minutes and I was already aggravated. Finally, in what could only be described as the middle of nowhere, we pulled into the parking lot of the restaurant off the highway.

Once inside, we were greeted by The Pfeifer House's maitre d', an older, thin, flamboyantly homosexual man. He looked at the two of us the same way I was eyeballing the entrees on people's tables. He guided us and sat us far away from where anyone else was sitting. The plates that had already been served were beautifully decorated with meals designed to be as satisfying to observe as to eat. I enjoyed the compartmentalized service: one person to seat me, one to bring water, another to wait on me, and even more to bring and clear the plates. It was the treatment I expected royalty to get every morning as they got dressed.

"You gentlemen enjoy your evening." There was something in his voice that indicated that he thought he was clever or had "figured us out." It made me want to trip him as he walked away; just to knock some sense and tact into him, but I did nothing.

I wiggled in my seat and grinned. The setting was downright romantic. The floors were dark and wooden, matching the beams that crossed the ceiling. White plaster walls wrapped around broken by windows in deep archways and dressed with long, gold, patterned curtains. The tables were covered with low-hanging thick white cloth. One wall had a heavily mantled fireplace displaying an assortment of apples and other fruits. Plates, murals, and stenciling decorated the walls and there were flowerpots mounted to the sides of the windows. The fragrance of rich Mediterranean food drifted through the air, warming the room and making my mouth water. I took the green cloth napkin off my plate and laid it across my right leg.

Our waiter approached the table. "Welcome to The Pfeifer House. Can I get you gentleman the wine list or anything else to drink?" Like any good waiter he made intense, direct eye contact. He was about eighteen with short gelled up dark hair, dark eyes, a sharp jaw, and a cleft chin. Although young, he was beautiful. I straightened up in my chair to let the shirt stretch across my chest and become a little more revealing. We were dueling peacocks spreading our feathers, only it wasn't Ron's attention he was trying to get. His eyes never broke with mine while Ron ordered a scotch on the rocks. Arching my eyebrows in intrigue, I ordered a tumbler of pineapple juice on the rocks. Waiters flirt to make their day more interesting. It's a game. It also makes them feel like at any moment they could be rescued from the job, that they'll be discovered and give purpose to having endured the occupation. With my date's nose in his menu, Ron never noticed our unspoken interaction.

When he walked away, I rethought my actions. The rudeness of them came over me harshly. Ron had been nothing but civil and almost considerate to me all day. Why was I repaying him by lusting after the waiter at the most romantic dinner we'd yet had? I resolved to concentrate on Ron for the rest of the night and do my best to block out the distraction of our server.

The table was too wide for me to reach my hand under to hold Ron's, which was too bad. The tablecloths were long, and no one would be the wiser. My engine was getting hotter, but I'd not been given a green light yet. Before too long we had our drinks. Pineapple juice always tastes more authentic in Hawaii, even when it comes from the same can. We placed orders for

Caesar salads and I requested a glass of water for each of us, which he again brought back almost immediately.

Since I know how to cook, eating off a menu is often a letdown. However, I generally seek out the chef, thus I am typically only limited by the available ingredients and his imagination. In my experience, getting the chef's attention was not exceedingly difficult. Someone who is passionate about preparing food, quickly becomes bored with manufacturing the same dishes every day. For this reason, most restaurants worth spending money at have a selection that frequently changes. Still, a chance to be different, even for one person, and enjoy the culinary art, can make the week bearable for a chef.

Ron ordered a filet, a boring and obvious choice. I decided to go outside the printed lines. Explaining that I was a vegetarian I asked if he could ask the chef and make something that was warm and filling. My only influence over his decision was that I liked pasta, and I liked cheese.

"I'll speak to Chef Franz and see what he can do."

I thought I'd handled the situation quite well. With a smile of satisfaction I took a drink of my water. I continued to smile at the appropriateness of Mediterranean food being prepared by a man named Franz. Someone with that kind of name was almost required to be artistic; it's difficult to picture a tax-accountant named Franz. My smile fell off my face when I tasted the tap water. Tap water, like coffee and beer, is another beverage that is an acquired taste. I had to drink the same water for months before my palette adjusted to the level of minerals and chlorine. When the waiter came back to confirm that my request would not be a problem I asked him to bring me some bottled water.

"Sparkling?" I had no idea what he meant, but it sounded good at the time.

"Yes, thank you." When I tasted the carbonated water he brought back, I wanted to spit it out and change my mind, but it was too late.

Ron ordered his second drink when we started our salads. The dressing was excellent and had a bite that was almost too much for my sensitivity to spicy foods. He ordered his third drink when the meal came.

While Ron's steak was served beautifully with a zigzagging line of thick, brownish-purple sauce and a sculpted side of rosemary mashed potatoes with peony petals topping it. Mine was miraculous. In front of me was a large round plate with a braid of angel hair pasta coated lightly in a butter lemon sauce. In the center was a whole red pepper with the top sliced off and propped open like a lid by a twig of rosemary. Tiny slices of lemon went half way around the bottom of the pepper and, on the other side, the slices went around the edge of the plate. Inside the pepper were mushrooms, broccoli, and other vegetables cooked between layers of baked cheeses. To say I was impressed would have been an understatement; I was flabbergasted.

After I'd groaned through half of the pepper, a man I assumed was the chef came out to the table and bowed slightly. Instinctively from Hawaii, I put my hands at my side and returned the honor. On the island, certain Japanese customs were so commonplace they were almost compulsive.

"Truly remarkable, sir. Thank you. You've exceeded any expectation I could have had."

The smile on his face was gigantic. I knew he'd enjoyed creating it as much as I had eating it. "I'm glad you enjoyed it." He bowed again and returned to the kitchen. This was the first great meal of my new life.

By the time dessert came around, I'd lost count of how many drinks Ron had put away, but I was having too much of a good time to care. The artistry of the deserts would be my indulgence, so Ron should be able enjoy his too. He hadn't really spoken through the meal and I'd been too involved to notice really. The thought that was most prevalent in my head was the look in his eyes after we kissed under the setting sun. It made me rethink why I was really here. Maybe Ron was interested in me.

He'd been warming up to me all day. Maybe he had brought me here for reasons beyond pissing off his sister.

Ron covered the check, a given. I was curious, having seen the prices on the menu, how much we'd really spent, but knew that it would have been inappropriate to ask. We walked back into the cold night and headed to the car. I'd started to consider the silver SUV as home base for us, and the visits, the stops, and the yacht clubs were only brief deployments. The moment felt like I could have even held his hand, but I didn't want to ruin it with the possibility of rejection. My belly was full, the day was going smoothly, and I was starting to identify myself as potentially Ron's boyfriend.

My moment of clarity came to a close when from the passenger side he directed us back north in the direction of Tahoe City.

"I don't want to go back yet. Let's go out."

That Ron didn't want to go home yet didn't bother me; nor did it faze me that he wanted to go out. It was where he pointed that worried me. The building at the end of his pointing finger was a local tavern. It was one of those local places, where everyone knows everyone else's name, and visitors are few and far between. I was somewhat of a connoisseur of bars, and I generally avoided these if at all possible.

The wind blew into the car and I wished again that I had a coat. Ron, on the other hand didn't; with the kindling of all the scotch in him, he was already warm from the inside.

***

26

GRAVITY

We opened the door of the bar. I didn't know what it was called since there was no noticeable signage outside or on the door. An audience of faces turned to see who was coming in. There is a distinctly different weight to the air of a straight bar. They are usually brighter and the lights more yellowed and less flattering. People organize into clusters that face away from one another and there are few times when they can cross gazes without instigating conflict. The differences were quite subtle, and would've been almost unnoticeable if I hadn't spent significant amounts in both types.

I didn't like to be in straight bars very much. Not because I wanted to alienate myself from heterosexuals. It was because of the hostile mood that slowed the air like honey. If cooking and chores were Cynthia's version of slumming, this must have been Ron's; drinking with the working class must have been some sort of getaway for him.

The bar fit my expectations of a local dive bar. The walls were dirty with smoke. There were mismatched posters of

Marilyn Monroe and Budweiser girls that alternated between cheap-looking neon signs. The drop ceiling had been stained yellow from years of tobacco and was splotched with darker spots from where the roof had leaked.

The pool table hosted a game between a young man with a shaved head and an older man with a ponytail. Next to the jukebox were two guys poking at the glass choosing selections of the noisy rock music that flowed out it and along the floor. In nicer bars, sounds of the music seemed to rain from the ceiling. In bars like this, it sounded like it came from my feet.

The balls on the table made a loud crack and I walked behind Ron up to the bar where he plopped down in a stool.

"Are we going to stay here long?" I whispered into Ron's ear but not so closely that it looked suspect. He turned to me blissfully drunk and cocked his head a little to the side. The bartender walked over to us. He was rough and looked drained as if the life had been sucked out through his sunburned ears, leaving his face hollowed and depressed. His belly hung over his belt and his shirt was spotted with spilt drinks.

"Captain and Coke." He knocked on the bar and bounced a little in his seat like a boy ordering a milkshake, anxious for the yummy goodness.

"And for you?"

"A glass of milk please." I thought about not ordering it. But, I didn't care about blending in here. Blending was a moot point since ours were the only four legs in the place not sheathed in denim.

"You got ID?"

"For milk?" I asked shooting back my best *"are you nuts?"* look.

"Oh shit, you're right. Never mind."

He was fast at serving us our drinks. Before I set mine down I shook some salt out onto my napkin. I did the same to Ron's while he took the first gulp of his drink. He really could just sit at the bar and stare at the wall of bottles with pour-tops and be perfectly content. Being as stir crazy as I was, and

260

uncomfortable, this was a point of view I could fake but didn't really get.

"What's your name buddy?" My thoughts now were along the line of "here we go again." I wondered if he still remembered the names of the cab driver and his children from the night we met.

"Ron." The bartender seemed uneasy answering this. From the location and patrons he probably didn't get asked much. It was likely everyone here was on a first name basis with one another.

"No shit! Me too!"

"No kidding." This was the bartender's way of saying "like I give a shit."

Ron's head was bobbing to the bashing noises that were supposed to be the drum beat of the music. If he didn't object to this music, what was so wrong with what I had tried to listen to? I guess I'd already considered the idea that he didn't want to listen to it simply because I did.

"I'm gonna use the head."

"What?"

"The bathroom. I'm going to the bathroom. I'll be right back." It was a little odd that he spent so much time around boats and didn't even know the basic Navy term for bathroom. Maybe it was only odd to me since I was more than familiar with Navy terms.

There are differences, beyond the air quality, between gay and straight bars. In a gay bar whenever I went to get anything I took the longest possible route to get there; even if I was sitting at the bar, it wasn't uncommon to walk to the other side of the bar to order my drink. Doing this ensured that the maximum number of people would get to check me out. This time I took the straightest path I could to get to the bathroom keeping my eyes on the floor.

On the way, my distractible nature got the best of me. A woman with thin dyed hair and grey roots blocked my path. She turned around, thick smoke fuming from the caked-on lipstick-covered hole in her face. In her arms she cradled a shaking Chihuahua puppy in a blue baby blanket. Two heavy-bellied men sat near her on barstools and looked at me in judgment.

"Can you say hi?" The woman said with a voice that had been carved into a gravely sound from hundreds of packs of cigarettes. She had too much eyeliner on and it had clumped on her eyelashes. I decided instantly she was either a Tammy or a Suzy. Her face ran deep with an intricate network of wrinkles, but her most notable feature was the tall curling thin dyed hair.

"Oh, what a little cutie." I responded and then flashed a look up at the two men, they still looked at me and I wondered if my response was too feminine, if I'd turned my voice up too high, or if baby talk somehow lay outside the bounds of gendered speech.

The defenseless dog stared back without blinking as the cascade of grey clouds plummeted from the wrinkly woman who held it. It was irresistibly cute the way its eyes were too big for its head, and it was sad to see the innocent animal's ears and paws trembling through the shifting waves of cigarette smoke. I reached out and stroked the silky hair on the top of its head. The men were still looking at me and I raced to find some joke that I could make that might negate any orientation cues I'd dropped a moment ago. As I scrambled in my mind and scratched the puppy's ears it occurred to me that maybe too much attention, too long of lingering over the trapped animal in the baby blanket was a tell itself. I started to move on but before I did I needed to say something.

"Isn't it funny how a little creature like that turns you into a baby-talking idiot?" I faked a laugh and moved away. It seemed important that I not look back for a response. At the end of the bar, I found the door with the half-destroyed black and gold sign to the men's room.

Opening the door I heard the sounds of someone in the stall. The sink and urinals were stained and there was a matching orange smear on the floor under the urinal. At least in McDonald's the sink would have been clean enough for me to navigate around the yuck; in this place there was no way out; I was trapped by griminess.

"I'm gonna go outside for some air." These words were my first to Ron when I came back. I wanted to be away from the situation and the bar entirely.

"Relax. Have a drink. It'll mellow you out."

Even if I did push boundaries with Ron earlier I thought his suggestion was a lot more out of line than mine was. Maybe I was hypersensitive to it, having been nagged for years by Marines, but that he asked it in that moment, already holding a new drink, got to me a little. I'd abandoned so much of myself as I molded to fit into Ron's world, but this was part of me I would never relinquish to him. The ill feelings I had towards the popular kids in high school was actually a cover, I told myself when I thought about my decision to be dry. The fact was I hated the idea of letting go or losing control of myself; I hated the idea that people might like the intoxicated me more than the real me, and I hated the idea that I might enjoy the sensation of drunkenness too much to return to sobriety.

Looking at my glass of milk I felt sad that I had wasted it. Drinking from a glass that I hadn't had constant supervision was something I did not do. A few swallows was all I'd gotten. My nearly full glass was left to waste on the bar. I walked away from him and out the door.

Outside my ears readjusted to the quiet and I figured out that my logistics for escape were severely flawed. It was very cold. Sitting in the car wouldn't support my statement about fresh air, and really, I couldn't go anywhere even if I did get pissed off. The car was his and I didn't have anyone's phone number who lived within a thousand miles.

Why would Ron have suggested something like that? It probably wasn't a big deal to him, but it still seemed insensitive. It is a cliché to claim that people change when they acquire wealth. I didn't believe that was exactly the truth. The truth was, in my view, that they stopped being afraid of saying what they really mean. Ron had lived his whole life without the fear of consequences. Why should his treatment of me be any different? If he treated me differently, wouldn't that be dishonest? That's not what I wanted.

After what was probably five minutes, but felt like fifteen, I went back inside, hiding how badly I was shaking. Another trait of being macho is not letting the weather bother me. This meant not wearing coats or gloves in the snow, not shivering when I was freezing cold, not turning away from the wind when it was messing up my hair, and standing in the rain while it soaked through my clothes and into my shoes. I didn't feel like I was not macho, but I hated the weather. I didn't hate it to the extreme where I needed to live in San Diego, where they gave the forecast annually as sunny and cloudless.

There were two guys next to Ron who he was talking to. Neither their look nor the company looked pleasant. They wore dingy jeans, stained shirts that bulged at the midsection, and had dark, unkempt, thinning hair. Either of them could have passed for a Dale, Buddy, or a Joey—the kind of name I had seen embroidered onto a greasy mechanic's uniforms. I walked over to the jukebox and pretended to browse the selection. They weren't acting hostile but they were standing closer than people normally would even with someone they knew at a bar.

Physical proximity between men has an interesting dynamic. There was a trained discomfort in American men with being to close to other men. This insecurity added to the hostile environment of bars like this one. I'd been known to say to guys who felt this tension and didn't like it, that they should approach their closest male friend and embrace them. Hug them and just stand there with as much body contact as possible. I'd tell them they should not let go until the fear leaves them; they'd be better, more compassionate friends for it. Wrestlers and Marines had a stronger bond because the boundaries of male proximity and discomfort of male-to-male physical contact were abolished in practice and in Boot Camp.

How close someone was to someone else was only part of the equation of male conflict. Alarms went off in my head when I saw the man next to Ron looking right at him. Between men, eye contact usually has two functions, one frequently is considered part of gaydar because the other pertains to mostly to straight men: the provocation of conflict. Men who did not know one another well did not look at each other. When males walk by one another they look away; if they don't it signals one of those two possibilities: either their interest in kissing, or kicking ass.

I stood where I was. My legs were parted and my arms were crossed over my chest, head high and posture directed at Ron and his current company. The entire bar could have been orbiting around them at that moment; they were all I could see.

Dale/Buddy took another step toward Ron and was now only inches away from him. I broke my stance and marched up to them, exaggerating my height and posture like I had when I marched in my graduation ceremony.

"You ready to get home, Ron?" Dale/Buddy and Joey looked up at me with unwelcome glares, as if I'd interrupted their fun. To my surprise, Ron looked oblivious to his situation. At least he stood up and started to walk with me. He stopped, walked back to the bar interrupting the men who were earnestly talking, picked up his drink from between them, downed it, and set it down as he staggered his way back toward me and the door.

Outside I walked toward the car ahead of Ron. "Where you going, rich man?" Dale/Buddy hollered at us.

Turning around with the driver door open, I saw that both of the men had come outside behind us and a third stood up against the wall as a spectator. Ron turned around and started walking toward them, confused and annoyed by their question. I thought "No, no, no, Ron. What are you doing?"

"What?"

"I thought we were having a good time. Why you leaving on us? You said you'd buy as a round."

"I'm not buying you a round." Ron looked to his left, where no one was, and pointed at the man talking. "Can you believe this guy? Ronny!" This was an inopportune time for Ron to be having a conversation with ghosts from his childhood.

"That's not very gentlemanly." I wasn't sure, but it felt like I was witnessing a "rich-bashing."

Ron was laughing to himself and not stumbling in any particular direction as he looked at the ground. The situation to him was comical but I understood how very real it was. "Ronny! I need some service here! Ronny!"

"Come back inside. We'll all sit down and have a drink." Joey reached out and grabbed Ron by the shoulder. Some scenarios prompt me to run away and some scenarios have a gravity that pulls me into them.

"Hey!" The growling shout of the corporal inside me blasted into the air. I walked up to them with measured steps. My heart was pounding and my hands were cold and sweating. Here we go.

"I wasn't talking to you. Mind your own business you ignant son-of-a-bitch." I would have to enjoy the irony of his mispronunciation later.

"You're god-damn right you weren't talking to me." Ron looked at me, confused by the hostility of my voice. I grabbed him by the arm and started to pull him toward the car like an obstinate child.

"Excuse me?" I kept walking.

Ron laughed as I dragged him along. "What are you doing? I need some service here! Ronny!"

"What did you say to me?" I heard their footsteps coming. Ron broke loose and I turned around to face Dale/Buddy, who was steaming towards me with tight fists. His right came at me fast and I stepped to the right of it, knocking Ron over. I grabbed the man's wrist as it missed my face, and pulled him past me, pounded an elbow to his kidney and causing him to fall onto my left knee and then to the ground. He grabbed onto my shirt as he fell ripping half of it off, including one of my sleeves. My face was full of flames and I was biting down hard enough on my teeth to break them.

"Come on, mother-fucker." Joey came at me with a left. Stepping left instinctively, I grabbed him by the back of the head

266

and issued three violent blows to his abdomen with my knee. After, I threw him to the ground and kicked him in the gut as he moaned. The two men were coughing and trying to crawl away. The bystander stood frozen against the wall with his hands up at his sides indicating he didn't want any trouble.

I stood over the two men crawling away from me on the ground. The sound of denim and shoes scraping against the dirty pavement circled up into the blackness. I looked at Ron who was still on the pavement where I'd knocked him over. His eyes were so scared he would have cried if he knew how. I picked him up, walked him to the car, and got in the driver side after shutting him in. The men still hadn't stood up by the time I'd driven around the corner, casually going the speed limit.

I was still breathing heavily and I concentrated on slowing it. I stopped clenching my teeth and stretched my neck from left to right. Fighting was something else I didn't usually talk about, because people assumed I couldn't do it. That I could was hard to prove, so I kept it to myself. I took pride in having a secret talent. A skill I had learned, through trial, that I was very good at. Talking about it also seemed counter-intuitive; I was concerned about people assuming I was just another dumb grunt.

My new favorite shirt was ruined, but I'd finally gotten some exercise. My mind was moving a million miles an hour and Ron said nothing but was as far away from me as he could be and still be in the car. At least showing up this late at night we wouldn't have to explain my appearance.

I took my half of a shirt off in our room, and Ron crawled immediately into bed wearing all his clothes. I went into the bathroom. On the way I noticed that the door to the kid's room was now closed.

I flipped on the light and shut the door. Bathrooms have a way of making me feel safe and alone. I turned on the hot water. I'd been sweating the whole way and my face felt greasy. Leaning over the sink, I swung my dog tags behind me and washed my face. I dried it with someone else's towel and stared hard into my eyes in the mirror. "I'm a good person, aren't I?"

The person in the mirror didn't answer. I turned off the light and left.

It wasn't for an hour or so that enough adrenaline had left my bloodstream to let me sleep. As I fell asleep, the first time I'd ever been in a fight came into my head. Other than a pushing argument, in junior high I'd never been involved in any kind of fighting. I'd seen two wrestlers go at it in high school, falling to the ground clutching one another, their fists making deep thuds as they punched each other in the ribs. In Boot Camp I could hear everyone outside the bunker chanting "Kill, kill, kill, kill..." while they padded me up and handed me a large pugil stick. When I was finally all suited up, I ran down the tunnel out. The other recruits were gathered around. Running at me just as fast was another recruit brandishing the same weapon. My mind filled with a rage I'd never known, and my feet dug deep in the sand as I went after him. With two sharp blows to his side and then his head, I knocked him brutally to the dirt.

I awoke from my dream, panting, and I saw Ron's face only inches away from mine. His eyes were full of sadness and maybe even understanding. He leaned in and kissed me with a closed mouth, stood back up, and got back into bed. I had my answer.

***

27

THE ANSWER YES

When I sat up in bed Ron was still sleeping, so I lay back down and stared at the ceiling overhead. It felt later than usual and the bright sunlight coming in was proof that it was at least nine in the morning. I hadn't seen Ron sleep in yet. That he was now seemed odd. Looking over at him, sleeping on his side facing the wall, I couldn't tell how asleep he really was.

"Good morning." My attempt to discern if he was sleeping was inconclusive since he didn't respond. If someone was actually sleeping, there was no practical way to figure it out. Sleeping is something that one can only prove someone is not doing.

"It's wake-up time." Babytalk was easier to get away with when I was sleepy.

"Go back to sleep. We don't have to get up early today." We didn't have to get up early any of the other days either but we had. I was confused what made today any different. I wasn't sure if it was Saturday or even what day of the week it was. Without some form of institution to report to Monday through

Friday, weekends become obscure and the days of the month blend together. I supposed it might be Saturday, but for some reason it just didn't feel like it was. The air smelled like a weekday.

I turned on my side and faced my own wall. I attempted to go back to asleep. Positioning the sheet to cover my eyes from the light as best I could, I tried to get comfortable and pretend to be in the dark. Feeling quite rested, I wasn't entirely sure how possible it was that I *could* fall asleep. The heat of the sunlight that had slowly moved onto my face woke me up and proved that indeed, I could. Somehow, I was more tired than I had been when I woke up before. Looking over at Ron I was a bit disappointed to see him in the exact same position he had been in. It still wasn't time to get up? I adjusted out of the sunlight and wiped the greasy sweat off my forehead. My elbow and knee were aching for a reason I couldn't determine until I remembered what I had done.

Now that I had engaged in violence, would Ron continue to expect that from me? Did he plan on bringing this up in front of Harold and Cynthia? What would they think of the fight we'd gotten into outside the nameless bar in Tahoe City? Images of Harold's disappointment and references to Gandhi flashed through my mind. I also saw the disgusted look on Cynthia's face as she had her validation that I was a common savage. There was a level of satisfaction in her figuring me out and being able to categorize me this way. The whole situation made me feel small and ordinary. I wanted to escape but I was helpless. Where would I go even if I did run?

Waking up again another half hour or so later, I was out of places to put my face where the sun would not hit it. The sheets were warm and damp where they had been absorbing my perspiration. My whole face was now covered in warm sweat. My choice to wipe the slime off with the loose end of my pillow case I immediately regretted when I remembered I was going to have to sleep on it again later; that was, if we were still here at the end of the day. Ron was still asleep, but I was done. My body felt groggy, like a saturated sponge. My arms and legs felt a little numb and unfamiliar. My mind felt clouded and I was almost depressed. Standing for a moment over my sleeping companion, I lost the desire to be on my feet. I wanted to crawl somewhere cool and dark and sleep more.

I made the bed, put on some clothes, and tried to zip the bag back up slowly and quietly. Softly stepping out of the room, I heard no noise from anywhere else in the house. The door to Cynthia and Harold's room was closed, indicating that they were probably still asleep too. Maybe it was Saturday. They wouldn't sleep in on a Sunday; they might have been cosmetic Christians, but that still meant attending Sunday services.

I continued downstairs in search of a glass of water for my sticky mouth. The dryness of my throat made it hard to swallow. The first floor was empty and felt slightly eerie. It was the first time I'd felt alone in the place. Everything seemed to be completely still. Even the air was motionless.

The silence amplified the sounds of my pant legs rubbing against one another as I walked into the kitchen. Using only fingertips I opened a cabinet, retrieved a glass, and closed it again. Letting the tap run slowly, I filled the glass with water. The moment it hit my lips I spit it back out. I'd forgotten the terrible taste of foreign tap water. I could still taste it in my mouth. Disgusted, I got a bottle of water from the refrigerator.

I dried off the glass and put it back. I put some of the cold bottled water in my mouth and let it warm up there. I swished it around once it became tolerable to my teeth and rubbed my finger across the surface of my enamel. Spitting it out into the sink, the fizzy dirty water looked a little disgusting so I washed it down the drain. I would have brushed my teeth but brushing right before drinking water made my throat too cold and made it difficult to hydrate. But I also hated the idea of swallowing any built-up yuck that had accumulated overnight while trying to quench my thirst. The finger brushing seemed a reasonable compromise.

271

I put on my shoes and took another drink of water. Unlocking the back door, I stepped out onto the deck and into the cool morning air. Once I'd gotten past the shadow of the cabin and into the light, the illuminated parts of me warmed up. I turned my face to the sun and let the corners of my mouth curl up into a grin. When I felt energized enough, I walked off the deck through the broken shadows cast by the high canopy and down to the edge of the water. The cabin was far enough away that the soft sloshing of the lake against the embankment couldn't be heard.

Stepping onto the dock my shoes made familiar hollow sounds on the wood. I could see down the lake where the store was. It appeared much closer from this vantage in a way that was typically deceiving when looking across water. In Hawaii I'd once decided to swim out to the Mokulua Islands off Lanikai Beach. When I finally made it to the shore the sun was already setting over the Ko'olaus. I'd realized it was getting later than I'd liked much earlier, but the longer I swam the closer they seemed. I swam back in the dark, alone, through what I knew were shark-infested waters. Unable to see any coral reefs or shallow rocks, I let the tides of anger drown me: I'd been so stupid, and feared that I was quite possibly about to die. I used the negativity to propel me to the shore, leaving behind me a trail of salty tears in the salty water. The current was relentless and I ended up swimming at an angle to the beach. It was completely black when I made it onto the sand. I was shaking, kneeling gratefully on the soft sand and sobbing in the tradewinds under the indifferent stars.

The door opened up again and I turned to see who it was. Harold made the way to his chair in what appeared to be a pair of patriotic pajamas. The look was a little silly, especially on someone that seemed to take themselves so seriously.

"Good morning." He seemed to be in a good mood.

"Good morning, sir." I took note that while Cynthia had politely protested my addressing her formally, Harold never did.

Cynthia emerged from the door in a matching set of pajamas with tiny American flags patterned over the entirety of the fabric. "Good morning."

Apparently it *was* a good morning; they were chipper in a way that made me suspect that they might have "privately" worked out some of their frustration. "Good morning, ma'am." She raised her eyebrows at me. I smiled sheepishly. "Sorry. Can I help you again with breakfast?"

"Today, we'll be having a champagne brunch." She said this like everyone knew what it meant, like she'd used the term a hundred times before. I still felt out of the loop: what is a champagne brunch? Were we supposed to drink champagne instead of eat?

"I see. That sounds wonderful." I said.

"We'll wait until Ronny is up to start. Can I get you some coffee?"

"I'll get myself a glass of milk if that's alright, ma'am. Can I get either of you anything?"

Harold grunted "coffee," as a single word request without looking up from his paper, and his wife asked for some bottled water with a wedge of the lemon that she'd sliced yesterday.

"There are some pajamas upstairs for you in your room, too, if you want." They bought me pajamas? Would it be rude of me not to wear them? I thought about it and it seemed like, if they'd gone out of their way to get them for me, I didn't have much of a choice.

I fixed their drinks, brought them out, and headed back up to our room. Unfolding the pajamas that I hadn't noticed on the dresser, my heart sank as I saw they were too short. I hated that pajamas, and many other garments for that matter, came only in small, medium, large, or extra-large without accounting for people's difference of height.

Ron was up now, standing next to the bed wearing only a pair of the same pajama bottoms. He was handsome and masculine standing shirtless in the loose-fitting bottoms that went all the way to the floor on him. "Well, good morning." I used my most hushed voice in case the kids were behind the closed door to their room. He swiveled his head over toward me with a half smile and slipped on the top. I removed, refolded, and put my clothes away.

"What are we up to today?"

"Not sure. We'll play it by ear. I think Cynthia has plans for us." The implication, I figured, was that we would be spending the day with his sister. That in a moment they would both begin drinking champagne felt like foreshadowing. Ron went downstairs and I went into the bathroom to brush my teeth.

Cynthia was down in the kitchen setting out brunch ingredients on the counter and almost bouncing as she went along. I couldn't figure out why everyone was in such a good mood; clearly, I had missed something. Watching her actually brought up my mood. I wasn't much into holding grudges against people.

Her head swiveled toward me, her eyes were bright, and with her hand on her hip she raised the other in a shrug. "What should we make today? I want to do something a little more involved." Meaning she wanted *me* to do something a little more involved. Funny how those who will be eating often take ownership of the preparation; I didn't mind as long as they gave me feedback, even if it were just a contented smile or a pleasured groan.

"How about…" I knew exactly what I wanted to say, but I wanted to give the impression that it took more effort than it did. I'd actually decided from the available provisions what I was going to cook today the day before. "Let's have poached egg with cheese on English muffins, and toast with jelly."

"Oh, and fresh fruit!" She glided over to the refrigerator and produced a pineapple. The large, spiky, fruit was something I was sure wasn't there last time I'd checked.

"Have you ever cut a pineapple before?"

"I thought of you when I saw it. I figured you could show me how." Would she slip me a few twenties again? The

274

idea of getting paid to do a little of the work was a little easier to swallow over breakfast this morning.

As I brought the water to a boil on the stove and stirred in white vinegar, I relaxed into the potential of my new morning ritual. Waking up each morning, enduring coffee, making breakfast, pretending to read the paper, and engaging in endless small talk. I watched the egg turn white and spin in the water as I turned down the heat and put a lid on.

Cynthia asked the predictable questions about life in Hawaii. Did I surf? Was I afraid of volcanoes? Did I eat a lot of pineapple? Did I get island fever? They were closed-ended questions that I could have answered with: no, no, yes, no. But, I elaborated on my reasons. I didn't surf because I enjoyed being *in* the water more than *on* it (and my fear that if I tried, I'd be terrible at it). The volcanoes for the most part were extinct, though I was apprehensive about being inside Diamondhead Crater; I had quickly become comfortable with the idea that my chances of being hit by a plane falling out of the sky were better. I was quite fond of pineapples, and especially of pineapple juice. I preferred to walk around with a glass of juice rather than a bottle of water; I'd rather people thought I was getting drunk than high on Ecstasy. The crowd I ran around with was a bit wild, and I'd learned to recognize the signs of those who used recreational drugs; people who consistently hydrated instead of tipping back cocktails were generally rolling. Island fever was a tricky animal. It is true that Oahu is a confined island with a limited number of people, getting to the mainland was hard and expensive, and I couldn't just get in a car and drive to another state (unless they built a bridge from Honolulu to San Francisco); but I'd never felt confined.

I took issue with Marines or locals that would complain about feeling trapped, and how they'd see the same people everywhere. The truth was that the places they'd go to were the same places inhabited by the same people. I had a propensity to frequent a variety of different bars that were popular among different demographics. I spent plenty of time in the gay clubs, but I preferred mixing it up a little. The Marine bars, the business-casual parties, and the local pubs freshly infused every weekend with new faces and different perspectives. I could see how exclusively attending any one of these groups could quickly grow old, but it seemed more their fault than the island's.

I juggled the saucepan and the toaster as I prepared each plate, wiping cream cheese onto the crunchy browned surface, laying on a slice of mozzarella, then finishing each serving by topping it with an egg, a squeeze of lemon, and paprika. To keep them warm, I covered them with plate lids, which, I was astounded, were already part of the new cabin's inventory.

When I looked up at Cynthia, I saw her with a butcher knife in one hand preparing for a confrontation with the pineapple. I'd been so engrossed by the eggs that I'd become oblivious to her even being there. Each of them was planning their next move but neither appeared willing to be defeated. I pictured Cynthia leaping into the air, doing a flip, landing, and then spinning around chopping the fruit's head clean off, juice squirting up into the air like a decapitation in a bad horror movie. Instead she walked up to it and laid it down on its side. The pineapple cooperated since it must have understood the futility of resistance. Drawing a chopping knife from the knife block was sufficient in communicating to Cynthia that her battle plan was flawed. She backed away from the fruit and I moved into the executioner position.

After I'd killed and skinned the hostage fruit, I cleared the cutting board and dissected it into edible bites. I had to frequently remove my hands from the pulpy core. It was cold from being imprisoned overnight in the refrigerator.

Once the carnage was done, we assembled the plates and brought them to the men waiting outside in the sun with their papers. "Who wants champagne?" Her enthusiasm answered the question on her part.

"That would be nice, thank you, darling." Harold seemed happy just from seeing Cynthia happy; this was another characteristic of the interaction of long-term couples. I was happy from the contact joy. Even Ron seemed content. The table looked like an adult-sized pajama party.

I started to enjoy my breakfast and the absence of the flavor of coffee tainting the taste of my food. Everyone was already eating when four classic champagne glasses were placed on the table. Three filled with bubbling gold and one with thick white; it was an unexpected nicety from my would-be employer. When I finished my toast she was up again to fill her and her brother's glasses. I wondered how long it would be before today got really interesting.

The chit-chat continued and after Cynthia and I cleared the plates from the table. In the kitchen we continued our routine of rinsing the plates and putting them in the dishwasher; this time with increased efficiency.

"What do your parents do, Brad?"

"They are business owners." This was another question that always sounded better to answer vaguely. "They've worked hard to get where they are." I was grateful not to have to grow up with parents who worked the shame of a big corporate cult.

"Ron, you guys should pick up some soda from the store for later." She phrased it as an order.

Ron nodded as he came in from the outside, squinting in the dark as if restricting his field of view was going to make the darkness easier to navigate. The momentum of the morning was picking up and it was also getting warmer. When I'd first put on the pajamas I'd still felt cool and clean. The heat that had driven me from bed had now warmed the rest of me and my shirt felt cold and sticky where it loosely touched my skin. Fueled by this dirtiness, I excused myself and went upstairs to take a shower.

The water was already running when I was coming up the stairs, so I made a detour into the room, picked out a shirt and shorts and set them folded on the bed. Looking down at them I rearranged them into a neat and comfortable stack, but was still unsatisfied. Unfolding the shirt, I laid it out on the foot of the bed tucking the bottom underneath itself and running my hand along the edge to smooth it flat. I'd practiced the pressure required to produce an edge that was crisp and straight. Pushing too hard would cause the fabric to stretch or wrinkle, leaving an uneven or curving line. Taking the shorts, I placed them just over the shirt, but it still didn't look quite correct. Doubling my belt over, I set it across the belt loops and stood over the preview of my attire for the day. It was a clean and composed outfit; the formalities of my new clothes were not unlike the uniforms I'd been wearing, but the detail required to meet the necessary standards was not comparable. All told, I enjoyed the precision of the creases, buffing the scuffs from my Corframs, the clean gig-line, and the shirts held tucked in with shirt stays. I felt clean, handsome, and invincible walking down the street dressed as a Marine. If I couldn't continue to dress in uniform, the wardrobe Ron had bought me was an acceptable alternative.

The shower stopped just as I'd placed the shoes next to the bed where the feet of the imaginary person I'd created would have been. I grabbed my towel and I waited outside the door until Ron came out and I took my turn in the steamy bathroom.

Allowing myself a little more time to clean my face, I hurried through the rest of my list of spots to clean and turned off the water. Once I'd dried off and shaved I unmade my clothing display and headed back downstairs.

"You could at least be considerate, Ron." Cynthia stood a few feet away from him in the kitchen with the same hand in the same place turned out in the same way.

"What are you talking about?" Ron's tone was annoyed.

"Do we need to pick up anything else at the store?" Asserting my presence seemed to provide the necessary distraction to blow away the superheated air that was radiating between the two of them. In theory, Harold and I could probably manage the peace in this manner indefinitely.

"Anything you think we'll need; maybe some potato chips." The fact that she called them potato chips instead of just chips was a giveaway that she rarely purchased or ate them. Snack food culture is one of laziness, and the avid participants adopt any shortened terms that would reduce the effort of talking, to free the mouth for more eating.

"Alright." I pulled the keys out of my pocket. When they didn't make much noise I hooked my finger into the ring twisting my hand back to get them to make a little and clue Ron in on my wanting to get in the car. I put my hands on the island and we all stood in a silence that was awkward for me but didn't seem to faze them. I took in a breath but I couldn't think of anything to say, it was almost comical and I considered laughing but that didn't feel right either. The fact that the relationship between Ron and me was not up for discussion limited any comments I could make as just a friend to lure him away from his sister. Without an ounce of grace, I stepped away from the island and walked outside onto the deck.

Harold was still sitting in the same chair, his paper put down, and his arms folded across his chest. He seemed to be part of the quiet steady ambiance of the lake so I didn't feel comfortable disturbing him. I had no idea what I should do, where I should sit, whom I could talk to or what I would say. This was an out-of-place feeling that always made me feel uncomfortably useless. Ron rescued me when his footsteps came up behind me.

"Let's go." Timing my footsteps to his, we walked in step out the front door and to the car. The inside air of the car was hot and stuffy from the sun glaring down on it through a gap in the trees.

Although I'd spent a lot of time in the car already, I was starting to like being in it and look forward to where it would take us next. When I'd finished adjusting the windows and had figured out how to work the air conditioner, I noticed that Ron was looking at me.

"How are you?" I asked.

He smiled the way someone did when they had a secret but were waiting for the right time to break it.

"What?"

279

Ron looked out the window and I resigned to the fact that today was going to be full of inside jokes I was on the outside of.

"What all are we gonna get at the store?"

"Just some junk food."

I put the car in gear and pulled out of the stall. My assumption was that we would just be going down to the same local store we had stopped at before. Would Diana with her giant diamond suspect anything if she saw the two of us together on a repeated basis? I didn't really know if in Ron's world everyone was actually clueless about it or if they were ignoring the subject intentionally.

"Turn off to the right just up here." I saw the small dirt road he was talking about which must have led to another store or part of the micro-neighborhood I hadn't yet seen. That there would be more to the community than I had seen so far didn't surprise me. I looked through the brush as the road turned back and forth, trying to see if there were stores, houses, or even a school around the next bend. "Stop the car just over there." My confusion was becoming frustrating, tiring, and was getting me a little annoyed.

The car lurched forward on its shocks a little when I pulled off the main road onto the dirty clearing on the side of the road. Ron opened the door and my patience was gone. "What are we doing?" I got out and went around to the back of the car to confront him. "What the hell are we doing out here?" The idea that he wanted to spontaneously hike through the forest in my new clean clothes was another in a compiling list of irritations. He opened the back hatch of the vehicle and let the door of it swing all the way up.

"Shut up and get in." My anger deflated like a hot air balloon after landing. I couldn't contain the smile on my face and it overflowed into a bit of a giggle. I started singing cadence in my head, a little caught up in the moment. "Dedicated, motivated, to the corps, ooh rah, ooh rah." We were *definitely* going to sex have again!

"Oh yeah?" I climbed into the back of the car and he climbed in after me. "Are you serious?" He looked at me with his head cocked at an angle again; then he pulled the hatch shut. I'd asked myself a question of whether we'd ever end up having sex again on this trip; the answer was yes.

When we opened the doors to the local store I saw Diana behind the counter. If I was worried that she'd suspected we were involved, I was even more worried that she'd be able to tell from our flushed faces what we had just finished doing minutes earlier in the back of the Mercedes.

Diana smiled at us warmly.

"Welcome. Happy Fourth of July!"

I turned to Ron as if world had been playing a cruel joke on me. "It's the Fourth of July?"

***

28

PROPAGANDA

"It's the Fourth of July?" My disbelief was coupled with my being frustrated that such an obvious holiday had snuck up on me. Ron and the woman said nothing. Instead they chose to stare at me the way people do whenever someone expresses something that they consider to be given knowledge. Like exclaiming in the dairy section of the supermarket "did you know that the calories in butter come from fat?"

My discomfort forced me to make one of those "oops" type smiles that exposed my bottom teeth. I did my best to look casual as a strolled into the nearest aisle. As I walked down it, pretending to be in deep debate over charcoal or motor oil, I hoped that neither of them realized I was faking it to look busy.

I slowly made my way down the row of car products and cleaners and headed toward the coolers filled with the familiar racks of chilled soda. It occurred to me that I should get Ron to decide what to pick out and hope he didn't choose something that I hated.

"What kind of chips should we get?"

"Whatever, you choose."

"How about I grab the chips and you pick out the soda." He didn't look at me but I could see him pinch his eyebrows together and squint his eyes. To him there wasn't really any decision to be made. He'd grab whatever cola was at eye level without putting any thought into it. He wouldn't worry about whether anyone else would enjoy his selection or what I might think of his choice, even if I did have an opinion. There was a freedom to his liberated apathy towards opinions others might make about his everyday decisions. I envied his lack of worry and grabbed the first bag I saw in an attempt to emulate it.

Walking away from the rack I looked down at the crinkling bag in my hand, which read "sour cream and onions." I couldn't do it; I couldn't just say "screw it" and plop the chips on the counter. Sour cream and onions seemed to be an acquired taste, one that goes best with people who would eat bratwurst and coleslaw. That didn't seem like Harold or Cynthia. I could see Cynthia enjoying the nostalgic plainness of salty ruffled chips or thinking she's going all out by crunching down some classic barbeque flavored potato wafers. Doritos's were too MTV for her, and their variety of flavors were suited to individual palates. Cheetos were too elementary-school lunch-box, not to mention too messy for those of us worried about getting stains on our clothes. After I checked to ensure Ron was not watching, I swapped the bag out for the jumbo sized bag of plain ruffled potato chips and brought them up to the counter, setting them next to the cardboard case of Pepsi.

Ron looked down at the bag and then at me. "Aren't you going to get dip?"

"Oh, sorry, I forgot." I didn't forget, I had no idea I was also supposed to choose one. "What should I get?"

"Cynthia and I like sour cream and onion."

After I brought the pop-top can up to the counter, Diana put them into the bag with her jeweled hand and pushed the paper bag across the counter towards me.

"Thank you, ma'am."

284

"You boys be careful. Don't light yourself on fire." We left the store to the sounds of the little bell on the handle jingling.

I could still smell sex in the car when we got back inside, only now it was heated up and musty from being baked by the sun. It was a little unpleasant, and so, given that we wouldn't be driving all that fast combined with the pleasant weather, I rolled down all the windows before I backed out of the stall.

It seemed like as good a time as any to attempt to try for an escalated level of affection. I leaned onto the right hand side of my seat and steering with my left hand I put my right on his leg. He didn't move. He didn't even glance at the intimate hand placement on his thigh. It was as if he was paralyzed from the waist down and ignorant to the touch of my hand. He just continued to gaze out the window watching the trees, cabins, and the lake pass by. His arm was out the window and his short hair blew in the wind. He hadn't acknowledged it, but at least he hadn't rejected it. I called it a victory and put a trophy smile on my face.

Inside, Cynthia and Harold had gotten dressed and out of their patriotic pajamas. There was a large woven picnic basket sitting on the island with one side open. The inside was lined in the standard red-and-white-checkered fabric. She had set out in front of the basket a cheese kit complete with different instruments for cutting the blocks of varying firmness, a wine kit with corkscrew and glasses, and a set of small trays that contained pickle wraps, miniature sandwiches, and vegetables. It was all quite elaborate.

"We've got chips and soda." I wasn't sure if there would be room for them.

"Thank you so much."

I set the bag down on the counter where I assumed it would be out of the way. I saw there were more empty individualized Tupperware-like containers sitting out. "Do you want me to put the chips in these, ma'am?"

"That would be so wonderful." I popped open the bag and filled each one just high enough so that the lid would not crush them when I closed them.

"How long have you lived in Hawaii?"

"About three years now. You said you've been."

"Oh yes. We go to Maui every so often." I wondered if they ever ran into Robert and Richard there, if they too were friends or what they might say about the wealthy flamboyant couple in private.

"I've been to Maui. I love Hawaii; it's not like anywhere else I've ever been. It's like when I saw a hitchhiker on the side of the road on the mainland, the first thought in my head was, is this guy dangerous, or I wonder if he's on drugs. In Hawaii I think, I wonder if he's going my way and if I can give him a ride. People don't have to lock their doors to feel safe."

"Well, they have less crime to worry about there."

"I don't think it's just that. I think that the culture is inherently nicer. Every year there is this May Day, Lei-Day concert down at the Shell, and all over the lawn people spread out their blankets so that the edges overlap, and they eat food. I could walk up to any one there and not only would they invite me to sit with them they wouldn't think twice about giving me a plate. People just aren't like that back here." I felt like I was rambling a bit too much, that I'd gone on too long, too passionately, to leave her with any way to appropriately respond.

"We go there to relax and always have a good time." It seemed a slight change of topic but that was alright. I really didn't want to come out too anti-mainland, so it was probably better this way. That she went to Maui to relax *and* she came to Lake Tahoe to relax I found amusing. Where was she the rest of the time, that she needed so many extravagant places for downtime? To me, I still couldn't imagine that anything in her life could be all that stressful. Then Ron walked back in.

Ron opened one of the containers that protected the finger foods and pulled out a pickle wrap. He popped it into his mouth and walked into the living room without closing the container. Before Cynthia could react my hands were pushing down the lid until each side made a gentle snapping sound.

"Can I get you anything to drink?" What I had meant to say was, "can I get you some water or juice?"

"Rum and Coke," he said. I had asked, so it wasn't like I could back down now.

"I'll have a gin and tonic." Cynthia said when I was getting Ron's glass. They were either overestimating, or at least assuming I had any idea how to make these drinks. I took the gin and rum out of the cabinet and retrieved the tonic water from where I'd seen it chilling in the refrigerator.

"How much do you want in it?" I'd paid close enough attention when they'd made Ron's drink that I could fake it but hers I was lost on.

"Not too strong" She wasn't helping. I assumed then that I would attempt try the same ratio as I did with the rum and Coke.

"I'm not *that* dainty, Brad." Clearly I wasn't doing it right but I knew I'd look stupider if I started dumping the bottle in or if I went little by little checking each time for her approval. I hated admitting not knowing what I was doing but I was left without any other option.

"I really have never made one before." She sighed and came over. I felt impotent that I had offered to get drinks, at least Ron's drink, or at least *something* to drink, and I wasn't able to follow through. It was as if I had my bluff called and hadn't even known my cards were bad.

I watched her fill the glass with a nearly equal amount of gin and tonic water and realized how funny it must have appeared to drown the tiny shot of gin in the sea of tonic water I'd poured over it. All of her motions revealed she was irritated at having to teach me how to prepare the concoction. I was equally irritated that I had to ask her for help.

She moved down the counter and opened a magazine, nursing her drink while she slowly perused the pages. Ron's head bobbed to the sound of the jazz that came from the covert speakers. I was again at a loss of what to do, so I stood with my glass of water and drank. I never much cared for drinking water with ice cubes in it. They would always get in my way, freezing my lips, slip into my mouth where I couldn't help but chew on them, freezing my teeth in the process, and the water became colder and colder the more I drank until in the end it froze the top of my mouth. Ice just didn't seem worth the hassle that the first few, perfect, refreshing, swallows provided.

I tried my best to chew on the ice as quietly as I could while I watched everyone in the cabin ignore each other: Cynthia with her magazine, Harold watching the lake, and Ron listening to the music. It seemed that they had avoidance down to an art form. Only when there was a knock at the door did I have any idea that somehow I'd joined them in ignoring one another. The knock was followed by the sound of the door opening and a stampede of small shoes on the concrete floor. The kids were home.

They headed straight for Cynthia, spouting stories that all seemed to begin with "Mom, it was *so* cool!" Not that it hurt my feelings any but they hadn't even acknowledged I was in the room. They'd thrown their bags on the ground in front of the stairs where someone might trip on them and went directly for the refrigerator where they pulled cans of Pepsi and greedily drank between shouting their encounters and gasping for air. Ron appeared as oblivious to them as they were of us, but when the woman who must have driven them came into view, she moved the bags up against the wall and looked brightly up at me. Her hair was blond with a multitude of highlights and lowlights in it. Her blue eyes sparkled and her smile gleamed, there was artificiality to everything about her presence; she was exactly what I'd expected a friend of Cynthia's to be like.

She came at me with her thin tan arm stretched out to greet me. The heels of her shoes made loud sounds on the concrete as she came toward me. She wore a modest skirt with a less modest top that struggled to contain her breasts and allowed an ample view of her cleavage. Apparently to distract people's attention, she wore a bold necklace with a large blue stone wreathed in diamonds. "Hi, I'm Julia…"

At that moment I wondered what reaction would have come if I'd only said back "Hi Julia" or "that's nice" and neglected to introduce myself back. Would her friend have cut in and introduced us? Would Ron have? Would she have taken it as the intended insult to her charade of niceness toward the strange militant-looking young man in front of her?

"Hi, I'm Brad." I liked her even less when I took her cold limp fingers into my hand. The handshake had been her idea; she was the one who had extended her hand and all she had to offer were a few icy, insecure digits. I wanted to clamp my grip down on her. It was the easiest way to teach a young Marine not to make the mistake of a half-assed handshake. Squeezing down on a couple fingers, not held firmly under deliberate control, was painful enough to get the message across in usually one go. A handshake is a gesture designed to bring two people into a close professional understanding, a symbol of respect. What she was doing was insulting the tradition and the slimy weakness of her touch left me feeling icky and mildly repulsed.

"No way!" One of the children shouted from upstairs. The sneakiness of kids was another one of the qualities I disliked. I had to be on constant guard as they snooped around and explored variations of pranks and practical jokes in their search to determine what was fun, what was funny, and what was rudely unacceptable. The other two children bolted up the stairs, their feet pounding heavily against the wood as they did their best to take the steps two at a time.

"I hope they haven't been too much trouble. Where are Ken and Charlie?" Julia's hand slipped out of mine.

"No trouble at all. Are you kidding?" She flapped a wrist and looked up at the ceiling. "Charles wanted to make sure we get a good spot on the beach, so he took Ken down there to stake out a place. Hi, Ron."

Ron raised his class and gave her a nod. After taking in a breath she turned back to Cynthia. "I can't get over this place, you guys have outdone yourself, it's fabulous." Her arms were out to her sides and she turned around to evoke her astonishment. "Where are *you* from, Brad?" What she really wanted to know was why I was there, who I was, and did I belong there.

"I live in Hawaii right now, Iowa originally. You live up here on the lake or just summer here?"

"Charles and I got a place up here years ago and it's taken us years to convince Cynthia and Harold to get their asses up here too. It's just such a relief from stress of the city." Again this was another reference to the harsh life she must endure in the city. All the women in this world seemed to suffer from anxiety and stress in the city, or was it just that pretending to be stressed was some form of modest or sub-cultural etiquette. In any case, I had yet to hear the men complain about it so I held back the natural comments of "I know," "it feels great to get away," or "finally some time to myself."

The kids, energy restored, thundered down the stairs at a dangerous pace, brandishing overstuffed bags of fireworks. This was apparently why their door had been closed, to preserve the freshness of the surprise by sealing it in. "This is *so* cool!" The kids landed on the couch, displacing Ron, and began to unload the succession of festively wrapped explosives.

"You kids be careful with those, some of that can be dangerous. No lighting any in the house."

"Can we light it at the beach?"

"You can bring some sparklers; the rest will have to wait until after. Now, go show your father."

The stampede of volatile children armed to the teeth with roman candles, bottle rockets, and starbursts, stormed out the door to unload onto Harold their excess of excitement. I watched their faces as their mouths gaped open to enable the words to escape, gleefully ignorant to the meaning of the holiday that was being celebrated around them or of the tension between the adults in their lives. I looked at the twins; they would never have to face a world of growing up alone. Even if they ended up hating each other they would never have to feel the heartache of knowing that there was no one out there just like them, who understands them, or knows how they feel. They would always have someone there who'd been around just as long as them and grown up the same way.

"So, where do your parents live, Brad?" My daze was broken by Julia's question.

"Iowa, ma'am."

"They are still together then?"

"They have had a few rough spots, everyone does I guess, but ultimately they decided there were more important things than holding stuff against each other. The whole 'look forward instead of backward' thing." I looked from Ron to Cynthia when I said this hoping they would pick up on my subtext. This was a deliberate attempt to campaign compassion between rivaling siblings, which was never really an outsider's place.

"That's wonderful. There is a shortage of people willing to put the effort in to make a marriage work anymore."

"Yeah, it's not always easy forgiving someone, but I've yet to ever regret doing so." I knew I was campaigning pretty hard for peace and maybe taking it too far, but that was only assuming my intended audience had any inkling that I was referring to the strained relations between them.

"Guess what we're having tonight?" A knowing and almost lustful smile came across Cynthia's face as she leaned back against the counter. She gave a nod in the direction of the bottle that sat there. Julia squinted at it and then shock exploded on her face.

"No! You're kidding?" She went over to the bottle and picked it up as if it were a Fabergé Egg, intensely fragile and beautiful, the way people admire frail and lovely things. "Are you sure? You're an angel. I love you! Are we going to open it now?"

"Come on, I have to build up a little more suspense than that."

I thought for a moment that Julia might do a little happy-dance to display her pleasure, but she didn't. "I've always wanted to…"

"Mommy, Dad said we could light some now before we go, where are the matches, where are the matches?" She set her glass down firmly on the granite and gave her husband the ninth degree through the window.

"I said nothing until after."

"Let them have a little fun." This could have easily passed for a simple game of good cop, bad cop but I had the feeling that she held genuine contempt for the challenge to her authority.

When Cynthia asked me to make Julia a gin and tonic the thought crossed my mind that mixing champagne, wine, and hard liquor, I thought, was supposed to make people sick. I did as was requested.

Harold came inside and everyone moved over to the windows by the dinner table to watch the children play with unstable chemical reactions. I stood and watched the children try to position the cartoonist missile up through the gap in the canopy, but most of my attention was on the grownups I stood next to. I eyeballed them out of the corners of my eyes: Cynthia's fingers gripping her glass, Harold's smile that went all the way through him, Ron's casual amusement, and Julia's anticipation as she bit her lip and strummed her fingers on her glass.

"I've been reading this book by this guy that has just been such an inspiration." Julia's vague statement was met with a scoff from Ron who raised his glass to his mouth. I was glad he'd scoffed so that I didn't have to and I was glad that she'd broken the silence. It was exactly the kind of empty comment that Ron hated, and I understood better the way he must have felt sometimes talking to me. More importantly I was uneasy in the silence of this particular crowd; the less they talked the more I knew they were thinking and the less I knew what they were thinking about.

Cynthia came to her fellow female's side, "I need to spend more time reading." The two of them walked over to the living room to sit on the couch, twisting over the back to continue to watch the children who'd gone through a number of matches already and had not figured out how to get the lit match down to the fuse without it going out.

"I wish we could get the kids to read more. You read much, Brad?" Harold asked.

"Not as much as I should probably, sir. But self-help books are not my thing."

"Oh yeah? Why is that?"

I was glad that I could respond in a conversation with him that seemed separate from the one initiated by and including Julia. "Self-help books are propaganda designed to dumb down readers using cultish methodology. I'm a Marine so I already have a cult. I don't need to be dumbed down any further." I'd worked on this for a while, having said it before, slowly manipulating the words and honing the sentence to perfection.

"They're all for poor black bitches with twelve kids so they don't have to feel bad about themselves." Maybe at this point I shouldn't have been shocked by Ron's attitude but I wasn't sure why he suddenly went to the race issue. Did he spend a lot of time thinking about it, or did he have a tragic racial book incident that had permanently scarred him.

Cynthia made a sound of disgust. "Ron you're so crass." I recognized instantly that it wasn't his statement she objected to it was only the manner that he said it. I was not in the company of people with whom the legitimacy of the racist comment could be debated. In the Marines, race had never been much of an issue; every Marine is green. I considered the merit to the civilian argument. There was some evidence to the idea that blacks were perpetuating their own culture of poverty and crime. Most of the experience I'd had around blacks was that they openly resisted conformity to what could be described as white society. To embrace this other side was to be excommunicated from mainstream black society.

There were screams of joy from the kids, and we all turned back to see the twins hiding behind their older brother who stood confident a few feet away from the sparkling fuse.

"Hey, not so close." Cynthia voiced resonated off the glass and she started to stand as if to run out, snatch them up, and move them to safety. In a stream of diaphanous grey smoke and sparks, the projectile hurdled into the sky; as it did the twins ducked behind their human shield and then in a chorus, the three gazed up into the twilight sky as the rocket went out of sight. A boom echoed out over the water and the kids jumped and danced, congratulating one another on the successful launch. Julia stood up and looked at her watch.

"Should we gather everyone up so we don't miss anything?"

"It's getting chilly. I'm going to put on something warmer and I'll be right back down. Harold, would you put everything in the car?" The kids ran back in. Their excitement had not diminished from the moment they'd gotten home; in fact it had intensified.

"What you've got on now is fine. Just put on a coat."

"Ron, shut up." Cynthia said as she walked up the stairs. Ron smiled to himself as if pleased at having irritated her. I could see that his drink was finally transforming him from the mild-mannered Dr. Jekyll.

When we finally all marched out to the car I let myself enjoy the fact that Harold again got into the passenger seat. Cynthia came out in a large pea coat after we'd almost finished situating the seatbelts on the kids.

"Are we all ready to go?" she asked excitedly, and after that the car pulled out of the stall with a full load of passengers and sloshed back and forth down the road. It was time to celebrate freedom for everyone, even those who had never known a world without it.

***

29

A NIGHT OF FIREWORKS WITH THE FAMILY

It had gotten dark quickly on the drive, so much so that it could be considered night. We turned into a parking lot behind what seemed to be some kind of bar next to the beach. When we opened the doors I could hear the sounds of patriotic music drifting overhead.

Being the youngest and most able, I went around back and volunteered my arms to be the ones that carried the large picnic basket. As we walked toward the beach, I could see endless families sitting on blankets on the sand. We came around the crowded outside area of the bar. It was partitioned off with one of those fences made of reddish wood planks bound together at a slight diagonal by metal wire. On the other side, young and old couples drank, laughed, and looked up at the sky, waiting for the first burst of brilliant light.

Alone at the corner table I noticed a kid my age in shorts and a T-shirt. He was strikingly handsome and fit. Everything else about him was ordinary and average. He was perfectly still, smiling to himself, perfectly content, devoid of ambition or disappointment in his being as such. I could never be content to be average and the sensation of being happy outside of a state of constant conflict, not to want to do or be more, seemed foreign to me. I wanted more, even if I was good; I wanted to be better, to be great and then learn to do something else. This state of discontent was as satisfying and fulfilling as it was demanding and troublesome.

What was not satisfying and what seemed silly was my contribution in the search for Julia's husband, Charles. Wandering onto the deeper sand of the beach, making our way through the maze of people, I joined them in looking for him despite having no idea what he looked like. It was pointless, but I felt powerlessly compelled to participate. Here and there faces would look back. When I made lingering eye-contact, my heart skipped a beat thinking "Ah-ha! I've found him." But then the person next me would wave at them, nudge past me, and my heart would sink back down in embarrassment.

"Julia!" A man's voice came out of the dark and a bright white burst illuminated the audience, revealing Charles, an average-height balding man in a polo shirt and khaki shorts beckoning with one arm, causing his belly to shake slightly. Next to him stood a child with the same brown hair, transfixed by the sparkling fireworks in the sky. We all wanted to watch, but for the moment, we needed to use the colored explosions to light our path across the beach. "We thought you guys might miss it. Hi, Ron."

"Happy Fourth." Ron said flatly.

Still enjoying the lack of cheer in Ron's "Happy Fourth" I extended my hand. "I'm Brad. It's Charles?" He was kingly and slightly absent as reflected by being named such a royal name. His wife was entirely undeserving of the hospitable, humble name she'd been given. Maybe she would be once she became a grandmother and was forced into a more conservative life.

"Pleasure meeting you."

"Brad just got out of the Marines, he came up from the city with Ron to visit." This was a fair introduction from

296

Cynthia, who could have said something more along the lines of "and this is Brad, Ron's secret lover."

"That's fantastic. Good man. Join us. Everybody sit, there is plenty of room." While Charles was talking to us he didn't seem to actually be paying attention. He was determinately occupied with seating and arranging his family and ensuring they all had snacks and beverages. It was like watching a horticulturist tend to his flower garden and ensuring that each and every plant received equal attention.

We all did our best to fit on the blanket with no one having to sit too close to anyone they didn't want to. I accidentally put my hand right in the sand and was immediately annoyed. I hated the way sand stuck to my skin. I seemed to spend days getting it off myself. Had I been in Waikiki and in board shorts it would have been different, but I was in my new clothes. I took off my shoes and set them to the side out of habit. In Hawaii, no one wears shoes on the beach. It was accepted to go just about anywhere barefoot.

"You'll die when I tell you what Cynthia's done." Charles wrapped a blanket around his wife and helped her down onto the blanket. His eyes were glued to her gratuitous endowments that he himself had, most likely, subsidized so that he could do so.

"Oh yeah? What are you hiding from us?" Charles wiped his chin in a pinching motion. On his hand he wore a plain wedding band and a thick-banded gold ring with a substantial emerald. Cynthia opened the basket and pulled out the bottle by the top and presented it to him, cupping the bottom with the other hand. He accepted it from her and held it similarly. "I'll be. Where did you get this?"

"I came across a case of them a while back. If we don't drink them, who will?"

There was a small pop as the cork came out of the bottle. Julia rubbed her hands together like a starving child waiting for the ice cream man to get a fudgesicle from the freezer. The powerful smell of the fruity wine was amazing. As she filled the miniature goblets she passed them out to the adults. Everywhere around me was the crimson perfume wafting in the slight breeze. Cynthia must have noticed my eyes following each glass as it floated into one hand and then next. She let a tiny amount slosh into a glass and handed it to me.

Her smile was one of generosity and compassion. I lifted it to my mouth and inhaled as I let some wine into my mouth the way I'd heard my mother describe to her friends. There was no fumy taste of alcohol. It was heavenly and delicious. I knew from the moment it touched my tongue, coating my mouth, that this was something truly spectacular. Even in the dark I could see the thick liquid sticking to the side of the small glass. It was darker than any wine I'd ever seen and almost looked like cold espresso. If alcoholics didn't consider wine *drinking*, then tonight neither would I; I let another small sip enter my mouth and I floated out of myself and into the sparkling bursts in the sky.

The colorful flashes of light picked up at an exponentially quickening pace as we listened to *The Star Spangled Banner* come across the combination of indoor and outdoor bar speakers and the dozens of radios down the blanket-covered beach. Against the kaleidoscopic waters of the lake were the silhouettes of the four children standing on the shore with their shoes off and pants hiked up to their knees splashing in the small waves.

Hands everywhere started to clap and I joined them even though I'd been too distracted by the fireworks on the ground to watch the grand finale over us. I could see the plume of smoke trailing off to the East and, in the distance, the less impressive show on the shore of South Lake Tahoe for all the less privileged locals. People stood up all over and started to fold up chairs, shake out towels, and collect trash. With two fistfuls of wrappers and empty soda cans from the kids, I searched out a trashcan. When I turned back around I saw that Ron was already walking away from the group towards the parking lot. I went back and continued to help pack up. Julia worked on getting the kids to put their shoes back on any way that would help reduce the amount of sand they would get in their socks and shoes.

Back in the car everyone was mostly silent. Charles and the kids rode in a separate car so that all the children could ride together. Behind us they giggled and moved around restlessly in their seatbelts as the poked at each other, made funny faces, probably recreating the sounds of exploding fireworks.

"The fireworks were wonderful this year." Cynthia chimed. Ron scoffed and turned his head out the window. "I'm thinking about cutting my hair shorter." She added as she touched her hair.

"You trying to look like a dyke?" Ron said.

"You're a total asshole, Ron." She snapped back. She looked like she was ready to turn around and climb into the back seat to scratch Ron's eyes out for talking back to her. I wondered if Harold was prepared to grab the wheel and steer if she did.

"Is there any more of the wine left?" Harold intervened predictably. Cynthia, instead of mauling Ron, simply looked ahead and gripped the steering wheel. Harold sat up a bit more in his seat and Ron sat, arms crossed, running his tongue on the inside of his bottom lip.

"I think it would look adorable on you. Harold, honey, what do you think of Cynthia going short with her hair? Maybe I should do the same."

"You'll do it beautifully whatever you do, darling, I'm sure," Harold said to Cynthia. "Excellent selection of vintage. It was the perfect choice," he continued, perhaps to distract her from Ron's attitude or in anticipation that Ron might follow it up with a scornful critique of the evening's lightshow and provoke Cynthia further.

I looked over at Ron who had unfolded his arms, put is head down, and was gently stroking the fabric on the door like it was a puppy that needed consoling.

Charles followed close in his car and his lights shined in the back windows making shadows dance through the interior. This continued until we made a sharp turn into their parking place by the cabin. The doors to the cars closed in an almost musical way.

"Mom can we, we want to stay at Julia's more, can we?" the children rang out immediately.

"Is that alright with you?"

"Absolutely."

The kids started re-boarding the vehicle, loading the bags of fireworks on top themselves, and plotting the evening mischief. Charles sat in the car talking what was probably business over his cell phone. He seemed strangely in control yet detached from the rest of them. The noise of the kids also didn't seem to bother him as it would have bothered me had I been trying to talk on the phone.

"Call me the moment they get out of hand."

With the kids in the car, Cynthia stood and waved goodbye before following us up to the house. She took off her coat and hung it up in the doorless closet. The lights were still on from when we'd left earlier. "It's so cold outside. Who'd like some hot chocolate?"

"None for me, thank you." Harold responded. The sound of ice in a glass that came from the kitchen I recognized as Ron making himself another cocktail.

"I'd love to have some as long as long as you join me," I said.

"I could do that."

With her coat off I could see that she was wearing a white turtleneck with a gaudy broach of the American flag in what were most likely real rubies, diamonds, and sapphires.

I was a little excited as I followed her into the kitchen. Ron walked over by to the windows and drank deeply from his glass. Harold sat down and pulled a cigar out of an ornate box on the coffee table.

Taking two mugs out of the cabinet, Cynthia opened two packets of powdered hot chocolate mix. I'd expected something a little more gourmet but I wasn't about to argue with the offer of hot chocolate. She then filled the mugs with water from what I'd earlier assumed was a soap dispenser on the sink.

"Wow, that's neat. I'm glad I didn't hold my hand under that earlier and try to get soap out of it." She looked at me and then decided to ignore that I had said something she thought stupid. I was glad she did, as clearly she didn't get my joke.

Cynthia handed me a ceramic mug that was steaming up into the air. Hot chocolate was more than just a warming beverage; it was a means of communing with one of my favorite things. I'd developed an intimacy with the dark brown substance, that I had cultivated over the years. At first I wasn't entirely sure I even liked chocolate. I would have it from time to time but always with something else. Chocolate chip cookies, chocolate covered cherries, and mint chocolate chip ice cream were among my favorite candy choices. I had thought that the chocolate was a nice afterthought of the confection but not an essential one. As I got older I realized that the cookies, cherries, and ice cream were just vehicles used to deliver the chocolate. I still was not ready to really enjoy a piece of dark chocolate, but I was working up to it. My mouth wasn't fully prepared for the message chocolate had to say. My consumption of products containing chocolate increased and I slowly found myself able to eat larger and larger percentages of all-chocolate bars. Before too long it had me. I could sit with a piece of dark chocolate and place it in my mouth, feeling for its texture, and appreciating the difference between it and other chocolates I'd had. Finally I could have a relationship with just the chocolate and me.

"You know how to play mancala, Brad?" Harold asked.

"Not yet."

"Good answer." He pulled out from under the coffee table a piece of wood with two rows of divots carved in it and larger ones at the end. Inside each one were small black stones. Following a brief history lesson that included a mention that a mancala board had been found in King Tut's tomb, he explained the direction of how to move the pieces. The game play I found actually quite satisfying. There was no sense of defeat like with chess, no endless game play like with Monopoly, and no feeling of stupidity like in Trivial Pursuit. It was a simple, well-rounded game. Knowing the history, I felt almost regal playing it there with him as he puffed on his cigar and tried not to blow it at me.

Neither of us heard how the argument had started or even had noticed Ron and Cynthia in the kitchen together, but once I did, I immediately positioned myself in their vicinity, hoping that perhaps my very presence might calm the situation. It didn't matter what the content of the argument was, two people who are mad at each other will be mad for whatever reason the situation presents.

"Get over yourself."

"You're a lousy drunk, just like our father." The words came out with an ironically subtle slur.

"Fuck you. I'm no drunk."

"Oh really? That's why you got so shit-faced at Dad's wedding you told me to fuck myself during your toast. I'm the one who's had to put all the effort in to invite her into the family. Spend time getting to know her. What have you ever done to help this family?"

"Please. You two bitches have been ganging up on me from the beginning trying to figure out how best to carve up dad's money and cut me out. That's why you've been spending so much time with that gold-digging slut."

"Stop being so melodramatic, you little cry baby. You always were such a victim."

"Oh, fuck you, you cunt. Look at yourself. Why don't you go fuck off with his new communist whore of a wife!"

"What did you call me?"

"Hey Ron." I did my best to sound calm and comforting as he stormed toward me. Cynthia came at me like one of the fireworks with its fuse lit. Ron stood on the other side with me between them. Did Ron expect me to beat up his sister for him to get back at her for beating him when he was little? Then, behind me, Ron walked out the door leaving it open behind him.

302

Cynthia stood with her face flushed with rage. "Ronny! Ronny, get in here! Ronny!"

Her voice was like a punch in my gut as I recognized the inflection immediately. This was the voice that haunted Ron's mind when he was overcome with intoxication. It wasn't his father's voice at all. It was the demanding, condescending, abusive voice of a sister who had been forced into the role of a parent in the stead of a father who was as absent in their childhoods as was his face in the photographs in the stairway. "Ronny! Ronny, get in here! Ronny!" resounded in my head replaying itself over and over. I saw the horror Ron felt with no one to turn to when faced with the abuse of his sister, how she'd even stolen from him his best friend and married him, turning Harold against him too. "Ronny! Ronny, get in here! Ronny!" I imagined the loneliness of living in a house where the only person not on the payroll was a sister forced to grow up too fast, who was really just as lost and just as confused as Ron was.

Then, just like that, the hatred fell from the air and the cabin was again silent except the sounds of three beating hearts. Cynthia ran her hand through her hair, put down her glass on the island and went upstairs.

Harold sighed and went up shortly after her. I took another drink from my hot chocolate and stood for a moment alone in the kitchen. I waited for a very long ten minutes before I went out the still-open door into the cool night. There was no sound outside either. Listening hard I tried to pinpoint Ron's location. Shifting my gaze to the darkest place I could find I tried to adjust my eyes so that I might be able to see him. What if, in his drunkenness he had wandered off and become lost in the woods, what if he got hurt, what if he didn't want to come back, what if he thought I was on Cynthia's side, too? Was I? I didn't think so.

I didn't see him until a twig snapped under his foot. "Are you alright?" Ron came into the light. He looked disappointed in himself and he kept staring at the ground in front of him walking past me and into the cabin via the open door.

It was possible that waiting for him to talk was a bad strategy as he didn't say a word in the cabin, on the stairs, in the hall, or while he undressed and climbed into bed.

Together we lay silently facing away from each other in our separate, child-sized beds. Despite out age difference, Ron wasn't really older than me at all. He had stunted his own growth by holding onto the resentment for his father and his sister.

I knew the next morning we would leave. I wasn't sure I understood everything that had really happened that night but our visit was clearly at an end. We were all but pointed in the direction of San Francisco, but I had no inkling of the direction either of us would go when we got there.

***

30

FOR THE ROAD

The street was paved in old bricks that had worn around the edges. I managed to walk on them without tripping. There was a slight breeze and there were no cars. I walked down the middle of a street lined in two story buildings with balconies, awnings, and umbrella-covered tables in front of them.

I looked up and down as I strolled along with my hands in my suit jacket pockets. The quietness and lack of people made the entire city feel like it belonged to me. I wasn't even sure exactly where I was, it could have been Italy, or Spain, or even Greece, but I didn't really care. I was at peace and it was a beautiful day.

A gust of wind came up behind me picking up a table cloth and knocking over a glass of wine left behind by whoever had just eaten at the table. I watched the red stain expand outwardly on the white cloth, growing impossibly large towards the end of the table. The wind picked up again and I looked behind me in its direction.

I opened my eyes to the light of the sun shining directly onto my face. I moved my head out of the way and looked around the room. I was in the cabin again, Ron's bed was empty and unmade, and his bag once again resembled a disemboweled animal.

Sitting up, I wiped the sleep from my eyes, stretched my legs, and arched my back. There was no sound coming from the shower so I knew Ron must have gone downstairs. Worry started to fill me. What was going on downstairs? Were we really leaving today?

My mind began a slow jog and before I'd realized it, I'd refolded all of Ron's clothes and made the beds, my head racing with scenarios of how the morning and this day might go. They varied from me being left behind as Ron pulled away, getting a handful of cash from Cynthia and being dropped off at a bus station somewhere, to Ron coming out to his sister, embracing her, and him proclaiming his love for me and that he would build a cabin next door so he could finally be close to his family.

Looking around, I saw the byproduct of my nervousness. Unless I was to start dusting the room there was really nothing left I could possibly do. My outfit was laid out in the shape of a person on the perfectly wrinkle-free bed and the bags were neatly sitting in their position, patiently waiting to be picked up with their handles folded over each other on top.

The smell of breakfast drifted into the room and my stomach growled a little. I hadn't really eaten much the night before, as the sandwich menu in the picnic basket did not include a vegetarian option. I decided to shower first and go down fully dressed, that way if the situation escalated I'd be clothed enough to make a break for it. In my mind's eye I got a flash of Cynthia leaping at Ron with flames coming out of her eyes while I jumped up and ran from the table so fast the plates smashed against the wall, bits of food slowly dripping down the windows.

After my four-minute shower and another four minutes to shave and dry off, I slid into one of the remaining unworn outfits I'd gotten. It was entirely possible that back in the city

Ron might continue building my wardrobe or even that we'd just buy new clothes everywhere we went. Assuming that we went anywhere. There was no sound coming from downstairs and as I buttoned up my pants; this too made me uneasy.

Coming down the stairs I did my best to move as stealthily as I could in order to continue to survey the conditions I was walking into. When it came into view, the sight was more shocking that any of my predicted scenarios could have been.

Harold sat outside reading his paper open, Ron was next to him with his paper folded in half, and Cynthia was in the kitchen carefully measuring ingredients. My heart skipped a beat while the déjà vu overwhelmed me. Everything was exactly as it had been before. Maybe yesterday didn't even happen. Maybe I'd dreamed it in a "worst case" version and today I'd have the chance to put it all right.

"Good morning, ma'am."

Cynthia looked up at me and smiled. "Good morning. Can I get you some coffee?"

"Could I just do a glass of milk please, ma'am?"

"Help yourself to it." She dumped a teaspoon of oregano into the bowl of eggs that had a whisk sticking out. I didn't entirely understand why, when someone offered coffee or tea, it was their obligation to get it, but everything else was self-serve.

With my glass of milk in hand I sat down next to the men of the house outside. Harold passed me the part of the paper he was done with and Ron just sat there reading through his dark glasses. The creepiness stemming from the lack of closure to last night's fight was driving me insane. Didn't they have anything to say to one another? Didn't they need to resolve their issues to move on from it? I hated to think that ignoring it was in fact them moving on from it. Picking up my glass of milk, the napkin stuck to the bottom. I pulled it off and dashed salt onto it.

Cynthia came out onto the porch with two plates of food in her hands. She set them in front of her husband and brother. "Eggs and toast, Brad?"

I swallowed my milk to respond. "Yes, ma'am. Thank you." I wasn't meaning to be so overly polite but I decided that the relation between all of us was still brittle and required extra gentility.

She sat down after placing a plate in front of me. "So, you guys have a long drive today. You should grab some bottled water from the fridge before you go."

After that, no one spoke as we ate, or at least said anything of substance. There were a few passing references to the weather, the headlines, and the show last night. There were a number of opportunities to finally have it out between the three of them in a sober environment, but all were left to lay fallow. I entertained myself by coming up with plays on words that might test the stiff fragility of the silent courtesy. Things like "not stormy like it was last night" or "did you hear they declared peace in Lake Tahoe" or "the fireworks in the sky were nothing compared to the ones when we got back."

"Would you like to help me clear the table?" Cynthia asked.

"Yes, ma'am. Sure."

After the plates were rinsed and put in the dishwasher—and my far-fetched hope that Cynthia called me inside for a heart to heart disappeared down the drain—I went upstairs to find Ron sitting on the bed staring out the window. Was he thinking about me? Was he as worried about the end of this trip as I was? When I came in he stood up. "Ready?"

The suddenness of this made a knot of my stomach. "Yeah, I'm ready. I'll take the bags down to the car." I picked up the bags and Ron pulled some wrinkled money from his pocket, still counting it when I carried the bags out. Once I had the bags secured in the back and shut the hatch I saw the front door open. Ron came out followed by Cynthia and then by Harold. They all walked slowly and talked too politely quiet for me to hear over the rustling of the trees.

"…anytime." Cynthia gave her brother a hug. "It was nice meeting you, Brad."

308

Cynthia came to give me a hug and her husband nodded at me. "It was a pleasure meeting you."

"Now, this is for your mother since you said she loved wine so much." Harold passed her a bottle that she then passed to me with both hands. I looked down and read the scripted word: *Inglenook*. I wasn't sure if she was only being nice because she felt exposed by having lost control last night or if she meant it. Although at times she'd been condescending and acted arrogantly toward me, in her position I might have treated me the same as she had. I hoped not though.

"Thank you very much." I had no idea how to convey to correct amount of appreciation for this gift I knew I didn't fully grasp the significance of. "Thanks for having us."

Harold put his arm on Ron's shoulder and then gave him a hug. It occurred to me then that maybe once they'd been more than just friends as they grew up that maybe Harold had been the one that had allowed Ron to discover who he really was; that maybe Cynthia even knew this and resentfully kept the secret safe for the two men in her life. Ron walked away and over to his side of the car.

"Drive safely." Harold raised an arm, Ron shut the door, and so did I. We pulled out of the stall while they waited to watch us drive off. The air in the car was stale and I turned on the air-conditioner, cracked the windows slightly, and Ron reached up and turned up the Jazz on the radio. Even with the tension that had occurred, it was a little sad to leave knowing that I might never see them again.

"Where to?"

"We'll stop for lunch again at Tinsley." I understood this to mean that we would not be stopping by Robert and Richard's again. There was a bit of relief in that, since it eliminated the possibility that he might just drop me off on their doorstep, but I was a bit disappointed as I did want to see them again to describe to them what had happened at the cabin as they were acquainted enough with the back-story that they would enjoy it in a way few others could.

Coming down the mountains on the winding road I was surprised to see a towering waterfall in full view of the road. The broad stream of clear white water rushed over it, falling what looked to be more than two hundred feet off the side of the mountain. It made me doubt that I was even on the same road. I knew I was at least where the navigation system told me I should be since I had to stop to program in our destination before pulling onto it. There were no signs identifying the falls. I knew I would go to a map later and try to locate it in order to add the credibility of its name when retelling the story.

The mountains flattened out and we sped across the central valley of California. The highway cut through the endless patchwork of fields. I saw the signs for Sacramento and again felt a few pangs of sadness knowing that we wouldn't be stopping there. It wasn't long after that the first signs for Stockton started to appear.

"Pick it up a little, let's try to hit the next ferry."

I glanced down at the speedometer and saw I was already going eighty-five. How fast did he need me to go? I saw the familiar intersection up ahead and flipped on my turn signal. Sometimes I don't really realize just how fast I'm driving until I have to slow down. Gravity pulled our bodies forward as we approached the turn and the needle measuring our speed moved from the right to the left. It was a straight shot from there, so once on the road I let the speed increase without pushing the peddle to the floor. The sound of the engine moving from gear to gear was admittedly a little exhilarating, holding the wheel in my hand controlling the heavy SUV as it rocketed down the road that made a straight slice westward through the fields. I reached my hand across the center console and put it on Ron's hand that was on his knee. It didn't move away nor did it react to hold onto mine. I didn't care. It felt good to be in control and not alone. I was floating in the air of the fast moving vehicle. This could work out after all.

I didn't even look at the speed until I saw the colored lights flashing in the rearview mirror. They glittered like sparkling Christmas lights, but unlike that holiday, they brought a sensation very different from cheer. Not only had I not driven before, I had neglected to tell Ron that I actually didn't have a driver's license.

I was more afraid of admitting this to Ron than to the officer who I knew would soon approach my window. How would I handle this? There were a variety of characters I could portray. I could be the hyper-respectful Marine constantly apologizing and calling him sir and thanking him for his patience, I could play the nervous wreck and grovel verbally through the open window with tears in my eyes, I could be the ignorant simpleton who simply didn't even know he was speeding without a license.

The figure dressed in black with dark glasses walked up from his car with a wide gait that swung his feet out to the side a little. His head went out of view in the side mirror before I could really get a look at him. I couldn't bear to look over at Ron and see exactly what type of disappointed face he had on. The situation seemed all too predictable. What were the odds that while speeding down a virtually uninhabited road through agricultural land to catch a ferry to an island reserved only for the elite, that a driver without a license would miss a cop behind him, on the side of the road, or from wherever he came? Why was the officer there to begin with? Exactly what kind of hooligan was he hoping to catch on this road? I found myself becoming irritated at this road being at all a priority for law enforcement. It seemed like a waste. I didn't see the benefit to society in stopping a Mercedes from speeding in the middle of the country and fine its driver a fee smaller than he probably spent on his golf balls!

I buried my anger behind a smile and reached my hand up to the button and the window went down. As the whirring sound propelled the glass down the agricultural ambiance from outside rushed into the car, changing the atmosphere.

"Good afternoon, sir."

"You know how fast you were going?" I wondered how boring it would be to ask this question all day and felt sorry that he had to ask it and that he had to listen day after day to people like me answer. Truth told, I had no idea how fast I was going; last time I'd looked I'd seen the marker pass ninety.

"I guess I wasn't paying attention, sir."

"Can I see your license and registration?"

The thought that came into my head was, "No actually, you can't see it, not unless you use your imagination and sense of humor." Instead I began to fumble my words and managed to get out "Well, actually, I don't know, see, I'm from Hawaii, sir, it's not my car, it's new, I don't know what—" Ron let out an irritated sigh that was intended either to be targeted at my stuttering or at the officer for having the nerve to stop us.

"Hey look, we're just trying to make the ferry to Tinsley." My mouth actually opened a little at the audacity of the tone of his voice.

"I don't have my license with me, sir, I'm sorry. I can give you my ID if you like?" I pulled the small green card from my wallet and passed it out the window.

"You're a Marine?"

"Yes, sir." Technically I was on terminal leave, so for another week, I was still active duty.

"I'll be right back, devil-dog."

I was getting another cardio workout. My chest was pounding again and I held onto the steering wheel to hide the fact that my hands were shaking a little.

"I can't believe you said that to a *cop*."

"Whatever. He's probably just upset he has to live a dead-end job and watch people who've made something of their lives drive by. He should go somewhere they actually need cops and do his job." Apart from the fact that was almost the most he'd said at once all week, his statement wasn't entirely wrong, but being that my ID and legal record was in the officer's hand I put aside any ill feelings about the cop's motives and concentrated on how to best keep my cool and generate the most positive outcome.

While we waited, the clock changed to ten past; we'd missed the ferry, removing any benefit we might have gotten by speeding in the first place. I rolled the window back down while he walked up to the car. Again the warm quiet air from outside blended with the air-conditioned air inside.

"You know, devil-dog, you need to carry your license with you whenever you're driving."

"Yes, sir. I'm sorry, sir."

"I'm not gonna give you a ticket for that. I'm not gonna give you a ticket for how fast you were going either. I had to go one-fifteen to catch up to you. I'm gonna give you a break. I'm writing the ticket for fifteen over instead of fifteen over a hundred. You keep your nose clean." He handed my ID back to me.

"Yes, sir. Thank you again, sir."

Either he knew about me not having a driver's license and wanted to spare me the embarrassment to some kind of incompatibility between the Californian or Hawaiian systems must have mistaken my learner's permit for a full driver's license. Finishing getting the license had never been much of a priority. Between public transportation and friends I'd never really needed one.

I rolled my window back up but wasn't sure if I should wait for him to drive off ahead of me, or if I should go first. Putting the car in gear seemed to be the right answer since he was still shuffling through something in his car.

The speed limit felt especially slow with the feeling of how fast we had been going still fresh in my memory. When we pulled into the parking lot at the base of the dike again, we both knew we were going to have to wait for the next ferry. We paced around in silence on the dock. Listening to the sounds of water sloshing under the planks I looked down and watched to see if I could actually see any fish swimming beneath the murky brown ripples. As I followed the edge I came upon a small candy machine that had been filled with fish food. Feeling in my pockets I was disappointed to discover I had no change. Why would I have? I hadn't really had any money the entire trip.

I gave up entertaining myself and resigned to sit on the bench under the late-afternoon sun to wait for the ferry to come to take us to our late-afternoon lunch. I wasn't even really hungry, but I would eat anyway.

Ron sat down next to me but not so close that it would have seemed strange. My butt sank into the spaces between the wood of the bench, making it uncomfortable. I knew from holding shooting positions on the rifle range that moving would only make things worse. Staying still and enduring the position I was already in was the best option.

We were the only ones on the ferry this time as we motored down the lake again. The island was also less inhabited so there was no line. Despite the lack of people, the buffet was stocked the same. Perfect stacks of soft buns, and chopped vegetables, glass condiment bowls with tiny spoons for ketchup and relish, terrines of soup and chafing dishes of pastas. Half-way down there were grilled cheese sandwiches and tomato soup as an option, so I took that instead of being ushered back into the kitchen again to get a custom-made meal. We set our plates down, and at that moment the lack of children running about or splashing really hit me. The island was almost abandoned. I assumed that people were dispersed across the country to enjoy the holiday with various relatives.

"I have to remember to get some toilet paper in the city." Ron's comment caught me off guard, as almost any time he spoke without direct provocation did. I'd never really thought about him, or anyone in his financial situation, having to buy their own toiletries. It was something I never heard of or thought about, like tornados in a foreign country.

I enjoyed being away from the hostility of the cabin but I missed the enjoyable parts of it. Mostly I missed the setting that implied the trip was not over, being back on the island felt too close to being back in San Francisco, back where he would feel

314

less guilt about dumping me on the side of the road, assuming he'd feel any guilt about that to begin with. My head was beginning to throb from the sterility of the environment and the energy it took to keep up appearances. I didn't want to have to worry about how close I was sitting to him on the bench anymore or if anyone would notice me checking him up and down or staring at his strong neck and shoulders. Mostly I wanted to be touched, and opportunities for affection between us were infrequent and would stay that way, in this place especially. Going back to the city was not a fix for this. There we ran the risk of running into his business associates or of him just running.

There was a coin suspended in the air over me flipping over and over. On one side was me standing on a sidewalk as the Mercedes pulled away, on the other the image of me standing on the bow of a sailboat wearing my dress blues with Ron behind the ships wheel. Over and over it was spinning. It made me dizzy and sick to my stomach. I stopped eating my grilled cheese and I'd barely touched my soup. Ron stood up from the table.

"Are you ready?"

***

31

DELORES PARK

"Are you ready?" His question was pointed. I didn't have an answer other than no. How could I be ready? I still didn't even know what ending to be ready for. The day was moving fast, so much so that I felt a sickening sadness knowing that it would be over before I was ready for it.

"Sure."

We walked back to the ferry that was ready to depart. I was relieved not to have to wait again but not relieved to be on it. Staring off into the distance I tried to clear my head. Meditation had always been an elusive concept; I was never sure if I was just spacing out or if spacing out was what meditation was. In any case I didn't want to be in that particular place at that particular moment, and attempted transcendence seemed to be a viable option. I never looked up to see the faces of the other passengers that time, but I knew they were there. The sky was a faded blue.

When the ferry got to the dock I stretched and let the four or so other passengers get off first. It crossed my mind that

Ron might figure out and become annoyed that I was stalling, but it didn't really matter at this point. We were already down to the ultimatum. Either we would have to label what we had going on between us or part ways.

The doors to the car shut with their usual thud that sealed the silence of the cab from the outside world. The air was hot and stale and I rushed to get the key into the ignition and the windows down. I looked over at Ron and let a smile linger in his direction. He looked back puzzled. What was he puzzled about? I knew that my glance was a little strange, as they tended to be, but was he puzzled because he didn't know how he should feel or because he knew exactly how he felt and didn't know why or what to do about it.

"Hi." I said. A huff escaped him and he put an arm out the window and turned his head. I could see a small grin on his face as he watched the world rotate around us pulling out of the parking stall. The small smile on his face I decided to count as an emotional victory in my favor, that maybe he didn't want to see me go either. I rolled up the windows as soon as we started to gain momentum and let the cold air from the vents fill the car.

Even though I had set the cruise control, I found myself repeatedly checking the speedometer and looking in the rear-view mirror. Why both of these precautions were necessary I wasn't sure. If I wasn't speeding what was I worried about? Situational awareness was important so I let that military cliché be the deciding vote and continued my paranoid verifications.

Watching my mirrors and my speed took a back seat when a semi pulled up on my right hand side. I hadn't seen it approach somehow, so I assumed it had merged from the right. It was right next to us now and continued going slightly faster or slower, keeping it at pace with us. In the rearview I checked for other drivers that might be annoyed by both lanes being occupied by vehicles traveling at the same speed. Maybe the driver of the semi was trying to get our attention, to warn us of police ahead, to hit on us and get us to pull over for a quickie, or maybe he got an eyeful of my hand on Ron's strong hairy leg. As these

318

thoughts circulated through my mind I was caught off guard when the semi started drifting into our lane. A small gasp escaped me and I moved over to the left as it came at me. Ron looked over at it without even being fazed, watching it come closer and closer. I'd never been through driver's education: was I supposed to slow down and let the truck pass or speed up and get around him. The driver in the lane next to me was either too tired or too drunk to know I was there and he was about to change lanes. I put my foot on the gas pedal, my hands closed tighter around the wheel, but I changed my mind and decided slowing down was the best option.

My foot pushed on the brake a little harder than I intended and we slowed down rapidly. Inertia pulled our heads forward but both our eyes were still on the road. The semi passed us and moved completely into our lane. Looking in the rearview now I just wanted to see if anyone else had seen us almost get killed. The cars behind us were so far back I doubted they noticed.

Until I let the air out I didn't even know I'd been holding my breath. I flipped on the turning signal and reset the cruise control to five miles over the speed limit instead of the ten I'd been cruising at before.

"Holy shit! What the hell was that?"

Granted that this was a rhetorical question, I felt that the situation and my obvious agitation deserved a comment of some kind from Ron. No such luck. Ron looked ahead of him as if I had said nothing. The sun raced against us down the highway as we headed toward the coast. Then, almost startling me, I felt Ron's hand wrap around mine. The sensation of this strong thick fingers molding to squeeze my own sent shivers down my spine. I wanted to wiggle in my seat or jump across the cab and kiss him; instead I just squeezed back.

We ended up passing the semi again later. I half expected to get a honk or a wave from the driver to apologize for almost destroying another of Ron's Mercedes, but he didn't.

It wasn't long after when we made our way up through the mountains that separated the central valley from the breezy Californian coastline. Once over them it seemed odd to be turning due south. When I saw the large, stately perfection of the Mormon temple halfway up the mountainside I knew we were traveling in the right direction, but I still didn't remember this when we came through the first time.

Lanes of traffic merged with other lanes, which joined up with even more as various highways and roads consolidated into one in preparation for crossing the San Francisco bay by way of the Oakland Bay Bridge. The route took us along the series of massive cranes used for loading and unloading truck-sized metal crates from the thousands of shipping vessels that were loaded and unloaded from here each year.

The first half of the bridge was twice as wide as the second half. The San Francisco side of the bridge had its East and Westbound traffic stacked on top of each other; a project that hadn't been completed on the Oakland side yet. Monolithic grey towers supported each span of the ten bogged-down lanes of traffic. The whole thing seemed impossible yet there we were, driving down a suspended lane of traffic over an inlet of water wide enough to be seen from space and crossing one of the most active fault lines in the world. Weren't we asking for trouble?

San Francisco is a city whose buildings go all the way to each of its edges. There is no suburban territory to gradually ease into. All roads drop off in the center of everything, a center that covered every square mile of dirt with skyscrapers, pavement, and Victorian houses. In moments, we were no longer over the water, and the road began to make swooping curves around the buildings of the bustling metropolis.

"Take this one." Ron pointed at an exit sign before I could see it. I merged. The road descended to ground level as our speed dropped. It felt like landing. We had officially arrived. Despite our having been together for days on end, we were not snapping at each other or in a panic to part ways.

Dangerously, I feigned confidence and made my way back to the top of Knob Hill. I vaguely remembered where I was going, driving in a city full of one-way streets and "no left turn" signs.

"Do you want me to pull into the garage?"

"That's fine."

Ron got out and entered a code in a metal panel on the wall that made the gate go up. Looking up at the top of the building I was scared we'd scratch the roof coming in but managed fine. His smashed car took his parking space, but since he owned the building, I imagined he could pretty much park wherever he wanted. I pulled up into a yellow-striped space marked "loading and unloading only" and turned off the car.

"Is this O.K?"

"It's fine."

Getting out of the car my hands were shaking. The air smelled different and familiar. The crisp blue and green pine smells of the mountains were absent. The city air was sweet with the aromas of food that permeated the dense blocks of concrete skyscrapers, and soured with the smells of exhaust and industrial shipping. Our movements echoed in the quiet parking chamber. I was a little startled when the gate started to come back down noisily, but being as on edge as I was, anything would have startled me.

"I'm not looking forward to getting on my flight." I said, fishing.

I picked up both of the bags and followed Ron to the elevator. Ron said nothing. I looked at the image of myself standing next to this short handsome man in the golden surface of the elevator doors. The two of us weren't a bad match. I didn't imagine there were many men or women who could tolerate his drunken rudeness, but it didn't really bother me all that much. If anything, it added a dimension of excitement and unpredictability.

We entered his apartment and I carried the bags down the hall to his bedroom. The apartment was even more barren, white, and empty than I'd remembered. Ron headed straight for the bathroom and didn't close the door behind him. It was relaxing to hear the familiar sound of him urinating. I set his bag next the closet and mine next to the door.

Sitting down on the bed seemed only natural since there was no other seating in the place. I laid back and stretched, smiling. The bed was cozy and big, unlike the small twin beds we'd been slumbering on at the lake. I grabbed a pillow and propped it behind my head. Ron finished and flushed the toilet. He came out of the bathroom and stopped to look at me. There was a small grin on his face, as he looked me up and down. My arms were behind my head, legs parted, the fabric of my shirt revealing the shape of my body better than the manufacturer intended. He came into the room, kicked off his shoes, and started to look through the plastic wrapped clothes in the closet.

"I'm gonna miss my flight if I don't get going soon." I stated trying to be more obvious.

"Or you could just stay and take a later flight." His sentence didn't entirely invite me to stay. He'd left the option of a later flight dangling there in the air. Did he want me to stay or did he want me to stay a little longer and then leave.

I didn't know if I wanted to go back to my life in Hawaii. I would have called it my *real* life but it didn't seem any more real than the one I had been living for the past week. I wasn't even sure what I was going back to. There was no job waiting for me to clock in, no duty desk to report to, I didn't even know if I still had a boyfriend or not. The ambiguous way we'd parted weeks before left me in a state where I felt unattached and not the least bit guilty about my time with Ron.

Finding someone sexually compatible wasn't all that easy between gay men. This was something that most straight friends found difficult to grasp. There was more to it than just physical attraction and personality. There were different areas of sexual compatibility beneath the surface that had to be exposed to discover if two men really were a good fit. Not all men could tolerate an aggressive Marine. The masculinity conflicted with their idea of what it meant to dominate. This was a subject that always bordered on being too graphic to describe to my straight friends, but my leaving it alone didn't help them understand.

I had never felt demeaned by our financial disparity even when I felt awkward with him paying for everything. The proposition was quite palatable. I could take him up on his offer, skip getting on the plane for the second time and leave with him right then. My mind trembled with doubts that told me to decline Ron's invitation and my fantasies blossomed despite the shaking ground beneath them. Either decision I would make, would I not somehow regret?

"Well, if I stay I don't think I could keep pushing my flight back." I needed for a more definite answer from him. I wanted to get a solid, "stay here with me, if it doesn't work I'll buy you a ticket and you can leave later."

"Then go."

His words smacked against my ears. The room was all at once silent. They were neither what I wanted to hear nor what my emotions could handle at the moment.

"I mean I could stay, but you'd probably have to get me a new ticket." I was backpedaling while I continued to fish. Ron scoffed, took off his shirt and shorts, and started to change. Standing up I walked over to the door; would he jump in my way and stop me? That didn't seem very Ron so I kept a close eye on him as I walked over to my bag, waiting to see if he did anything to signal me to stop. "Well, I guess I should get going then."

"It's up to you if you want to stay." What did that mean? How could he think it was up to me at all? How could it possibly be? I didn't have any means of supporting myself, Hal's apartment didn't seem like a good backup plan for a living situation, and changing my flight arrangements felt like a stretch the first time I did it, let alone doing it repeatedly for who knows how long.

"I'd stay, but like I said I'd need a new ticket, I can't just keep changing my departure time every week." Letting the comment linger in the air didn't help anything. I picked up my bag and headed to the door. Ron started picking up some of the clothes on the floor and tossing them on top of the giant pile of dirty laundry in his room.

"I'm gonna take off then."

Ron said nothing. Did he even care? Of course he did, I watched him move around his room tidying things and making the bed, this was definitely not typical Ron behavior, but I needed to be sure, I needed him to stop me. I opened the door and hesitated.

"I had a great time."

"So did I." Ron said from around the corner.

"Bye." I pulled the door closed behind me, slowly, and held the knob for a moment, waiting. I went to the elevator.

Fantasy scenarios that would have all played well in *Pretty Woman* stormed through my head. I saw Ron throwing open the door and stopping me before I got into the elevator, waiting for me at the bottom when the doors parted, shouting at me from on top the roof or out a window to come back, or even already at Hal's apartment or the airport waiting for me to tell me that he didn't say goodbye because he didn't want to ever say goodbye. None of this happened, but as I walked away from the building I looked up and listened carefully just in case.

At the bottom of the steep hill I boarded the BART, bought a ticket with the money Cynthia had given me, and headed toward the Castro. When I got off I headed back to street level and started walking up hill towards Noe Valley. Up ahead I saw Delores Park. Nicknamed the "waterless beach," it could frequently be seen populated with beach towels and scantily clad bodies absorbing rays of the California sun. Today it was empty and I was glad for it. There was a narrow passage made for the train tracks that made a convenient shortcut from the park to the street Hal lived on. I was sweating a little after climbing the incline and slowed down to catch my breath.

Crying was something I had done only a few times over the last four years. I'd cried with everyone else at the top of The Reaper when my drill instructor put my first Eagle Globe and

Anchor in my hand and turned me from a nasty recruit into a Marine. I'd cried the first time I'd seen the pride in my mother's eyes when I came up to her after graduation, and then I cried again when I saw the same look in my father's. I'd cried when my close friend told me he was in love with me because I wanted to love him back in the same way but I couldn't. The last time I'd cried was when my best friend who I confided in told me she was returning to the mainland when her enlistment ended; I knew this meant it would be years before I would see her again. No time I've ever cried before feels as significant and painful as the moment I was crying in now.

Walking up the trolley tracks back towards Hal's apartment, I stopped and let my back fall hard against the wall. From this spot I could look out across Delores Park and see the skyline of San Francisco looking back at me through the hazy air. I looked up and felt the world rise out and above me looking down on me. All I could think was "this is so fucked up." I didn't even know exactly what I was crying about. Did I miss the situation, the thrill, the endless variability of what might happen? Did I miss the escape from a life that had fallen apart on me and that I had done everything in my power to forget about in the last week? Did I miss Ron? Did I have feelings for Ron or not? I pushed away from the wall and continued walking over the hill. The tracks took a long turn around the corner, and behind me the city went out of sight.

***

BRETT EDWARD STOUT

32

SUGAR-BABY BRIDGE

Returning from somewhere "exciting" people always ask each other how they are and what that they were up to. It's easy to get into talking about oneself and forget to ask the same questions back. When you live on an island, anywhere else is somewhere exciting.

I'd sent the bottle of Inglenook back to my mother. She greeted its arrival with suspicious jubilation, pointing out that it was worth several thousand dollars a bottle. I passed it off that she should enjoy it since it was a gift. It was wine after all, if she didn't drink it, what else was she going to do with it? All the while I was on the phone with her I stared into my closet looking at my oversized Tinsley Island shirt hanging next to the dark form of my dress blues blouse.

It was a week before I'd said hello to everyone and another before I'd felt up to going out to Hula's, the bar I often spent part of the afternoon in when I had a day off. My last paycheck, that I thought wasn't coming at all, had come through late and it was enough for me to get by for a little while. I was a

327

little glad that I hadn't known about it as I probably would have spent it frivolously back in California.

The afternoon sun flooded into Hula's through the long open window that ran the length of the bar. The Hawaiian breeze wafted in the smell of plumeria blossoms that mingled with traces of bleach used to clean the floors each night. Going to a bar during the day and not being assumed an alcoholic was a benefit to island life, and Hula's was a place that felt right any time of the day or night. It was a bit like a tropical coffee house that served beer and frozen cocktails instead of lattes and shots of espresso.

"Aloha, Spicer!"

Hearing the name was comforting like a warm beach towel. Back in Hawaii everyone called me by my last name; it had become an unofficial first name I'd assumed after living a life in sports and the military. Even as Ron had called me Brad I'd never actually associated with the name. In some ways, maybe it had made it easier to play whatever part Ron had needed me in his world, which seemed even further away across the thousands of miles of ocean. Here, I was once again safely protected by the sexy persona of Spicer.

People often talk about the "real world" and insist wherever you are, you're not in it. For me though, the real world had been Oahu; it was home. When you're home, nothing is quite the same as when you are visiting somewhere. On vacation, it is easy to be whoever I want to be. The possibilities of the personality I choose to show are at my discretion. The excitement of escaping my life and pretending to be someone else can be very alluring. This liberating phenomenon can most acutely be observed in two places: Las Vegas and Waikiki.

Hula's was at the end of the Waikiki strip near the zoo. It was the second location of the bar and like the "Old Corps" saltier Marines often reminisced, older patrons would comment on how much better it used to be. I'd never been to the "Old Hula's" but, the new location was clean and the view relaxing. The entire side of the building opened out to the fresh breeze of the tradewinds. From the long bamboo bench that spanned the wide opening I could sit and look up at Diamond Head to watch it change from brown to green in the spring and back to brown again. It was also popular for watching tight-bodied surfers come in off the beach and back to their battered cars in the parking lot across the street. From above, there was little worry that they or any passing members of your unit might notice your gawking.

"I've got a message for you?"

"What?" The bartender slid a piece of paper over the bar towards me. Unfolding it, I was shocked by its contents. On the yellow slip was a name followed by a number. The note read "Ron" and the number beneath it began with the area code eight zero eight. It was a Hawaii phone number. A closed chapter had suddenly reopened, its pages fluttering about in the once-soothing breeze of the tradewinds. Although I was back in Hawaii, I might have well been still sitting on the edge of Ron's bed in his giant empty penthouse vacillating over what to do and waiting for... who knows?

I walked out to the payphone in the hall, put in some change. It rang. "Hello?" Ron's voice came over the earpiece.

"Ron?"

"Brad! I'm on Maui. I'm going to New Zealand. You should join me." He spoke as if we had never parted at all; as if, even to him, I *was* still sitting on the edge of his bed awaiting instruction. After getting over the initial shock of his voice, I smiled at the flattering nature of the statement. Here was the voice I'd stood outside the building on Knob Hill waiting to hear, talking to me over the distorted telephone line. What did it mean, and why two weeks later? Obviously he had gone to the trouble to try to find me by leaving a message at a bar I'd mentioned I liked and that knew me. Here Ron was, an Island away. I took a moment to think. Isn't this what I had wanted? Didn't I want him to ask for me to stay, to extend the invitation beyond the week in Tahoe? I felt the need for clarification.

"Really? That sounds great. You buying me a ticket?" Although it never felt that way before, this time it did; it felt degrading to ask him to pay my way.

"Don't worry about that. Grab your passport and a bag. Fly over to Maui and we'll leave from here this weekend." It all seemed like a joke, I'd have thought it was, had I actually told anyone anything about Ron. The parts of my vacation that included him I'd kept to myself. Part of me wondered where my threshold to his persistence was. If he continued to ask, I was afraid I'd give in. Just sixty seconds earlier I was sure that I didn't want to go down this road with Ron again but hearing is voice snapped the suspension lines that had earlier grounded me.

"Why don't you call me when you get back or, come over to Oahu; we'll have dinner?" I said this without considering the idea that he might actually come.

"Oahu sucks. I like it here on Maui."

I paused for a moment. "I really can't take off just now."

"That's too bad. Call me if you change your mind." As the phone conversation ended and we both hung up my mind scanned his voice, still reverberating in my ear, for traces of regret or sadness or any emotion at all. I found nothing, which was maddening. I was almost angry at how difficult it was to read him, especially over the phone. Call him if I changed my mind? I hadn't even made my mind up let alone been prepared to change it. The seriousness of his proposal was too intimidating for even the Marine parts of me to handle. I folded his number and put it in my wallet. I couldn't bring myself to just throw it away; I wanted to keep it to prove that I hadn't dreamt it all.

Ron lived a life of impossibilities that spanned the Pacific much like the gargantuan bridges of San Francisco. In Hawaii we often joke that life on the island would be easier if there was a bridge back to the mainland. The task is impossibly large to accomplish. Ron seemed like someone who could manage it, but walking on a road that precipitously clung to his support seemed contradictory to the idea that on the other side of the bridge would be a destination for both of us. Ron had put in front of me plans that would build that bridge for me, a bridge that meant no body of water, no border, no ocean would be impossible to cross. Each span supported by ideas and aspirations. While I romanticize the idea of its possibility, its likelihood was as heavy as concrete and on it I would be dependent on the steel cables to hold me up, and ultimately it was a bridge with no visible end. Though the choice seemed both easy and appealing, it was neither.

I walked back into Hula's and leaned forward against the bar. "The usual thing, Spicer?" I was again wrapped in the comfort of that name. I smiled and nodded. The bartender leaned over and took a jug of milk out of the cooler. "So, are you auctioning yourself off in the bachelor auction tonight?"

"Tonight, huh…?" I smiled at the bartender as he poured the white liquid into the cold glass, setting it on the bar top. I took it in my hand. Lifting it to my lips I took a deep drink. As I set the glass down I let the cool fluid wash through me. The moisture from the frosty glass was enough to make my entire hand wet. I shook the water off, wiped my hand on my jeans, and picked it back up. Looking the bartender right in the eye, I took another long swallow and looked out at the green sides of Diamond Head. The idea of auctioning myself off seemed ironic after the conversation I'd just had. "What do *you* think?"

A wide grin came across his face and I slammed the rest of my milk.

***

A preview of Brett Edward Stout's
new novel, *The Lives Between*,
coming soon

1

THE GOING RATE

ow much would someone pay for me? What would they expect me to do? If they paid enough, I'd feel obligated not to disappoint them. I hated knowing that people were disappointed in me. It was a rotten feeling that saturated my chest and left my eyes heavy and my head light. The feeling was intensified when the disappointment came from a stranger; and even more so with a stranger I'd probably never see again. I reviled the idea that someone's memory of me might forever be disappointment. With random strangers, there was no opportunity for redemption. In this place, there were endless chances of such everlasting disappointment.

The air in Waikiki was warm but not humid. The light breeze carried the faint scent of plumeria blossoms and saltwater. Night in Hawaii enhanced the sensation of being on an island. The world of plain concrete hotels with sporadically lit windows and randomly occupied balconies reached into the blackness without touching it, leaving me standing on the brightly lit concrete streets of the city. It was as if the ocean was rising up overhead and swallowing the sky.

Above me, the throbs of dance music poured out of the open wall of Hula's Bar & Lei Stand and into the streets like waves flooding into a tide pool. Hula's was at the far end of the bustling tourist destination and contrasted the quiet black trees of the adjacent Honolulu Zoo and Kapiolani Park. In front of me, the moon reflected on the ocean. The soft glow of the moon lit the sky just enough to reveal the iconic slanted crater of Diamond Head volcano.

Hula's was the only bar in Waikiki lucky enough to have this view. It occupied the second floor of the Waikiki Grand Hotel and faced both the park and dormant volcano. To capitalize on the view, the bar had a long bank of windows that could entirely be opened to let the sweet, constantly pleasant air of the island in.

Clusters of dressed-up twenty-somethings walked from the dark parking lots, heading to the city's numerous clubs, bars, and restaurants. Their faces filled with anticipation and hope, expressions that were quite different from the tanned, shirtless, surfers with boards under arm, who's satisfied grins with were stained with the sadness that dusk had brought their leisurely fun to an end.

Truth be told, I'd always wanted to surf but, unsure of success, I instead watched from the safety of the sand. I admired with restrained jealousy as athletic bodies mounted long, bladelike sheets of fiberglass and danced on the unpredictable swells of the sea. My joy-watching was perforated by moments of anxiety. When they wiped out it made me nervous they were injured and I wouldn't be able to reach them even if I tried.

Tonight, looking out into the bluish black, it wasn't the surfers that filled me with nervousness. It was the reason I had come to town that caused the tremble in my hands. I was about to stand in front of a crowd of people, many of whom I knew, and listen as they assigned a monetary value to me. It was a fear that had plagued me from the moment I'd agreed to participate in Jack's charity bachelor auction.

Saying yes was far simpler than enduring the unease between then and now. For days the trembling had grown, as did the doubts and list of excuses I might use to back out. When my name was published on a flyer at the door, the stakes for reconsidering were raised substantially. The embarrassment of breaking my now public promise outweighed the humiliation that I would potentially endure.

As I climbed the wide, sand-littered stairs into the lobby of the Waikiki Grand, two middle-aged men with bellies stretching their tank tops came around the corner. They walked in step with one another and shook their heads as they laughed at a joke I didn't fully hear. Their laughter stopped when they saw me. I watched their eyes trace up and down; their lips pressed tightly together in judgment.

Straightening my posture, I clenched my abs, flexed my chest, and let my mouth form into a small innocent smile. I'd always found I got more attention when I feigned naive stupidity in the company of random gays.

I looked away before they'd finished checking me out to avoid any uncomfortable eye contact as we passed. The sand under their flip-flops scratched against the steps and slapped at their heels as they walked down and out of the hotel, turning down the street.

The lobby of the Grand had soft yellow walls and was almost overly lit. There were comfortable rattan loveseats, chairs, and coffee tables just inside, and hung here and there were brightly colored paintings of bold ginger flowers and lush tropical leaves.

Rounding the corner, my eyes met with the front desk clerk as he looked up to check if I was a guest of the hotel or the bar. I was always a little embarrassed to walk past the desk clerk. I knew he must see hundreds of more garishly dressed and flamboyant men walk by, but his familiar gaze still felt like it was condemning me. In the past I'd often worried that he'd been posted there by some church on the hunt for gay men to brutalize or even worse, that he'd be stationed there by my command to report back proof of the private life I'd tried so hard to conceal. I knew this was paranoid projection but it didn't stop my mind from fantasizing the worst. The reality was that he'd probably fallen into the job due to a lack of other options and he likely got a charge from the gaudy parade of muscle bunnies, closet cases, and drama queens. His mind probably wandered just as much as mine, filling with entertaining back-stories behind each guilty pair of eyes. For him, it at least broke up the monotony of being behind a thankless desk checking in customers and handling complaints.

Walking past him I came to the open stairwell door. I'd seen people take the elevator before, but it seemed impractical.

The bar was on the second floor. The time wasted waiting for the elevator and the electricity of operating it seemed to outweigh the energy spent climbing two flights of stairs, even if it was less glamorous than having an elevator all to yourself.

The second floor hallway was wide and ended at the large blue doors to Hula's. In the stale air outside the doors one could smell the faint odor of fog machines, bleach, and cocktails. Opening the doors I moved from the bright hallway into the encompassing atmosphere of the bar. The music in Hula's was always slightly out of date but unquestionably upbeat. Instead of the oppressively cutting-edge house and dance tracks of most bars, the poppy, familiar, somewhat-campy songs of Hula's were a relaxing accompaniment to the friendly ambiance. Everything about the bar had a laidback feel that encouraged people to laugh, hug friends, and introduce themselves to sun-burnt tourists who themselves were hoping to meet the cabana boy of their dreams.

The regular doorman stood behind a counter and smiled at me the same way he'd done for the last several years.

"Aloha, good night tonight?" I asked. I was never sure if Jack, who owned the place, would change his mind and ask me to start paying the cover charge imposed on everyone else.

"Same as always." He smiled through his thick, black, well-groomed beard. He always smiled as people entered but his eyes always seemed placid and ambivalent. With a motion of his hand, he waved me past.

The bar was not as full as I would have preferred for a Saturday night but, being that it was still early in the evening, I knew things still might pick up. Despite the sparse crowd, I put on my best smile and walked inside.

This was the *new Hula's* and many were still jaded for having lost the old one. The old bar had, for many, symbolized gay life on the island. I'd never seen the old Hula's first hand but I'd heard enough about it that it sometimes felt like I had. Every time I mentioned never having seen the old Hula's, I would endure rolling eyes and detailed stories of a magical outdoor bar that teemed with life under the protective cover of a giant banyan tree strung with lights. The image was admittedly romantic and glamorous, but nostalgic stories would never bring it back no matter how many times people told them.

The new bar was a large open space that ran the length of the Hotel. The structural pillars that might have formerly been hidden within the walls of hotel rooms were now covered in mirrors. A long rattan ledge, wide and strong enough to sit on, ran down the entire length of the open wall. The ceiling was black with a smattering of club lights. In the center of the room was a giant rectangular rattan bar under cabana-like canopy with a full-sized, koa wood outrigger fixed to it. I'd been told once that a boat like that could easily fetch forty-thousand dollars, making it what I believed to be the single most expensive piece of decoration I'd ever seen in a nightclub. Along the back wall the dance floor was contained in a soundproof glass room that many referred to as the coffin. The acoustics were great and it held in the fog, but dancing in it made me feel isolated from everything else going on and quickly became boring.

"Spicer!" a voice shouted.

All eyes were usually on whoever just walked into a bar. This seemed the same at every bar I'd ever been to. Playing it cool and stepping to the beat of the music, I walked in, pretending not to hear whoever had called my name.

Leaning forward, I was careful not to touch the bar top. Even though I'd personally seen the entire place bleached, and knew that this was done every evening, the filth that might have accumulated through the day made me uneasy.

I smiled broadly hoping to get the bartender's attention, which usually didn't take long. The bartender that night was a polite, muscular, handsome man named Chuck. Chuck was the kind of name I imagined a lumberjack having. This Chuck's brawny build and large hands fit with that picture perfectly. He wore faded jeans, boots, and no shirt. I actually wasn't sure I'd ever seen him wearing a shirt and was certain I'd never seen him leave the bar with anyone despite his handsome appearance.

339

Bartenders were expected to be insatiably slutty the way that writers were expected to be bat-shit crazy. The combination of Chuck's flirtatious behavior and possible celibacy made him even more attractive the way that defying a stereotype always seemed to. Leaning in a little further Chuck looked up and nodded at me smiling. "Hey, Spicer."

"Spicer!" the person who had called my name earlier came up behind and wrapped their arms around me. I hated when people touched me like this. I'd always felt direct human contact should be deliberately asked for before initiated. There didn't seem to be any polite way of communicating this before or after the fact, so I usually tried to suppress my aggravation. "How are you, honey?"

Turning around, I saw it was one of the young Asian cocktail servers that I was on good terms with. He was already drunk and his fingers wandered the grooves of my lower back and the muscles of my arms. I worried that his groping might wrinkle my freshly ironed shirt. I'd known he was interested in me for as long as I'd known him. His body was sculpted and his back handsomely decorated with one of those broad dragon tattoos I associated with the Japanese mafia. But, his manner was too soft and too friendly for me to find attractive.

"I'm good, man. You look like *you're* doing well." I knew he had told his name a dozen times, it was embarrassing that as many times as he'd said it, I'd never actually learned it. That fact was easy enough to avoid and it wasn't like I didn't remember his face or our conversations.

"I am *drunk!*" He dragged out the word drunk to emphasize how seriously he meant for me to take his being intoxicated. The words held a tone of hope that perhaps, since I was sober, I'd take advantage of his drunken state and carry him home for a night of unbridled, meaningless sex. That was to say that the sex would have been meaningless to me. Sex without attachment was like frosting without cake. I got to enjoy creamy goodness without all the heavy substance. In excess one might become high from the satisfaction, or bored from it. Despite the

340

risk of overindulgence, I didn't really want to stop or switch to a cake only life. I'd always loved frosting and I was determined to keep on loving it.

When Chuck finally came towards me, I used the opportunity to pry the cocktail server off. Checking my clothes in one of the mirrored pillars, I saw that they were thankfully wrinkle free.

"The usual glass of milk?" Chuck said through his grin.

I smiled back and winked. "Sure thing." I made a habit of not taking my money out preemptively here in case my drink was on the house, as it often was. If he asked for money when he came back I'd gladly pay, but if I didn't have to I wasn't about to give away the little money I still had. My last paycheck from the Marine Corps had been delayed but it had come. Living without it on terminal leave in San Francisco had been a good lesson in being frugal.

"One dollar." He said, setting the tall glass of thick white milk on the varnished bamboo bar top. I kept my smile to hide my disappointment to see another few dollars slip away and laid two tri-folded bills next to the glass.

"Thanks, Chuck."

He winked back and quickly moved on to the man waiting at the end of the bar leaving my money where it was. Alcohol consumers seemed to have an unspoken honor code. When it came to paying for drinks. Money left on the bar was not up for the taking either because they were afraid someone might catch them or because they genuinely believed it was off limits. I admit that I'd considered reclaiming cash that had sat longer than I deemed appropriate, but it was an impulse I'd never acted on. Stealing seemed a slippery slope. If I gave myself license to take something in one occasion, who was to say in which other circumstances I'd allow myself a similar transgression. I imagined that, like smoking, it was easier to never start than to try to quit later.

"Kevin!" The young Asian boy next to me exclaimed and moved on to another regular who had just come in the door.

I was a little relieved not to worry about him groping, wrinkling, or causing me to spill my freshly purchased milk. The glass was cool and dry. I glanced around to ensure there were no other random cocktail servers who might suddenly and unwelcomely embrace me. When I saw the coast was clear I took a drink of the thick pleasing refreshment.

Licking the residue off my lips I continued to look around for people I knew or visitors I might want to know. As the foggy taste of the milk transformed in my mouth, figures moved in and out of the pulsing pockets of light. In the few minutes I'd been there, the population of the bar had grown considerably. Men shuffled between smiling circles of half-a-dozen or more, reaching out to hug, kiss, or fondle one another. They laughed and talked story, but all the while kept a keen eye on the moving shadows for the same reasons I was.

There were a few guys I recognized, but for the most part it was a collection of unfamiliar faces. These were the strangers who I risked disappointing, the strangers by whom I'd be judged, the strangers who would permanently have an opinion of me from this one night.

It was then I saw the familiar beaming smile of perfectly white teeth glistening from across the room. Marty was the most cheerful person I'd ever encountered; I had often wondered if it was even possible for him to be sad. Every time I'd seen him, he was smiling that same elated smile, laughing to someone's bad joke, or hugging random people who he counted as friends. One time I'd gone home with him only to learn he both climaxed and slept smiling. In the back of my head I thought would make the perfect spokesperson for Prozac. Seeing this likeable figure here tonight, instead of filling me with the usual contact joy, heightened my fears of disappointing strangers; I was sure he'd also be on the block tonight. Side by side with him, I felt a bit plain and ordinary.

The bar was busier near the open wall. People tended to collect there either for the fresh air, the view of the sky, or the view of pedestrians below. I suspected many just congregated there because everyone else did; the way animal herds group together for no reason other than to be part of a collective.

A group of younger guys, possibly underage, leaned over the window railing and heckled the lean-bodied surfers below. It was a sight that contrasted that of the other, more centralized, gay bar, Angles, where the curious and insecure pedestrians below would gawk, make faces, and shout the occasional insult. Neither situation seemed appropriate. In fact, I didn't think it mattered who started it, but I would have thought one side or the other would have learned to be considerate by now.

For the next few minutes I performed obligatory mingling. I moved from one circle to the next, smiling, sipping, laughing, and making funny faces to people's comments I thought were amusing, unamusing, or that I was only pretending to have heard over the energetic music. Each gesture, pose, or reaction was executed keeping in mind that someone in another circle might be watching. I negotiated hugs, pats on the back, and remarks on my physique that were mostly just excuses for people to grope me.

I usually didn't talk much when I was out. It was easier to be judged by my appearance than by my intelligence. Having someone dislike me because I wasn't smart or witty enough was like loosing at chess; it defeated through and through. Superficial rejection was easier to ignore.

"Corporal Spicer, or should I say Mr. Spicer?" I heard Jack's loud, deep, charismatic voice behind me and turned to him opening my arms for a hug. It was hard to get my arms around him. Jack was dressed in his usual aloha printed shirt and light khaki shorts. Tonight's shirt was black with patterns of bamboo and hibiscus flowers. Jack's skin was tanned, he was slightly overweight, his once blond hair was thin and grey, but his demeanor was stately and professional. My favorite of his features was his cool blue eyes that were perpetually listening, forever thinking, and brimming with integrity. Hugging him, my dog tags pressed flat against my chest and the metal chain tugged on the back of my neck. The metal felt cold and my heart sank a bit. His words brought attention to the fact that ón Monday I wouldn't have to iron my utilities, spit shine my boots, and run as one of the anonymous members of my former unit. "Hey, I wanted to ask you, are you for sure doing the auction tonight?"

"Yeah, definitely, sir. Anything I can do to help." I'd rarely turned down any favor Jack asked of me, he'd always been nice and, unlike most older men, had never taken advantage of or misunderstood my being friendly. I admired him. He held a respect from others that I very much coveted.

"Excellent, I want you to know I really appreciate it. Look, I have to run to my office."

"Hey, no worries. When does everything start?" I didn't want to sound overly excited or nervous even if I was both.

"In about thirty-forty minutes or so."

"Alright. Mahalo, Jack."

I was a bit disappointed that the event would still be a ways away. I'd spent a lot of time in the Marines waiting for things, but it didn't mean I enjoyed it. It occurred to me that I should leave and come back closer to show time. I jokingly thought that if I stuck around and everyone got a look for free, who would want to pay for me later? I chugged the last of my milk, a feat that would have been more impressive with a beer. The smooth milk coated my mouth and throat. Picking up a clean napkin I wiped my mouth, folded it in fourths, and stuffed it into the glass before heading for the door.

Just as my hand gripped the filthy handle, the young Asian cocktail server's hands stopped me. His palms were sweaty from drinking and dancing. I felt slightly repulsed by how they were soft like a woman's. I pulled my hand away gently and slid it into my pocket. Unless I was shaking someone's hand, having my hands touched was too intimate to perform with acquaintances.

"You're not leaving are you?" He asked with slurred desperation.

"I'll be back."

344

"Good, I'll see you when you get back, baby." He smiled, planted a clammy wet kiss on my cheek, and winked before walking backward away from me. Drunk people were always hyper-affectionate, although not as bad as people on ecstasy. Both felt like road hazards I had to swerve around.

Waving to the doorman, I headed down the stairs, out the lobby, and down the street. I walked with a determined stride as if I had somewhere important to be. Each step was measured, even, and deliberate. Even though I knew in my head I wasn't a Marine anymore my heart disagreed. I was still compelled to wear a belt and tuck in my shirts, I still felt the urge to exercise in the morning, and I still automatically offered help to anyone who seemed like they needed it. I also compulsively followed the rules of general polite etiquette: don't walk on the grass, call everyone ma'am or sir, don't eat and walk at the same time, and to always act as if someone was watching. The last of these examples carried into the way I was walking now. I'd always been ordered to "walk with a purpose," swiftly and as if I know where I was going, even if I didn't. I hadn't gotten far down the block before I had chosen a destination where I could wait out the time till the auction.

I came up to the corner. The main drag abruptly dropped from four to two lanes where it met with the park, symbolizing the end of the city. Kalakaua Boulevard's lanes stretched out to my right along the newly revamped palm sidewalks. The entire length of the road was now lined with palms, sculptures, and waterfalls that separating the calm waves of Waikiki Beach from the towering hotels. Here and there, small construction projects were still underway. The intention was to expand the beach in order to beautify the city and thus promote the suffering tourist industry. In order to accommodate the wider slate sidewalks, trees, and tiki torches, a lane of the busy street had been sacrificed. It seemed a fair trade to the industry that fueled life on the island. Many local inhabitants disagreed and voiced their concern almost daily in the paper. I hoped that I would never be so short sighted to look a gift horse in the mouth the way they did.

Standing on the corner, I looked far out into the ocean trying to spot anyone surfing by moonlight. A woman laughed loud and obnoxiously through an open window of a restaurant behind me. I was glad to see the white walk signal so that I could escape having to hear her repeat the annoying sound. Laughter was as individual as fingerprints. I'd often swallowed my own chuckles in case someone else found mine as unattractive as the uncensored noises that issued from the woman's mouth. I was all too eager to get away.

Turning left, away from the city lights, I headed down the newly finished sidewalk that separated the grassy expanse of Kapiolani Park from the beach. The sand cushioned the shallow southern waves creating the ocean's familiar swoosh. It was a beautiful stretch of pavement with green streetlamps and the occasional ocean-facing bench so that people could rest and watch the waves or take in the sun as it set into the Pacific. The light tradewinds blew unendingly in from the ocean, creating a harmony between the rustling palm fronds and the rhythmic rush and retreat of the water.

This was one of the first places I'd come to when I arrived in Hawaii. On my first day, I'd been dropped off at this end of Waikiki and followed this same sidewalk. Since that time, the concrete had been repoured, the sod replaced, and fresh sand added to the shrinking beach. Even before the beautification projects, I had been enchanted by how handsome it was.

I'd learned from an online map that the gay beach was near this spot, but it hadn't been my reason for coming. It was another feature that piqued my interest. At the point where the sidewalk veered around a snack shop, a path crossed the sand to towards the sea.

Reaching out into the ocean was a long jetty built from large volcanic rocks. The top had been paved for easy walking. When I reached the far end of it, I turned around to look back at the majestic city rising up from the sand. It was just as breathtaking tonight as it had been the first time I'd come here.

Watching the waves roll towards the shore, I felt as if I was floating by the city, an observer on a concrete catamaran drifting by the twinkling buildings. While I knew that people flew to the outer islands to admire the views of unspoiled nature, I didn't see how anything made by nature's hand alone could be better than this. The jagged Ko'olau Mountains provided a backdrop for the marvelous manmade structures; each one filled with relaxed hopeful people, on their honeymoon, on business trips, or just escaping from the mad days of home.

On more than one occasion time had slipped away from me at this place. Sometimes, I would sing, sometimes I'd take off my shoes and let the water lick my feet, but usually I just stared. Not just at the site of it, but at the subtext: the possibility it symbolized, the utter improbability my ordinary childhood in Iowa had landed in a paradise such as this. Somehow, here I was. In this spot, nothing brought me down. Under any other circumstances, the chance of getting my shoes, feet, or pants wet drove me into rage, but not here. Here it didn't matter. Here I was home. It was perfection.

I wasn't sure how long I'd been standing there, but I was pretty sure it was time to head back to the bar. Reluctantly, I walked to shore watching the palms slowly block my view of the mountains past them. Turning left, I headed back down the sidewalk toward Hula's.

Before I'd gotten inside I knew that things had picked up considerably. From the sidewalk, I could hear that the voices were more numerous and excited than when I'd left. With a spring in my step, I went through the lobby, up the stairs, and into the crowded bar.

The air inside smelled of skin and liquor. I considered treating myself to another milk, but I wasn't sure I had the time to finish it before being called on stage. I had a rule to never drink from a glass that hadn't been in my positive control the entire time. The risk that my drink may have been used as an ashtray or tainted with drugs wasn't one I was willing to take.

Inside the room that encased the dance floor I saw Jack, Marty, and a few others talking. Jack now wore two leis around his neck, one of folded leaves and kukui nuts and the other of yellow plumeria blossoms. It was customary for people to present Jack leis throughout an evening. On a few special occasions they had even piled so high you could hardly see his face.

The group Jack was with was presumably the other men up for bid in tonight's auction. Even though the event was for charity and not designed to be a competition, I couldn't help but look at it that way. Coming through the dance floor turnstile I gave each one a quick once over. From the looks of it, I didn't have much competition. Marty's tight body and irrepressible smile were still my greatest threat.

Jack turned towards me as I entered. "Oh good, Spicer, you're here. Danny, Spicer here is one of our boys tonight." Jack laughed at the end of his sentence the way he always did when he was in a good mood.

"Enchante de faire votre connaissance." The man Jack introduced as Danny came toward me like a character out of an old movie. He wore thick-rimmed rectangular glasses and his dark hair was slicked back. As he walked closer, he led with his right arm extended. Taking my hand, he kissed it and smiled. His peculiar decorum was strangely non-threatening and bizarrely natural. Though I'd never met him before, I couldn't imagine him greeting anyone in any other way.

I wasn't sure if it was for my benefit or Danny's, but Jack introduced us to the rest of the men. Until he said his name I hadn't even noticed the presence of Doyle, a thirty-something, relatively fit, but not particularly appealing man, who'd I'd met in passing. Doyle was Marty's ex-boyfriend. Knowing this lessened my opinion of Marty's standards, which by transference of my having hooked up with Marty was an insult to me.

"Now…" Danny turned towards me, cocked his head to the side, and folded one arm across is body to prop the other up to put a finger on his mouth. "You strike me as straight; are you?"

I found his comment, even if contrived, to be flattering. In my periphery I could see Doyle's eyes rolling far back in his head. Why having my sexuality mistaken was a compliment I didn't entirely understand. Somehow being taken for straight made me feel normal. It was a discreet way of being labeled as masculine, which was hypocritically perceived by gay men to be superior to the flamboyant alternative. To pass for straight was to be considered worthy of manhood. Right or wrong, it felt good.

"I'm afraid not." I replied, unable to contain my smile. I felt childish and transparent, stupidly grinning from ear to ear, in front of Marty and the other guys.

"Oh, I see. Hum… Clearly you've been with women though. I'm getting that playboy vibe from you." He said, peering through his glasses with a perfectly straight face. For a moment I wondered if he actually meant it.

"Well, Spicer here *was* a Marine until just recently." Jack interjected.

"Technically I still am. Once a Marine, always a Marine." I responded, trying to get control of my stupid smile.

"Yes, yes I see. Well, I should put you all in order for the auction."

Danny lined us up and then walked back and forth with his hands folded behind his back, as if inspecting us. Jack went into the DJ booth and was whispered in the DJ's ear what I assumed were instructions for the event.

Standing in line, my heart started to race, the longer Danny paced back and forth, analyzing and rearranging us, the more adrenaline flooded my veins. He sorted the group so that less attractive guys were at one end and the more attractive at the other. I grew eager for him to single me out the same way I'd longed for my name to be called out in grade school dodge ball team.

When Marty, Doyle, and I were the only three he hadn't arranged he paused, stepped back, and then reached into his pocket. My stupid smile came back when a long seamstress tape dropped to the floor and he sternly pretended to measure us. He measured, stepped back, looked us over, and then measured us some more. He shuffled me to the end of the line, then third from the end, then in the middle with Marty last. After stepping back for another moment he switched Doyle and Marty so that Doyle was last.

"That's perfect." He said to my confusion. If we were in an order of relative attractiveness, I was insulted that Doyle took the top position.

"Are we almost ready to go here?" Jack said, emerging from the DJ booth.

Danny instructed us to wait until we were called out to take our places next to him on the stage. After he finished, the music was turned down and the stage lights came up. Without the colored lights, the room where the dance floor was seemed small and dirty. Smudges on the mirrored walls that were once invisible became obvious and grotesque, scuffs on the floor formed patterns where people had danced in place, and the once-black ceiling appeared dull and grayed with dust.

Preserving our order, the group moved to the dance floor's backdoor so we would be out of sight until called. Danny walked up onto stage with a microphone in hand. I could barely make out what he was saying through the soundproof glass until one of the guys near the front cracked open the door.

The anticipation continued to build in me as one by one the boys were washed onto the stage by the call of Danny's tawdry commentary. However, as bidding on the third guy ended, my elation drained out of my chest, leaving a sucking hollow sensation. Where once my blood coursed with vigor, it now curdled with horror.

"Alright, that was Alex. Sold, to the gentleman to my right, for twenty dollars."

***

25908228R00229

Made in the USA
Middletown, DE
15 November 2015